INVISIBLE BLOOD

ALSO AVAILABLE FROM TITAN BOOKS

Dark Cities: All-New Masterpieces of Urban Terror
Dead Letters: An Anthology of the Undelivered, the Missing, the
Returned...
Exit Wounds
New Fears
New Fears 2
Phantoms: Haunting Tales from the Masters of the Genre
Wastelands: Stories of the Apocalypse
Wastelands 2: More Stories of the Apocalypse
Wastelands: The New Apocalypse

Sherlock Holmes: The Sign of Seven
Associates of Sherlock Holmes
Further Associates of Sherlock Holmes
Encounters of Sherlock Holmes
Further Encounters of Sherlock Holmes

SEVENTEEN CRIME STORIES
FROM TODAY'S FINEST CRIME WRITERS

INVISIBLE BLOOD

EDITED BY **MAXIM JAKUBOWSKI**

Leabharlanna Poiblí Chathair Baile Átha Cliath
Dublin City Public Libraries

TITAN BOOKS

Print edition ISBN: 9781789091328
Electronic edition ISBN: 9781789091335

Published by Titan Books
A division of Titan Publishing Group Ltd
144 Southwark Street, London SE1 0UP
www.titanbooks.com

First edition: July 2019
1 2 3 4 5 6 7 8 9 10

A CIP catalogue record for this title is available from the British Library.

Printed and bound by CPI Group (UK) Ltd, Croydon, CR0 4YY

TABLE OF CONTENTS

Introduction

BLOOD, ON THE STREETS AND IN THE MIND

MAXIM JAKUBOWSKI

We are experiencing a Golden Age of crime and mystery writing, when every single week at least two-thirds of the US and UK bestseller lists are populated by mysteries and thrillers, notwithstanding the profusion, excellence and diversity of so many other titles originating in the genre that don't reach such a status. Indeed, I would argue that since what is considered the traditional Golden Age of crime, as represented by Agatha Christie, Dorothy L. Sayers, Margery Allingham, Ngaio Marsh and countless others (and wonderfully foreshadowed by Sherlock Holmes and his rivals and foes), there have been further ceaseless, if not continuous generations of Golden Ages, epitomised by the likes of, successively, Raymond Chandler, Dashiell Hammett, Erle Stanley Gardner and later the emergence of Ed McBain, Ruth Rendell and P. D. James, all the way through to our modern times where James Patterson, Lee Child, Ian Rankin, John Grisham and so many wonderful contemporaries excel on a regular basis. The Golden Age has never gone away!

Why is that?

Because crime and mystery writing, at its best, entertains, intrigues, and on many occasions also makes us question the world we inhabit, the way we live.

I have been reading crime and mystery since my teens and have gone on not just to read it on an epic scale but also throughout my career in the world of books to edit it, publish it, sell it (when I owned Murder One, London's foremost mystery bookstore), write it, judge it on behalf of major literary awards, collect it, even, and it has never disappointed. All the world is there – in the form of fiendish puzzles – scary in the description of crimes beyond the newspaper headlines, fascinating when it gazes into the face of everyday evil, conjuring abominable and worryingly often super-intelligent villains, enlightening when it delves into the psychology that tips the balance between good and evil, as well as educational and also entertaining.

I have had the opportunity to edit many anthologies, whether selecting best-of-the-year stories or focusing on a particular theme amongst the wild selection the genre offers, from cosies to noir, from police procedurals to amateur sleuths and private eyes, from spy thrillers to psychological thrillers, from famous fictional detectives to their counterpart villains, from domestic drama to action and suspense, and so many other variations in the almost unlimited palette crime and mystery writing allows. But, on this occasion, I decided to offer carte blanche to some of my favourite writers and friends, asking them to come up with a brand new story to celebrate the genre, irrespective of theme, period, or style, and I'm truly delighted to say that each and every one came up trumps with a tale that epitomises their storytelling talent.

We have authors from the US, the UK, France, and even Israel, and all are at the top of their form. Some are major stars in their own right, others are still emerging talents, but all have established a sterling reputation previously with their fascinating books and ably demonstrate how wide the range of ideas, imagination and readability is that contemporary mystery writing has to offer.

Not all the stories actually feature blood, of course, but I guarantee each will have you glued to the page!

MJ

ALL THE SIGNS AND WONDERS

DENISE MINA

William Halligan looked from the flashing tip of the knife to Claire's hand on the white handle. He wasn't afraid but his brow rose a fraction, sceptical. He thought she wouldn't do it, that she was just upset, that she had no reason to hurt him. But Halligan didn't know her. Claire was willing to risk it all. She had killed the king before.

When young she had jumped on a man's back and punched him in the back of the head over and over. She broke a knuckle, but she didn't notice at the time because she was so carried away, in the moment, not afraid or sorry, not worried about what would happen next, as she usually was. It felt as if she had dared to walk through a doorway and become one of those people who refused to accept what was given to them.

She'd been thinking about doing it for so long, imagining, rehearsing. She knew the arithmetic of violence was not who was the strongest but who was willing to get most hurt. She did get hurt.

The man tried to get her off, twisting and spinning as if she was a spider he could shake off. He clawed up at her face: "Claire! Get off, you stupid girl!" But Claire was young and fit, and her legs were strong. She managed to stay up there for quite a long time, get a lot of blows in. Then she fell heavily into a table, landing on her side, bruising a rib and her hip.

The man who threw her off was her Dad. It was a seminal moment in their family. Claire had always been afraid of him, but after that futile gesture she was never afraid of him again. She'd turned it around.

While she was up there, part of her mind stayed calm, rolling through possibilities, formulating a defence in case she killed him. This is what she would tell the cops: Claire walked into the living room and found him kicking her mother in the stomach. Her mother was on the ground, lying curled on her side, holding tight to his shin as he kicked her with the other foot. No daughter could watch that unfold without being moved to action. These thoughts were rattling around her head as her thighs burned at the effort, her hands numb from hitting bone.

It would be a good defence. Claire was fourteen and looked younger. She would weep in the dock. She would wear a blouse. They had the intensive care reports from the time he broke her Mum's jaw to back it up.

It was true: that was the scene Claire had walked in on. Normally she'd have backed out and shut the door and left them to it. It was futile to intervene. But standing in the doorway she'd heard a small "no" pop in her head. A tiny "no", like a twitch or a burp. No. She would not play her role tonight. Not tonight. She would object, not to him doing that to her, not to her doing it to him, but to Claire having to see it.

She didn't kill her Dad. She fell off and even before she hit the ground she knew what would happen afterwards. He sat down, holding the back of his head where she had hit him, gasping with pain, looking shocked and wronged, deeply offended at the breach of protocol. "What are you think—what the *heck*?" He didn't approve of swearing. They were trying to raise her right.

"Claire!" Her mother was up off the floor, bent double, arms crossed over her bruised stomach. "You could have really hurt him!"

Claire had broken the ritual of silent acquiescence. She had stopped being the passive child, lost her special role, but it was worth it. They were looking at her.

Her Mum crouch-walked over to his side, cupping a protective hand near the back of his head, not quite bold enough to touch him. He looked up at her, eyebrows tented. "Why? I mean, look what she made me do!"

"I know!" said her Mum.

Her Mum's lower jaw was swelling up. The wires were not long out. He'd shattered it and knew better than to hit her there again. They didn't want to end up back in hospital with all the questions and the exasperated

7

policewomen trying to convince her Mum to bring charges.

He hurt Claire. Her cheek was scratched, pierced with two of his fingernails, drawn down an inch. She could feel the skin swelling around the cuts and the warm blood dripping from her jaw.

Claire said she was sorry and backed out, but she wasn't sorry. She felt wonderful. She had thrown off a spell by daring to defy the consensus.

After that she walked taller. At school she started to do well. No longer cowed, she became quite popular. People sensed the shift in power.

She left home at sixteen and got a job, worked hard, got a flat: life was good. She started to attend a church with a flatmate and found great comfort in her faith. There was no drama to it. She didn't have to give anything up because faith and the practice of prayer, attending Mass, taking the sacraments, they filled a hole that had always been there.

In the years to come she thought about the moment often, that "no" and how it changed her life. She wondered if it had been God-inspired. That moment laid eggs in her. She told no one but she was proud that she'd dared. The arithmetic of daring.

But Halligan didn't know that story. They'd never met before. He didn't know how daring she was. He seemed old, though she knew he wasn't. He was deeply freckled and his pale blue eyes were rimmed with red. The boundaries of his lips were indistinct. A pale-skinned man who had spent a lot of time in the sun.

Claire pointed the knife at his heart. It was a big carving knife, long and sharp. Halligan held her gaze, so sure she wouldn't do it that he didn't even raise his hands to defend himself.

"What are you doing?" he said quietly.

"I should have done this a long time ago," said Claire.

"I've done nothing to you."

He was right. Claire stabbed him in the heart.

Halligan's eyes widened with surprise, his mouth dropped open. He didn't believe it. He blinked over and over, trying to reboot reality.

She was still holding the knife. She thought of Halligan with an ambulance crew gathered around him, the knife still in his chest, lifting him, shocked and blinking still, onto a stretcher. But Claire thought *No. Kill the king. Dare.* She pulled the knife out not out of a wish to undo, but because she knew it would make her actions irreversible. She dared. She killed him.

A bloody mist sprayed her face and she turned away, startled by the sudden sensation of warmth, spluttering to get the blood off her lips as he crumpled to the floor.

Claire stood over him, watching blood scorch the white square of his priest's collar. She could hear his mother humming along to the radio in the kitchen.

She stood there, for what might have been a second or an hour, and then took her phone out of her pocket and called the police on herself.

A second or an hour or a day later, she couldn't say which, they arrived and broke down the door and found Claire still standing in the living room, soaked in his blood and Father William Halligan dead on the floor.

"I killed him," she said. "It was me."

In prison, held on remand, Claire had time to think. Far from the sense of euphoria she had expected, her mood was very low. She felt at first shocked by herself, by the visceral nature of what she had done. Then disgusted. She lay on the bed-shaped slab of concrete, feeling the cold seep in through the rubber mattress, awake, ceiling-staring, mind blank. This was not what she hoped would happen. She had hoped to walk taller, do well, be popular. Oddly enough, she did become popular for a brief spell because people thought they understood what she had done.

"A priest, aye?" This from a grizzled woman in the refectory. "Child-abusing bastards. Kill the lot of them."

A lot of people made assumptions, of course. He was a priest, after all. People like to think they know things. Then it came out that Halligan had just returned from working in the Sudan. He had been teaching young children at a chaotic refugee camp on the border. Everyone thought they knew why Claire had killed him. She knew something, had heard rumours, knew there would be no consequences for him within the church.

During that phase Claire got letters of congratulations from strangers, survivors of abuse within the church and also random people who couldn't bear what had gone on. *Thank you for taking a stand*, they said. Some told her their stories. Claire skipped the abuse details and only read the aftermath: drugs and drink, depression, sexual misdemeanours, self-harm and suicide. She was looking for herself in the aftermath, for a comradely sense of fellowship, but none of the stories were as bad as her own. She didn't reply to any of them.

Because she didn't contradict any of it her reputation as a defender of children snowballed. Auntie Mags, the heavy-set drug dealer who ran the convicted block, sent a lackey to give Claire the gift of a phone card and a box of teabags. Don't worry if you get convicted, said the lackey, Mags is saying you'll get looked after. They didn't know what she had done.

A rumour went around that Halligan had been abusing Claire's own children. *Good for her*, was the consensus of opinion. *Finally someone took a stand.* She seemed to stand for all of the women who'd been through that. A lot of the women on remand had come from abusive backgrounds, some of them had children who were abused and had been either too ignorant or powerless to stop it. Claire became a hero to those women. She got extra potatoes at lunch from a young woman who made eye contact for too long. She got extra books from the library trolley.

It was nonsense. Claire didn't have children. She was twenty-six and couldn't have children. She'd had a full hysterectomy when she was first diagnosed at twenty-two. It was a brutal treatment option for such a young woman, but best in the circumstances. Cut the cancer out completely.

No one knew that, though, because she didn't speak two words. She was shocked and waiting for God, who never came. He just never came.

They must have realised that she didn't have children at some point, but those who needed the redemption story hung on to it regardless of the evidence. No children came to visit her. No one but her church friend Valerie came to see her. Still Claire didn't speak. Just as her star was waning, Lilly Spenser declared herself Claire's lawyer.

Spenser wore lipstick the colour of a village burning at night. She wore trouser suits the colour of stab vests and had ironed black hair that hung down her back like chain mail.

"I am going to save you," she said.

"I don't need a lawyer," said Claire. "I'm guilty."

Spenser sat across the table from Claire in a rarely-used room. The sun shone in through the window all day and super-heated it. Where the mildew smell was coming from was anyone's guess.

"Had you met Father Halligan before?"

"No."

"Did you know people who knew Father Halligan?"

"No."

"But you'd heard of him?"

"Yes."

"What had you heard about him?"

"He was a priest."

Spenser frowned and sat back in the chair, her sharp suit buckling outwards between the buttons, showing a pink nylon blouse underneath. Claire thought Spenser knew it was visible and probably hoped it looked sexy. It was disconcerting. She was not a sexy woman. She was all defences and corrugated iron.

"You're not helping me very much, Claire."

"Why would I?"

"I'm defending you."

"I don't need defending."

"Then you'll die in prison."

Claire smiled at that. "I'm dying anyway. Stage four. It's in my lymph nodes."

Spenser was shocked at that. She bundled up her notes and went away, undoubtedly going to check out the veracity of what Claire had told her.

But Spenser didn't stop coming to visit. She tried to weave it into the mitigation case. Briefly, she tried to convince Claire that they should claim that she wasn't herself and defend the murder on the basis of diminished responsibility, but Claire said, "I'm guilty. I want to plead guilty. I don't want to put his mother through a trial, she's done nothing to me."

"What did he do to you?"

"Nothing."

"He must have done something."

"I'd never met him before."

"Then why kill him?"

Claire sat back and read the yearning on Spenser's face. This is why she was here. She wasn't here for Claire's defence. Spenser was here for answers. She wanted the story to make sense. It bothered her enough for her to turn up for these fruitless meetings. The need for order. The need for narrative closure. But it didn't make sense to anyone but Claire and God. *No.*

"Look," said Spencer, "you're not mad. You're previously of good character. You're not familiar with prison. You're ill and you need treatment. I know you've investigated experimental treatment in the past, and you can't pursue that in here, so *why*?" Spenser sat forward again. "I've interviewed very high-powered people in that charity and they all say that Father Halligan was a blameless man. That he never abused anyone. His pupils have written open letters talking about how much he helped them."

"Fine."

"The consensus is that he was a good priest, a good person."

"Was he?"

They looked at each other. Spenser found a fresh tact. "We have been investigating your past too, Claire."

Claire felt her stomach tighten.

"You had quite a hard time of it, didn't you?"

No, she wanted to say. No, I didn't. I thought I had a hard time of it, but no. I didn't have a hard time. I only thought that I had.

"With your parents, your father murdering your Mum."

Shut up.

"I believe there was a long history of domestic violence?"

You don't know.

"I have—" she opened a file in front of her "—a report here about the time your father broke your Mum's jaw. The police report said there was a child present?"

The file had a police incident picture of her mother with a grotesquely swollen jaw, two black eyes and a crust of blood around the left side of her mouth. She was lying down in the hospital bed, her eyes swivelled sharp to the right, and

Claire remembered that she'd been looking to Claire's father who was sitting there, tight-lipped and furious. It took her back to the night, to the intrusion of the cops, to the questions and the refusal to understand that all of it was a conversation her parents couldn't have any other way. Maybe they shouldn't have been talking to each other at all then, that was a legitimate point, but it wasn't about her Dad hitting her Mum. It was about them hitting each other and him winning all the time.

She didn't want Spenser to know how the photo made her feel. She tried to seem uninterested, but she overcompensated and was slouching so much that her foot slipped and she nearly slid off the chair.

"Where is your father now?"

"Dead."

"He died in prison?"

"Mh-hm."

Spenser closed the file and put it away, watching Claire to see the effect it had on her. Claire tried not to react, but her eyes followed it into Spenser's briefcase and stayed there as Spenser put all of the other papers in there too. The table in front of them was clear. Claire thought she was leaving, but she wasn't.

Spenser laced her fingers together and leaned on the table.

"Claire," she said quietly, "my job here is to present facts to the court in your defence. You're pleading guilty and now they want to hear about mitigating factors. You know what 'mitigating' means?"

"I know what 'mitigation' means."

"Okay. I want to know if you think there is some reason for the court to make your sentence shorter."

"No."

"The doctor here told me that your cancer is terminal. You've got four months, he says."

Claire didn't feel herself standing up. She didn't feel her arms rise in front of her, she didn't feel her fingers as they laced through the dry hair at the side of Spenser's head or her shoulders as she slammed the face into the table.

She did feel prison officers grab her and lift her and lay her on her stomach. She did feel the weight of a knee in the small of her back. The taste of hot dust was deep in her lungs, scorching her throat. She felt hot vomit come up through her oesophagus, burning her mouth and the cheek that lay on it.

When they got her up she glimpsed Spenser at the scratched window in the interview room. She was bleeding from her forehead and her hair was a mess, but her expression was beatific. Claire knew she would never see her again and not because she'd attacked her. Spenser had no reason to come back. She got what she wanted. She understood. The story made sense to her now.

Claire had just received the final diagnosis. The three doctors sat on a settee, elbows on knees, nodding. It was unanimous. Nothing more could be done. A box of tissues sat on the table in front of them. The top tissue stuck vertically out of the hole at the top. A prompt. *Now is the time to cry. This is the weeping time.*

Claire didn't weep. She said okay. She nodded too.

"How do you feel?"

"Okay."

They gave her numbers, Macmillan Cancer Support, a counsellor, a support group.

Okay.

But they could see she wasn't okay. Maybe they could see the anger in her, the phosphorus burning on the surface water, the sense of injustice.

Did she have someone who could come and get her from the hospital? She lied. I have a friend waiting outside. One of the doctors wasn't sure that was true and offered to walk with her to the car park. I want to be alone. They couldn't argue with that.

She walked home in the rain.

She had spent the last eight months on her knees in the chapel praying. She'd become a daily communicant, attended the rosary and prayer groups, did a daily round of prayers. Please, God. Valerie, her friend from chapel, had told her that "please, God" was short for "if it should please you, God". It didn't mean *please, God, gimmie*. God wasn't Amazon. He didn't just deliver what you wanted. Claire understood that, she did; she was praying for the fortitude to cope with whatever God put in front of her. But in this one instance she thought God might understand. Her life had been so grim, so unremittingly hard and knock-filled, that she did mean *please, God* this time. Let me live. Let me thrive. It's so unfair. But God ignored her.

Days later, not answering her phone or opening the door to the Macmillan nurses, she went out. It was raining. It was cold. She was in the street and stopped, thought she might just stay here until it was over, in this Godless place. Then God sent her a sign.

"Come with me. I'll make you a cuppa."

A lady, quite old, genteel, had seen her in the street and recognised her from chapel. Claire knew the face but couldn't remember her name. Maybe she'd never known it.

The woman took Claire to her house that was nearby. It was a bungalow with peonies bursting around the door and a mother-of-pearl name plate. She peeled the wet coat off her, hanging it on a radiator to dry. It was a nice house. Tidy. Lots of religious imagery and cushions.

"There now." She gave Claire a hot mug of tea, a half cup because she was shaking quite hard. She cut her a slice of dense fruitcake and placed a napkin on her knee to catch the crumbs.

"Your eyes are tinged yellow," she said to Claire. "Are you ill?"

Claire nodded.

"You've had a shock, haven't you?"

She nodded again.

The lady made her drink her tea and gave her another half cup. Kindness from a stranger, coming at a brutal, lonely time, felt like the hand of God on her back. She looked around the room. Doilies. A cat curled on a chair. Framed pictures of family. A cared-for garden through the back window. It was nice.

Would Claire like another slice of fruitcake? It was very heavy, sunk in the middle, and she had to use a big, white-handled carving knife to cleave the slice apart with the tip and then saw at it. She put it on the napkin on Claire's knee. Claire could feel the heft of it weighing down on her leg.

"Why were you standing in the rain all alone? You must feel awfully sad."

"God let me down," said Claire.

The lady nodded as if she understood. "Hmmm. Well, that's not good."

"I know," said Claire, putting her teacup down on the saucer. "It's not good." She felt understood. It was a sign.

"I've felt let down, sometimes, but I came to understand that God gives us what we need, not what we want. Prayer helps me."

"I see you at Mass all the time."

The lady put her hand on Claire's forearm and smiled. "And I see you. Would you like to pray together?"

Claire's face soured. She would give nothing back, not now, God could take nothing else from her. She had given and given and given and got nothing back. In fairness, Claire should take something from him.

The lady saw her face and was afraid of her. She withdrew her hand and the warmth on Claire's forearm evaporated.

"God has taken everything from me," said Claire. Then they sat quietly as she ate the chewy fruitcake.

When she had finished eating the lady tried to reach out to her again.

"My son is a priest, you know," said Mrs Halligan. "Just back from the missions in Sudan. Would it help, at all, if he came downstairs to speak to you?"

THE WASHING

CHRISTOPHER FOWLER

The first time the bell rang, Linda was supervising the packing of the last of the crates. The front door of the flat was wedged open, so she was surprised that someone had bothered to ring at all. *Spain*, she thought, wiping her hands and heading along the corridor, *they're more formal here than at home. Their circumstances are different.*

The man standing before her was sixtyish, sturdy and balding, with a wart the size of a marrowfat pea on the side of his nose. He wore a dark grey suit with a formal waistcoat and a watch-chain, and must have been boiling. He regarded her over the top of his half-moon glasses and did not smile.

"You are new," he said in heavily accented English. He pointed accusingly at the door. "This is wrong."

She looked at the wet paint in surprise. It was a warm brown, the colour you'd get if you mixed plums into chocolate.

"We just painted it," she explained. "It's the same as all the other doors in the building."

He was taken aback by her English accent. "It is not like the others at all, Madam. It is the wrong colour. It must be repainted at once." He managed to suggest that there would be dire consequences if it wasn't.

"The painter assures me it will dry lighter," she replied cheerfully.

"No, no, no." He wagged a nicotine-stained finger at her. "It is not right. Did you check your lease for the correct colour reference?"

"I don't think so." Miguel had taken care of the rental agreement. She had not been shown the paperwork and knew there would be an argument if she asked to see it. The best thing with men, she found, was to give in and agree. It usually worked with Miguel.

"I'm sorry," she said. "I will have it repainted."

He left without another word. Five minutes later, he returned to issue another statement. "Your removal van is blocking my car."

"I'm sorry," she said again.

He pinned her with a gimlet stare. "Two sorrys is two too many." With that he turned and vanished into the gloom of the landing.

The stairwell was unlit. Already she had miscounted the steps and fallen both up and down them. The building was over a hundred years old. Even on the brightest summer day the flat was so dark that she had to put the lights on. The sun reached a peak of fierce intensity at 4:00 pm, when the shops were only just opening after their siestas and the breeze from the sea had burned away, leaving hot dead air behind.

There were no cooling ceiling fans because they were not needed; the building's thick brick walls and lack of internal light kept it naturally cold. After the removal van had gone, she set about tidying up and putting away the crockery. Unwrapping her mother's coffee cups with great care, she set them out along the kitchen dresser. She had hoped Miguel would help with the unpacking, but he regarded the home as a woman's domain and avoided all forms of household maintenance, as if helping would somehow impugn his masculinity.

The days passed more slowly than they did in England, where the solstices offered fewer than five hours of daylight and five hours of darkness at their extremes. Here it was always summer. 4:00 pm was the hour for staying out of the searing sunlight and tackling household chores as slowly as possible. Miguel did not get home until 8:00 pm, which meant that the afternoons would become interminable if she failed to find a way of occupying the time.

When the bell rang she knew it was someone from within the building, because the inside door had an old-fashioned clockwork bell. There were twelve flats, but she had yet to meet anyone other than Carlos the janitor and Mr Two Sorrys.

She opened the repainted door to a slender young woman with cropped hair, a long thin neck and slightly protuberant eyes. At least this one knew how to smile, and what a smile!

Its corners seemed to reach her ears. "I am Pippa and I am so sorry," she began, darting forward to formally offer her hand. "It is my fault. The baby's sock."

Linda shook her hand. "Please, come in."

Pippa checked the threshold as one might look before crossing a road, then took an exaggerated step inside. "Oh, this is nice, you have no walls. All this space! We have many more walls, for the children's bedrooms. I have two boys and a baby girl. You must hear them at night. I hope they don't disturb you too much."

She headed straight for the open windows of the back bedroom. "The clothesline," she explained, pointing out and down. Each flat had a rack of three clotheslines outside, attached to the wall with metal arms. A pulley allowed the clothes to be moved some ten feet along the side of the flat. Linda followed her neighbour's pointing finger. "I live above you," Pippa told her. "I go to peg the baby's sock and poof—it fell down onto your line."

A pink sock not much larger than a man's thumb had landed on one of her towels. Pippa snapped it up and came back inside.

Linda had heard that this technique was used whenever someone needed an excuse to visit a new neighbour. "Would you like a coffee?" she asked.

Pippa threw up her hands in horror. "No, no, I do not want to make you work."

"I'm having one."

"All right then, just for a moment." She seated herself swiftly enough and looked around. "It's nice. You are married?"

"My husband Miguel is from here," she explained. "We met in England. He came back to his old job. His company supplies military equipment." She lit the hob, glad of the company. The building was grave-silent during the day. At night she sometimes heard dinners being prepared on other floors, and tantalising smells of fried fish, pork stews and *albondigas* drifted up from the courtyard.

"And you, you could just leave everything and come here?" Pippa asked.

"I had to give up my job, but yes, I'm afraid there's no arguing with Miguel. He can be very forceful." She laughed a little too gaily.

"Have you met the others?"

"No, only a rude man who complained about the colour of our door."

"Ah yes, he is the *prepotente*, you know this word? He thinks he is the boss, yes? Because his brother is a friend of the Generalissimo. I am no friend of Franco. One day he will be gone and then we will speak of better times. But the others here, they have been here since *la Guerra Civil*, they love our great leader, so you must be careful what you say."

"Oh, I am an outsider. I try not to get involved." Linda liked her instantly. Pippa was open and honest, with an innocence that took risks by showing itself. "Who else should I know in the building?" she asked.

"Come, come." Pippa rose and headed back to the window. The building formed a large U shape. The apartments opposite were no more than twenty feet away. Twelve racks of washing lines extended from the rear windows. Some bore bedsheets. Others had rows of shorts arranged in ascending sizes. Not all of the lines were used.

"You must always look at these." Pippa pointed to the racks. "You may not see anyone on the stairs but you can tell who is in and what they are doing. Look, my two boys." She pointed up at her own clothesline, upon which were strung two matching football shirts. "And over there."

The washing line opposite was full up with stockings, two red blouses, some pairs of frilly knickers, a pretty lace brassiere and a flared white dress covered in blue and yellow irises. Half a dozen paper windmills, red, orange, gold and silver, turned in a flowerpot hooked to the railing.

"That is the apartment of Maria. She is a dancer at *El Nacional*. She is so pretty." She shook out her fingers at the thought. "*Muy bonita*. But very poor. She needs to find a husband but the attractive ones are also poor, I think."

After coffee, Linda thanked Pippa for coming down, and they agreed to meet again.

Miguel was nearly always late home. She had expected it would be like this at the start, but hoped they might settle into more regular hours. After the flat had been decorated there was little else to do, and the streets were too hot to walk through on summer afternoons, so she seated herself by the open bedroom windows. They were shaded by 4:00 pm, so she could sit and read without having to fan herself. She was trying to revise her Spanish from a schoolbook but the effort invariably made her sleepy.

She hardly ever saw anyone on the gloomy central staircase. A couple of times an old lady passed her without saying a word. Pippa came down for coffee once or twice a week. At night Linda heard the squeaking of the pulleys, and knew that her neighbours were hanging out their clothes. Each day she found herself checking the washing lines to see who was in and who had been out the night before.

One afternoon she sat in the shade with a translation of Cervantes' *Don Quixote* in her lap, and her eyelids grew heavy. A squeak from the window directly opposite woke her. The floor-length glass was always heavily curtained and was never left open more than a few inches.

In place of the usual blouses and the iris dress was a long white cotton gown, a man's formal shirt and a pair of black socks. Down in the courtyard she could see pink and yellow specks of confetti.

"Who is Maria seeing?" she asked Pippa on their next coffee afternoon.

"Didn't I tell you?" Pippa dropped her jaw, appalled. "She has married *El Prepotente*."

"Mr Two Sorrys? No!"

"Yes, very ugly but very powerful. His name is José Masvidal. He's in the military division, the one I told you about with the brother who knows Franco. I don't like him so I did not go to the wedding. Better to smile from a distance than lie close up." Pippa pulled a face. She was full of peculiar sayings that probably had more impact in their original language. "Now Maria is married he will never let her go anywhere. She is much younger. She is my friend. I say to her, come dancing with me, and now she is too scared to go."

"So she's going to stay in all the time?" Linda asked.

"Oh yes, she will not be allowed out in the evenings. It is not respectful, it is *vergonzoso*. You know, shameful. Because she was a dancer and he is a good Catholic in the government."

Summer turned to autumn. The shadows changed their angle but the temperature barely seemed to fall. She saw less of Pippa because her friend had taken a part-time job in the *mercat,* working in one of their grain stores.

Outside the building opposite, the washing on the line had changed.

Now there were always four large spotlessly white shirts, vests, an old man's drawers, black socks, a shapeless black shift dress and what she'd assumed was underwear belonging to an elderly lady; an arrangement of baggy, beige cotton sacks. The paper windmills had been removed from the flowerpot and a heavy lead crucifix had appeared on the back wall. The woman who passed through the shadows moved with a supple, fluid grace. *She's so young,* Linda thought. *Don't let that happen to me.*

In the late afternoon the clock in the kitchen seemed to slow down. The sun took hours to set. It reached a low point in the reddening sky and just hung there without moving. When Miguel returned he asked her how her day had been and proceeded to tell her about his without waiting for her reply.

"The man opposite has stopped his new wife from going out," she said one evening over dinner. "He's making her wear old lady clothes because they're more respectable."

"A nightmare of a day today," said her husband, looking around for his cigarettes. "Put the radio on, will you?"

The clothes on the line opposite changed from fancy to plain, from bright blue flowers to charcoal grey, from French scanties to beige drawers. How easy it was to dismantle a woman's personality and replace it with something that smothered and suffocated. In all this time she hardly ever saw the woman behind the washing. She heard the pulley squeak a little before midnight twice a week and always went to look, but it was too dark to see, so she waited until the next morning to look at the line.

One morning she caught a glimpse of Maria in full sunshine, going to the *mercat*. She was slender-waisted and had tumbling auburn hair that shone in the fresh early light. She walked happily, bouncing slightly, swinging her basket, glad to be free.

Linda waited for her return. As Maria approached the building with her groceries she looked apprehensive, as if all her fears were held inside its dark stone walls.

"Your friend doesn't dance anymore?" asked Linda casually over coffee.

Pippa stirred her cup thoughtfully. "I asked her to come with me but she won't. Sometimes I go by her flat but she doesn't invite me in now." She lowered her voice as if worried that someone might overhear them. "It's the husband. He doesn't like me. He's had the walls repainted and has changed the furniture. All of her lovely bright things have gone. He moved in his grandmother's dresser and her armchairs. So dark and heavy. I saw them taking her lovely pink dressing table down the stairs. Such a waste."

The rains came. Miguel had to travel on business. The trips could last up to a week. For the first time she wondered if she was like Maria, willing to clip her wings for the love of a man. Sometimes she watched Miguel dressing for work and wondered how well she really knew him.

When she went back to her seat by the window and looked across the courtyard on the next washday she was in for a surprise. Maria was at the window. She looked furtively behind her as if to make sure that she was alone, then hung out her old red panties and blouse, taking them in the second they were dry, which in the afternoon sun was only a matter of minutes. Linda wondered if she had taken to going out while her husband was away.

"I've met him a couple of times," said Miguel over dinner one evening. "José moves in high circles. He is greatly respected."

"José from across the courtyard?" she said, surprised, her fork halfway to her mouth.

"He married the local beauty. A bit fast, by all accounts. He had to rein her in a bit."

"Perhaps it was her job to let him out," she said defensively.

"I don't know what you mean," Miguel replied, placing his knife and fork together.

*

There was now a pattern, she noted. Whenever there were no white shirts and black socks to hang out, her old clothes reappeared. José Masvidal's schedule was not unlike her husband's. He had to travel most at the weekends.

Christmas came and the flat was closed up while they visited each other's families. Pippa went home to see her mother. The building was mostly empty. In January the old pattern continued, but in the middle of February there was another change in the clothesline opposite. A man's shirt with bright blue stripes was hung out to dry beside Maria's sexiest items. José Masvidal would never wear such a shirt. As soon as the items were dry they were hurriedly taken indoors.

"It was a tiring journey," said Miguel, settling into his armchair beside the radio. "Across to Zaragoza, and on to a military facility outside Teruel. José was there. We had quite a talk. He's a very nice man."

"How are things going with his 'fast' wife?" she asked, keen for news. It seemed as if the men sometimes found out more than the women.

"He never mentions her," Miguel admitted vaguely. "José plays bowls and golf. He likes to tell me when he beats his rivals."

"Does she go with him?"

"I can't imagine she'd want to watch a group of middle-aged men playing games." Miguel carefully refolded his copy of *El País*. "We're visiting military posts over the next four weekends. Make sure you go to church on Sunday mornings."

She studied his face to see if he was joking but found nothing.

All through March the brightly striped shirt appeared on the washing line. Sometimes it was accompanied by racy blue swimming trunks. One afternoon when Pippa came down, Linda asked her about the owner of the clothes.

Pippa's eyes widened. "You mustn't say!" she cried, shocked. "Do you know what would happen if he found out? Why, he would have her killed."

It was Linda's turn to be shocked. "You don't actually mean—"

"Do you have any idea what goes on when those men go out together? They're on military business." Pippa pushed her coffee aside and leaned in closer. "The noisy ones in the towns they visit just disappear. I'm not saying they don't bring it upon themselves, but they're certainly sent away somewhere, and often they don't come back. A man is always a danger, but like-minded men in a group—they can go too far."

"Perhaps we should visit Maria to make sure she's okay," Linda suggested.

"Trust me," said Pippa, "she's fine." She held her painted nails level to the table top. "So long as everything stays like this. No upsets. It's best for everyone. And it's best you don't know any more." She flattened her red lips and held a finger against them. "Yes? For all of us." There was a bang on the ceiling and a slow rising wail. She listened for a moment, then shrugged. "*Los niños*. Always the boys. One day I swear they will kill each other."

*

The flat was so silent at night that the sound of the key in the lock was enough to wake her. She turned on the bedside light and sat up. Miguel came in and set down his briefcase.

"You're back early," she said. "I wasn't expecting you for two more days."

"The trip was cut short." He unbuttoned his jacket with great concentration and hung it on a chair.

"Oh? Why?"

"It's complicated," he said wearily. "Do you really want me to try and explain?"

"Did you come back with your friend José?"

"It's because of him we came back." He pulled off his shirt and threw it on the floor. "I need to get some sleep. I'm in early tomorrow."

By the time she awoke he had already left. She picked up his shirt, washed it and hung it out. The other washing line was empty, and the glass doors remained closed all day.

Later she sat in her seat by the window and read a trashy thriller. When her attention drifted she raised her head and looked across the narrow courtyard. The line was still empty. If José had come back, where were his shirts? She waited by the window, fully expecting that at any moment the glass door opposite would open and the washing would appear, but there was nothing. Miguel called to say he would be later than usual, so she ate alone, the sound of her cutlery ringing in the empty flat.

Just as she was climbing into bed, she heard the squeak of the pulley. She waited until it had finished turning and the door had shut, then crept over to the window without putting on the lights. The white shirts were back, four of them, with four pairs of black socks. And so were the beige old lady drawers. Maria ironed everything first; the creases in the shirts had perfect sharp edges.

The bright striped shirt stopped appearing on Saturdays. The red blouses and lace underwear did not return. One afternoon the glass door was left open and she could see inside the apartment. It had been painted grey and was dominated by the lead crucifix on the back wall. Linda tried to imagine what had happened. Mr Masvidal had returned early and thrown out the lover. Now his flighty wife was being made to repent her ways. Maria never even went to the shops anymore. Twice a week a crate of groceries appeared outside the door of the Masvidal apartment.

Linda heard from her friends in England. "When are you coming back?" they asked, but she was unable to give them an answer. Miguel had been promoted and his prospects looked good. Her desire for a child returned, but the doctor had advised against trying again for the sake of her health, so she contented herself with looking after Pippa's boys from time to time.

She missed her old job in England. She had only been cataloguing records in a provincial newspaper office, but she had lost herself in the stories they told. The local library here had a pitiful selection of books in English, so she relied on her sister to send the latest novels from London. She wondered if she could write something herself, perhaps about the dancer who had married the military bureaucrat, hoping for a better life. She bought a notepad and a fountain pen, and sat by the open windows plotting.

The day she started writing, a new dress appeared on the line. It had a little colour, pale primroses around the hem, but its main feature was its size. It was a maternity smock.

Linda could not wait to take coffee with Pippa. "How far gone is she?" she asked, setting out freshly made *coca de forner* in thick oily slices.

"Five months at least," said Pippa excitedly. "Even I didn't know. She's so skinny that she's only just started to put on weight. I thought, so, she's eaten a few cakes, but no, she tells me just the other day."

"You think this will bring her and José closer together?"

"How can a baby make that much difference? You know what they say: *Lavar cerdos con jabón es perder tiempo y jabón.* Washing pigs is a waste of time and soap."

"I think it loses something in translation," said Linda, pouring coffee.

Every Wednesday evening she attended a writing course run by the British Embassy, from one of the chambers in their amber stone wedding cake of a building behind the main plaza. There she learned about murders and motives and mysteries with a handful of bewildered elderly expats and a couple from Kenya who found sexual suggestion in every passing remark.

After her latest effort had been picked apart by a stern patrician from Henley-Upon-Thames who had never recovered from ending up here after failing to get his novel published in England, she went home and prepared dinner for Miguel. It seemed perverse to want to dash through the flat and check the back clotheslines for the latest update, but lately the washing had come to act as a lifeline to the world, a jungle telegraph that told her there were real emotions flailing behind closed curtains and shut windows. Tonight, there was nothing. The primrose maternity dress, which always made an appearance on Wednesday nights, failed to materialise.

"Terrible," said Pippa, barely able to gasp in enough air with the shock of it all. She had brought their usual coffee hour forward to the morning, so desperate was she to share her news. "She has lost the baby. That pig—" She went to spit but remembered where she was just in time. "He kicked her. In here." She waved a bony tanned hand over her own non-existent stomach.

"Did Maria tell you that?" asked Linda, wide-eyed.

"No, of course not. She says she slipped on the stairs, but I know it was him. She told me the baby was not planned and he has three of his own, from his first wife. Did I never tell you that?" She waved the missed information aside. "So, she is in Our Lady of Grace, recovering. The most terrible bruises, right from here to here."

"But if you think it was her husband, something must be done," said Linda firmly. She looked around the sombre room, trying to imagine a course of action. "I can talk to my husband and ask him to find out the truth."

"You must not do such a thing," Pippa insisted. "If you tell him, then José will know it was me who told you. Promise me you will say nothing."

Linda promised and the confidence was kept. But the windows opposite had taken on a sinister air that perversely drew her attention, because after Maria returned from the hospital, Linda noticed that something had changed.

Washdays still arrived twice a week and the shirts were pegged out as they always had been, but now they were badly ironed and no longer bleached to a fierce whiteness. The sleeves were grey and patchy, the collars washed without the studs being removed. Each one was hung with a single peg so that it creased badly as it dried. The maternity dress reappeared, but had been taken in so that it fitted tightly. Maria was not about to let her husband forget what had happened to their unborn child.

Summer arrived once more and the temperature soared back to its lethal intensity. The sky was so blue above the rooftops that it looked like the atmosphere was evaporating into space. Rectangles of light slid slowly across the drawing room's polished floor and over the kitchen tiles, marking off the hours of the day.

One evening Miguel came home in a strangely sour mood. Whenever he was like this she knew it was better to keep away, but tonight there was something about his face that made her ask.

"They say he fell," Miguel told her, half under his breath. "The man was as strong as an ox. Every morning he lifted weights, even when we were away attending conferences. I refuse to believe it."

"Who?" It was so rare that she asked questions, she wondered if she could still be heard. Perhaps her voice had shrivelled to nothing without her noticing.

"José Masvidal," he snapped back at her, striding about the room. "He was found at the bottom of the stairs with his head—" Miguel grimaced at the image that had formed inside his own head.

"You mean the marble stairs at the ministry?"

"No, our stairs—the stairs outside his own front door!" Miguel shouted.

Linda had experienced the treachery of the unlit staircase often enough, and had wondered if accidents had occurred in the past. She had not ventured up the opposite staircase but could tell it was the same.

"They should put lights on them," she said. "The skylights need cleaning and hardly lets in anything. I've nearly fallen there myself. Who found him?"

"*She* did." He could not bring himself to say her name. "She says he left for work and something made her go back to the front door. He was lying with his head down, what was left of it. He'd fallen from the top to the bottom. A man like that, as strong as an *ox!*"

She went down and crossed the vestibule of cracked black and white tiles, heading for the other side of the building. As she climbed the darkened stairs she heard a metallic thump and a slide. Carlos the janitor was working his way across the landing with a galvanised bucket and a mop. Water flooded across the tiles.

She looked at the patch he was cleaning. The sticky dark stain on the lowest step was, she noted, roughly the shape of Spain. Carlos was mute, and as a consequence his features were highly expressive. He shrugged at her, rolling his eyes at the door above. He had successfully scrubbed away the marks on the landing. Now he tipped soapy water across the last step, dissolving the Spanish map.

Pippa was next, of course. As Linda started the coffee she stood in the doorway looking up at the ceiling, listening. "They're asleep, thank goodness," she said, coming in. "I brought cake." Her wide brown eyes spoke volumes. "I shall be sent to Hell for saying it, but the answers to prayers come in many disguises. He beat her all the time and she did nothing. That was why she could never go out. Her body was black and blue."

"Have you talked to her?" Linda asked. "How is she? It must have been awful finding him there."

"Yes, probably. She is at the police station."

"Why?" Linda brought over cups and plates, setting them in their usual places. "Surely they don't suspect her?"

"What, you think she bashed in his head and dragged him to the stairs? Where would she get such a weapon to do this?"

"You've thought it through, then," Linda observed.

"She is at the police station because she must make a statement," said Pippa, unwrapping the cake. "After all, she found his body. I myself think she is in a dangerous situation. Her husband was friends with the captain of police." She raised a knife over the cake and cut it. "When Maria was younger and even prettier she was arrested. But the handsome young policemen did not press charges and let her come home." She left the implication hanging in the air. "Your husband is also friendly with the police, no?"

"Miguel? He never told me that."

"There are many things he doesn't tell you, I think."

"Is there anything we can do for Maria?" she asked, feeling as useless as all who merely observe. "Perhaps we should go down there and vouch for her character."

"And how can you do that when you have not properly met her? No, we must pray for her," said Pippa with finality. "That is all we can do. It is as my mother said: The men do the work and the women do the praying."

An argument of such simplicity was hard to refute. They ate their slices of cake in silence and tried not to glance across at the washing line.

"At least she will be a rich widow," said Pippa, munching. "We have a saying: The new wife comes before the old children."

The next afternoon, as Linda sat in her chair by the windows and read, Maria's glass door opened and sunlight suddenly fell into her room. The great lead crucifix had gone from the wall. There remained a single bare nail.

It was washday. She heard Maria singing "*Bésame Mucho*" as she hung out the washing. Linda tried to catch her eye but as usual the girl kept her head bowed modestly. The iris dress, white and blue, had reappeared. She hung it out and went back inside.

Linda wondered where the crucifix had gone.

The afternoon sank into a state of overheated enervation, but she found herself unable to settle. It felt as if a storm was breaking somewhere nearby. She read a few pages, then tried to plan the evening's meal, but found herself pacing back and forth across the drawing room.

At 5:00 pm a car pulled up in the street outside and two policemen got out. One of them was carrying a large wooden box with a leather handle. They looked up at the building, then went to the entrance. Linda knew who they had come for and why they were there; they would question Maria and examine the scene of the death. The box contained forensic equipment.

When she went to her chair by the open windows she glanced across and saw that the iris dress had gone, although the pegs were still in place. Leaning over the edge, she looked down. The dress had slipped free of its line and had fallen into the centre of the little stone courtyard.

Latching the door, she ran downstairs, carefully counting the steps as she went. At the bottom a small back door opened onto the outside area. She quickly gathered up the light cotton dress and took it upstairs to her flat. When she examined it in bright sunlight she saw that it was no longer just blue and white but had several irregular pink patches, including one geometric shape that, to her mind, resembled the upper half of a crucifix.

Maria had scrubbed the dress, but not with the right

detergent. At the hem were several carmine spots she had completely missed in her panic.

Linda poured a solution of soap and bleach into her sink, adding boiling water. While it was soaking she went to the windows and looked across once more. The men were pacing around Maria, asking her questions.

She acted quickly and without hesitation. Running back to the sink, Linda rinsed out the dress, noting with satisfaction that the fabric had been restored to its crisp white background. Even the hem was spotless. She squeezed out most of the water, but the dress was still damp and heavy. Laying it across her arms, she left the apartment and went across to Maria's building.

On the way, she stopped in the courtyard and dropped the dress back onto the dirty stone floor. Then she picked it back up and climbed the stairs. Carlos had made a good job of the stonework. The steps had already dried. Approaching the partially opened door, she could hear the detective's questions.

"One last thing, Mrs Masvidal. You were up and dressed when your husband left for work, yes? What were you wearing when you went to the front door and found he had fallen?"

She barged in, acting as though she had no idea that there was anyone else in the flat. She spoke loudly and confidently to cover her nervousness. "Maria, darling, your lovely dress fell off the washing line. I'm afraid it will need another rinse."

The astonished Maria accepted the wet dress from her.

"She washes her clothes every Thursday," Linda explained to the severe-looking gentlemen. "I see everything. I live in the flat directly opposite." She turned her attention to Maria. "One of your pegs broke. Such a pretty dress. I saw it fall from the line." She gave everyone a nice friendly smile. "Well, I can see you have friends over. Perhaps if you'd like to have coffee later?"

She smiled again and left them all standing there in the middle of the living room. When she reached her own flat, she put the coffee on. After a few minutes she heard the throaty ignition of a car engine and got to the front window in time to see the police drive off.

Linda unlatched her front door, then made the coffee and set out three cups. She unwrapped some chocolate cake she had been saving and cut three thick slices.

When she looked up, Maria and Pippa were standing in the open doorway, waiting to be invited in.

BLOOD LINES

STELLA DUFFY

Three nights in and the pain is almost too much.

Every joint aches, every place where bone rubs on bone, sinew reaches into bone, where muscle twists around bone, I feel as if I am splintering into myself, cracking within from the depths of me. The places that hurt are all of the usual joints where any of us may rub away a lifetime of cartilage and find ourselves left with bone on bone, the places that get us all in the end—knees and hips, lower back, shoulders—but for me the pain is more than simply the aging of my skeleton and what surrounds it. This pain rises up at every point where a human body might bend or twist, reach or stretch, ricocheting internal agonies from bone to flesh and back again.

Each one of the knuckles on my fingers and my toes is a site of concentrated suffering. She shall cry wounding wherever she goes. My neck, my elbows, my wrists, are racked from inside. Every one of the knobbly vertebrae counting down my spine sing out their individual pain-name as I try to rest, give myself to the ground. I hope that lying might be easier than sitting, standing easier than lying. Decades of this pain have taught me that there is no easier way, have shown me the steps I must pass through to come to ease, and still I shift in my chair, lift in my bed, turn in my pose in vain hope.

My body moves because it cannot be still in pain, my mind a labyrinth of pointless suggestions, each one tried a dozen times or more. I know there is no remedy, no solution, just the pain, standing, sitting, sleeping, not sleeping, living with pain and, even so, I search for respite. I practise giving in to it, I meditate on ignoring it, I attempt revelling in it because there is nothing to be done, yet maybe this is the one thing that can be done, and I greet my pain as one long-known.

There is no way round but allowing it and eventually, every other option tried and failed, I do. I cede. You would think that after all these years I would have learned to give in sooner, taught myself to accept, to stay with, instead of trying to outrun, the inner mutilation. But I am not that evolved, have not yet become one who, confronted with her own mortality, can stare it in the face with equanimity. I look away, shadow my gaze, blink in coyness and fear and, eventually, as ever, pain takes my chin in her firm grasp, turns my lined face to hers and demands I look her in the eyes. Then, finally, I yield, give in, surrender. This pain is all of me. And what it heralds, what it reveals, is all and only mine.

Of course, I had a choice. I could have taken myself to the highest bridge and jumped into the abyss beneath, or thrown myself in front of a speeding train, a rush-hour bus heavy with urgent passengers. I could have filled my pockets with sea-smoothed stones and laid me down to welcome the rising tide. I have done none of these things because in the months or years between bouts of pain and revelation I lived as easily as you do, as normally as you do.

(Are you easy? Normal? No, neither am I, but we are all so skilled at the pretence, aren't we?)

I did not kill myself, I had no choice but to bear it. I have borne it for decades now.

The first time it happened, I was a girl edging into a woman. Given what comes after the pain I have often thought how useful it would be if I could link these bone and muscle and tissue pains to the pain of my own bleeding, one linked to the other, blood to blood in a womanly echo. That is how nice stories go, but it is not what happened and this is not a nice story. I was well into my fifteenth year, accommodated to my personal lunar cycle when the pain cycle began, the other rhythm that has ruled my life for more than five decades.

The orbit of my torment is not regular, it matches no heavenly bodies even though it is deeply ingrained in earthbound ones, bound for the earth. The irregularity means that even after all this time it creeps up on me and I can be in the throes before I realise I am part of it again, my darker cycle.

Since I became menopausal this has been my only cycle and it has come more often. In my youth I experienced it just once or twice a decade, more than enough for a growing person, one already feeling too fiercely the shifts and uncertainties as we begin to make our way in our teens and twenties, those awful years of no belonging, no true home. When my children were small the episodes of pain came more often, but I attributed that to any mother's mortal fears for her child, every mother's excessive imaginings—though I did not need imagination to understand excess. The children left home, their fathers went too, and since I have lived alone I have paid more attention to this other pattern, the pattern only I possess. While I cannot track when it will arrive, it does not match weeks or months, count in sevens or twelves, I have come to know intimately the path it will follow once it is with me, when it takes me up, fills me up.

Today is my third day of pain, tonight will be the third night; I know I will sleep very little if at all. When I wake tomorrow the world will look quite different.

I didn't know any of this the first time. I had the pains, yes, but my mother called them growing pains. My father thought I was trying to get out of school. My sister complained I'd kept her awake all night with my groaning, even though we had separate rooms by then and I knew that her nights were disturbed by her dreams of Clyde Forster, not my suffering. Before I understood that the pain was easier to bear by giving in to it, I tried to walk through it, work through it. I found that concentrating on something else, anything else, was useful if not entirely successful.

That morning I concentrated on the awful blood on the heavy boots of the lollipop lady. I imagined we would get to school and there would be an assembly about the dreadful accident that had happened before we all arrived. When no assembly was called and we trooped off to English, Biology, French with no call to come together and offer up prayers for the dearly departed, I decided the blood must have come from one of her cats. We knew the lollipop lady had a dozen cats or more. Her house was the old and smelly one at the end of Marshall Road, right where our ordinary town streets hit the beginning of the big dual carriageway. It must have been one of her cats, squashed beneath the wheels of an uncaring businessman's company car as he raced to the meeting that would finalise his bonus, or broken beneath the huge tyres of the buses that drove factory workers from our little town to the dark new city four miles west. By the time our school day ended with ninety minutes of quadratic equations, the room and my brain slowed down by sun pouring through the afternoon windows, the pain had receded to less than a memory. It was a past itch of hurt, once there, now nothing even to remind me it had gone.

It came back three years later. By then I was training as a nurse. I was not drawn to nursing as a caring profession, nor was my own experience of pain the reason I had decided to train. I wanted to leave home, to get out of our stifling little town. I thought myself better than our parents and their factory jobs in the city. I knew I was neither as capable nor as interested in learning as my sister with her university place, and took the only route open to girls like me from people like mine.

Nursing paid a little while we trained and offered a small room in the nurses' home; it was a way of getting out while not risking too much. I did not yet understand that there is no cocoon against risk.

Two years into my training I believed myself an independent nineteen-year-old. I had a prescription for the pill and a boyfriend in his third year of medical school; we were starting to weave dreams for a future together and thought ourselves very fine indeed. Our plans to share a small flat the following year would have been daring if my parents had been at all interested in what I did with my life, if his Nigerian family had any suspicions that he was wasting his precious study time with a poor white girl from a small town family. Mine were not and his did not and so we rolled into an easy two-step that allowed each of us to believe we were braver than we were while also offering ready access to the frantic and fulfilling sex our youthful bodies demanded.

The nurses' home backed on to a graveyard, a crowded place of angels with broken wings standing sentry above young wives taken too soon in childbirth, dead children alongside them. Elizabeth aged nine years, Charles aged six years, Mary Alice four months, much beloved. Beyond the long dead babies was an Edwardian monstrosity of a church with no redeeming features. In a nod to the twentieth century the hospital trustees, a fat group of great and good who prided themselves on bettering this tired city and lifting it above the factories that enabled their largesse, had installed in the church tower an automated bell that tolled each hour from six in the morning until midnight, with a tedious peal at midday. No matter how late we nurses had gone to bed after our night shift, crawling back to our cupboard rooms with aching feet and eyes gritty from the night, the church bell assured us of our location and the exact hour we were failing to sleep.

My shift finished as usual at eight that morning, we talked through the handover until eight thirty, I left the hospital and made the short walk to the nurses' home, rubbing dry eyes with hands that stank of liniment and bandages from my stint on the elderly ward, all arthritis and wasting lives. I sluiced away the worst of the night in the communal bathroom that served eighteen young women, pulled the thin curtains against the damp summer day and lay myself down on my bed. I had not even pulled up the covers before I fell asleep.

When the pain woke me the church bell was tolling midday. I came to, groggy and uncertain. By our second year we prided ourselves on hearing the bell every hour, noting its lunchtime alarm, but doing no more than shifting in our beds, turning the pillow to the cool side to sleep on. This was not an ordinary day.

The pain arrived with the repetitive peal and it did not leave me. It was different from the pain I experienced at fifteen, somehow both more on the surface of me—this time my skin hurt as much as the places where my bones met—and also deeper, in the marrow of me. It may be that by my second year of training I had words for these parts of me, for the capillaries that opened to allow burning blood to flow through, for the specific nerves ripping at me from deep inside muscle fibre, and that knowledge may have made my suffering more specific.

I lay for a full hour and marvelled at what was happening within me. From midday until the one o'clock bell I twisted and turned, sweated and froze, uttered guttural groans with my fist in my mouth to leave my neighbours sleeping and whispered into the foetid air of my tiny room the worst curses my Nigerian lover had taught me. I did all this and somehow lifted above the pain. I watched myself, observing from far within my mind while simultaneously experiencing each interminable second.

By early afternoon the pain had ebbed a little. This was to become the pattern for many decades of my life, a sudden onslaught, a slow leaving and then a pulsing of the pain, to and from my body, to and from myself, to and from the me that resided in the body and the me that cowered in my mind, watching pain run its course in morbid fascination. By the time I was washed and dressed ready for my shift the pain had receded to searing blossoms of agony every five to seven minutes, one burst in my lower back, the next in my left shoulder, the third stabbing between my intercostal muscles on the right-hand side, the fourth a solid burn at the back of my right eye. It travelled around my body, taking up residence for three, four, five impossible breaths and then moving on. I knew I could not explain it and therefore I would bear it. I thought I could bear it.

That night I sat beside an old man shunted out of the medical ward to a side room where he might more privately die of the disease that was choking him, locking air out of his lungs until all he could breathe was blood, his nose and mouth dripping with it. He died just after four thirty as the summer sun was making its way up over our tired city, his wife fifteen minutes too late to kiss him goodbye. My body kept on with the pulsating pain throughout his last hours and into that waking day, the wife's first without him for fifty-two years. I was in the process of tidying him away when there was an emergency in the ward. I left the old lady with her dead old man and, as I had been trained, came running at the call of "Nurse!"

The call came from a surgeon I had not met before. I had done a brief surgical rota in my first year, but our longer training was yet to come. He wore surgical scrubs, mask, cap, but it was the blood that showed his profession, blood on his gloved hands, blood on the front of his gown, blood on his forehead where a clumsy surgical nurse must have wiped his brow during a tense procedure and mingled a patient's blood with the sweat of his work. Two of my fellow trainee nurses were fussing over a middle-aged man. He'd been in for gallbladder surgery two days ago and was healing far too slowly, his drains were clogged, his scar red and inflamed. The surgeon shouted at them to step back, lurched forward to look at the man and roared as his leg caught on the patient's catheter drain, urine spraying his scrubs a dark blue that made the blood stand out all the more.

He practically spat his instructions to the two flustered nurses, rattled off a list of drugs the sister needed to order up immediately, demanded the man be brought to him in theatre in four hours if the drugs did not take effect and turned on his heel, tearing off the filthy scrubs as he went, dropping them at the door to our ward so we could watch him stride away in a suit of arrogantly elegant midnight blue.

Sister Watkins glared after him and ordered one of the two nurses to deal with the man's catheter and the other to pick up the scrubs. She wasn't having her ward stinking of urine for the morning handover, she knew exactly what Sister Murphy would think of that.

"Not to mention all the blood on his scrubs, Sister," I said, rushing to help my fellow trainee.

The first-year nurse looked at me. "What blood?"

Sister Watkins hissed at her to get on with the cleaning and hadn't the patients been disturbed enough, before turning to me with an odd look on her face. "Were you with the old man when he died, Nurse?"

"Yes, Sister, but his wife's in there now and I heard the call for a nurse, so I came to help."

She smiled. Unlike Sister Murphy, Watkins was kind to us new nurses.

"I don't imagine you've had too many dark deaths yet and his wasn't a pretty sight, of course you've blood on the brain. Not to worry, you go and take the wife to get a cup of tea now. I'll send someone to wash the man down with you, and then you can tidy up the room and hopefully their children will be here soon. Off you go. It will be easier from now on. The first nasty death is always the worst. I think I saw blood wherever I looked for a fortnight or more after my first."

She was gone then to a call at the other end of the ward, the poor men in Surgical Three were not to get any sleep that night. I went back to look after my widow, to tidy up the dead man, and to marvel that my pain had disappeared in the more immediate fuss caused by death and piss. The rest of the shift was busy but without incident and I was in bed and listening to the church bell toll nine before I realised that Sister Watkins had been reassuring me because she thought I hadn't seen blood on the surgeon's scrubs at all, that it was simply a result of having been so close to a bloody death. Perhaps she was right. As I fell asleep I remembered the blood under his fingernails. Caked and dried brown.

The twins were three and my baby was six days old when the health visitor arrived and I refused to let her touch the baby, screamed blue murder as she reached out for him with her crimson blood hands. When my marriage broke up, when our daring, sex-centred love had not proved strong enough to withstand colicky twins, sleepless nights, the ongoing grind of daily racism, he moved home to Lagos and I found a job in a small town with a strong need for a part-time practice nurse and far enough from my family to no longer feel their 'told you so' looks.

I knew the health visitor; we worked alongside each other. She was ten years older than me, middle-aged well before her time, and had been kind about my marriage break-up, my need for part-time work, generous with her baby-care advice for the twins. She had turned decidedly sniffy when I told her about the pregnancy. Her words were that she'd have thought twins were more than enough for one woman on her own, but I know she was more annoyed that I was screwing the town's only eligible single man. When I became pregnant and chose to keep the baby, keep the man as a friend and for sometimes-sex, she was horrified.

"Look, you're a modern young woman, you don't have to have this baby, you know."

"I know."

"I mean," she hesitated, "I could help, if you like. There's a woman I know, I assist her sometimes. Only young girls, you understand, or where things have gone wrong, the girls from the special school or up at the psych unit. Or some of these farm girls," she said, warming to her theme, "they've seen plenty of it with the animals, think they know everything, and then they're as surprised as Christmas when they fall."

"But don't some of them want…?"

She smiled. I think she thought the smile was coy but it was cruel. "Oh, they all think they want their babies, but they're only children themselves, not old enough to know. Anyway, I just wanted to say, I could help, no one needs to know."

"You mean you perform abortions on them without their consent?"

She was cold now, sharp. "A twelve-year-old cannot give consent. Her parents do."

We did not speak again after that. We passed each other files and folders in the surgery. I paid particular attention to agitated mothers and young daughters in the waiting room and our health visitor's subsequent half-days off. I should probably have told someone, but I was seven and a half months pregnant, alone with twins, my eligible lover had gone off me as the bloom faded and the heavy ankles and tired face flooded in—I didn't have the energy. And in the weeks that followed, the cow-time weeks when I became slower and daily more nesting, settling, gathering in, I forgot everything but my little ones and the baby to come.

It was an easy birth compared to the twins; my lover was generous in his gifts if not his time or interest. I went home quiet and comfortable and happy with my lot, baby-love hormones flooding my body. Yes, I felt pain, but of course I did; the twins had been a caesarean birth, this was natural in its agonies, natural in its tears and rips, natural in its slow time too. But I welcomed that, I had wanted that experience. I went home and felt every moment of my uterus contracting, my body re-finding itself. It did not occur to me that these pains were those pains.

She only came to my little house down that long country lane because it was her job. I had known she would have to, I'd thought we would be polite, get it done, all would be well. But I could not hand him over to her, I couldn't let her hold him, touch him. She was blood-soaked, wet with it, from her fingertips to her elbows.

They decided it was a post-partum psychosis, moved me to the hospital, put me under the observation of a psychiatrist and two nurses. I was fine, outside of her presence I was fine. When they mentioned her name I began to shake, all I could see was the blood.

For a single mother back then, with no partner, two brown babies and one white, I was very lucky. I had made a good impression in that town, everyone loves a practice nurse who remembers their name, takes care to be kind to them. I was not sectioned: it was a one-off incident; I promised to take it easy; I promised to be a good girl.

I kept that promise. I had worked it out. There was blood on their hands, their clothes, their faces, caked in their nails and pooled around their boots. They had been deep in blood and I could see it. My pains were a harbinger of their guilt. I had three children to look after, I did not mention the blood again, I did not scream when I saw it, I simply paid closer attention to any twinge or ache, to the blossoming pain when it finally arose, years apart each time, and then I looked out for the person I should avoid. The next person whose guilt I could read in red.

Five years later it was the twins' PE teacher, a fit and strapping young man who had been, they said, a hero in the army. I went to a parent-teacher meeting and met him stuffing his face with Victoria sponge, blood running from the centre of his forehead into his eyes, nose, mouth. He munched on blood-soaked cake and I went home via evensong, found Jesus in the heart of a secretly evangelical Anglican vicar. My children left the state system that week and I became a dedicated church-goer until the end of their primary schooling.

My youngest was twenty-one and away at university when I married again, the twins travelling on two different continents. We had a register office wedding, our signatures, his oldest friend for witness. She was the best friend of his first wife, the wife who'd died of cancer over twenty years ago. Theirs had been Love Story and he the perfect grieving Ryan O'Neal who waited two decades to find me. He'd waited far beyond the acceptable period of mourning, everyone was delighted for him, delighted for us. I had not experienced the pains for sixteen years. I was almost forty.

I was careless.

I let down my guard, let him love me into a relaxation that meant I almost forgot the pain, forgot what I knew about it. Memory does strange things, it reduces the extremity of hurt, dampens down once-intense fear. It made me believe that perhaps they were all right when they told me it was my mind seeing things, not truth in blood. Nothing had happened, I was seeing blood that wasn't there, I was wrong, mad, not bad, mistaken, not quite sane. The kind psychotherapist explained that my axis was tilted ever such a little and I saw things that were not hidden, as I had once assumed, but actually non-existent. I saw things invented by my over-active mind or spirit or heart, perhaps all three.

I almost allowed myself to believe them. It was so much nicer to believe them, to be part of it all instead of standing outside, watching for blood. But my body knew, even when I denied what I had once understood, my gut knew, my muscles knew, my bones and tendons and sinews, my organs and the grey matter that is my brain, every piece of me that is solid and fibre and real, that is not thought or feeling, but real, actual, all of that part of me knew.

And one day that part of me, body-me, real me, insisted I see the truth, pulled me out of my soft mattress of complacency to show me the truth again. I hated my body for doing this to me.

Don't we always? Wouldn't we all prefer to go with the tide, float on gentle waves of trust and faith in each other, prefer not to see the truth, especially not the secrets our loved ones have hidden so well?

Whisper it to yourself, you know the answer.

My son came home from America. My first-born who arrived ten minutes before his sister and yet was always the shyer, quieter of the two. My son came home after four years away, living in a desert ashram, a forest retreat, a commune in a mangrove swamp. He had sent letters and emails, totems hand-carved from the driftwood of his journeying into himself. I felt his arrival. An hour before his delayed plane finally landed at Heathrow, forty minutes after it had started lazily circling London waiting for permission to land, the skies too busy that cold Tuesday afternoon, my pain had begun. It started in my uterus and this time I didn't lie to myself. It was not period pain, it felt everything and nothing like period pain. This was mother-love revealed in terror. Not my boy, please not my boy.

But yes, of course, my boy.

Why not? Why should my family be immune? Why should any family be immune? *Why should yours?*

I held him and wanted to vomit. He was tall and fine, very beautiful and so tired. I stroked his matted hair, his tattooed back and his triple-scarred shoulder. He told me every cut line meant something and I believed him. I sat beside him in the back of the car, my husband driving ahead, a taxi-driver for our reunion, and my beautiful boy who was a blood-stained man lay his head in my lap and fell asleep. I sat perfectly still, pain coursing through every breath of me, and stared at the places where blood was marked on him. Both hands. His left foot. Each of the three shades of blood were slightly different, one to match each scar on his upper left shoulder at the front, just where it turned into chest. I could read the blood as easily as I could read the lies he had fed me in his emails and postcards home.

A week later, when he had caught up on his sleep, eaten everything I put before him with an appetite more voracious than anything he'd ever had as a child or teenager, when I was still in pain, while I still saw the blood on his hands, his foot, saw it smeared from him to his bedsheets, rubbed into the towels he left on the bathroom floor—no doubt the ashram and the retreat and the commune all had staff, he had a mother—I decided it was time to ask him for the truth. I told him to come with me for a walk along the beach and, perhaps it was my tone, perhaps he was just tired of sitting inside. He agreed easily. My husband and I moved out here two years ago; my husband is a painter, he came for the light. I came because I could not risk being around people, there is too much blood that I do not want to see. And then my son brought it home.

We walked along the shore, the North Sea smacking and punching at the sand, dragging it deep, and I asked him to tell me everything. I told him I was his mother, there was nothing he could not tell me. He told me nothing. He talked about his spirit and his senses, prattled about early-morning yoga and late-night chanting, of shared values and a hope for humanity. He assured me that he had not given up, but that it was a hard life in community. It was too tough to continually give of himself to others with no respite. My big boy, a foot or more taller than me, scooped me close to him with his bloodied hands and held me tight, telling me he had come home to rest with me, find his strength, enable him to go back out there and make the difference he was born to make.

I stood with my back to the roaring sea and I looked up into his beautiful face and I begged him to tell me about the people he had killed. I asked if it was an accident or murder. I promised him I would love him anyway but that I had to know. I told him how clearly I could see the blood on his hands, on his foot, how I lay awake at night imagining him stomping someone to death, the boot in the face, the steel toecap to an exploding liver, toxins and bile and death. I sobbed in physical pain and heart sorrow and the agony of a body that had grown him inside me, pleaded with him to tell me what had happened, give me the stories, whatever they were. I had never felt the pains so strongly, never been so sure I was right.

He was confused, bewildered. He denied it all at first. But I took his arms, his hands, I showed him where I saw the blood, I traced the lines of it, described the different shades. I knelt at his bare feet as the tide came in and tried to knock me over, knelt and showed him the blood that was not washed away, how it stayed on his skin. I promised him I could hear the truth, my hearing it would make him well again, whole again. And then we were both on our knees, he crying and clawing at me, shaking all over, me scrabbling in the sand, trying to beat the tide, pull the truth from him before the sea dragged me away.

My boy could not swim. He never got the hang of it. Even as a little child, he sank straight to the bottom of the pool. He was a little precious stone. A tall, thin, broken precious stone, soothed and shaped by rough sand on his soft scarred skin, rolled in roiling waves. I didn't want to let him go but the pain in my arms was too deep, too much. My hands were seized up with cold and a deep bone ache that meant I could feel nothing else, I could not feel his skin on mine, his hand in mine. I could not feel his hand.

They said we looked like the Pietà. It felt more like solace. It must have been unbearable for him to be in the world, knowing what he had on him, death on his hands, his body. No wonder he had marked his skin with such ferocity, but all the tattoos did was make the red of the blood seem deeper, richer. The waves washed us both clean. When they found us I was almost gone myself, holding him close and feeling his body get colder and colder. The sun was long gone, the tide that had left us was on the turn. But I did not hurt, it was as if the water had peeled his crimes from his skin and at the same time had washed away my pain. For the first time in decades the pains were truly gone. Yes, they had receded for many years at a time, but I always had the fear of a return. This, giving my son to the sea, accepting ease in return, this felt like an exchange. I was spent.

I explained about the blood, of course, but I do understand it was hard for them to believe me. They were surprised that neither of my husbands knew of what I had endured, nor did my work colleagues, friends. When they went further back they noticed certain connections. A PE teacher who left the school in such a hurry, a rumour put about that he had been caught looking at the children as they undressed; he had left in order to escape questioning. A health visitor, nearing retirement, who had sent a typed letter of resignation and never gone back. It was on headed notepaper and she was definitely nearing the end of her time. A surgeon who had been asked out by a young nurse, presumably left his lovely wife and lovely home and lovely life for her too, no word, no message. A lollipop lady who one day toppled down the steep stairs in her old house, undiscovered for ten days, her half-feral cats left to fend for themselves, to feed themselves on her corpse.

When a woman is quiet, kind, unassuming, when she has a nice job and a nice enough life, nothing too bright, nothing too glamourous, it is easy to ignore her, easy to think that she has nothing to do with the big dramas of life.

When a woman can no longer ignore her own pain, can no longer ignore the evidence of her own eyes, then—perhaps— it is time to pay attention.

They are very kind to me here. All of them, the staff and the other residents. They prefer us to say residents, they say it makes the place feel less institutional. But I know where I am, I know who I am, what I feel, what I see.

Three days ago the pains began again. I'm looking forward to seeing the young woman who comes to visit on Wednesday afternoons. We talk and she takes notes. She thinks she is listening to me, and I'm sure she is, in her own way. But now that my pain has started, now the sap of agony is rising, my eyes will see more clearly. I am looking forward to what she shows me.

SMILE

LEE CHILD

The guy who put together the video evidence highlight reel was a nerdy young timeserver named Skelton. Every day, rain or shine, warm or cold, he wore a checked flannel shirt and a knit tie. No one liked him. But pedantry and exactitude were required in his role. Juries still regarded video evidence as vulnerable, especially when it got blurry and out of focus. And the recent algorithmic add-ons were mostly seen as woo-woo filmflam, without a serious guy in a knit tie to explain them all. Facial recognition, gait analysis, and so on and so forth. Very complicated, down at the scientific level. Skelton had his uses.

He started out by saying, "Obviously we're lucky because this is London, and this is its main long-haul airport, which means we have at our disposal more cameras than literally anywhere else in the world. We can follow along, in real time, virtually every step of the way. Ready?"

Nominally in charge of the investigation was a Detective Chief Superintendent named Glover, but all morning he had been accompanied by three unknown associates, all with visitor tags around their necks, all younger than himself, two of them women, one believed to be from the Foreign Office, and the other from MI6. The third unknown associate was me, believed to be from the American CIA. Whatever, the women and I seemed to make all the final decisions. As in right then, when Skelton asked Glover, and Glover looked at the women, who looked at each other, and then at me, and I nodded, whereupon Glover said to Skelton, "Yes, ready."

A uniformed officer closed the door. The room went quiet. We were in the basement underneath New Scotland Yard. Skelton started the highlight reel. The first shot was a downward angled view along three drop-off bays at the first-class end of BA departures. The picture was huge, on a monitor bigger than most home TVs. It was in bright colour. It was crisp and detailed. Nothing like the old days.

On the screen a car pulled into the furthest-away bay. A late-model Bentley Flying Spur sedan. Not quite black. Some kind of dark gunmetal grey. Both rich and sinister.

"Looking for attention," a detective said. "Or he would have come in a black S-class Mercedes, like everyone else."

On the screen two men got out the front of the Bentley. The driver walked around to the trunk. The passenger stood for a second, glancing all around, and then he opened the rear door and stood back, respectfully, but still glancing all around.

"Bodyguard," the detective said. "Somewhat superfluous. That's the safest location in England."

On the screen a big bulky man in a dark wool overcoat got out the back of the Bentley. He stood for a second, half turned away, facing his bodyguard, adjusting the fit of his coat on his shoulders. Then he turned toward the rear of his car and looked down, as if at something low to the ground about ten feet away, and then he turned more and looked up, as if checking on his driver's progress, hauling luggage out the trunk. For a steady second, his face was clearly visible.

Skelton froze the playback.

"That's Anenko," he said.

"Are we absolutely sure?" Glover asked. "We'd look like fools if we misidentified the chap right from the beginning."

"Watch this," Skelton said. He rolled the action back, frame by frame, to where the guy in the coat was once again turned mostly away, looking down low. He froze the picture like that and said, "Heathrow is thick with cameras, but what you need to remember is, for every one you can see, there are probably fifty more you can't. Because they're hidden. They're disguised as other things, or built into things. Lots of them are waist-high, looking up, so a wide-brimmed hat doesn't work so well anymore. Some of them are knee-high, looking up."

He clicked a mouse and the picture changed to a new view of the same instant. Now the camera was head-on to the guy, low down, so that the more he hunched away from his car, the more he leaned in toward the new lens, as if welcoming it, as if embracing it.

Skelton clicked again on a couple of options, and powerful software froze the picture and rotated it up a little, and left a little, until it was like a head-on mug shot of the guy. All kinds of fine pulsating lines darted here and there, as if pointing out areas of interest, and then finally a graph appeared, printed in glowing green, above a caption that said *Level Of Confidence 100%.*

"It's Anenko," Skelton said. "No doubt about it. We ran it through three separate facial recognition systems and they all agreed. Between them they had more than a hundred images to compare against. Some of them dated back to the Soviet era. Most are recent and undeniably authentic."

"Good enough," Glover said. "I suppose."

On the screen the scene picked up again from the original high angle. The driver pulled a suitcase out and set it upright and extended its handle. He followed it with a briefcase. The bodyguard took charge of both pieces. Anenko led the way, and the bodyguard followed, like a porter. They walked to the edge of the frame.

"Now watch," Skelton said.

On the screen a black S-class Mercedes sedan pulled into the bay behind the Bentley. At the top of the picture the terminal doors opened for Anenko and his bodyguard. At the bottom of the picture the rear passenger door opened on the Mercedes. At the top Anenko and his bodyguard stepped into the building. At the bottom the passenger stepped out to the sidewalk.

Skelton froze the image. He chopped the screen into three separate panels and loaded each one with a different angle, the first being Anenko and his bodyguard walking down the approach corridor, which led from the street to the main departures hall itself. They were walking head-on toward a camera, which was also bright and in colour and crisply detailed. Insanely detailed, in fact. Beyond the bodyguard, back out through the glass door to the street, tiny figures were clearly visible, moving about. Who they were was made clear by the centre panel of Skelton's array. It showed the same high-angle scene as before, now with the driver getting back in the Bentley, and in the bay behind it the passenger from the Mercedes closing his door and stepping toward the terminal. He took nothing with him except a small canvas messenger bag on a leather strap. He walked with his shoulders back, his head up and his eyes front. He wore no hat or glasses.

"He knows there are cameras," the detective said. "He's been well briefed. He's been told he can't beat them. So he's not even trying."

On the third panel Skelton froze a suitable head-on shot of the guy's face.

"Now they all walk for quite a long while," he said. "It's an airport terminal, after all. That's the longest most folks walk all year. We might as well use the time."

He clicked his mouse. The frozen image on the third panel tilted and rotated and arranged itself into a mug shot, and the same thin pulsating lines darted about, followed by a graph identical to the first, with the same caption: *Level Of Confidence 100%*.

"Who is he?" Glover asked.

Skelton said, "First I need to make clear this conclusion is based on only five known images. Statistically that's enough for the algorithm. But a jury wouldn't understand the arithmetic. The numbers are too far apart. A hundred per cent but only five pictures."

"Who is he?" Glover asked again.

"He's an American citizen."

Glover glanced at the Foreign Office woman, who glanced at the MI6 woman, and then they both glanced at me, and I shrugged and nodded, both at the same time, as if to say, what did I care?

Glover asked, "Does he have a name?"

"Jack Reacher," Skelton said. "Jack not a diminutive for John, and no middle name. He's a West Point graduate. He was in the U.S. Army for thirteen years. There are two military ID photographs in the system. Plus two passport photographs. The fifth known image is from French intelligence. They photographed him at his mother's funeral, in Paris."

On the screen Anenko and his bodyguard were about to walk under the camera recording them. Jack Reacher was about twenty paces behind them. He was a big guy. Not a circus freak, but enough for a double take. Skelton changed the angle to a new camera set well to the side of dead ahead, so that the walking figures seemed likely to pass out of the frame, until they changed direction, in a long curve, homing in on the camera itself, as if it was their exact destination. Which it was, in the short term, because Skelton's next change showed it to be high above the perfumed air of the dedicated first-class check-in area. Anenko stepped past the concierge at the velvet rope, without showing paperwork, as if obviously entitled. Reacher followed. He showed his printed-out itinerary. The woman smiled and waved him in.

Anenko's bodyguard put the suitcase on the check-in scale and handed the briefcase to his boss. Then he stood back a pace, respectfully.

"Not going with him," the detective said. "Operationally a no-brainer, I suppose. I'm sure he has regional specialists waiting at his destination. And as soon as he's through security, he's in a sterile area anyway, by definition. He doesn't need anyone now. And air fares for the help add up, you know, whoever you are."

The hidden cameras in the check-in desks had microphones with them. Anenko was headed to New York. All was in order. He was in plenty of time. Two desks away Reacher was checking in for San Francisco. All was equally in order, but he had much less time. The West Coast flight left much earlier than the East Coast.

Skelton hopped sources again, to a head-on camera above the entrance to the dedicated and very genteel first-class security line. The bodyguard stood back and watched his boss walk on without him. He stayed in position, motionless, like a wistful relative. Reacher stepped around him and followed Anenko, about ten feet behind.

Skelton paused the playback.

He said, "With all due respect to whoever you all really are, surely we need to admit the first mistake has already been made."

Glover said, "Careful, now."

"What mistake?" the detective said.

"This man is flying from London to San Francisco with nothing but a tiny little messenger bag. That should have been profiled."

The woman from MI6 whispered to Glover.

Who said, "We used to, but we had to abandon it. All we caught was billionaires. Tech people with homes in both cities, and sleeping pills in their bags to get them back and forth."

"No sleeping pills in this bag," Skelton said. He clicked a couple things and an X-ray photograph of a bag came up. Taken from directly above. All green and orange, like the agents saw. There were three rectangular shapes inside.

"A hardcover book, a boarding card, and a passport," Skelton said. He called up a second image, of ghostly items in a dog-bowl container. "Plus a clip-together toothbrush, a credit card of some sort, a wad of paper money, which seems to be about half pounds and half dollars, plus what looks like twenty-nine cents in American change, and thirty-three pence in English money. Altogether not much for a long journey. And he isn't a tech guy. He's a retired military cop, currently under the radar."

Skelton switched back to a moving picture. A guy one ahead of Anenko and two ahead of Reacher was holding things up at the metal detector hoop. Something beeped. The guy tried again. It still beeped. Anenko's briefcase was already out the far end of the X-ray tunnel. It rattled down the rollers and came to rest among a small but growing pile. Then Reacher's canvas bag came out and jammed up behind it.

In the end the guy got through the hoop with his shoes off,

and after that it was plain sailing first for Anenko, and then Reacher. Anenko stepped ahead and shook his briefcase loose from a minor tangle of straps and handles and walked away with it into a glamorous corridor, which according to a discreet little sign led to the first-class lounge. Reacher stepped around the guy putting his shoes back on, picked up his own bag and followed Anenko.

Skelton switched from angle to angle, accounting for every second and every step, like a prosecutor building his case. Anenko entered the first-class lounge. Reacher entered the first-class lounge. Anenko sat down. Reacher sat down, far enough away to be in the background, but close enough to watch what was going on. Which for a long time wasn't much. Attentive waiters took orders. Tea for Anenko, coffee for Reacher. That was about it.

Skelton watched the clock in the corner of the picture, and he said, "The San Francisco flight is taking off right about... now."

On the screen Anenko drank tea, and Reacher drank coffee.

"Watch now," Skelton said.

Anenko stood up and glanced around. Looking for something. His bearings, possibly, or a discreet little sign. To the men's room. He saw it and set off. In the background Reacher also stood up. He chose a direct and nimble route through the chairs. He arrived at the bathroom just a step behind Anenko. Anenko went in. Reacher went in.

"This is where we run out of luck," Skelton said. "There are no cameras in the bathrooms. I mean, we could do it. No one would ever know. But if they ever found out, obviously there would be a huge scandal. Especially the women's bathroom. So we've never done it. Right now they're both in a dead zone."

One of the detectives laughed.

"Careful, now," Glover said. "Show some respect."

On the screen the shot stayed static on the outside of the men's room door. Time ticked by. A guy came out, a guy went in. Then Reacher came out. A total of almost five minutes inside.

"OK, spoiler alert," the detective said. "Anenko doesn't come out again, never ever. In fact about four hours from now he is discovered dead on the floor of a cubicle locked from the inside. Dead with a broken neck. Discovered by an ear-witness who at the crucial time was facing the opposite direction, taking a leak, but who heard a sound he describes as exactly like a fat man falling off a chair, and he turned around to see the dead guy's face jammed in the gap at the bottom of the door. Kind of leering out at him. Naturally the gentleman made a considerable fuss about it. We were called in. The initial assumption was Anenko had died there and then. Maybe a heart attack, and a post-mortem break of the neck in the subsequent fall."

Another detective said, "But then they worked out he had missed his flight by hours and had checked in much earlier in the day, so the doctors took a closer look, and they figured he had died right back at the beginning. Mostly because the toilets are automatic. They count the flushes. That stall saw no action all day long, because Anenko was dead in there."

"Of what?" Glover asked.

"Could still have been a heart attack, just four hours earlier than initially assumed. Maybe it came on peacefully, and then hours later the gases swelled up and tipped him off the throne and bust his neck for him."

"What do the doctors say?"

"You know how it is, sir. They'll say whatever we tell them to say."

"Would a neck break that way, post-mortem?"

"Medical opinion says it's very unlikely."

"Then what really happened?"

"No one liked Anenko," the guy said. "Even his friends didn't like him. Certainly not his enemies or his customers. We didn't like him. I'm sure no one in this room liked him. But there was nothing much we could do. Too many rules. But those don't apply to everyone. Maybe Anenko made the wrong kind of enemy. Maybe someone hired a contractor."

"This Reacher guy?"

"The timing is exactly right. Reacher follows Anenko into the bathroom, wrestles him into a stall, breaks his neck, props his body on the can, leans over from the outside and locks the door, then leaves. The airport is the one place in the world they don't take their bodyguards, and the one place in the airport with guaranteed no cameras is the bathroom. This was planned. Reacher was recruited. He's not a first-class kind of guy. The airline never heard of him. He's not a frequent flier. He's an old bruiser. His army record shows he did this stuff for a living."

"Circumstantial," Glover said.

"He was right behind Anenko, going in the men's room.

An arm's length away. He wanted to be there. He made up a lot of ground. He took a direct route through the seating arrangements."

"Still circumstantial."

"At least he's the last person to see Anenko alive. We should talk to him."

"He has an alibi," Skelton said.

"What alibi? How could he?"

"He was en route to San Francisco."

"Bullshit. You showed us when that flight took off. He was sitting right there, drinking coffee. He missed it."

"He didn't miss it. He was on the plane. His passport, his boarding card, both checked by competent officials at the departure gate. Which is a rock-solid government-backed alibi."

"How is that possible?"

"Watch this," Skelton said.

He clicked around and came up with a completely new picture. Passengers, getting on a plane. On the right of the screen was inlaid a read-out of what the scanning machine was saying. The competent official was matching names on boarding passes with names on passports. But not passports with faces.

A man in a blue suit stepped up. The agent checked his names and dabbed his boarding card against the reader. The right of the screen flashed in green: *REACHER, JACK.*

The guy walked into the jet bridge.

"Watch this," Skelton said again.

He switched back to the first-class lounge and rewound

the timeline all the way to the security line. All the way to the guy who had to take his shoes off. He was wearing a blue suit. Skelton stopped the action and put a still frame through the tilting and rotating software until the view seemed to be from directly above the far end of the X-ray belt. Where the small but growing pile of hand luggage was accumulating. Which contained Anenko's handsome leather briefcase, and two identical canvas messenger bags, with leather straps.

"He swapped them here," Skelton said. "Reacher took the other guy's bag. The other guy took Reacher's bag, which had his passport and boarding card inside. No doubt the reverse was also true. The other guy got on Reacher's plane, and no doubt Reacher got on the other guy's plane. It's incriminating behaviour in itself. And it's all easy enough to prove."

Glover looked at the Foreign Office woman, who looked at the MI6 woman, who shook her head very slightly, and then they all three looked at me, and I shook my head very slightly.

Glover said, "No, I think Anenko had a heart attack. Then later the thing with the gases toppled him over. Natural causes. He was certainly overweight."

"Sir, the evidence allows for other possibilities."

"There are always wild rumours. Generally better to ignore them."

"Just because no one in this room liked Anenko? Does the end justify the means?"

Glover shook his head.

"I don't like loose cannon," he said. "Usually they're a royal pain in the neck. I would be happy to find Mr Reacher and have a word. But we can't prove a case without busting his alibi, which we can't do without telling the world we let people get on planes here in London with the wrong boarding card and the wrong passport and the wrong face. In the wider picture it's probably better we don't do that. In the sense of possible damage to an important economic sector. And as you mentioned, no one liked Anenko anyway. So, all things considered, I think we'll let it slide."

Skelton was quiet a beat.

Then he said, "Reacher knew you would, right? He knew you would think the thing about getting on the plane was more important. That's why he didn't care about the cameras."

Glover looked at the MI6 woman, who nodded, so he nodded too.

"Reacher took a couple of intelligent chances," he said. "But overall it was beautifully executed. By which I mean, how the aftermath was handled. The deed itself was routine. What came next was perfectly predicted. But also manipulated. He's daring us to help him. Just this one instance."

"Will we?"

"Probably better the world doesn't know we let the wrong people on planes."

"Plus we didn't like Anenko anyway."

"There's that."

"And Reacher predicted all this?"

"Apparently."

"Is it us, paying him?"

"Good lord, no," Glover said. "We don't do things like that."

Skelton sought me out. The American.

"We don't either," I said.

"But you're going to help him."

I said, "Kid, you need to learn, this whole business is about choosing between a very bad thing and an even worse thing. There are no good answers."

"OK," Skelton said. "Anenko died on the toilet."

"Like Elvis."

"There's that. All I'm saying is, the evidence could be used against you."

"Delete it," Glover said. "We had no need for it in the first place. Anenko died of purely natural causes."

"Including his neck?"

"He was a big heavy man. He suddenly pitches forward, literally a dead weight, purely naturally his neck breaks on impact. It's simple physics. We don't need hours and hours of recordings. It's a routine event. We just mentioned Elvis. I'm sure there were thousands more."

"OK," Skelton said, and he deleted it all right then and there, which is how Anenko stayed dead, and Reacher stayed free. Later he mailed short and cryptic thank-you notes to both Skelton and Glover. Neither officer turned over the notes to the investigation. Both kept them private.

FALLEN WOMAN

MARY HOFFMAN

Afterwards, my dreams were haunted by the sight of her, a sight I never saw. A woman in a white dress, falling, falling, almost graceful. I always woke with a jolt before she hit the ground.

In reality what happened was a man roughly pulled me away and there was a hideous sound behind me. At first, I didn't relate the two and assumed I was being assaulted, mugged for my wallet. In fact, he was saving my life.

Did you ever see those videos of 9/11 before they cut out the sound? The sound of the men and women who jumped hitting the pavement? It was like that, though I didn't recognise it at the time. My attacker/rescuer pulled me to his chest in a bear hug, then led me away to the nearest café, took me indoors where I couldn't see the Campo, and ordered a double espresso, stirring so much sugar into it that the spoon could have stood up.

I brought the tiny cup to my lips with a shaking hand and drained the bittersweet liquid in one gulp, like an Italian. I recognised that I was in shock. Something had happened. I had no idea what.

"Better?" he asked, with an Italian accent. "Now alcohol."

He ordered two brandies and encouraged me to sip mine slowly.

It was 11:30 am and I had been on my way to get coffee in one of the many overpriced cafés that fringed the Campo. But, like the English traveller I was, I would have ordered a cappuccino.

Now I sat sipping the fiery spirit, hearing the noise of an ambulance arriving. I turned to look, as I had my back to the window, but my new friend stopped me.

"Don't look," he said quietly. "Eat something. You need sugar."

I couldn't believe I would ever need sugar again after that coffee but I bit into one of the ricciarelli biscuits the waiter had brought and let the soft marzipan taste melt on my tongue.

"What happened?" I asked. My hands had stopped shaking. "Who are you?"

"Just a passer-by," he said. His English was perfect. He leaned forward and offered me a hand to shake. "Roberto Cagni."

"Nicholas Appleton," I replied automatically. "You saved me from something. But I still don't know what."

He shrugged. "I saw a girl jumping from the tower. You were right in her path. I pulled you out of the way."

"Jumping?" I said stupidly. "A suicide?"

The Torre del Mangia of the Palazzo Pubblico was over

three hundred feet tall. No one would survive a fall—or a jump—from the top to the ground. By a great effort, I didn't turn round to look at it.

"It happens," said Roberto. "There are a few suicides a year from the tower."

"A girl, you say?"

"A young woman in a white dress."

"What could make a young woman so desperate?"

"I don't know. Maybe she was pregnant?"

I laughed. "This isn't the 1960s. She could have got rid of it. No need to kill herself."

Roberto spread his hands. "An unhappy love affair, then. How do I know? I didn't know her."

That somehow made it worse. His not knowing her immediately conjured up the possibility of knowing her, as a real separate human being. Not just an unforgettable sound and a whoosh of displaced air.

It was dawning on me how certainly her death would have caused mine if it hadn't been for Roberto's intervention. He must have had the reactions of a top ten tennis player. How many seconds were there in which he sized up the situation, saw her trajectory, realised my danger and lunged forward? What if he hadn't been there and been so keen-eyed and quick-witted?

The caffeine and sugar must have begun to wear off; I felt myself trembling.

Roberto handed me his card.

"Go back to your hotel and lie down," he ordered. "The shock is getting to you."

I looked at the card.

"You live in Rome? You aren't Sienese?"

"No. I'm a tourist like you."

He took back the card and scribbled on the back.

"This is my hotel. Come and find me if you need anything."

I gave him my card with my mobile number on it, and as an afterthought wrote my hotel on the back too.

"But I'm not a tourist," I said. "I'm a journalist."

He looked at me sharply for a moment then regained his unruffled appearance. He beckoned to the waiter for our bill and rejected my offer to pay my half. We walked cautiously out of the café and turned left, trying not to look at the police tent in front of the Entrone to the Palazzo Pubblico.

At the slope up to the Banchi di Sopra we separated, Roberto gripping me briefly in a bear hug.

"Thank you," I said, suddenly emotional, "for what you did. I can't really thank you enough."

"Forget about it," he said. "I'm glad it worked." He turned and walked away, an urbane figure in his butterscotch-coloured linen suit and white shirt, looking like any other prosperous Italian on holiday in Tuscany. I guessed he was about fifty but very well preserved and fit. I wouldn't forget the heft of the tug as he whipped me away from certain death.

It was quite a walk northwards to my hotel near the Porta Ovile. By the time I got there, all I wanted was to shower and lie on my bed with the air-conditioning on. I was hungry but couldn't face the restaurant so ordered room service and switched the TV on. I was showered and in a towelling bathrobe when the food arrived. The television was still chuntering on.

"*Terribile!*" said the waiter, nodding towards the screen.

I saw the sight I was trying to forget—the Campo, the Palazzo, the tower and the police tent. I shuddered.

"*Sì*," I said, not wanting to let the waiter know I had been there. It was something I didn't want to acknowledge.

There was a stream of rapid Italian coming from the newsreader.

"What did he say?"

"He said the police want witnesses to come forward, especially one man who left the scene quickly just after the woman fell. That man and an older companion."

He meant me. There was a phone number to call, which I memorised. I tipped the waiter heavily and hurried him out of the room.

My appetite had gone. Why did the police want to speak to me and Roberto? I knew nothing about the girl, or young woman, who had fallen, not even her name. And he hadn't known her either; he had said so.

I got dressed and picked at my meal. I no longer wanted to lie down. I wanted to ring the police, but not without talking to Roberto first. I needed his advice. If I didn't contact the police I might seem to be hiding something, but what would he do? If we didn't give statements, or whatever, it might look bad but, if we showed up at a police station, would they detain us?

I phoned the number on Roberto's card and it went straight to voicemail. I didn't leave a message. I slipped my passport into my jacket and went out. I couldn't stay still and do nothing, so I decided to walk to his hotel.

It was smarter than mine, very near the Duomo. The reception area was marbled, with brocade sofas and armchairs. I asked them to ring through to Signor Cagni's room and the message came back that he was out but his wife would come down and meet me.

His wife? Of course. Why not? I sat and waited on a blue and gold sofa until an elegant woman in her fifties came to greet me.

"Signor Appleton? I am Maddalena Pacini. My husband told me about you. He is not here, I'm afraid. Shall we go to the bar?"

That was the best idea I'd heard for a while.

We sat in comfortable chairs and Maddalena ordered Aperol spritzes then sat back and looked at me appraisingly.

"You had a—straight escape this morning?"

"A narrow escape, yes. Your husband saved my life."

"You are a journalist, he told me. So, are you on holiday or working in Siena?"

It seemed a strange thing to ask. I hesitated just a bit too long before answering and knew she wouldn't believe me if I said I was on holiday after that pause.

"I'm covering a story," I said slowly, "but I can't tell you any details."

In fact, I was investigating a high-level drugs dealer, an Eton and Oxford Englishman called Jonathan Hill who was very well-connected, married to the daughter of a minor aristocrat, and squeaky-clean as far as evidence was concerned. A lead had brought me to the unlikely setting of Siena, which was not famous for drug crime. But my gut instinct had told me I was on the verge of a scoop.

Maddalena's eyes widened and she patted my knee. "*Segretissimo!*" she whispered.

I did not need much Italian to understand that. But I was saved from any awkwardness by the arrival of Roberto, who kissed his wife on both cheeks and then did the same to me.

"They told me in reception I would find you both here," he said, snapping his fingers at the barman and indicating another round of spritzes. "How are you, Nico? You wanted to see me?"

"Well, yes," I mumbled. Somehow, I didn't want to talk about the death of the young woman in front of Roberto's wife, but I blundered on. "I saw on the TV that the police wanted to speak to us. At least, it sounded like us…"

"It was," said Roberto. "But it's OK. I've been to see them and told them everything I know—which was practically nothing. And I told them about you. I don't think they'll want to talk to you now but I gave them your number."

He took a big swig of his drink.

"What did they say?"

"Suicide for sure," said Roberto. "She had a note in the pocket of her dress."

"Who was she?" asked his wife.

"Caterina Peretti," he said, and I thought I saw a look pass between them.

"What did the note say?" I asked.

"They didn't tell me," he replied smoothly, but there was something I didn't like in his manner. This man had saved my life but I suddenly felt uneasy about him. I decided I would go to the police myself.

Soon afterwards I made my excuses and left them drinking in the bar. I was a little light-headed myself, having eaten little that day. I wasn't going to make a hard-nosed, hard-drinking reporter at this rate.

I looked up the nearest police station on my phone and walked there instead of phoning the number on the TV. I was eventually seen by a polite English-speaking officer who listened to my story. I wondered whether to show him my NUJ card, but held back for the moment.

"So you were walking past the Palazzo Pubblico when this man, Roberto Cagni, pulled you out of the way of the falling woman?"

"I know it sounds fantastic," I admitted. "But that's exactly what happened."

"Do you have this man's address or number?"

I started to answer, but then said, "Wait. He told me he'd been to see you."

"Not at this police station," said the officer. "We have nothing on file here."

"But he told me her name. He said you'd found a suicide note in her pocket!"

The officer suddenly became very interested and leaned forward. He was about thirty, with dark brown eyes—just my type, in fact. I wondered if I was his before registering he was saying something.

"I'd like to take a statement from you, Signor Appleton. Just tell me everything again from the beginning, including what Signor Cagni told you this afternoon."

By the time I left the police station I was really rattled. I didn't know what to believe. The officer, whose name proved to be Ettore Alessandro, had confirmed the suicide's name and that she had a note on her but would say no more. He also said that this information was at the moment classified and confirmed that Roberto had not reported in to any police station in Siena, as he claimed he had.

Every journalistic instinct I had told me there was something fishy about the man who had saved my life. But what did he have to hide? He had told me he didn't know the woman who jumped and yet he knew her name—and not from the police as he claimed.

I must have wandered around the city for hours, but in the end, as I knew they would, my footsteps took me back to the Campo. It had a dread fascination for me now and I wondered if I'd ever again see it as a neutral space, a beautiful medieval piazza in the shape of a fan.

It wasn't closed off and the police tent had gone. Of course, the body must have been taken away for an autopsy by now. I looked at my watch. It was only nine hours since the jump, or fall as I preferred to think of it, and my sudden rescue by Roberto. There was some sort of industrial cleaning machine working on the cobbles beneath the tall tower. It was getting dark and the swallows were screaming round it, their silhouettes black against the deepening blue sky.

I realised I was very hungry and decided to eat at one of the restaurants in the Campo, even though they were overpriced and I knew I could get better food in a dozen other places. I was feeling reckless. I deliberately chose a place right opposite the tower and was about to sit down outside when I froze.

A few tables in, Roberto Cagni was sitting with his wife—and Jonathan Hill.

I turned and left so quickly they couldn't have seen me. I chose a restaurant further down and sat where I could just watch the group in the other place without easily being seen myself. I ordered a plate of pappardelle with wild boar sauce, a salad and a half carafe of the house red. I wanted filling male food, red meat and carbs and strong wine. My blood was pounding and my pulse racing.

I had come to Siena to find Hill and there he was! I wouldn't have thought anything about seeing him dining with friends, but I could hardly go and give him my card now, asking for an interview, now that I knew those friends.

My wine came and I started stuffing breadsticks into my face as if I hadn't eaten for a week. I was uncomfortably close to the tower and the cleaning machine. But I kept my eyes fixed on Hill and the Cagnis. They looked just like any other group of Italians eating in a restaurant, relaxed and smiling, drinking wine and eating pasta.

A waiter came and took away their empty bowls as my waiter brought my food. What did it mean? If Hill was what I thought he was, then a friendship with him was unlikely to be innocent. And how did it involve Caterina, the woman who fell from the tower this morning?

I rapidly ate my pasta as I watched the group in the other restaurant cutting into steaks and ordering more wine. I was feeling better. I wasn't traumatised Nicholas any more; I was Nick Appleton, newshound, and I smelled something worth chasing down.

But a sixth sense told me I was going to have to be careful.

I left the Campo by the lower exit, making sure Hill and his friends wouldn't see me. Of course, he didn't know what I looked like, but I had researched him extensively. There had been no sign of his aristocratic wife so I guessed she hadn't accompanied him to Siena.

Back in my hotel, I opened my laptop and typed in *Caterina Peretti + Jonathan Hill.* It directed me to her Facebook page. It was a shock to see her photo, even though I knew it would be plastered over the papers tomorrow morning. She was young, about twenty-two I guessed, with dark hair and a pretty face. My limited Italian wasn't up to understanding most of what was on her page, but I looked at her friends list and Hill was there.

I took a beer from the minibar to celebrate and checked my emails. Then I thought I'd check if Roberto Cagni had also been Caterina's Facebook friend. But when I typed her name in again I got a 'No results' message. Caterina had been wiped out. Still, the police, or whoever it was, hadn't been quick enough. I had what I needed.

Rapidly I typed her name again, into Italian directory enquiries, and there was her address. I wrote it down before it too was pulled and then called my editor in London. He was a bit flustered at being phoned during a family dinner (I forgot I was an hour ahead) but listened carefully while I told him about Peretti and my hunch that Jonathan Hill was involved in her death.

"Be careful, Nick," he said. "If you're right and it wasn't

a suicide then Hill is more dangerous than we thought. And that Roman sounds dodgy too."

It was getting late but I decided to go to Caterina's address. It was a ground-floor flat in a house not far from my hotel and when I got there I saw the tell-tale police tape across the front door, but no sign of an officer guarding it. I was about to turn away when I saw a light flicker in one of the windows. Not an electric light, the distinctive sight of a shadowy figure moving in and out of torchlight. Someone was in Caterina's flat and it couldn't be the police.

I ducked into a bar and ordered a *digestivo*. With fumbling fingers, I took out the card the police officer had given me and dialled his mobile phone number. It was after hours and I felt sure that it would go straight to voicemail so it gave me a jolt to hear his voice say, *"Pronto!"*

"Inspector Alessandro?" I asked. "It's Nicholas Appleton." I lowered my voice. "There's someone in Caterina Peretti's flat."

I heard his sharp intake of breath.

"Where are you?" he asked.

"In a bar opposite the flat. Bar Mancini," I added, looking at the coaster under my drink.

"I'll be there in ten minutes," he said and cut the call.

From my bar stool I could see across the road to Caterina's flat. But no one was going to come out of that front door; the police tape was intact. I wondered if they had been equally professional about any back entrance.

Ettore came into the bar and took the stool beside me. It was disconcertingly like a date. He didn't wear a uniform but

I was aware he carried a weapon. He had a jacket on now but he had been in his shirtsleeves at the station and I had seen the Beretta at his belt.

He ordered two coffees and I was glad not to have more alcohol. He inclined his head towards the house across the road.

"Anything?" he asked.

I shook my head. "I think they would have got in and out from the back."

"Let's take a look," he said, knocking back the coffee and tossing coins on to the bar.

I felt like a character part in a cop movie—the poor sap who gets shot in his second scene, some random informer or low life.

I thought we'd be going round the back but Ettore tore down the tape and fitted keys to the front door. It opened on to a short passageway and he snapped the light on.

"Which room?" he asked and I indicated the door on our left.

I was hoping he would kick it open, with his weapon raised in that double-handed stance I'd seen in too many cop shows. Ettore turned the door handle and we walked in on a scene that lived up to my lurid imaginings.

As soon as he switched the light on we saw that the room had been comprehensively turned over. Ettore signalled to me to stay and swept the rest of the flat.

"Kitchen window," he said when he returned. "They've gone."

"What do you suppose they were looking for?" I asked.

He shrugged. "We took her laptop and printer," he said. "The one the note was written on. And there was a thorough search before these clowns got here. I don't think they would have found anything."

I looked round Caterina's ravaged living room. It might have been quite an attractive space before it had been trashed. It was hard to tell. I sat down heavily on a sofa that had had its cushions ripped open. I didn't want to know Caterina as a person. She was nothing to do with me. I just wanted to get the story about the drugs ring.

"Come on," said Ettore. "I'll have to file a report on this, but then I think you and I need to talk."

He wasn't flirting, unfortunately. We walked back to the police station and he wrote up the evening's incident then put Caterina's keys into a safe and locked it.

Then he stretched his arms and cracked his knuckles.

"It's late," he said. "You should go back to your hotel. But I think there is much you are not telling me. And it might put you in danger. I'll walk back with you."

It was comforting to be escorted back to my hotel by an armed guard. He wouldn't come up to my room but he said he would come and talk to me first thing in the morning.

I fell into my bed exhausted and slept fitfully, dreaming over and over again of a woman in a white dress, falling.

I was having breakfast at 8:00 am the next day when Ettore came into the hotel restaurant. He didn't look much more rested than I felt. I had a window table for two, looking over the garden and the path to the swimming pool. He joined me and a waiter brought another setting and coffee.

He looked quizzically at my Englishman's breakfast of bacon, sausage and scrambled egg, but got himself a couple of mini croissants and drank lots of sweet black coffee. I self-consciously ordered another cappuccino and finished my toast and jam.

"What do you know about Roberto Cagni?" he asked, as he watched me eat.

"Only what I told you yesterday," I said. "I never saw him till he saved me from the falling woman."

But then I told him about seeing Cagni and his wife in the Campo last night.

"Look, do you mind if we go outside?" he asked. "I need a cigarette."

We walked down to the pool, which wasn't open to guests yet, and sat on two loungers. He offered me a cigarette and I accepted. I am trying to give up but after meals is the hardest time.

"What is it you are not telling me, Signor Appleton?" he said.

"Call me Nicholas," I said. "Nico, if you prefer. I'm a journalist. I want a scoop. If I tell you what I know, will you give me something in return?"

His eyes flickered, amused. Maybe he *was* flirting now?

"Nico," he said. "You know I can't promise you any information that might compromise the case. But tell me what you know and I'll share what I can with you."

So I told him about Jonathan Hill and his connection with the dead woman and the Cagnis.

I thought he was going to whistle through his teeth,

he was listening so eagerly. He took his notebook out and scribbled in it. Again, I felt an affinity with him.

"I can tell you that we don't accept it was suicide," he said. "There were traces of sedative in her bloodstream."

"Couldn't she have taken something to make it easier to face that jump?"

"She could. But not Rohypnol."

We stared at each other.

"Is there CCTV on the tower?" I asked.

"Unfortunately, no."

"Witnesses?"

"We've put out an appeal for anyone who climbed the tower at the same time as Caterina, but I'm not hopeful. They would mostly have been tourists and might not be watching Italian TV."

"So, we may never know what happened up there?"

"Well, there is something else. Caterina Peretti had a criminal record."

Before I had a chance to find out more a hearty voice was greeting me.

"Hey, Nico! It's too early for a swim!"

Of course, I had given Roberto the address of my hotel. But how was I going to introduce him to a policeman?

"Roberto," I said, to warn Ettore. "I was just out here for a smoke."

"Me too," said Roberto, sitting down on my lounger and lighting up.

Ettore took control of the situation. He leaned over and kissed me on the cheek.

"*Ciao*, Nico," he said. "See you lunchtime. One o'clock? Usual bar?"

And then he was gone, waving to both of us. I couldn't stop the blush rising on my face.

"I see you've found a friend," said Roberto.

"We met yesterday," I said.

"And yet you have a 'usual' bar?" he said.

I shrugged. "You know romantics," I said. "Do something once and it's a tradition."

I hoped I'd carried it off. At least I was sure Roberto hadn't realised Ettore was a cop.

"How are you feeling?" Roberto asked. "Has the shock worn off?"

"Not great," I said. "I didn't sleep well. Nightmares."

"We're going back to Rome tomorrow," he said. "I wanted to check up on you before we leave."

"Thanks," I said. "Holiday over?"

I tried to remember what was on his card. Something like *Imports and exports*?

"My business here is done," he said. "And we've seen the sights."

"Not the tower," I said, shuddering.

He put a hand on my shoulder. "Go home, Nico. Try to forget it. You're young and alive. You can do nothing for that poor girl."

Did he know I had been trying? I was as sure as Ettore that she hadn't fallen voluntarily to her death. If she had been pushed, who had done it? Not Roberto, who had been waiting to save me in the Campo. I was sure he had known it was going to happen. And surely not Jonathan? Even without CCTV, he would hardly have taken such a risk. But why had anyone killed her? Maybe my new cop boyfriend could tell me.

I had to play dumb with Roberto because, although he had saved my life, I found I couldn't trust him. And it was odd that he had come to my hotel to say goodbye when he could have phoned. I felt he was checking that I was taken in by the suicide story.

He took a folded newspaper out of his pocket. It was the *Corriere di Siena* and there was Caterina Peretti's photo on the front page.

"Shocking suicide at the Torre del Mangia," he translated the headline for me.

"I suppose we'll never know why she did it," I said.

He seemed satisfied with that. He threw the paper down on the lounger and stood up, putting out his hand.

"*Arrivederci*, Nico," he said. "Put it out of your mind and you'll soon be sleeping well."

"*Arrivederci*," I said, shaking his hand, hoping that I never would see him again.

After he left, I felt a strong sense of foreboding. I didn't want to leave the hotel. After half an hour, when the pool guy came, I went up to my room for a towel and my trunks. I spent a couple of hours ploughing my way up and down the pool till I was exhausted. Then I showered in my room and slept until I woke with a jolt at 12:30 pm. It was time to go and meet Ettore. I guessed by our "usual" bar he meant the one opposite Caterina Peretti's flat.

I got there a few minutes before 1:00 pm and took a table

by the window. I looked idly at the menu while I waited for Ettore. I wondered how to greet him when he arrived. That kiss had been for Roberto's benefit but I had still liked it.

The doorbell jangled and he came in.

"Are we really having lunch?" I asked, to get over any awkwardness. "Or was that just a front?"

He sat down and took the menu from me. "We might as well eat while we talk," he said. "That is if you have any room left after that breakfast."

We ordered pizzas and beers.

"Are you off duty?" I asked and he shook his head.

"I'm never off duty," he said. "Even when I'm having a beer with a good-looking man."

He had the nicest smile. But I couldn't relax and think it was all going well. He was a cop and he wanted to know what I knew and what I suspected. It was in his interest to have me off guard.

"What were you going to tell me when Roberto arrived? About her record?"

"It wasn't my division," he said, wiping the beer moustache off his lip. "It was the drugs squad. She was a mule and an informer."

"I knew it!" I said triumphantly. "She worked for Hill, didn't she?"

"We think she was about to shop him. At least she was going to tell us the name of her boss. If what you tell me is right, it must be him." He looked at me curiously. "Have you ever climbed the tower?"

I shook my head.

"Let's do it when it opens after lunch."

"It has re-opened?" I stalled.

He nodded. And then our food came. My swim had made me hungry and it soon vanished. Then we drank tiny cups of coffee and ate the small, sweet biscuits that came with them.

Ettore insisted on paying, which made it feel even more like a date. What was his game?

It was quite a walk to the Campo and I started to drag my feet when we got close to the tower. There was a queue at the box office, but Ettore flashed his police ID and we were both gestured to by-pass it.

On the first floor was a place with free lockers. You weren't allowed to take anything up the tower with you—not even a bottle of water—except a camera. We had no bags but Ettore waited till the locker space was empty.

"We had this sealed off pretty quickly after she fell," he said. "You can imagine the chaos. People rushing down the narrow stairs while others were still going up, not knowing what had happened. The people coming down wanted their bags. There was one Englishwoman screaming that she must have her bag. She had a plane to catch and her passport and tickets were in the bag."

"Did you find anything belonging to Caterina?"

He nodded. "We got the master key and unlocked all the lockers. It took a long time because we had no idea what we were looking for. The people were kept out but all the owners of bags in the lockers waited on the ground floor. Except for Lady Gaga, who was still screaming about her flight."

"Lady Gaga?"

"She talked like a woman, what do you call it? A posh one. Like someone from *Downton Abbey*."

Something stirred in my mind. "An aristocrat? Did she get her bag eventually?"

"Yes. It all took time. We released all the bags that had male ID in them. That left ten lockers. Most had something to identify them so we called the names out."

"And the Englishwoman?"

"The third name we called. She was not lying about the passport."

"Lady Frederica Hill," I said.

He looked stern. "We had no reason to suspect her or detain her. I checked this morning and she did take the plane back to London. First class from Florence."

"What about Caterina?"

"After we'd called out all the women's names, there was one bag left. There was just a purse, some make-up and a mobile phone."

"You have her phone?" I asked, excited. He nodded.

"It was easy to trace her name from that. We got it unlocked and checked her calls. There was one that morning from a Freddie, arranging to meet her in the queue for the tower. *Like tourists!* it said."

I had been wondering how poor Caterina had been lured up there. Now I thought I knew. Jonathan knew she was going to shop him to the police so he sent his wife to do the dirty work. What a cold-blooded bitch!

"We assumed it was a man but now I think it was that

Englishwoman," said Ettore. He turned towards the narrow stairs.

"We're really going up?" I asked. I felt a bit sick. I'm not afraid of heights but there was something grisly about tracing Caterina's last steps.

"Of course," he called down and I hurried to follow him. I wasn't claustrophobic either, but the stairs were really tight and I couldn't help wondering what would happen if we met someone coming down.

It was a relief to reach a sort of viewing platform on a landing and to see that Ettore had waited for me.

"You are not very fit, Nico," he said, laughing, as I wheezed and waited for my breath to settle.

"Says the smoker," I replied as soon as I could. But he wasn't at all out of breath and soon took to the stairs again.

I had researched Torre del Mangia after Caterina jumped and knew there were 400 steps. I could believe it.

Finally, we were at the top, with very few other people around. They were all clicking cameras and phones and took no notice of us.

We waited till they had all gone back down. You are not supposed to spend more than fifteen minutes at the top but it was strangely peaceful up there, looking out over the Tuscan countryside, until the next batch of selfie-happy tourists came up.

"What now?" I asked. I was looking down at the spot where the woman had fallen and Roberto had performed his life-saving grab. Was there still a stain visible on the stones or was I just being over-imaginative?

Then I felt myself being seized from behind. This was no rough play from Ettore. I was wrenched round and could see him holding his Beretta but looking very uncertain. There was another gun pressed into my neck. I knew by the smell of his cologne that my captor was Roberto.

"So, your new boyfriend is a cop, Nico," Roberto growled. "I guessed as soon as I saw you both at the tower box office."

"You were following me?" I said, careful not to move my neck.

"I didn't trust you," he said. "I thought there was something fishy about your interest in the Peretti girl."

I would have laughed if I hadn't got a gun waiting to be fired in my carotid.

"That makes two of us," I replied quietly.

"What do you expect to gain by this?" asked Ettore, strangely calm. "There will be lots of people coming up here any minute now. And you'd have to kill us both before they get here."

"He's right," I added. "You haven't thought this through." Roberto twisted my arm.

"Shut up," he said, but I thought I heard his voice falter.

"You'll be caught for sure," I said. "Why go to prison for what Hill and his stuck-up wife have done?"

I realised he was moving me to the open part of the tower. He wasn't going to shoot me. He was going to throw me over the edge and down to the Campo. Ettore moved too.

"Stay back!" Roberto shouted at him. "You're right. I don't have much time."

Nor did I. Without any warning, I found myself in the

last minutes of my life. I'd never get my scoop now, never have a relationship with Ettore, or anyone else. But maybe Roberto was going to kill this nice, gentle policeman too?

Self-preservation kicked in. Caterina had been an unsuspecting young woman. I knew what Roberto intended and I was twenty years younger than him. OK, Ettore thought I wasn't fit but I reckoned I was fitter than my attacker. He had only just climbed 400 stairs too; I could hear his ragged breathing.

He was going to push me over and then shoot Ettore. He would have thrown his body over too, then hidden the gun and hurried down the steps and away before anyone realised what had happened.

But I wasn't going to let him.

He had me half over the barrier and suddenly kicked at my legs then began to heave me over.

But I was ready for him. I braced and ducked at the same time. I rolled away as the gun fired.

It was so loud in that small space that at first I was deafened and wasn't sure which of them had fired. I was on all fours, panting and shaking my head like a wet dog.

I felt gentle hands lifting me up.

Roberto was lying half over the barrier, blood soaking through his shirt and suit. Ettore propped me up against the wall and then pulled the body down. He was shaking too. He picked up Roberto's gun and pocketed it.

And then the space was filled with hysterical tourists, who had heard the shot as they climbed the last few stairs. Naturally they assumed Ettore was a crazed killer and it took some minutes for him to calm them down and show them his police ID.

I remained hunched over against the parapet, my head in my hands, while Ettore called his colleagues and the emergency services. I heard him phone down to the box office to tell them to stop any more people coming up and to close the tower again.

Incredibly, some of the tourists, who had just minutes before regarded Ettore as a dangerous terrorist, were taking selfies and shots of the view. All while there was a bloodied corpse in their space. Ettore sat down next to me and offered me a cigarette.

"Filthy habit," I said, accepting one and drawing deeply on it. "Thank you for saving my life, by the way," I added.

He put an arm round my shoulder. "My pleasure," he said. "I didn't think either of us were going to get out of here alive."

"What now?" I asked.

"My colleagues will bring Signora Cagni in for questioning and they'll be on to your police in London to arrest Signora Hill."

"What about Jonathan? He might still be in Siena."

"Ssh," said Ettore. "It's all taken care of. All the local airports are covered and every police officer in the city has his description. You're quite safe now."

And with his arm still round me, I felt it.

It took hours to get all the tourists out of the tower and the logistics of getting Roberto's body down once forensics had finished with it were horrendous.

Ettore had to help me down the 400 steps and my legs were shaking when we got to the bottom. My brush with death had left me exhausted and drained. There was a police car at the bottom and Ettore commandeered the driver to take me to my hotel.

"I have to be back at the station for the rest of the day," he said. "Shall I come to your hotel, after work? We can eat in the restaurant there if you don't want to go out."

I nodded, unable to speak. I knew I had to call my editor and write up the story but I didn't know if I could. It seemed as if, for the last couple of days, I had been living on adrenaline and I was having the worst comedown.

Back in my room, I couldn't sleep or even rest. I kept replaying the scene at the top of the tower—something more to add to my nightmares. If I hadn't moved when I had, Roberto would have pushed me to my death and then shot Ettore, I was sure of it. His gun must have had a silencer. I didn't know; I had no idea what a silencer looked like. I wasn't cut out for this sort of life.

I thought about Roberto's wife. Had she been in on everything? Whether or not, she would be devastated by his death. Would she blame me? The only time I had met her, she had been perfectly nice to me.

But Caterina Peretti must have had family to mourn her, maybe a boyfriend too.

My thoughts went round and round and the hours dragged through the day. I slept fitfully, waking several times with nightmares, until I didn't know if I was asleep or awake.

At seven, my phone rang and it was Ettore.

"Shall I come up?" he asked and they were the best four words I'd heard for a long time.

After sitting and talking and even kissing for about an hour we went down to the restaurant. I felt at ease in his company. He was Sienese born and bred and was from the Contrada of the Wolf. Amazingly to me, he still lived in his parents' flat but he seemed very sorted, comfortable in his own skin.

We were getting to know each other and it seemed natural for him to come back up to my room with me. We got into the lift and, just before the doors closed, someone else ran to squeeze through them.

It was Jonathan Hill.

"Hello, lovebirds," he said pleasantly, then hit the stop button. We were between the ground and first floor and he pulled out a wicked-looking knife.

"Which of you shall I slice first?" he said.

"There are two of us," I said, more calmly than I felt.

"And I am armed," said Ettore.

"Yes, yes, I know. You shot my operative, Roberto. But I am a desperate man in a small confined space. I'd stab you before you could reach your weapon."

All this was said in a light, bantering upper-class English drawl. But neither of us doubted he'd do what he said.

"And I'd stop you," I replied in the same tone. "We seem to have reached an impasse."

He looked at me appraisingly. "You probably have about seven years on me," he said. "And you clearly work out. But I am the one with the greater motive. I don't fancy your chances."

He was obviously high, but whether on adrenaline or from one of the drugs he peddled I couldn't guess. Either way, he was very dangerous. He was standing with his back to the door and Ettore and I were on the other side, about two feet apart.

For the second time that day, I was very close to death.

"I think I'll take the cop first," said Hill. "Before he can get to his gun."

He took a step forward. Ettore braced to take him on.

But Hill was like a wild animal. It all happened very quickly.

He flung himself at Ettore, who fought back bravely, getting cut on his forearms. Blood splashed on the floor of the lift. I hurled myself at Hill's back, trying to pin his arms, trying to buy time for Ettore to reach his gun.

The small space inside the metal box seemed to be full of a slashing blade and spurting blood.

Then I heard a grunt like someone being punched in the chest. Ettore was down and bleeding all over the floor. Hill was crouching over him, wrenching the blade out of his chest. I was hanging on to Hill's back and arms.

He twisted towards me, raising the knife stained with Ettore's blood.

I didn't hesitate for a moment. I blocked his lunge, then punched him in the kidneys as hard as I could. The knife flew out of his hand on to the floor and we both scrabbled for it. But I got there first and plunged it into his chest.

Hill slumped to the floor and I crawled to Ettore and cradled his head in my lap. I hit the emergency button but I knew it was too late for him. Too late for us.

The whole thing had taken only a few seconds and my

description makes it sound clearer than it was. Like all amateur fights, it was messy, uncoordinated and wild.

The only reason I can even begin to describe what happened was that I saw it all again at the police station the next day, on the CCTV footage from the camera installed in the lift. It was clear who the criminal was, and who were the victims.

But as I sat on the floor of the lift weeping, with two bodies for company and a clear view of how one of them could have been mine, I knew none of this.

I had killed a man.

So had Ettore this day. I knew it was the first time; he had told me at dinner. It was the only thing he could have done but he hadn't had long to live with the consequences. I had the rest of my life.

When the emergency services got there and raised the lift to the first floor, I was at first arrested. I didn't blame them. There were two dead men, one live one and a knife in that metal box.

After one night in a cell, I was released. Ettore had filed a report on what had happened at the top of the tower and there was a phone call from London to say that Frederica Hill had been arrested and charged with the murder of Caterina Peretti.

Once I had given my statement and been released, I went to see Ettore's parents. A colleague of his had, probably against all the rules, given me the address.

It was the worst hour of my life, even worse than seeing my potential boyfriend killed before my eyes.

It was a relief to get back to London and my tiny flat in Bermondsey. I buried myself in my work. It was quite an exclusive for my editor to have a piece on a public-school-educated drug dealer, who had been killed by the journalist.

I even won a prize.

Sometimes I still dream of the woman falling, falling, as her white dress billows up around her. But it's better than the other dreams, in which I'm trapped in a metal box with a madman and a knife. Or the ones when Ettore dies in my arms over and over again.

I wonder what dreams Jonathan Hill's wife has in her prison cell.

BLOOD ON THE GALWAY SHORE

KEN BRUEN

"That's a fine boat"
Said a guy sitting on the dock of The Claddagh
My trawler, the *Kate*
Once a thriving fishing vessel, pollution, foreign illegal
boats and, of course, EU directives effectively killed the
Galway fishing industry
Stone dead
I had toyed with the idea of selling her, fucking off to
Australia like the rest of the young but a chance gig of
ferrying tourists to The Aran Islands rescued me
No way was I going to retire on the proceeds but it kept me,
forgive the pun, *afloat*
I loved the sea, like nothing else
Heading out across Galway Bay, the sun just rising, you
could believe all kinds of shite

Like God

Love

Success

Then come evenings, tying up, the whole ritual of mooring,
battening down hatches, made me feel alive, then a stroll
up Quay St and pints in Naughton's

Was that happiness?

Fuck knows

My father had been a captain of a large merchant ship and
was known to all as *Skip*

All I inherited was his nickname, he drank everything else
away, had said to me

"'Tis the seaman's fate to drink"

Right

He talked a lot of other bollocks but mostly, thankfully, I
forget it

As I try to forget him

My mother was as they used to say

"On tablets"

Not anything to do with Moses, or even Catholicism

No, it was tranquilisers

Do I blame her?

Yeah, a bit

She left me and my sister to the mercy of a violent drunk

His excuse

"I've no work"

Pity the fuck

Years later on a chance rapid view of *Judge Judy*, as I channel
surfed, I heard her say to dead beat Dad

"Can you say, you want fries with your burger?"

Man, I loved that

My sister, never recovering from all the abuse, killed herself
    on the White Strand beach, it's really lovely there,
    picturesque even

She used my father's merchant navy knife, a long serrated
    vicious blade, bit rusty then but hey, you make do

Cut her wrists in the correct fashion, she Googled it, then lay
    down, looking at the waves, her blood making a crescent
    shape on the sand

Coroner told me

"Took her a while to bleed out"

I stared at him, asked very quietly

"You felt the need to tell me this, why?"

He was filing papers, not once looking at me, said

"Full disclosure"

Weeks later, I saw him having dinner with a very foxy young
    lady

Wife/daughter/hooker?

Who the fuck knows

Or cares

I waited until he took a toilet break, came up behind him as
    he splurged a stream of very expensive champagne piss
    against the urinal

Hit him twice, fast, hard in the kidneys and he shot forward
    into the bowl, I leant into him, whispered

"Full disclosure?"

Pause

"You're some cunt"

I stole his wallet and fuck me, it was jammed with large
    denomination notes
What were they paying civil servants these days?
I'm not a criminal and I don't give much heed to the adage,
    crime pays but I do believe that criminals should pay and
    the coroner committed the crime of gross insensitivity
I used his money to streamline the engine on the *Kate* and for
    a headstone for my sister with the inscription
...*full disclosure*
I had one close mate
Finn
A wild colonial boy
He had a shock, and I mean *shocking* in its ferocious redness,
    of hair and since being an extra on *Game of Thrones* up
    north, he'd a full flaming beard
He'd been a shoo-in for *Vikings* shooting in Wicklow but was
    so hungover that he burnt out, he did say to the casting guy
"Aren't Vikings like, supposed to be hungover, generally
    wasted?"
The guy, all snot and vinegar said
"But they are required to at least be able to stand up"
Finn, not easily discouraged, said
"I can do good pillage and bro, my plunder is a thing of art"
He is not in *Vikings*

Finn, if he'd lived in California, would have been your out 'n'
    out stoner

He certainly had the language if stoner words can even
     remotely be connected to articulation
Dude
Chill
Like (always seeming to end in open-ended question)
And the ubiquitous
In response to direct questions
"*I wanna say*"
Of course he loved his weed, bongs 24/7
But he had my back, always
A time when I was gradually taking over the boat, my father
     managed to drag himself from his daily stupor, gave my
     mother a beating, spat at my sister then headed down to
     the pier to *deal* with me
I was near the wheelhouse, bailing water as is a constant part
     of my trade when he launched, if unsteadily, on to the deck
     and did that thing that bullies learn in intimidation classes
Make a show of taking their belt off
When you're a child few gestures hold the horror, terror of
     that
Even now, the memory can bring a shudder
He snarled, froth leaking from the corners of his mean
     drunk's mouth
"You gonna get a whipping now boy"
Finn, below decks, making spliffs, appeared like a wrath of
     ferocious red fury
Picked my father up like a toy, said
"Dude, you got to like chill"
And threw him overboard

*

I began to stockpile my mother's pills, the sleepers
I crushed them and began to add them to a bottle of Crested
    Ten
My father's tipple of choice if he had a choice
He'd drink out of a wellington if he had to
I *borrowed* a car from long-term parking at Jurys hotel
I intended to put it back
On *Daddy's birthday,* I said to him
"Get your coat; I have a treat for you"
He growled
"Hope it's fucking cash"
I showed him the bottle of Crested, said
"A little libation for the trip"
That's all she wrote
He was in
My mother did her usual gig
Nothing
Nothing at all
As I drove, he nipped from the bottle, cursing every driver
    on the road
I put on music
"For whom the bell tolls"
Metallica
He near spat
"What's that shite?"
I said
"That is your knell"

*

We got to White Strand, the beach looking deserted
Forlorn
A lone heron stood sentry
I stopped the car, produced a flask, said
"This has poitín and coffee"
Plus a wee smidgen of Rohypnol

Got it from Finn, the walking pharmacy, who inquired
    mildly
"Dude, you do know this is like, the date rape gig?"
Added quickly
"Not like I'm judging or shite"
I said to my father
"We'll have this on the sand"
He could give a fuck, long as the booze flowed
He headed off, staggering wildly as the Crested Ten took
    effect, and he sat/collapsed near the water's edge
The ocean was coming in fast, high tide in about an hour;
    I knew from Google maps, I watched him for a moment,
    feeling nothing
Nothing at all
I pulled on my battered Barbour jacket, near blond in colour
    from years on deck, grabbed the can of petrol from
    behind the driver's seat, headed after dear old *Daddy*

He had collapsed right at the water's edge
I suddenly recalled his manic viewing of a TV quiz show

where contestants choose between three coloured doors, prizes varying according to the choice; during this show, my sister and I were literally crushed into silence as he roared at the TV

"Pick the red bloody door moron"

And more in that vein

He looked at me, snarled

"Gimme some of that shite in the flask"

I did

His eyes got wild and I indicated the petrol can, said

"You get three choices

1... I pull off my belt"

Asked

"You remember that action you liked so much, when you beat us, well door one is, I strangle you with said belt

2... Door two is I pour petrol over you and whoosh, you burn like the deepest hurt"

I took out a battered Zippo, had the insignia, *Brónach*, I flipped the hood to get his full attention then said

"3... Door three is, you lie there and the tide will drown you in about... Hmm, an hour"

He gurgled something and I said

"Think of it like this

1... Red door

2... Yellow door

3... Blue door"

He tried to rise, failed, the water reached his shoes, wetting the ends of his frayed trousers and that tiny thing nearly caused me to abort

Nearly

I pointed my finger, said

"See, over in the sand there, you can almost still see a crescent shape, that's where her blood ran"

I flicked the Zippo, said

"Time's up, I think the yellow door is your best fit"

Then I met Skylar

Gorgeous, American with a Brit accent

What was not to love?

And I did

Love her

Hard

I was working on the *Kate*, painting the hull, not long after my Dad's funeral

A girl approached, in her fine mid-twenties with a wonder of long dark hair, like a ferocious raven and indeed, fierce she would prove to be

Her face was marred by a badly broken nose that appeared to only recently have been slight repaired

Her eyes were dark blue and she had what they call in literary works, *a full mouth*

She might have been pretty before the nose disaster but she was better than that as she exuded an air of menace and heat

She asked

"You Skip?"

She was wearing those skinny jeans that no one save a Ramone can carry off but she was close

121

Black biker jacket as is the current trend and ping T with the
    slogan
#meattoo
I stared at her a moment too long then asked
"Who wants to know?"
Letting a hint of hard granite leak slightly over the words
Saw it in a movie and liked the effect
She laughed, said
"Oh I do like the bad boys"
I said lamely
"I'm Skip"
She studied me for a tense moment then
"What's a girl gotta say to get a drink?"
I snapped
"Please would work"
So it began
A frenzied dance of pubs, clubs, trips on Galway Bay, and
    when she finally saw my home, she exclaimed
"Is this like for real?"
The old fishermen's cottages, you have to be
Of
From
Related
To Claddagh
To have one
I had restored it to its previous look
Poor
Everything white, wicker furniture and precious little of it
I went for the Zen look

She said
"Bare"

She went by the name of Skylar because of *Breaking Bad*
She said she grew up in Oakland, California but was
    educated in London
Thus the curious blend of accents
She was twenty-five and in Ireland to write a book titled
The Galway Girl
Because she said
Gone Girl still had some mileage despite the hundreds of
    writers who leapt on the domestic noir wagon
So put *girl* in the title and
Hey
She was in fucking Galway or vice versa so borrow Steve
    Earl's song title
What would he do?
Sue?
He didn't sue Ed Sheeran
Later, after I had bought her a damn wedding ring, and
    paid rent on a flat for her, plus down payment on a Ford
    Corsair, I discovered all of the above was false
What was true was she was banging Finn

Time later, I was more than a little drunk, sitting on the
    beach near the *Kate*, had done some lines of coke and it
    makes me homicidal, that's why I took it, my right arm
    was pouring blood from the deep slash I carefully cut
    into it

A bottle of poitín in my left hand to fuel if possible the
    maniacal ferocious rage
And a sawn-off shotgun with two shells primed
I had texted both of my *mates*
Finn
Skylar
Asking them to meet me for a wonderful drop-dead surprise
As I waited, a picture of almost calm, I whistled
What else
Galway
Girl

#METOO

LAUREN HENDERSON

Mary Poppins. That's what he called me. Book my car, Mary Poppins. Get me the penthouse suite, Mary Poppins, and stay there with me pretending to make notes until I want to be alone with the latest actress wannabe and give you the nod to leave. Get my Viagra out of the fridge. Pour me a shot of tequila. Suck my cock, Mary Poppins.

He must have told me to suck his cock a thousand times. But it was reflexive; he spewed out that command to everyone, men as well as women. No, that's not true, now I think about it. He never said it to women over thirty-five.

The first time he told me to do it, on my starting day as his latest PA, I raised my eyebrows and said, "I'm sure you're joking, Mr Van Stratten, but I don't find that very amusing," and he roared with laughter and said, "Jesus, they hired me Mary Poppins! Where's your umbrella?"

Thank God, by then I'd been in New York long enough

to learn how much Americans love a posh British accent. My own is bog-standard middle class, now I've smoothed out the rolling Cambridgeshire accent that had people at university asking me rather snarkily where I came from. I wanted to be neutral, not to stand out; that's always been my preference. I'm an observer, not a participant. It's what makes me such a good PA. I always say that in interviews, and it always gets me the job, because people can see it's true.

In New York, being English in itself is laden with meaning. They think you're more intelligent, more sophisticated, more educated than they are. And if you can manage an upper-class, *Downton Abbey* above-stairs accent, that puts ten grand on your yearly salary right away.

I could never pass for posh back home, never. There are a million little things that give you away. We're so attuned to accents in the UK, so aware of the tiniest inflexion or turn of phrase, the inability to spell *hors d'oeuvres* or *per se* correctly. I don't even think I could pass for upper-middle: you need to know about opera and ballet and classical music for that. Posh people don't do culture, necessarily, but upper-middle ones do.

I said I was an observer.

But here in New York, I watched other Brit expats and poshed up my accent, and it gave me power and money. Not only that: for Jared Van Stratten, I was Mary Poppins, and no one wants to have sex with Mary Poppins. As Jared once said, she could kill your boner just by looking at it.

Which suited me fine. It was protection. He had such a choice of starlets available to him that office workers were far, far down any list of women he'd want to have sex with. But Jared was an animal. I never believed in sex addiction until I started working for him; I thought it was an excuse that men use to cheat on their wives. I had never seen anything like his behaviour before, and I still can't quite believe it. Trust me, if you'd been sitting just outside his office and regularly gone in there after one of his sessions to clear up, you wouldn't have believed it either. And yes, if you're wondering, he got a big kick out of strolling out of that office once the starlet had left, adjusting his trousers, watching Mary Poppins snapping on a pair of latex gloves, picking up a box of disinfectant wipes and heading into a room that smelt of semen and poppers and fear sweat and sometimes, slightly, of urine, to clean bodily fluids off his leather sofas.

America has introduced me to the near-miracle that is Scotchgard. With the job I do, its ridiculously long hours, its frequent travel, the possibility that Jared may call me any time. When I'm at home I mostly eat takeaway comfort food on my sofa in front of the Bravo Channel. I love reality TV. Scripted stuff is a busman's holiday for me; reality, fake though it may be, soothes my nerves. The shows I like the most feature people screaming at each other, because they're trapped inside the screen, under control.

They can't, for instance, reach through the glass and yell at me to fill the script for their dick shots, an immortal line that Jared uttered to me on the first day I worked for him. I had no idea what he meant, and I stared at him, baffled, aware my mouth was hanging slightly open. It sounded as if he wanted an update on a porn movie they were shooting, but Parador, as far as I knew, specialised in popular, feel-good art films, the kind that won Oscars because they made the viewer feel intellectual and sophisticated.

'Script', it turned out, was American for 'prescription'. And 'dick shots' was American for 'penis injection'. I'm fairly sure that even if I'd understood what he was saying, I'd have goggled at him in exactly the same way.

It's amazing what you can get used to, given time, and, more importantly, everyone around you taking outrageousness for granted and expecting you to do the same.

Anyway, Scotchgard. All the catered food at Parador is extremely healthy and protein-rich: sushi rolls made with brown rice, superfoods and quinoa coming out of your ears. Jared's a health nut. So at home I tuck into messy, sloppy, delicious fatty food: enchiladas, pad thai, General Tso's chicken. After I got my first bonus, I went to West Elm and spent it all on a top-notch velvet corner sofa that practically fills my living room. And I ticked the Scotchgard option. Best money I ever spent; spilled takeaway wiped right off the velvet.

Pad thai, however, isn't a biohazard. Jared's sofas were replaced regularly and I used disinfectant wipes every single time I touched them.

Every year, my bonus went up by a considerable amount. Not only did I scare HR rigid with my euphemisms, Jared loved my work. (My actual work, not my sideline as a sofa cleaner and needle disposal technician.) I didn't mind the sideline that much. I waitressed through university to help pay my tuition fees. And university towns don't have the best-behaved clientele. I had to clean a lot of very gross restaurant toilets after students staggered out of them. Now that I've got my degree, if my job requires me to wipe up other people's bodily fluids, it had better come with a great salary, huge yearly bonuses and the best health and dental care plan available to humanity. Which it does.

Besides, the office manager told me the real reason we had a personal copy of the *New York Times* delivered every morning, when Jared never even glances at it. It's a thick stack of paper with several supplements every day, more than enough to wrap up the used syringes for safe disposal. I did suggest a sharps bin in the toilets, but the manager gave me to understand that this would make the situation too blatant. I had a whole system for making sure the needle was driven through layers and layers of paper, completely covered, so that the cleaners would never get hurt.

"Mary Poppins!" he yelled, striding into my office, the antechamber to his, with a couple of elegant, beautiful twenty-something women behind him, arrow formation. As always, with the particular type of assistants Jared called his wing women, their hair was long, their heels high and their smiles bright.

"Present and correct," I said in my Mary voice. The more formally I talked, the better he liked it.

"Get me the latest version of the nun script!" he shouted. This was his normal pitch, so I didn't even blink.

"Absolutely, sir," I said, extracting it from the stack of scripts on my desk and carrying it through to his office.

There was a pile of head shots, which I had printed out earlier, waiting for him there. Everything was done electronically nowadays, but Jared insisted on having them on paper. It wasn't because he was old-fashioned; no, he had a ritual he always performed with the latest batch of young female possibilities. Standing in front of his big glass table, he reached out one hand, placed his palm on top of the pile and smeared it over the surface with a sweeping gesture until every face was visible. He didn't care if he covered the text, their names, their accent and dialect skills, their performance skills, whether they could ride side-saddle, dance the Argentine tango, shoot a bow and arrow; all he cared about were the faces.

Then he stared down at them and touched the tip of his tongue to his bottom lip, entirely unselfconscious, a glutton contemplating an all-you-can-eat buffet.

The wing women were sitting side by side on the leather desk chairs. No one went near the sofa unless they had to. They were scrolling through their phones, busy surveying casting agencies' offerings of the latest propositions for a demanding gourmet: fresh meat between eighteen and twenty-five, thin and white and coercible. They knew his tastes perfectly. Jared would have gone younger, of course, but he was self-protective enough to limit himself to legal flesh.

Having picked out several options, they would present Jared with the list. Calls would be placed, appointments booked, reservations made at the hotels in London and New York and LA that Jared favoured; young women who might be nervous of meeting a famous film producer in his hotel suite would be reassured by the presence of another attractive young woman taking notes, clearly there in a professional capacity.

Until she got an urgent phone call and had to excuse herself, a couple of drinks later...

"What do you think, Mary P?" Jared asked, and I looked down at the latest crop of sacrificial victims, still holding the script, careful not to look anywhere near his crotch area.

Colour photos, luminous skin, as natural looking as possible, any retouching minimal. No overt grooming, hair shown off if it was luxuriant, or pulled back if it wasn't. Only the slightest of smiles, nothing provocative or enticing. These weren't modelling shots. They were supposed to be neutral canvases onto which producers and directors could project their fantasies and desires.

I hadn't looked at them before, apart from checking that they had all printed out clearly. There were so many. There were always so many. But as I stared at the latest offerings, young women to be considered for the lead in the nun film, one face stared right back at me, and I could not take my eyes from hers.

She was strong-featured, sculptural, her brows straight dark lines, her cheekbones slanting upwards towards them, a perfect triangle which echoed her wide forehead and pointed chin. Her wide-set eyes gazed directly at the camera, very distinctive. They were pale blue, but the irises were rimmed by a circle of darker blue, extraordinarily striking. If she photographed this well, she would pop on screen.

I knew straight away that he would want her. It was obvious in the set of her chin, the way her lips were pressed lightly together, that she had both character and personality. He liked ones he could break; he loved a challenge.

His hand was at his crotch now, and the three of us women were pretending that it wasn't.

"Script," he said to me, holding out the other hand.

I gave it to him and left the room, closing the door behind me. I knew I'd be needing the gloves and the wipes in about half an hour. At least he wasn't requiring me to give him the injection, the way the nurse had shown me, into the side of the penis, avoiding the head and underside and any visible veins. One of the wing women would take care of that.

I sat down and stared at the screen in front of me, on which a complex spreadsheet ranked a long, long list of women's names in order of current preference. The ones at the top were those who would snag the coveted parts they had been through hell to achieve. At the bottom was the blacklist: women who had turned him down, fought him off, got to the door of the suite before he could, possessed some God-given instinct which had kept them from ever being alone with him in the first place.

Many of the names would make people's foreheads pucker, wondering what had happened to them. They had burned bright, been talented and charming and charismatic, made the cover of *Vanity Fair*, seemed on track for stellar careers. The answer, of course, was Jared. Jared had happened to them.

If a male director or producer was a predator, he just had to tell him that the women wouldn't bend over the casting couch. If the guy had some scruples, he spread the word that the women who had rejected him were unreliable, emotional, *difficult*—that word which attaches so stickily to a female that it's almost impossible to peel it from your skin. There were so many easy women to choose from. Why pick difficult when you didn't need to?

No one ever made it off the blacklist.

But I wasn't looking at the screen. I was seeing her, Siobhan Black, the name that had been at the top of the headshot. Irish, with a whole list of accents. She could ride a horse, drive a carriage, play the violin, cycle and rollerblade, had basic screen combat training.

Well, she wouldn't need any of those for the nun script. The part mostly required the nun to lie on her back, crying and screaming while she was being gang raped. It was one of the hottest scripts of the year: young women were lining up to compete for it.

It was called *Ave Maria,* and it was written by an older English director, who was well known for his defiantly eccentric films, often involving a great deal of nudity, featuring malleable up-and-coming actresses who would be unlikely to push back against unscripted additions or "improvisations" he might make once shooting started. He had been struggling for a while, falling out of fashion, making films that seemed almost wilfully obscure.

Realising that, he had cleverly come up with this pitch. Jared loved it. All his male cohorts loved it. Ostensibly, it made a strong feminist statement: a young nun was raped to death by monks in the Middle Ages as punishment for defying their authority and trying to save a witch they were persecuting. The witch was forced to watch the rapes before being burned to death; she and the nun then proceeded to haunt the monastery, their ghosts increasingly vengeful, inflicting a series of nightmares and hallucinations on the monks, turning them against each other with grisly results.

It was a horror art film, by far the director's most commercial idea to date. But, of course, it wasn't merely the potential returns that so powerfully attracted Jared. He was licking his lips at the prospect of the auditions. One thin young vulnerable white woman after another, lying on the floor of a rehearsal room, feigning being raped, sobbing, pleading, struggling; stripping down in front of Jared, the director, the casting director, Jared's buddies at Parador, a couple of money men, so they could "see if she looked physically right for the role"; and then, if Jared liked them, trooping into his office, his suite at The Plaza or The Ritz-Carlton, nervous but reassured by the presence of one of his wing women. Until she had to take that urgent phone call.

Or by my presence. I must be honest. I had been summoned to those suites several times when the wing women weren't available. I knew what was expected of me, and I did it. It was part of my job.

But this time...

I don't know why Siobhan Black affected me so much. She was part of a long, long line of young women just like her.

No, not just like her.

Who knows why one face in particular calls out to you? After the myriad faces I'd seen spread out on Jared's desk, a smorgasbord of availability, who knows why hers and hers alone affected me so much? I never had a type. Never felt especially drawn to strong straight eyebrows or white skin or light blue eyes limned in darker blue. It wasn't her looks, though of course I was drawn to beauty. Who isn't? It was something in her gaze.

Maybe she reminded me of my first-ever crush, but who was that? How can I possibly remember? Some little girl at kindergarten sitting opposite me on the bus, playing with me at the sandpit at the local park? Features that imprinted on me, formed some image of my ideal woman before I was even able to remember, some alchemical combination of elegance and strength, straight eyebrows, pointed chin? A babysitter, a friend of my parents, a next-door neighbour?

Perhaps there was never a template. Perhaps it was just her, Siobhan herself. Something in the way she looked at the camera, something that made me fall in love with her without knowing anything about her. If so, she would be a wondrous success as an actress. I couldn't be the only one in whom she stirred these feelings, this need, this desperate compulsion to protect her from a predator who had stared at her photograph and licked his lips and stroked himself through his trousers, picturing her naked on his leather sofa.

There was a commotion just outside my office and I braced myself, recognising the particular quality of bustle and noise. A few seconds later in swept Mrs Van Stratten, over six foot tall and looking, as always, like a finalist for Miss World in the Trophy Wife dress category, hair over fur over silk over skinny jeans over heels barely thicker than a darning needle, on which she moved as easily as if she were barefoot.

Gold and diamonds dripped from her ears, her throat and her wrists, and flashed from the designer sunglasses holding back her thick blonde-streaked tresses. Behind her trailed the Van Stratten twins, a matched pair of five-year-old boys who were biologically hers but had been carried by another woman, as Natalia Van Stratten's irritable bowel syndrome had prevented her from being able to do so.

I know. Me neither.

They were adorable children, if you liked that kind of thing, which I didn't. Each was shadowed by his own nanny, silent Filipinas whose eyes never left their respective charges.

"His door's closed, Mrs Van Stratten," I said, but she had already come to a halt in the middle of the room.

Natalia Van Stratten knew the situation perfectly well, had served her time, I had been told, as an aspirant actress on a previous incarnation of that sofa. Now she was happily ensconced in Jared's twenty-two million dollar penthouse in one of the Richard Meier-designed towers on the edge of the West Village, the twins and nannies sequestered on the lower floor of the duplex. She gave him respectability, accompanied him to red carpet events and premieres, trotted out the children when he needed family-friendly publicity, wore the latest designers and smiled a lot in public.

In private, she compensated for the smiling.

"Ugh!" she complained, frowning as much as her Botox permitted. "I need to talk to him right away! The doctor rang me and he's skipped his appointment *again*!"

I knew that, of course. I had texted his driver to confirm and reminded Jared first thing that morning, an hour before the car was due, and on the driver's confirming he had arrived. At which point Jared had told me to fuck off, because he wasn't fucking going.

"You should have made him go!" she ranted, and I nodded in agreement with her, because what alternative did I have?

"I'm so sorry," I said humbly, and as I did I noticed one of the nannies shoot the other a glance that said: *Look, they yell at the white women just like they do at us for completely unreasonable things we can't do anything about. It's not personal.*

"It's important!" Natalia said, stamping her foot. "This crazy new diet's putting such a strain on his kidneys the doctor says he needs to stop it immediately! It could be dangerous!"

Honestly, I thought, *what do you care if he drops dead tomorrow?*

And I was pretty sure, from their blank stares at the floor, that the nannies were thinking exactly the same thing.

Jared was always trying new diets, as if there were some miracle fix to be accessed, though he knew perfectly well, from working with actors, that there was no substitute for lean protein and a hardcore personal trainer. His weight fluctuated wildly; he could come back from a weeklong business trip a stone heavier, fly to Canyon Ranch for a few days and starve himself back down again, then pile two stone back on when he got back to New York.

To me, it didn't seem that big a deal. But I had very swiftly learned that rich Americans could be obsessive about their health. Sometimes I thought that they secretly believed they could live forever if they ate the right food, took the right supplements and exercised compulsively. Besides, if Jared's doctor fussed about the yo-yo dieting, kept calling him in for check-ups and tests, it spiked the bill, so it was in the doctor's interest to take it more seriously than it warranted.

However, if the doctor's concern turned out to be warranted, enough to worry Natalia Van Stratten like this, it had to be the case that her pre-nup wouldn't fully pay out if she couldn't keep her husband alive for another few years. New York had been quite the learning curve for me. Trophy wives regularly signed agreements that gave them bonuses per every five years of marriage, for instance; maybe Natalia came into a major lump sum at the end of her first decade with Jared.

The office door swung open, and the wing women emerged, sleek as always, quite as if nothing had been going on in there that shouldn't have been. They acknowledged Natalia with deferential nods, gliding past her, their heads bowed like subservient swans. She ignored them completely in magnificent style.

"Jared!" she yelled, and one of the twins ran over to his nanny and drove his head against her waist in a primitive need for comfort. "You need to go to the doctor, now!"

"Fuck you!" her husband yelled back, appearing into view. "If I wanted some bitch who nagged me about going to the doctor, I wouldn't have married a Russian, would I? I'd have picked a Jew or a Chinese or an Italian!"

Natalia set her hands on her waist and threw her head back, ready for combat. The other twin took refuge with his nanny, who started stroking his curls. And as my employer and his wife continued screeching at each other, I did a

Google search for branches of the New York Public Library in Harlem.

I live in Brooklyn.

It took a fortnight. Michael, the British film director, flew to NYC so that he and Jared could start initial auditions with an enthusiasm that was marked even by their standards. Video clips of young women sobbing and pleading not to be raped by invisible monks accumulated in my inbox, self-taped by prospects who were unable to present themselves in person because they were working on another job. Appointments racked up for the young women available to sob and plead in person. One of them was Siobhan, who had been flown over by Parador from the UK, together with several other prospects, every one of whose agents knew exactly what her client was in for.

As did the female casting director. The only extenuating circumstance for them all acquiescing to this was that, as I had learned from office canteen chat, women blocked by the boys' club from the opportunity to be editors, producers and directors became agents or took casting jobs instead. Roles that were traditionally perceived as female and which, not uncoincidentally, paid considerably less.

This afternoon, Siobhan was booked into the casting suite. We had our own, a large meeting room with cameras and lighting permanently set up; other production companies used rented space, but Jared loved auditions— technically called "meetings", I had learned when I came to Parador—and he wanted to be on the spot for as many as possible. It was my job to meet the actors in reception, to calm their nerves, bring them up to the suite, reassure them with my lovely manners and my Mary Poppins voice. After all, what could be more calming than being escorted by Mary Poppins?

Jared was highly predictable. If an actress piqued his interest in the casting suite, he would bring them back to his office straight afterwards. And as soon as I saw her in person, I knew that was what would happen. She was even more beautiful in real life, which isn't always the case. Her Irish colouring was very strong, the black hair, the light blue eyes, the milk-white skin so pale it almost had a bluish tinge, a delicate Milky Way of freckles across the bridge of her long straight nose.

She was dressed in the usual way for actors coming to meetings, like models for go-sees. Casual, functional, showing she was there to work. Faded jeans, a black roll-neck sweater, form-fitting enough to reassure everyone that she was as slim as leading actresses needed to be. A black leather jacket was slung over her shoulders, and her hair was pulled back from her face in an artfully messy twist.

"Oh, you're English!" she said, smiling at me, holding out her hand. "Nice to hear a familiar accent over here."

Mine shook as I took hers, but hopefully not enough for her to realise. It was cool and dry, a little too much so; she needed to moisturise more.

"Nice to have an Irish person be happy to meet an English one," I said in response, and she grinned like an urchin.

"Hey," she said, "I'll take what I can get in a foreign country."

"Is your hotel okay?" I asked, the standard question I asked everyone, as I turned to lead her through security. The big glass gate swung open for us.

"Oh yeah, thanks," she said, a little too casually.

They had put her up in the latest hip place on The Bowery, I knew. I had checked the travel department's reservation for her. It had the usual complement of try-hard décor and gimmicks: single shots of gin, made in the hotel's on-site distillery, served from a machine in the check-in area; an entirely gluten-free menu; a dedicated ballet barre studio in the gym. All charges to Parador's card. Siobhan couldn't fail to be impressed, but she was doing her best to act cool, for which I couldn't blame her.

"I haven't been there yet," I said at random, trying not to babble. "Is it nice? How's your room?"

Was that creepy? No, I decided. It sounded like small talk, not as if I were asking her for a photo of her bed so I could imagine her on it.

I didn't need it. I already saw it on her Instagram a couple of hours ago.

"Small but perfectly formed," she said with a lilt of amusement. "And some things I've never even heard of in the minibar."

"They'll be very healthy and taste a bit like seaweed," I said, pressing the button for the lift. "Just don't look at the ingredients."

This was small talk at its finest, words intended merely to spackle and plaster over any awkward silences, pure filler. And yet it felt to me as if every word that dropped from her lips was a diamond, or a pearl, like a fairy tale I remember, where the heroine is given that blessing in return for her sweet nature.

I led her into the casting suite, and I saw Jared and Michael's expressions as they took her in, that particular toxic flicker in their eyes, the burning darkness inside them crawling out for a moment, a flash of feral red. And she thanked me for bringing her to them as sweetly as the girl in the fairy tale would have done.

I couldn't access the video recording system from my computer to watch it live, not until the recording was finished and it streamed automatically to my database. I sat in my office in a pool of sweat for half an hour. It was the longest thirty minutes of my life. I took handfuls of antiseptic wipes and dabbed myself down under my blouse. They stung; I welcomed the sensation. I had seen some of the other auditions for *Ave Maria*. I knew what kinds of things she was having to do, the questions she was being asked.

Finally the door opened and Jared walked in, Siobhan following directly behind him. On her face was the identical expression I had seen on so many starlets accompanying him into his office: dazed, disbelieving, afraid to hope her dream was coming true, struggling to keep her spiking optimism under control. And just a little apprehensive.

Jared didn't look at me as he passed. He didn't need to tell me not to disturb him or to hold his calls. I was very well-trained, and I knew exactly what to do.

The door closed behind them. His office was practically sound-proof. I had barely ever heard anything through the thick wenge wood walls, the door with rubber flanges that enabled it to close with only the faintest sigh and click.

I went through two more handfuls of disinfectant wipes.

Then the door flew open with such force that my heart slammed just as powerfully into my ribcage. Siobhan stood there, wearing only a small lace bralette on the upper half of her body. The top button of her jeans was unfastened. Her eyes were wild, the pupils hugely enlarged.

"He-he-" she stammered.

I was on my feet, running towards her in stockinged feet. Jared made his female employees wear high heels, but I had kicked them off as soon as I sat down. I caught her and pushed her back into his office, guiding her to one of the chairs in front of his huge desk. She was shaking like a birch tree in high winds.

Jared was collapsed across one arm of the sofa, face down, trousers and boxers down. The kidney-straining diet had been effective, I noticed; his bare buttocks were slim and toned. From the floor, I grabbed her sweater, the thin T-shirt she had been wearing underneath it, and shoved them at her, telling her to put them on and button her jeans. As she obeyed, clumsily fumbling to pull the clothes over her head, I dived for the used syringe on his desk. All I had to do was substitute it; I had kept the one he'd used a couple of days ago, hidden at the back of a drawer, his fingerprints on it, and now I pulled that out, switching them over.

I was very fast. Siobhan wouldn't have seen me; her head was buried in her black sweater, her arms struggling to find the sleeves. I dashed into my office and buried the syringe

Jared had just used in the usual crumple of newspapers in my desk bin, which the cleaners were briefed to empty carefully.

I was back in his office as her head emerged from the neck of the sweater. She was in shock, I thought, her pupils still dilated, so pale that her freckles were even more visible than they had been an hour ago.

"Sit still," I said to her, going round the desk, taking up his cell phone, dialling the direct line to our head of security, Caspar Petersen, the man who knew the precise location of every single Parador corpse. "It'll be okay. I promise you, it'll be okay. Everything's going to work out fine."

Petersen was there in five minutes. By that time I was sitting in the other desk chair, having drawn it next to Siobhan. I was holding her hands, murmuring quiet words of reassurance.

I had felt for Jared's pulse. There wasn't one.

Then a whole crowd of Parador employees whirled in like a tornado that picked us up and whisked us into the outer office, the head of HR cooing over us, asking us how we were. Siobhan was clinging to me, and I put my arm around her narrow waist. If I shook when I touched her now, like this, no one would realise why.

Petersen was making phone calls to the Mayor, the state governor and Jared's guy in the NYPD, a deputy chief. I heard the fridge open and close and one of Petersen's henchmen emerged from the office, carrying a stack of boxes of loaded syringes, other medications, popper vials, and something on top wrapped in hand tissue. The used needle.

He was moving very gingerly, and I couldn't blame him.

A wave of relief hit me; I would never have to touch those things again. It was extraordinary that I hadn't developed a phobia of injections myself. Through the open door, I saw two more of Petersen's men wrestling Jared's corpse off the sofa, dragging up his trousers, returning him to respectability, a film magnate tragically struck by an unexpected heart attack.

They brought us water. We drank it. A doctor summoned by Petersen examined Siobhan briefly and offered her some pills that she refused. Petersen and the head of PR told us we would be taken care of and not to worry. One of the henchmen guided us out of the building, and, with considerable irony, into Jared's waiting limo and thence to his suite at The Plaza. There we were ensconced in unbelievable luxury high above the city as the storm broke a few blocks below us. We watched it on New York 1, the local channel, Jared's body carried out of the Parador building, journalists shouting questions, the ambulance lights flashing bright, Jared's partner delivering a brief, grim-faced statement about what a terrible loss Jared would be to the industry.

They said it was a heart attack, and they were quite right, though no autopsy was conducted, as nobody wanted there to be a record of what precisely had been in Jared's body. I had seen them cover up plenty of scandals. I knew I was safe there. More precisely, he died of hyperkalemia, which, according to the New York Public Library computer in a particularly obscure Harlem branch, occurs when you already have weak kidneys and you inject yourself with a huge dose of potassium chloride, thinking that it's your erection drug.

To be fair, the New York Public Library didn't quite put it that way. But it did also tell me that potassium chloride is a generic drug and you can buy it in liquid form at any health shop, after I Googled 'weak kidney die' and it gave me the answer to my unspoken question.

I didn't need to be told to wear a baseball cap and a faceful of make-up in the library and then at the Vitamin Shoppe, plus layers of clothes that made me look a lot bigger than I am. I had no intention of being recognised on CCTV. Nor did I need to be advised to pay in cash without using my loyalty card, and to remove all traces of potassium chloride and the packaging from my apartment after I filled that syringe and took it back to the office. I read a lot of mystery novels.

With Jared's death, Parador was in a positive scramble to sanitise his memory, literally and metaphorically. Natalia sobbed on cue for the benefit of the paparazzi, her arms wrapped around the adorable twins. Everyone on the long list of employees and actresses who had signed non-disclosure agreements with Parador for lucrative settlements was contacted by lawyers and gently reminded that those agreements were just as valid whether Jared was alive or dead.

Siobhan and I, visited in our suite by the NYPD deputy chief, recounted how Jared had suddenly collapsed while talking to Siobhan about the part. Through the open doorway, I said, noticing his approving nod at this, I had heard her cry out, seen him clasp his chest and fall to the sofa.

She was superb at improvising. That was her RADA

training, I suppose. I followed along, careful to add nothing to her story, simply agree. We had been heavily coached, of course, by the head of publicity and a media handler who were both present during the entirety of the pro-forma interview. The deputy chief left, expressing his sympathy to both of us and assuring us we would not be bothered again. The head of publicity told us to charge anything we wanted to the room, and not to leave it until they told us we could, and the media handler told us not to answer any call that wasn't from Parador.

Jared's partner rang Siobhan and told her that she could have her pick of roles on Parador's upcoming roster of films.

The head of HR rang me and said I was being given a hundred grand hardship bonus for my loyalty and the exemplary way I had handled matters. Would I like to transfer to the LA office, all expenses paid? The precise nature of my role was still to be confirmed, but was I at all interested in producing?

I booked an Ayurvedic aromatherapy in-room massage for two. We ordered tuna poke and sweet potato fries. We got into the master bed, drank Tattinger and watched a Bravo series with attractive young people working on a luxury yacht, bickering, getting drunk and serving exotic cocktails to entitled guests. Eventually, we made love.

Siobhan had a boyfriend back in London. Some young actresses were coming out now, as lesbian or bisexual, but only women who had already had major Hollywood blockbuster success and now wanted to work in art films. One of them took the part of the nun in *Ave Maria*. She said in interviews that, like Jodie Foster in *The Betrayed*, it was much easier for her, as a gay woman, to play the victim of a male gang rape, than it would have been for a straight one.

Siobhan asked for and got the coveted part of a sexy assassin in a well-received thriller, which led to a role in a Marvel franchise. I moved to LA and got into production. It had been a nominal job title, given to me under the assumption that everyone wanted to produce, but to my surprise, I turned out to be very skilled at it. I have a sense of how to sell a story, what people will believe, what they won't. And there's quite the lesbian network in Los Angeles. They're all big fans of Julie Andrews and Mary Poppins.

I was Siobhan's maid of honour at her wedding to her understanding long-term boyfriend. We're still very close, though I'm married now myself, to a writer/director who was nominated for an Oscar last year. The boys' club has realised it needs to let in more than a token couple of women, and we're shoving hard at the floodgates. Siobhan and I don't talk about that afternoon in Jared's office. We spent four days holed up at The Plaza, talking, crying, sleeping, working through it, and then we were done.

She didn't realise then that I was the one who filled his prescriptions, stocked his fridge with them, cleaned up the used needles, provided the starlets' contact details for the lawyers to move in smoothly with their NDAs and settlement offers. It may have occurred to her since, but she's never brought it up to me. Why would an actress unnecessarily antagonise a producer?

Sometimes I think I see a little flicker of speculation in her eye as we hang out on the terrace of my house high in the Hollywood Hills, the lights of downtown glittering below, Katrine grilling a Paleo-suitable slab of meat over our fire pit, Siobhan and I sipping dry, low-sugar red wine, the fountain playing beside the vertically planted living wall of our garden. But that could so easily be a glimmer reflected from the leaping flames, the glint of light on moving water.

It's very unlikely that she's wondering if I emptied out that syringe of erectile dysfunction disorder medication and replaced its contents with heavily condensed potassium chloride, boiled down on my kitchen stove. That she's remembering my passion for her in that huge bed at The Plaza, and asking herself whether, after all the starlets I'd seen come and go, I finally killed him to protect her, putting that syringe in his fridge, the last one in the box, after I took her to the casting suite.

Because then it would dawn on her that, if my only motive had been to protect her, I hadn't done the best of jobs. I had subjected her to his aggression, his insistence that she show him her tits, unbutton her jeans, as he sat at his desk chair, pulled the last syringe out from the packet, unzipped his trousers, discarded the plastic needle cover and stuck the needle into the side of his penis—avoiding, of course, the head and underside and any visible veins.

I had forced her to watch him stand up, lurch towards her, tears forming in her beautiful eyes as he told her that good girls get leading roles, and to strip down, get on her knees and show him what a good girl she could be. To stand there, paralysed, terrified, conflicted, before he gasped and grabbed his left arm, his own knees buckling, his torso bending forward, hitting the wide leather arm of the sofa, his head crashing down like a heavy weight, pulling his body with it. To watch him die.

If I had truly done it out of pure love for her, I wouldn't have put her through that. I would have loaded that syringe for another actress's 'meeting' with him in his office and spared her the entire experience.

But then, she wouldn't have owed me. I wouldn't have been the one who rushed to her side, comforting her, telling her everything would be all right, and was as good as her word. I wouldn't have been holed up with her in The Plaza for four beautiful, miraculous, heaven-sent days. Wouldn't have been perfectly positioned to take advantage of her when she was in a state of extreme shock and vulnerability.

In my defence, however, she had sex with me entirely willingly. On that score, at least, I'm morally superior to Jared.

THE LIFEGUARD

JAMES GRADY

Cari knew there'd be a murder even before she saw him walk into that May afternoon backyard party in his honor. Soft blue sky. Purple lilacs. Freshly mown grass. Him gliding through the American heartland crowd. A polite nod here, a handshake there, a shy smile as they led him toward the microphone.

She didn't stand with teary-eyed parents from the elementary school, nor with still-married couples from the halls of her high school, nor with their small hometown's Big Men and Boss Wives where *they* said she now belonged.

Cari stood alone at the back edge of everything.

Saw him.

Finally, *oh finally*, saw *him*.

OK, *yeah*, he was lean and keen-eyed, a mouth that made her loins ache like never before and *for sure* never after her wedding. And *oh yes*, she knew he was a *librarian* who fostered the wonders of *what if* and *what is*. But what pulled her out of only one possibility of murder went beyond *him* to the sum of *them*.

"Hey, everybody!" said Mayor Mel into the microphone. "Great to be here to thank Jeff Gage. What a guy! Only come to town five weeks ago, sees a school bus full of second graders drop its driveshaft, crash into a bridge. Climbs onto the bus tottering over a fifty-two-foot drop. Pulls the kids out. Gets everybody safe, and when he jumps clear, *whoa*: that school bus tumbles down into the river!"

Some man shouted: "*Woo-hoo!*"

"We already gave Jeff a plaque down at City Hall. The photographer drove eighty-seven miles from the *Herald Tribune* to take a picture for those of you who still read newspapers. But now here with just us folks, let's let Jeff say what he wants to."

Cheers. Applause.

Jeff stood in front of the microphone.

His blue eyes locked on *her*.

Cari knew he felt it, too.

Jeff said, "I did what I had to do."

Stepped back from the microphone: what more was there to say?

Applause, cheers, calls for beers. People shake Jeff's hand. Pat him on the back. He slides through groups of friends and neighbors and in front of the whole universe, steps up to Cari.

She held out her hand. He clasped it with the strength of softness.

They whispered their names. Held each other's flesh until remembrance of their where and when made them let go, a release to propriety that triggered the townspeople to turn away from what they *might* see to what they *should* see.

"I don't know what to say," whispered Cari.

Only she heard Jeff reply, "This is crazy."

"Crazy like jumping on a wrecked school bus that's going to fall off a bridge?" Cari shook her head. "My whole life I've done what's sane and it's trapped me here, but now there's nowhere else I'd rather be."

Cari said, "No bullshit. No *polites*. Please, *please*: talk to me true."

Jeff stared at this woman with hair like the summer sun, who held him in her river eyes. "How much trouble am I in?"

"You're not alone."

"Rings on your fingers."

"I'm sorry!" Tears glazed her vision. "I had to. And now I'm even sorrier, because maybe I pulled you into your own murder."

Jeff said, "I didn't die when our lightning bolt hit me, I came alive."

"No, I'm talking for real, I—" Cari trembled. "Can we just have *now*? Just for a little while? Not talk about…murder?"

Trust filled his face as he nodded *yes*.

"Is it true you never married? All these years?"

"They were years without you. Drifted around. Drifted in and out of being not alone. But I was always lonely. And sure wasn't because I'm gay, like an element in this town is afraid of. Hell, them being wrong is maybe why they're leaving us alone so we talk. A bookish gay guy and a married woman, no threat to civic order."

"We're a threat to all the orders."

"All I want is for you to be free."

"*All?*" she whispered.

"I want you to be able to start there."

Microphone voice, Mayor Mel: "*Hey everybody, something's happening!*"

The microphone stood in front of Mayor Mel and an orange-haired man.

"Baden's got something great to tell us!" said Mayor Mel as he turned the microphone over to the beefy, handsome, orange-haired man.

Whose voice boomed, "Me being inspired by Jeff over there..."

Cari and Jeff felt a hundred million burning eyes.

"As president and owner of the First National Bank and Trust, I'm donating $10,000 for the schools to repair and upgrade the buses for our kids!"

Mayor Mel led cheers.

Cari said, "That's my husband. Grabbing the applause."

Jeff gave a wry smile. "He owns the buses the county rents. Is supposed to keep them repaired so crankshafts don't break and crash a busload of kids into a bridge. And *oh* will he collect on the insurance!"

"I wonder if the ten K will be his money or the bank's," she said. "I wonder where it will really go. No matter what, he'll claim a tax deduction. And you better believe that ten thousand dollar kisses sweetheart deals made by his golf buddies."

"Main Street, U.S.A.," said Jeff. "We get the bad with the good."

"You have no idea," said Cari.

His nod led her eyes through the crowd to near the microphone, where husband/bank president Baden stood in a cluster of well-dressed males, *big wheels* who posed shoulder to shoulder and blocked a gaunt man from intruding on this wonderful moment of charity.

Jeff said, "See that shrunken guy in the flag patches windbreaker trying to talk to your husband? He keeps glancing over here. At you."

"That's Dave Maynard. Owns the dry cleaners and laundromat."

Cari swept her eyes over faces she knew and mostly liked, even if they often turned away from her out of what might be pity.

"I should have gotten out when I was young," she said.

"And gone where?"

"Wherever it's us on the road, not the road on us."

"Please don't ever stop talking to me," he said.

Mary Cutler, who worked as county clerk and recorder and ran a *feed-our-local-hungry* volunteer program, sent Cari a smile.

"I wasn't always like this," said Cari.

A woman slid from the crowd, slick ebony hair and crimson lips, diamond studded velvet shoes crushing the grass under their soles.

"*Cari*," purred the blood-mouthed woman, "there you are."

Cari's eyes never left the creature in front of her as she told Jeff, "Regina Swanson is our host. I'm sorry, Regina, do they still call you '*Mrs.*' if you're a widow?"

"Well, you'll never have to worry about that, will you Cari? Now please take good care of Jeff here, this is his day to be important."

Cari blinked. "His *day*? His one day to be important?"

"Why else would we be here?" said Regina. "And you must be bursting with pride for your husband! Baden's ever so wonderful."

Regina sashayed away hissing orders to the wait staff of scared high school girls in white blouses, black pants, and dollars' need.

"Wow," said Jeff.

Cari said, "Even if she hadn't hit town last year with Ncil Swanson when he came back from Las Vegas before his heart attack—maybe from being forty years older than his new wife—even if Regina wasn't around, I'd still be murdered."

"Do you want to tell me now?"

"What I want has never much mattered."

"Does now."

"What I want… This isn't the *me* I wanted to be."

Cari said, "I was a lifeguard.

"At the city pool. I was seventeen. Wore a red swimming suit with a white circle insignia on the front, a red cross inside it right between my breasts.

"All that meant something. I had a reason to go to work besides money. Days perfumed with chlorine and coconut oil. Blue sky and burning sun. Light shimmers in a turquoise pool. Walking barefoot on warm cement.

"*Yeah*, whistleblowing at wild kids splashing cannonballs. Eyeballing some toddler ambling off while mom talks to the woman on the next lounge chair. Wrestling floating dividers into lap lanes. A dozen boring *gotta-do*'s every day.

"But I belonged there. High on a white wooden chair so I could see what was going on. Decide what to do. Mirror sunglasses. And *yeah*, I knew guys licked me with their eyes. They always had. Boys my age, and now them plus grown-up married guys and even grampa guys, *but so what*, I wasn't there for them. I was there getting to put all of me on the line to save lives."

Cari shook her head.

"I never had to. Until...

"My Mom. Youngest woman in town to ever have a stroke—strokes. My run-off father used to hit her. She fought for me. All the way to my senior year summer. Then the strokes. Us alone, mountains of medical bills, food, rent, her needing somebody there all the time, us headed for the streets, no other options.

"Except Baden. I'd told every other guy *no*, but I *really* told Baden *no*.

"And that made me more important for him to get. Eleven graduating classes older than me. Biding his inheritance time at the prince's desk his bank-founder father gave him. Needing a queen or at least a trophy so he could be king. Baden never gets told no. *'One way or another'* is his rule. Has to keep showing people he wins. Can't let anybody see that he ever lost.

"But I used our rent for that month, hired a smart lawyer who Baden and his attorney figured was *'just a woman'*. Pre-nup. *'Saved myself'* until after Baden set

Mom up in the nursing home because of the pre-nup. *Saved myself* until after the marriage certificate was signed and sealed. Cue the wedding bells and I'm still hoping. O'Hara Manor hotel, then…"

Cari's eyes filled with a horizon that made Jeff flinch.

"After we found out I couldn't work as a breeding bitch, he mostly stopped bothering." She blinked. "Mostly."

"Leave him," said Jeff. "Right now. We'll walk out of here right now."

"Then Baden'd have to kill us both sooner rather than later."

Gaunt Dave pushed his way up to them.

"Hey, Cari, seen your Mom up to the nursing home, doing good, gonna be around for a long time, but I gotta talk to you," blurted this skeletal man who smelled of chemicals. "Talk to Baden, you gotta talk for me, 'cause all of 'sudden, 'can't get to him."

Cari said, "How are you, Dave?"

"How does it look? I'm fucking cancer dying. Hell, 'be better if I died before dawn. That ain't crazy. Then there'd be something left for Sheila and the girls, but the insurance won't let me push it, and Baden, your husband, he won't let me set up so's my family won't lose everything.

"He says the bank's gonna call my mortgage *right now* on the dry cleaners. Hell, I took it out with an escalating clause like he said *back when* so as to fold in all the fees the bank kept charging me. Now the monthly's sky high and if the bank calls the mortgage before I die, instead of Sheila getting the mortgage pay-off insurance the bank made me buy, I leave nothing behind me but pain.

"Plus, Baden's on the private prison's board. The government don't give a damn about those locked-up guys they zoo with that back-East corporation. Tax dollars pay whatever bills get sent by the prison. Politicians write laws to keep the cells full. Now Baden says the prison is going to start doing its laundry inside. Make the cons do it. Take in other contracts, too, like how I do for the nursing home, though where the hell the prison's gonna get laundry machines cheap enough to make a go of it right away, damned if I know."

Dave shrank into himself. "Or maybe damned 'cause I *do* know.

"What I know… Never said nothing 'bout folks who signed petitions to keep that soul-sucking prison away from our town then gettin' after dark calls about how their home mortgages and car loans could be hurt if they didn't change their politics, erase the choice they made. 'Never said nothing 'bout a lot like that.

"A lot." Dave shook his head. "You know what'll happen when the bank takes my dry cleaners? Guy I know shovels for the city crew let me know. Gonna pave it into a parking lot. 'Prison's gonna rent it, make whoever's got the cheap-money guard jobs park there, ride some rental bus the three miles to work behind them electric razor wire fences. Make any visitors to the locked-up guys park there. In Baden's lot. Charge 'em all."

Someone laughed on the far side of this backyard party.

"My dry cleaners ain't just what keeps my family alive," said Dave. "It's my life. My work. How I got to be a free man and raise a family and not fuck anyone over or get fucked by just being alive. You gotta talk to Baden. Make him let me play it out, leave Sheila and the kids something to salvage. Please, Cari."

Cari touched the man's thin arm through the cloth of his windbreaker decorated with flags and politically conservative slogans. "I'll do what I can."

The dying man's nod fought off tears as he melted away.

Alone with Jeff, she said, "One more hollow truth. Wish I could have lied."

"We all get enough lies," said Jeff.

"That prison," said Cari. "I feel like I'm behind its razor wire. Did you know all the prisoners' accounts have to run through Baden's bank? That he handles all the banking for the prison, too?"

"We can get away," said Jeff.

"The pre-nup," said Cari. "Baden was so clever he trapped us both. He figured I'd ask for a divorce, so he put in a clause that gives most everything to 'the aggrieved party'— meaning him, not thinking the split could set up the other way. He made adultery no penalty because he knew before the wedding he'd be fucking around. Divorce means he'll stop paying for my Mom. Not even you and I together could cover that. He'll toss her out on the street.

"Beyond money, he knows he'll lose if we split—even if he hooks up with Regina, merging with her widow's inheritance so he's even more of a big shot. But if I walk free, then he's stuck being a loser. Plus, he can't risk me out from under his thumb with what I might know and what a public divorce might show."

Jeff frowned. "So you think he's going to kill you?"

"And now maybe you, too. Our *us*—which everybody at this party must see—that makes you a perfect fall guy for the murder. Or makes you somebody who'd come after him for killing me. Hell, he probably wants to kill you because, this afternoon, you got what he never did from someone who's legally his."

Jeff glowed.

Said, "Everything changes in a heartbeat."

Shook his head. "But *murder*..."

"Reporter from the *Herald Tribune* drove up here in January, he—"

"I remember," said Jeff. "He was out doing some story about oil field leases, the pumpers out on the prairie. Car broke down. No cell service. Froze to death."

"He was working a story on bank deals and public lands and oil rights," said Cari. "I'd never seen Baden scared before. Then..."

"Then the night before they found the reporter frozen dead trying to walk out safe from his broken-down car, that night Baden stormed into the house, stinking of whiskey, grin on his face. Grabbed me, dragged me...

"When it was done, he... He stood beside the bed, said, *'You best remember, sugar isn't always so sweet.'*

"The next morning when I heard about the reporter's car breaking down on the empty prairie where he went to meet someone or maybe get a picture of something... Baden used to brag about how in high school, he'd pour sugar in the gas tanks of anybody who pissed him off."

Jeff started to reply—

Sensed *someone coming* and turned from Cari in time to send a smile to Sid Stiffarm and shake that chiseled cheekbones man's hand.

"Just gotta say, Jeff," said Sid, "helluva thing you did. Thanks."

"You'd have done the same," said Jeff. "I know about you in the Corps."

"Hi, Cari," said Sid, and a light flashed in his eyes as he turned back to Jeff. "You know how smart this woman is?"

"I'm lucky to be finding that out." Jeff watched her.

"Week or so back, she calls me down the shop, insists I come up to her place, that big house on the hill overlooking town. They keep all Baden's cars in their garage, Cari's car being that old—*I know* it's what you brought owned to the wedding, so you don't wanna give it up, nice old Ford *from the last century!*"

Sid laughed.

"Anyhow," Sid told Jeff, "Cari here called me up 'cause when she went to get in her car to go see her mom at the nursing home, she spotted a trickle of wet run down the road out past her front bumper. Last few years, rainy season ain't but half of what it was and it'd been weeks since, so instead of doing the regular thing of bringing the car into the shop—hell, most people wouldn't even have noticed that trickle—'stead of driving off, she calls me. Insists I come up there.

"Cari, she makes up her mind, *Katie bar the door!* Cari's been like that since she was a little girl. Lived across the alley from us, so I drive up to see *what's what*. Come to find out, her old car's worn a gash in the brake line and it's trickled out plumb empty. She'd've just driven off like most folks, she'd've gone full tilt boogie down Knob Hill into who knows what. Maybe career all the way down to the train tracks.

"Now I don't call that *lucky*," said Sid. "I call that *smart*, and she's—"

"What *is* my wife, gentlemen?"

Baden lumbered into their trio, his orange hair laying strong and stiff in the breeze, his handsome florid face all smiles and his meaty paw clutching a clear goblet of white wine.

"Hey, how you doing?" said Sid. "Just thanking Jeff here—and *hey*, thanks to you, too. Helluva thing you did, donating. Good thing."

Sid held a *beg your pardon* hand up toward Baden. "Can I get you to do another good thing?"

"You never know," said Baden.

"That guy from across the mountains who you said works for you, 'come by my shop and like you asked, I cut him in ahead of the line 'cause he needed to go, paid me cash and come to find out, he paid sixty dollars too much. Can I get you to ask him to call the shop so I can figure out how to get his money back to him?"

"Can't you just keep it?"

"Hell, it ain't mine."

Baden said, "I'll let him know."

"Much obliged," said Sid. "And thanks again for everything."

Baden kept his eyes on the service station/garage proprietor walking back into the party crowd, sent his gravel voice to Cari and Jeff.

"Our Indian brothers," said Baden. "A good one is a good one."

Jeff threw his words like stones: *"People are people!"*

Anyone could see Cari rise to her full height.

Neither of them flinched when Baden drilled his gaze into them.

"Look at you two. Standing here. Together."

Jeff said, "Free country."

"So they say." Baden grinned. "But everywhere I look, there's a price tag."

Baden laughed, and Cari smiled. "Speaking of price tags, what *'man from across the mountains'* works for you—or the bank? Doing what?"

"Don't worry your blonde." Baden leered at Jeff. "She's an all-over natural."

Cari felt Jeff go cold, burn hot.

Quickly said, "Since when do you drink white wine, Baden, or is that your new natural?"

"This," said Baden swirling the golden fluid in his glass, "this is class. Right time. Right place. *Right, dear?*"

"What you got is a chance to do one thing right," said Cari.

"And *you* get to choose? *One thing?*"

All the *options* in the universe froze Cari in that tick-tock.

She fought through a thousand thoughts, chose to say, "Dave Maynard. The dry cleaners. His dry cleaners. Leave him be."

"Oh, I am. There's nothing on earth gonna stop me from leaving him be just like he is and is gonna be after we finish the business the law lets me do."

Baden grinned and raised his white wine in a toast. "And you can take that to the bank—my bank. You two got nothing to take nowhere else."

As he walked away, his chuckle turned to a modest and benevolent smile for the crowd in this hometown backyard.

Jeff whispered to Cari, "What the hell are we going to do?"

Invisible in the crowd, a woman with an extra white wine in her laughed. Just let the hell go. Laughed at herself. Laughed at what was, what wasn't. Laughed at the everything of this fine spring backyard afternoon.

Cari looked away from Jeff. Looked back.

Said, "Don't say what I'm dying to hear and say or I won't be able to do what I've gotta and then you'll—*we'll* both be trapped, just waiting for some man from across the mountains.

"Get out of here," she told Jeff. "Right now. Don't look back. Leave town tonight. Fuck your job at the library, *go*. Stay away. You know other folks here, you can check with them, they'll tell you what happens."

"I'm with you," he said. "Together for whatever."

"Even murder?" whispered Cari.

"He can try."

"Not him," she answered. "Me."

She shook her head. "It's gotta be me. I've got to be first. Murder him."

Cari looked at this man who was all she dared not name.

Jeff didn't look away. Didn't flinch.

From across the backyard came a chorus of chuckles as the town's big men ratified something Baden said. Regina's fingers touched Baden's forearm and quivered the white wine in the glass he held, a connection that lingered as their linked gaze said they knew the heart of the big joke.

"Wait," said Jeff. "How did her husband die?"

"Naked and not alone."

Regina turned from the pack of important men and their supportive wives, gestured with her wine goblet that matched Baden's.

"Hello everyone!" Though no microphone amplified her voice, no ears in that backyard missed what she said. "Thank you so much for coming! And for letting me introduce you to this wonderful California white zinfandel. Oh, and a special thanks to our guest of honor, Jeff!"

Courteous applause rippled through the crowd in this hometown backyard as faces turned to smile at where Jeff stood. Cari saw Sid Stiffarm flash Jeff a proud thumbs-up. And maybe it was just her imagination, but she thought she saw Donna in the crowd hold her fist close to her own heavy breasts to send *Cari* a thumbs-up.

"Sadly," continued Regina, "the board meeting for the civic development corporation was scheduled *way* before that school bus, and these things are always so difficult to change. Mayor Mel and the others and I, we have to follow those rules, but we also wanted to take the time to honor our local hero."

Tired applause. Baden beamed.

"However, now I'm afraid this party must end so the real work can begin," said Regina. "One of those boring dinner parties, but don't worry, I'll make it through—a-*gain*."

No one laughed.

"So I have to ask all of you regular—"

She laughed like she'd goofed. "Could everyone who's not working the board dinner please leave now? Sadly, that means even some of you wives."

Jeff saw the ebony-haired widow's eyes hit Cari.

The crew of big wheels backed Regina like a Vegas chorus line.

Mayor Mel nodded to his wife, who carried her practiced smile out of this backyard.

Neither reluctance nor rebellion stayed the crowd of citizens as they shuffled toward the narrow funnel of departure.

Sid Stiffarm cleared a path for Mrs. Jenkins working her two canes over the lawn. Jeff saw Mary discreetly dump a plate of plastic-wrapped, store-bought brownies into her purse for that night's *feed-the-hungry* dinners. Busty Donna whispered something to high school teacher Britene as they eased toward the exit. Skeletal flag-jacketed Dave Maynard pushed his way through the flow of the crowd to where Jeff and Cari stood.

"Saw you," Dave told Cari, his face determined, grim. "Saw you talking to him, and I gotta, you gotta—"

All the *gotta*'s of this world gripped Cari. She struggled to find the right words. Spoke them as flat and hard and true as bullets to the dying man's heart.

"I'm sorry," she told Dave. "You're not crazy. You're right. Baden's going to take your dry cleaners. Take it before you die. No insurance for Sheila and your two girls. Nothing for you and them but eviction notices. I did all I could. I'll do— *you know this*—when whatever happens *happens*, I'll do all I can to save Sheila, the girls. But you know Baden down in his bones. I can't do what I can't do."

Dave's face screwed into a desperate pained plea.

Blink.

Dave blinked again.

Looked at Jeff. Nodded.

Looked at Cari, said, "You're a good person. Thank you."

The doomed man stepped back into the crowd.

"What are we going to do now?" said Jeff.

She gave him no answer as the crowd shuffled out of here.

No one beyond where Cari and Jeff stood saw what was happening until—

BAM! BAM! BAM!

Screams. Hometown shoes scrambled to escape.

Baden crashed to his knees, his face in shock, his chest a mush of red from bullet holes Dave blasted into him after stepping from the crowd at *can't miss* close range. Dave let his pistol fall to the grass, his eyes full of the big man on his knees before him, the banker's eyes fogging with what he couldn't believe.

Regina bolted from the killing stage in her backyard, pushed a high school girl server out of the way and trampled a seven-year-old boy as she fled.

Sherriff Warren engulfed the shooter in a bear hug.

Hell, that lawman knew Dave. Poor guy didn't deserve to be blasted down, which would have ended things a whole lot better for the town, because all Dave's medical costs got transferred to the jail holding him for the murder trial that never had time to happen before he died a legally innocent man.

Screams softened to *"Where are you?" "I'm OK!"* shouts.

Cell phones whipped out of back pockets and purses as much to snap photos or film the scene as to message loved ones: *Didn't get me.*

Nobody typed *This time.*

Neighbors reached out to help neighbors.

Eyes turned to Sherriff Warren's capture of—*Oh, my God it's Dave!*—in a bear hug.

Nurse Vicki knelt over Baden, who'd repeatedly unsuccessfully pressured her for sex. She fulfilled her medical oath to her best, but failed to staunch the blood spurting from his chest. Then that pulsing red flow... Stopped.

Jeff stood where he was.

Waited until Cari blinked. Saw him. Knew he wouldn't run.

Before the roar of events swept her away *until*, he had to ask.

"Did you know Dave had a gun?"

The wealthy and powerful new widow said, "Isn't this America?"

THE GHOST OF WILLIAMSBURG

JASON STARR

When Lexi dozed off I knew it was time to bail. The sex had been pretty good, but I knew she liked me way too much and that waking up together, having sex *again*, and then going to brunch, or at least coffee, would be super awkward and get her ever more attached. It would be way better for both of us if I just ghosted her now.

As I wriggled my sweaty body free from hers, she said groggily, "Hey, are you okay?"

"Yeah." I already had my boxer briefs on and I was feeling around on the floor for my pants. The only light in the room came from the scented candle she'd lit to help set the mood. "I just have an early morning tomorrow, unfortunately."

I had just the right amount of disappointment in my tone to make this bullshit sound believable. Actually, I had nothing to do tomorrow, Sunday, except pick up my laundry, maybe hit the gym.

"Oh, okay," she said skeptically.

The key to a successful ghosting is to leave on an upbeat note. You need the other person to believe that nothing is wrong and they'll see you again soon.

"But I had an amazing time and it would be great to see you again. Sometime next week?"

"I'd love that."

"Awesome."

Did I feel bad for her? Not really. Online dating can be brutal, but I didn't make up the rules, I just played the game.

That said, I usually didn't ghost after first-time sex. I mean, hooking up takes a lot of time and energy and I wanted to get as much return on my investment as possible. Ordinarily I'd have sex with a woman at least a few more times before vanishing, but in this case I could tell that Lexi was into me, and was looking to be in a relationship, which complicated things. Since we'd only been out a few times, and had sex once, there were no deep feelings yet. She lived on the Lower East Side and I lived in Williamsburg, so we were unlikely to ever cross paths. The beauty of dating in a big city.

"Wait, come here." She pulled me back onto the bed, on top of her. She had a great body, no doubt about that, and I figured, *Why not*? I mean, I'd brought two condoms anyway.

Afterward, I didn't want to be a total asshole, so I snuggled with her for about ten minutes. Then I said, "I should really get going."

I put on my clothes as quickly as I could without looking like I was rushing. I kissed her one last time on the lips, then said, "I'll reach out tomorrow," and took off.

Riding in a Via back to Williamsburg, I checked my dating apps. On Bumble, Emily who was currently three miles away, had sent me a short message: *Hi would love to hear more!*

She was twenty-eight, three years younger than me, and although she'd put 'No HUs'—no hook-ups—on her profile, this wasn't a deterrent to me. In fact, I'd found that I had a much higher close rate on No HU profiles, as opposed to the more casual sounding ones. My theory was that the sluttier profiles got more responses than the No HU profiles, so there was less competition.

I responded with one of my usual replies: *Great meeting you here. Drink sometime soon?*

I liked to keep it short and simple and take the conversation off-line ASAP.

On OK Cupid, three new women had liked me—one cute, one lived too far away, one had a kid. I deleted the one with the kid and the geographically undesirable one and sent the other one my usual first message: *Wow, amazing profile! Let's meet sometime!*

None of my new matches on Hinge excited me, but on Plenty of Fish a very cute blonde whom I'd already matched with had agreed to meet for a drink at six in Midtown on Wednesday. It was a perfect time because I already had a date with a woman in the West Village on Wednesday at eight.

I responded: *Awesome, excited to meet!* and instructed Siri to add the new date to my calendar. Now Monday, Tuesday, and Wednesday were totally full, but I had an opening on Thursday and Friday early. Later Friday I had a third date in Park Slope that I was about eighty percent certain would lead to a hook-up and, as always, I had Saturday night open, keeping the time free for whomever seemed like the hottest prospect after my weekday dates.

The Via dropped me in front of my apartment, not far from the river. It was a walk-up, but it had "city charm"— the broker's words, not mine—and it had a river view that scored a lot of points on dates. The apartment itself was small, but it had the two most important things—a couch and a bed. I spent a lot of time and money on decorating, not because I cared how it looked, but because I wanted to impress women. My apartment was always clean—I had a maid come twice a week—and smelled fresh. I had a big fish tank with exotic tropical fish because an article I read online about how women were attracted to guys with fish. I didn't know if this was true or not but if it gave me an even slightly higher chance of getting laid, then hey, why not?

I wasn't always a player. At high school in Livingston, New Jersey, I was awkward and didn't date much, and in college at Michigan I had a couple of girlfriends, but I didn't feel fully in control of my dating. I over-pursued women and was easily manipulated and controlled. Women jerked me around and ghosted me all the time. I was a decent looking guy—not ugly, but not hot either. I got by with my personality and sense of humor, but I often wasted time chasing, and spending money on, women who were out of my league and just using me for attention.

When I moved to New York after college, I had a few mediocre dating years. I worked as a coder for various startups and lived with roommates in shitty apartments in bad neighborhoods. Then one of the startups took off and went public. I got stock and a higher salary and money changed everything.

I moved to Williamsburg into my own digs. Although I still wasn't in great shape, and had gained weight since college, I made up for it with confidence and game. I got a cooler haircut and a hip wardrobe, but most importantly I spent hours every day watching videos from dating coaches on YouTube. I utilized their strategies to create my own game plan, raising my SMV—Sexual Market Value. I began to see results—getting more dates and having more sex. I didn't get attached to women the way I used to in college because now the dynamic had shifted, now I was in control, and it felt so much better to be the ghoster rather than the ghostee.

In bed, I was back on Hinge, when Lexi texted me:

Hope you got home safe, sexy.

Of course, I didn't respond.

I wound up sleeping in and blowing off the gym. I spent the rest of the day watching Netflix and messaging women. I had a pretty full dating schedule next week, but I booked a couple of dates for the following week.

At around five, I hit the shower and started getting ready for the night's action. I had a double header: drinks with

Jessie from Bumble at six-thirty, and then back to my place with Sophia, the woman I'd been dating for a few weeks. I hadn't ghosted Sophia yet because she seemed only into me for sex. She was a busy nurse with only one or two nights free every week, so she had no interest in a relationship.

The date with Jessie went well. We were making out at the bar and I probably could've hooked up with her if I didn't already have the date with Sophia. I could've cancelled with Sophia last minute, but what was the point of that? I had a one hundred percent chance with Sophia, and maybe a fifty percent chance with Jessie. It was only my second date with Jesse, though, and I was confident I would score on date three.

Back at my apartment, I was chilling on my couch, listening to Pandora, waiting for Sophia to arrive, when I got a text from Lexi: *Didn't hear back from u How's your day?*

It was annoying that she'd sent me a second text. It was always cleaner when, after I didn't respond to the first text, they got the message. The *Didn't hear back from u* was obviously loaded with anger and resentment, which was also a pain.

Some people might block the person they're trying to ghost: not me. Even when a woman blows me off, I don't cut the cord fully. I figure that, if my schedule thins out, who knows? I might have to recycle them.

A few minutes later another message arrived from Lexi: *Helloooo?*

Two texts was annoying, but three was a total pain in the ass. She had definitely realized that I was ghosting her and wasn't taking it well. At this point, I had two choices— respond or continue to ignore her.

Responding would be the nice, respectful thing to do. I could text her that although I think she's a great person with so much to offer the right guy, I just don't feel enough of a spark and we're not the right long-term match. But if I sent her a thoughtful note, she would probably respond with a question or, worse, want to talk on the phone. Then I'd have to blow her off anyway, so wasn't it best to remain silent? Besides, she was a big girl, thirty-two years old, and had done a lot of online dating. It wasn't like I was the first guy who'd ghosted her, so it seemed unfair that she was even putting me in this situation.

I ignored her, hoping that my silence would be her answer.

Sophia arrived. We had drinks on the couch, then moved swiftly to the bedroom. After having sex twice, she left.

I never check my phone during dates, but when Sophia left I looked and saw that Lexi had sent me yet another text: *You ghosted the wrong girl, bitch*

I officially had a problem.

I debated it in my head and concluded that silence was still my best option. She was getting obsessed and with obsessive people, engaging was enabling. My best strategy was to continue to ignore her and hope she got distracted by someone else and forgot about me.

The next day was mellow. I only had one date planned—coffee with a woman in the neighborhood. We met at a place on Bedford, but I could tell right away that we had no connection. I still feigned interest. Even when a date didn't work out, I liked to stay in control, so when we were saying goodbye I said, "Let's do something soon," even though I had no intention of ever seeing her again.

As I entered my apartment, turning my key in the door, I knew something was wrong. I usually locked the deadbolt as well as the latch, but only the latch was locked. Was it possible that I'd forgotten? It was unlikely, although I had taken out garbage and it was possible I'd been distracted, because I had OCD and forgetting to fully lock my apartment was unlike me.

When I entered, everything seemed normal. My TV was still on the wall, nothing seemed out of place and as far as I could tell nothing was missing. I felt silly for getting paranoid about the locks; I'd probably been distracted.

Then I heard something. It sounded like something shifting in the kitchen. Was the super in the apartment?

"Hello? Anyone here?"

Silence.

I was thinking about the door again, but maybe I was just driving myself crazy. The noise from the kitchen could've come from the upstairs apartment. The ceiling wasn't thick and I often heard noise from up there.

Still, I entered the kitchen area cautiously. Nothing seemed off, and then it leapt in front of me. At first I thought it was a cat—a big, gray cat. Then, right about the time I screamed, I realized it was a large rat.

It dashed behind the table, slid on the floor and then came right toward me. I turned and dashed out of the apartment, slamming the door behind me, and fled down the stairs as fast as I could.

I was shaken. I'd never seen a rat or even a mouse in my apartment, and as far as I knew there was no rat infestation in the building.

I knocked on my super's door. George was an older, scruffy, Greek-American guy. He was in sweat pants and a wifebeater and the TV was blaring in the background, some sitcom. I told him what had happened and he was surprised.

"A rat? In *this* building?"

"Can you do something?"

"What do you want me to do?"

"Get rid of it."

"I can't catch a rat. Gotta call the exterminator."

I didn't want to return to my apartment so I waited in front of my building for almost two hours until the exterminator— Latina, surprisingly good-looking—arrived. No rings, I noticed. If I were in a different mood I might've hit on her.

"What's the issue?" she asked.

I explained about the rat.

"I can put down traps and poison, but I can't catch it."

"Then what am I supposed to do?"

She shrugged. "Wait till it dies?"

I didn't want to stay in my apartment with an aggressive rat. I could probably have stayed with my friend Steve for a couple of days, but not having access to my apartment was going to be a big pain in the ass.

As the exterminator placed traps around my apartment, I asked her how she thought the rat might've gotten in. She examined the pipes in the kitchen, in the bathroom and the kitchen and around the radiators.

"Apartment looks tight," she said.

"Have there been other rats in the building?"

"Been working here three years, never seen a rat. Mice, water bugs, and silverfish, yeah."

"How do you think it got in?"

She looked toward the partially open window that looked out on the fire escape and said, "Coulda come in from there?"

"How?" I asked.

"They can scale walls."

"You've seen that before?"

"Not really, but it's possible. Otherwise, I don't know. Maybe there's some space somewhere I can't see or somebody put it in here." She smiled. "Got any enemies?"

I knew she was joking, or at least trying to joke, but my mind went right to Lexi, and the last text she'd sent me: *You ghosted the wrong girl, bitch.* The text certainly had a threatening tone, but to put a rat in my apartment she'd have to be full-blown insane. It wasn't impossible, though. She, or someone else, could've gotten to the roof somehow, dropped down the fire escape and entered the apartment through the window. And what about my front door? What if I didn't forget to lock it after all?

When the exterminator left, I knocked on the super's door. He seemed annoyed to see me again, like I was ruining his Sunday with my stupid rat drama.

"Hey, just a quick question," I said. "Earlier today, did you happen to see a woman trying to get into the building?"

"What?" he asked, not like he didn't hear me, but like he didn't understand me.

"A woman," I said. "About thirty, thin, straight dark hair just below the shoulders."

"I don't know," he said. "I mean, somebody was ringing buzzers this afternoon, but I didn't see anybody."

Sometimes delivery people buzzed every apartment in the building to try to leave a package in the vestibule, but there were rarely deliveries on Sundays.

"Thanks," I said.

I packed a small suitcase and went to my friend Steve's apartment. He also lived in Williamsburg about ten blocks away.

I told him about the rat and Lexi and my theory that she might've been responsible.

"It sounds possible," he said. "Some women go crazy when you ghost them."

I knew I should probably forget about the whole thing, continue to ignore her, but how did I know this wasn't just the beginning? If she was crazy enough to put a rat in my apartment, who knew what she was capable of?

A couple of new women had written to me on Bumble, but I didn't feel like responding. Freaking Lexi—she was throwing me off my game.

Finally I decided to text her, with a simple yet firm note: *Please stop contacting me*

The message didn't display as *Delivered*. It was possible she was on the subway, but after a couple of hours went by I still didn't see a *Delivered* notification. I realized she'd blocked me.

Now my annoyance had turned into rage. *She* was

blocking *me*? The act of blocking me seemed to confirm that my suspicions about her were correct.

I knew what I had to do now.

I got up before six and took a Via to Lexi's building on the Lower East Side. I waited in front for her, figuring it would be best to run into her casually when she left for work.

At a little after eight she left her building. I followed her to the corner. "Hey, Lexi."

She turned around, as if startled to see me.

"How are you?" I asked.

"What… What're you doing here?" she asked, more concerned than confused.

"I was just seeing a friend nearby," I said, although I knew this didn't make much sense for so early in the morning. "I noticed you blocked my texts."

"Maybe it's because you weren't responding to mine."

"Yeah? Is that the real reason?"

She glared at me then said, "Leave me the fuck alone," and walked ahead.

Rushing up alongside her, I said, "What about the rat?"

"Rat? What rat?"

"Yeah, like you don't know."

"I said go away."

"You put a rat in my apartment yesterday, why don't you just admit it."

"Stay away from me!"

"Tell me the truth," I said, accidently pushing against her a little.

"Stop it!" she screamed. "Somebody help me! Help me!"

A big, sweaty garbage man across the street heard her and rushed over.

"He just grabbed me," she said to him.

"Hey, get the fuck away from her," he said to me.

"I didn't grab her, I just—"

I didn't even see the punch coming. Just felt the impact as I fell onto the concrete. He kicked me hard a bunch of times, mainly in my ribs and face. I couldn't catch my breath. I tasted blood.

"Fuck you," he said, and finally left me alone.

People were passing by, but no one offered to help me. I managed to get up to my feet, but it hurt to walk. I called in late to work and went to a walk-in medical clinic. They didn't think I had any broken ribs, but I needed stitches for my lip.

Back in Brooklyn, I stopped by my apartment and checked the traps. Sure enough, one of them had a nearly decapitated rat in it. I put it in a garbage bag and put the bag on the curb, then I got my stuff from Steve's and returned to my apartment.

It was nice to be back in my own place again. My lip hurt and I had to keep icing it, but in a calmer mood I realized that I'd overreacted and might've gotten it all wrong. The rat could've scaled the building and I could've forgotten to lock the door. The more I thought about it, the worse I felt for confronting Lexi.

I cancelled my dates for the week and decided that maybe it was time to take a break from dating. I focused on work, which was much less stressful without the distraction of a complex dating schedule. Still, I felt bad about what had happened with Lexi, and couldn't stop rehashing that morning in front of her building. I felt like I had to do something, at least let her know how remorseful I was.

I handwrote a note on a plain piece of paper:

I'm sorry for showing up at your building, that was my bad. I realize I jumped to a lot of conclusions and if you'd ever like to meet for coffee sometime, I'd love that, but if you never want to hear from me again, I get that too.

I knew that showing up at her apartment again would be a bad idea, so I mailed the note instead.

A couple of weeks went by and I didn't hear anything.

Then she texted me: *Okay. If you want to talk, let's talk.*

I texted her immediately and arranged to meet her at a coffee bar in Midtown, near where she worked. I was expecting awkwardness, but amazingly there was no tension at all. I apologized for going to her place and accusing her of putting the rat in my apartment, and she apologized for sending me the nasty text.

"I think what I did was much worse than anything you did," I said.

"Touché," she said.

We began talking about other things and hit it off. When we'd dated, I had no idea that she loved comics and anime as much as I did. We also both loved sci-fi and horror movies.

When we said goodbye in front of the coffee shop, we began making out. I didn't plan it; it just seemed natural, organic.

We began dating again. I didn't have any agenda this time. I wasn't looking to score with her, nor was I trying to come up with an exit strategy. I actually liked her and wanted to spend time with her, and she felt the same way.

The sex was off the charts. We attacked each other like we couldn't get enough. I'd finally, improbably, met the woman who made me want to delete all of the dating apps from my phone. We agreed to be exclusive and it was my suggestion, not hers.

The next several months were bliss. We laughed, dressed up at comic-cons, met each other's parents and took a trip to Bermuda. I used to think that I could never be satisfied with just one woman, but my mindset had changed. I'd found my soulmate and I didn't want to let her go.

On the anniversary of what we endearingly called 'Rat Day' we took a walk in Central Park where I kneeled down in front of Bethesda Fountain and asked her to marry me.

Trembling with happiness, she said, "Yes. Yes, of course."

She didn't have a lot of money in savings and wasn't close with her family, so I footed the bill for our wedding at The River Café under the Brooklyn Bridge.

It was a perfect, cloud-free day. I mingled with our guests and then later waited at the altar, alongside my best man, Steve.

Lexi was supposed to walk down the aisle at 2:00pm, but by 2:15pm she hadn't arrived. At three, I knew something was very wrong.

I thought the worst: Did something happen to her? Was she in an accident?

Then I heard a commotion near the entrance to the restaurant; my aunt Claudia even screamed. As I rushed over, I had no idea what could possibly be going on. In retrospect, I probably should have expected to see the large dead rat.

I imagined Lexi's gleeful expression, pleased that she'd patiently and successfully played the long game, stringing me along for over a year, to finally get the ultimate revenge.

She was right.

I'd ghosted the wrong girl.

BLACK DOG

CATHI UNSWORTH

That night, he saw the dog again. In his dream, the years had fallen away and it no longer pained him to walk, despite the clay weighing down his boots from a day behind the plough. His stride was easy as he followed the path of the setting sun and the curving course of Ceon Hill, a path carved out of the hillside centuries before by the hands of his ancient forebears.

It was still said that their old King Arawyn, the Lord of Departed Spirits, hunted his pack here at night, a howling swirl of phantasmagoric beasts with pricked-up red ears. But the dog that leapt across his path just then was as black as midnight. The young boy's heart jumped in his chest as the animal turned its head, he could feel its hot breath on his cheek. The old man jolted awake, into the morning of Wednesday 14 February 1945.

*

"One for you, sir."

Detective Chief Inspector Edward Greenaway looked up from his desk.

"Telegram from the Chief Constable of Warwickshire." The sergeant who relayed this news would, once, have been a much younger man. But the War had gone on for so long now that it was all they could do to keep things running with staff who had come back out of retirement, like the whiskery old bloodhound putting the memo in front of Greenaway's nose.

Can Scotland Yard assist in a brutal case of murder that took place yesterday? the DCI read. *The deceased is a man named JOSIAH STONE, age 75, and he was killed with an instrument known as a slash hook, used in his trade as a hedger and ditcher. The murder was either committed by a madman or one of the Italian prisoners in a camp nearby. The assistance of an Italian interpreter is requested.*

"A madman," said Greenaway. "Just what I need."

In the mortuary at the National Forensics Laboratory at Birmingham University, Professor James Willis laid out the remains of Josiah Stone, and the implements of his trade that had killed him, for Greenaway to see. The old man hadn't gone down easily.

He was attacked from behind with a walking stick. It had an oval dome at the end, something that would fit comfortably into his palm. It also made an excellent cudgel. Though the blood had been washed away, there was a dent to the back of the head that looked like it had been caused by a cannonball.

"He must have had some strength," said Greenaway. "Some anger in him."

"And he didn't stop there." The Professor deduced that, as the blows rained down, Stone dropped the implement he was using to cut the hedge, the fearsome, double-bladed slash hook. As he raised his hands to cover his head, his assailant grabbed the hook and attacked—there were lacerations and bruises on Stone's hands and forearms. Overpowered, he fell onto his back, where his opponent straddled him—two ribs were broken in the struggle—and slashed at the throat with the concave edge of the blade, severing the trachea and leaving a row of jagged ridges. Then he pulled open Stone's waistcoat and shirt, even undid the fly on his trousers, so he could cut open the torso with the straight edge of the blade.

Greenaway winced as he surveyed these wounds. Stone was carved from his collar to his pubic bone, then again straight across his chest.

"Opened him up like a butcher," he said.

The Professor nodded. "He left the slash hook embedded in the guts, rolled him over and drove Stone into the ground with the points of his own pitchfork." Willis demonstrated the action with his fingers. "One on each side of his neck. With such force it took two men to pull it back out again. So yes—" he pulled the sheet back up "—I should think you are looking for a madman."

Greenaway drove south from Birmingham, away from the factories and foundries, and into the undulating Warwickshire countryside. His destination was Upper

Pendleton, a village in the Cotswold Hills, where he was to meet with the Head of CID from Stratford-upon-Avon, the ominously named Detective Inspector Alex Tombs. Tombs and his men got to the scene a couple of hours after the local police, but the body had been left in situ until Professor Willis arrived at 11:30 pm.

Greenaway had seen some terrible things since his transfer to the Murder Squad at the beginning of the War—and scores of atrocities caused by the conflict—but nothing quite so macabre as the corpse of Josiah Stone. It put him in mind of Smithfield Market, its rows of bone white and blood red carcasses. There was something primordial about what had been done to this man. Despite the stick he'd used to ease rheumatic knees and hips, Stone had not been your typical 75-year-old; his battered husk still testified to the muscular strength of his arms and shoulders, his above-average height and a head of hair that was still as black as a raven's wing, still as thick as thatch.

His corpse yielded one clue—the angle of the indentations on the back of the head told Willis that Stone's attacker was a foot shorter than his target, which would make the madman around five feet tall. But that was all the Professor could give him to go on. He had not been able to lift any fingerprints.

Darkness was falling as the DCI reached his destination. Upper Pendleton was a huddle of thatched cottages surrounding the Norman church of St Oswald's, whose Perpendicular steeple, built from the local Cotswold stone, reached far into the gloaming, though not as high as the summit under which it nestled, the anvil-shaped Ceon Hill. He stepped out into the dreg end of the day. Like everywhere else in Britain, Upper Pendleton was observing the blackout, the blue lamp outside the police station unlit. But though the street appeared deserted, he felt as if many eyes watched him cross to the front door.

If all was still outside, inside the station was anything but. Stratford CID were doubling up with the local force, and as a result everyone was sharing an office. Greenaway had been given a desk alongside Tombs, a slim man with fair hair, pale blue eyes and deep lines on his forehead. He went over what they had so far.

For the past nine months, Stone had been employed by one Mark Hackstead to work at Yew Tree Farm for four days a week, depending on the weather. The morning of 14 February had dawned fine and fair, so he began to work in a field on the lower slopes of Ceon Hill called the Conanground. Stone was seen by a number of witnesses, passing through the churchyard at 9am on his way there.

The last time anybody saw him alive was at noon, when Hackstead observed him working on the hedge as he passed on his way to feed livestock in the adjoining pasture. He estimated Stone had cut six to ten yards of hedge by then, but he hadn't had time to stop and talk, because he had an urgent job to attend to: one of his heifers had fallen into a ditch.

Stone shared his home, one of the thatched cottages by the church, with his 33-year-old niece Meredith, who worked as a printer's assembler in Stratford. She had come home on the bus at 6:00 pm to find the place empty. This was unusual—Stone was of regular habits, always back by dark. Alarmed, she called on her neighbour, Harry Chapman, another casual employee at Yew Tree, and they went up to the farm together.

There, Hackstead took them to where he had last seen Stone, using torches to pick their way over the rough ground in the dark. Finding his body in its shocking state, Meredith broke down. Fortuitously, another farm hand called Calvin Peachey came round the other side of the hedge on his way home and Chapman had him fetch the police while he took Meredith home. Hackstead was left to guard the remains until PC Matthew Ramsey arrived at 7:05 pm, roughly 20 minutes later.

The position of the body, annotated on a large-scale relief map of Ceon Hill pinned to a corkboard behind Tombs' desk was, by Hackstead's estimation, four yards distant from where he had last seen him, a progress that would have taken half an hour. Crime scene photographs graphically displayed how the body had been pinioned to the earth. The resultant tableau had a feel of ritual about it, rather than the random carnage of a passing maniac. But why would anybody do such a thing to the old man?

"Did he have a lot of enemies?" was the first thing Greenaway asked.

"Good question," said Tombs. "Probably easier to say he was not a man who had many friends, though I believe that was out of choice. He'd worked on the land here all his life and they say he preferred animals to human company. His wife,

Isobel, died 18 years ago and Meredith's kept house for him ever since. That's the most recent picture she had of him." He passed across a small print, a record of the man Stone had been: a long, angular face with high cheekbones, bristly hair and a thick moustache and whiskers filling in the contours, no doubt weatherproofing them, too. Eyes as dark and sharp as flints stared through Greenaway, revealing nothing.

"They brought her up, you see," Tombs went on. "She's Isobel's brother's daughter. Her mother died when she was just a kid and I gather he dumped her there and did a runner. The Stones were already more grandparent age themselves by then, but they never had any of their own. Perhaps having Meredith made up for that."

"And how is she now?" Greenaway asked.

"Considering what she's been through, she's been very co-operative. She's identified everything she thought he had on him that day. His pocket watch is missing, which I think is significant."

"Was it valuable?" asked Greenaway.

"Not really," Tombs said, "but it's got one unusual feature—a glass lens kept under the casing, that could be removed without impairing the mechanism. We've circulated a description of it, but my feeling is that, if it turns up at all, this part will be missing."

Greenaway frowned. "What would you need the lens for? Like a monocle, you mean, to see with?"

Tombs raised a flaxen eyebrow. "I think that's the idea," he said. "It belonged to his grandmother, and Meredith said he never went anywhere without it."

"I'd like to speak to her tomorrow," Greenaway said. "And if the watch is this important, we should do a thorough search for it," he said, nodding at the map. "The army are normally pretty helpful and they'll have mine detectors we can use, in case it's been dropped or buried up there—I'll get on the blower to them. I'd like to go up there myself, soon as it's daylight."

Tombs nodded. "I'll get PC Ramsey to show you. He knows the ground better than anyone else and he's taken a lot of initiative so far."

"Good." Greenaway lifted the phone.

"Then perhaps I'd better take you to your lodgings," said Tombs. "The only place I could find for you was the local pub. I hope you won't mind too much."

The Cooper's Arms was across the churchyard from the station, so Greenaway took his bags and left the Wolseley in the police car park, letting Tombs be his guide. He'd managed to enlist the Royal Engineers to send a team of sappers with some mine detectors across to them the next day, and an Italian speaker had been found to interview the POWs—Sergeant Keith Saunders from Special Branch.

"Have you got any serious suspects so far, or do you think it could have been a deranged Italian roaming the countryside?" Greenaway asked.

"It would be very convenient if it was," said Tombs. "But I've got a horrible feeling we're looking a bit closer to home. The way he was killed wasn't the work of an opportunist— he would have been bashed over the head, robbed and that would have been it. Whoever killed Stone spent some time doing what they did to him and they didn't take his money, only his watch. They must have had some sort of personal connection to him, even if he was a man with no friends."

Greenaway nodded. "You ever seen anything like that before?"

"No," said Tombs, "but I was born in this village, I've heard all the legends. They say the Devil himself built Ceon Hill. That the Lord of the Underworld hunts with big black dogs up there and if you see one, it's a portent of death." Tombs' eyes shone as pale as the thin crescent moon. "Josiah Stone saw them more than once."

Greenaway shivered. "You trying to put the frighteners on, bringing me through a graveyard and telling me this?"

"Just giving you a feel for the place," said Tombs. "The reason I think the watch is important is that they say Stone's grandmother was a witch. If that was her watch, the lens would be what they'd call a scrying mirror—used to see into the future. I never saw the thing myself, but the glass was supposed to be black. The grandmother, Janet Setch, was murdered in 1875, by a man wielding a pitchfork."

They came to a halt by the lych gate, Greenaway's mind going off in a hundred directions. "Is any of that true?" he said.

"Janet Setch was killed all right." Tombs spoke quietly. "By a fellow called John Bilton, who you might call the village idiot. He claimed she was the head of a coven and stabbed her through the head with a pitchfork. She was eighty years old at the time. The story about Stone seeing the black dogs was in a book I've got; you can borrow it, makes good bedtime reading. I don't think any of that's true, but it does feed an idea about Stone. Maybe he was killed by someone who thought that watch had supernatural powers, that it could bring them good luck or wish ill on their enemies. Maybe the way he was killed was part of a ritual, too."

"Christ," said Greenaway. "You're serious, aren't you?"

"We might as well be in the Middle Ages," said Tombs. "But at least the landlord runs a decent pub."

The former coaching inn was made from the same, golden-hued stone as the church, that seemed to Greenaway to glow with a light and warmth of its own. A feeling that quickly evaporated when Tombs pushed open the door. The babble of the crowd around the copper-topped bar abated almost instantly as heads swivelled and eyes ran appraisingly up and down the two detectives. Tombs got a few nods and greetings, the conversation level gradually going back up in volume with a lot of sideways glances thrown at Greenaway.

He let his own gaze roam around the timber-beamed room, taking it all in. There were not many youngsters here, and there didn't look like there was much wealth to spread around either. This was a world of patched-over elbows and trousers held up with string, hobnail boots plastered in red clay, spotted neckerchiefs, poachers' pockets and Staffordshire bull terriers. It seemed exclusively male—not even a barmaid in sight. The landlord, a man of around 30 whose checked shirt, waistcoat and cravat put him a social notch above his flock, raised a hatch in the bar and stepped out. His countenance, at least, was friendly.

"Evening, Alex," he greeted Tombs. He had reddish, crinkly hair, red-veined cheeks and round hazel eyes. "Inspector Greenaway?" he said. "George Mayfield." Greenaway offered his hand. The landlord's palms were dry, his grip not inconsiderable. "If you want to come through, I'll show you to your room and then you can have your supper, if you like? The wife's made plenty."

He led them to a doorway at the side of the bar. As they passed beneath it, Greenaway could see strange marks scored onto the lintel, a flower-like pattern of overlapping circles and the initials *VM*. He knew what they were; he'd seen them before in London, on buildings of a similar vintage—witch marks.

Greenaway set off early the next day. The night had passed peacefully enough. Mrs Mayfield's rabbit pie, served to him and Tombs in the snug, tasted good with the pint of ale the governor pulled to go with it. They shared this smaller back room, adorned with horse brasses and Staffordshire pottery, with two old boys who puffed on long-stemmed pipes and gazed into the fire, a sleeping terrier between their feet. Above their heads, the mantelpiece was scored with more witch marks.

Greenaway's room was in an extension built onto the back of the pub, and there he went through the witness statements with Tombs, outlining his thoughts and concerns. Tombs left Greenaway with the book he had mentioned. *Strange Tales From Shakespeare Land* by the Reverend John Harvey was published in 1929, though the story it related was much earlier, from 1885. It told of how the young Josiah Stone had met with a phantom black dog on his way home from work ploughing Ceon Hill for seven nights in succession. On the last occasion, the hellhound was accompanied by a headless woman in rustling silks. Arriving home, the lad was informed that his sister had just died.

No phantoms, demon dogs or hags had come to disturb Greenaway's sleep. After a pleasingly hearty breakfast, he retraced the last journey of Josiah Stone, out of the village, through a kissing gate and onto the farm track that led upwards to the Conanground. It was a grey and smudgy dawn; February's drab palette of dun, oatmeal and moss unenlivened by the sullen sky, clouds scudding overhead fast on a northeasterly, trailing icy slivers of rain. The hill rose and fell in deep contours that, he had learned from his bedtime reading, had been dug to fortify the highest point in the district during the Iron Age. In this weather, he could easily imagine how legends of witches and devil dogs could spring from such eerie surroundings.

PC Ramsey was waiting at the spot. He had the same thick black hair as Stone, but the face that greeted Greenaway was wide and freckled, spreading into a cautious smile. "Inspector Tombs said I should meet you here," he said.

"I appreciate it," said Greenaway. As well as being the first man to the scene and to take a statement from Hackstead, Ramsey had done seasonal work at Yew Tree while he was still at school, knew the lay of the land and the men who worked there.

Beneath the section of the hedge that Stone had been cutting was a patch of dull brown grass, about three feet long and a foot wide. The dew might have risen three times since the murder, but the ground still bore its imprint. As Greenaway knelt down for a closer look, his nostrils filled with the iron scent of blood.

"So this is where Meredith Stone found her uncle," he said, picturing the scene from her point of view, her panic mounting as the torch picked out strange shapes in the dark, the realisation of what they were—and the smell that must have gone with it.

Ramsey's dark blue eyes were earnest. "I don't know how she'll ever get over it."

"And Hackstead," Greenaway asked, "what was his reaction?"

"Agitated," Ramsey recalled. "Hopping about, complaining about how cold it was—and he kept looking over his shoulder. At the time, I supposed he was frightened, or in shock from what he'd seen. But now I've had time to think about it, I'm not so sure."

"Why do you say that? You've known him a while, ain't you?"

"Since I was fifteen," said Ramsey. "Hackstead's always seemed fairly cocksure to me. Never heard him complain about the weather before—he's out in it day and night. It was a horrible sight, but it's not like he's squeamish either—he said he spent half the morning castrating calves, then he had to shoot one of his heifers that afternoon. He's seen his share of blood and guts."

Greenaway saw dangling carcasses. A man who knew how to butcher.

"He buggered off again the minute I got his statement," Ramsey went on. "I don't know about you, sir, but I think I'd have shown a bit more concern if a man had been found in that state on my land."

Greenaway got up, brushing grass and clay from his knees. "How much of his statement have you been able to check so far?" he said.

"I know he was with another farmer, Eric Barlett, all morning, helping him with his calves. Hackstead did the slicing, Eric said. Gave him a thirst, so then they went in the Cooper's Arms. George Mayfield confirmed they were there between eleven and twelve."

"Then after that?" said Greenaway. "Between twelve and one?"

"I'm not so clear about that. He said he was in that field there—" Ramsey pointed "—feeding his sheep, and then he went up the hill to meet his cattleman, Stanley Batchelor, about that heifer."

"Professor Willis estimated the time of death was one o'clock," said Greenaway. "Will Batchelor have clocked on by now? Can we have a word?"

They found him forking a barrow-load of marigolds into a trough while beasts nosed around him, lowing and stamping, exhaling clouds of white breath into the damp air. He talked to them as he worked, peaked cap pulled over large red ears.

"Morning, Happy," Ramsey called. "Got a minute?"

"Oh, morning, Matt." Batchelor eyed them warily.

"This is DCI Greenaway from Scotland Yard," Ramsey said. "He's come to try and help us find out what happened to Mr Stone."

Batchelor laid his pitchfork down in his barrow carefully, as if to demonstrate he wasn't the type to go on the attack with it.

"Bad old business," he muttered, shaking his head.

"We were just saying how hard it is to believe that it could have happened in daylight," said Greenaway, trying to catch his eye. "I don't suppose you saw anything untoward yourself Wednesday morning?"

"No." Batchelor scratched the back of his neck. "It was quiet up here Wednesday, for me anyway. It was Tuesday afternoon I had all the bother." He finally looked at Greenaway, his brown eyes liquid with sadness. "Lost one of my best girls, I did."

Greenaway didn't know what he meant, but Ramsey did. "That heifer you talking about? The one that got stuck in the ditch?"

Batchelor nodded. "Terrible, it was. Twisted a gut trying to get back out, Mr Hackstead had to shoot her in the end. Got in a right temper about it."

"And that was Tuesday," Ramsey repeated, gently.

"That's right," Batchelor said. "I wish I could forget it, but…" He shook his head, looked down at the ground.

"Mr Stone was murdered about one o'clock Wednesday afternoon," said Greenaway. "Laid there with a pitchfork sticking out of his neck, until it got dark."

Batchelor shrugged. "I never had nothing to do with Stone," he said.

"You didn't see anything of him that morning, or notice anything strange as you passed? Did you go near the Conanground in daylight hours on Wednesday?"

"No, I come up here and fed my girls, like I'm now doing." Batchelor addressed this comment to Ramsey. "Then I went back down and mashed up some more feed, brought them in for milking and come back up here. That's it."

"All right, Happy." Ramsey spoke gently. "You can go back to your girls now."

"All right, Matt." The farm hand pulled his cap down still further. "Sir," he muttered towards Greenaway before moving rapidly across the field.

The two policemen exchanged glances. "Tuesday not Wednesday," said Greenaway. "That blows Hackstead's alibi. And he ain't what I'd call Happy."

"He's scared," said Ramsey. "I wonder what of."

"I've got an idea," said Greenaway. "Go and pay Hackstead a friendly visit, before he gets the chance to find out this conversation took place. Tell him the army are coming today to search his fields for that watch, and the fingerprint man from the Yard's going to take a look at the murder weapons. See how he reacts."

"Is he?"

"There aren't any prints on the weapons, unfortunately," Greenaway told him. "Which an innocent man, of course, wouldn't know…"

*

"He always loved the horses best, did Joe. Had a way with them, with all animals." Meredith Stone had clearly prepared for Greenaway's visit. The thatched cottage was spotless, the hearth swept, the table set with starched linen, laid with her late aunt's best china. She smiled sadly as she passed the tea, a small woman with a round face and blue eyes like a doll. "Help yourself to milk and sugar, I've got plenty. Harry next door's been looking after me."

"Thanks." Greenaway added a drop of milk. "Had your uncle been upset about anything lately?" he asked. "Or had anyone been upsetting him?"

"I've been trying to think," she said. "If he had troubles, he wouldn't have shared them with me—he never liked to talk about things like that."

"Did he talk to anyone? Harry next door? The landlord at the Cooper's Arms?"

She shook her head. "Never. He didn't go in for that kind of thing."

"What, had he signed The Pledge?"

"No, Joe always made his own cider in the autumn, better than anything you could get at the pub. He did used to let Harry have a glass sometimes."

"But he didn't have any close friends?" said Greenaway.

"Only old Sid," said Meredith. "Sid Higgins, the stone mason, lives a few doors down, a place called Hill View. They've known each other since they were boys. Not that I've seen him since Christmas, mind. Sid's a bit of a loner, too."

"All right." Greenaway jotted in his notebook. "What can you tell me about this watch?"

"He didn't have it, did he?" Meredith's expression changed, anger flaring. "When I came in Tuesday night, he was asleep by the fire. Poor old soul, he looked so tired I let him be until I'd made supper. It was only when I went to wake him I noticed it wasn't in his waistcoat. He never went anywhere without that watch."

"It was already gone *before* he was murdered?"

She nodded. "It's the only thing I can think of. I did see him take it out of his pocket a few times and fiddle with it. What I'm wondering is whether it had stopped working and he took it to be repaired. Or if someone else offered to get it done for him." Her eyes rolled, anguish replacing anger. "If only I'd asked."

"He couldn't have just dropped it somewhere?"

Meredith shook her head. "He would have noticed and gone looking for it."

"Sorry for asking, but he wasn't a rich man, was he?"

She gave a hollow laugh. "He used to pay me a pound a week for keeping house. Which left him seven shillings. The rent on this cottage is three, and on top of that he paid for all the coal and the meat. Probably didn't have more than a couple of coppers to rub together by the end of it."

"Well, I know it ain't much by way of compensation, but if we find that watch on the hill, it might give us some fingerprints. Or, if it turns up at a pawn shop, it could lead us to our man that way. Maybe it can still come good for him, somehow."

Greenaway found the house called Hill View after he left Meredith's, but the door was locked and no one was home.

Neither were any of the neighbours. Before going to see how the search was progressing, Greenaway stopped back at the pub to ask George Mayfield a few more questions. Then he walked back up the hill through the pasture Ramsey had pointed out earlier, where he encountered some of the sappers and local coppers bent down to their tasks, to a chorus of bleats and gurgles from the sheep. Greenaway walked round the field himself and discovered how deceptive the hill could be. The only clear view he could find of where Stone had been working was from the gate that separated the two fields. It was possible that Hackstead had seen him from there, but only if he had been looking to check up on the hedger's progress.

Greenaway worked his way up the hill anti-clockwise, until the light began to fail and he could see the troops begin to come back down. By that point he had reached the summit, looking down on the huddle of buildings below, on top of the steep ditch where Batchelor's heifer came to grief. He thought about Tombs' book and the young Stone's nocturnal encounters.

"This where you saw it?" he asked the wind. His eyes travelled thirty degrees to the right, where an old stone barn had been scaffolded for repair, and saw a figure emerge from it, a bundle on his back, and begin walking down the hill. He hadn't noticed this building on his route up so he made his way towards it.

Once more, the dips and curves of the hill proved deceptive—it was not so close as he had imagined and he had to get his torch out to see his way. By which time, the figure he had been following had melted into the gloaming.

*

"He seemed quite relaxed at first," Ramsey reported. "Said he'd heard it was one of the fascists up at the POW camp who did it and that Scotland Yard were coming to get them—shows you how fast word travels. Then his wife asked me if they could get fingerprints off Stone's clothes. Hackstead started getting that look again, all shifty, like. Said Chapman had told him to go up to the corpse and make sure he was really dead, so he might have touched something. He never said this before and neither did Chapman. When I checked with him he said it was obvious that Stone was dead."

It was seven o'clock by the time they had a chance to reconvene at the station. Tombs had been looking into Hackstead's financial affairs. It was his father, Leonard, who owned Yew Tree. He also ran a boozer in Chipping Camden that was favoured by the county set. In Tombs' opinion, the old man wanted his son out of his hair. Mark had got himself into bother before, debts to bookies and at card tables, and acquired an expensive-looking wife. Hackstead Senior had hoped a bit of horny-handed toil might straighten him out. But talk at the Cooper's Arms was that wages from Yew Tree had been slow in coming lately. The previous year's harvest had not been a good one, and the small agricultural community had all felt the pinch of it. A glimpse at the books showed Tombs that Hackstead had been claiming more in wages than he had been sharing among his staff. About double the amount, in fact.

But it appeared Ramsey had made the best progress.

"I wonder what made her ask about fingerprints?" Tombs considered. "Course, he could have had anything he was wearing cleaned by now, but Stone's clothes all went with him to Brum. Is that where her mind was leading?"

"She started calling him an idiot, said the police would suspect him if his fingerprints were found on the body. He told her to shut up and got up and left. When I followed him out, he said not to take no notice, all she ever did was nag. Then he made himself scarce—went off to shout at Happy, probably."

"So." Greenaway made notes. "We've got the heifer that died the day before he said it did and now Meredith Stone's telling me her uncle's watch was already missing then, too. What do you make of that?"

"I've got another statement on that heifer," said Ramsey. "Happy's got one good friend apart from his girls, Bill Dyer. I went to see him after I'd left Hackstead and he confirmed Happy went to see him on Tuesday night, all upset because of it. Hackstead told him the animal died because it had been cursed by Stone."

"Why would Stone do that?" asked Greenaway.

"They had an argument," said Ramsey. "Something about a watch."

The atmosphere had subtly changed in the Cooper's Arms that evening. The range of expressions that greeted Greenaway were less like the appraisal of a farmer looking over a bovine fit only for the knacker's yard and more akin to the leer of a spiv, hoping to lure a young lady down a dark alley.

"They've been talking," Tombs deduced as they made their way to the snug. Sergeant Saunders was joining them, after his first day's interrogations. A room at the inn had been found for him too and there was jugged hare for their dinner.

"How many bloodthirsty maniacs did you meet today then?" Greenaway asked as they sat down. The sergeant shook his head.

"We had one brief moment of excitement," he said. "Giuseppe, little bottle-washer used to work up in Soho, was seen that day with blood on his hands. Turned out he'd been snaring rabbits. They don't keep much of an eye on them there. Let them roam about all over the place."

"Evening, Inspector." A hand touched Greenaway's arm. "Might I have a word?"

It was one of the little old boys, whose slightness of stature, bulbous nose and shock of white hair made him look closer to gnome than man. He took a long-stemmed pipe from between the two lower teeth he had left. "Outside," he whispered, pointing it at the door. "We shan't be overheard."

Greenaway left his plate steaming on the table. The old boy led him into the darkest corner of the graveyard before he would divulge.

"Something you might want to know about Stone." His voice was so low Greenaway had to bend down and cup a hand to his ear. "He used to keep toads."

"Toads?" repeated Greenaway.

The old man's eyes shone in the moonlight. "To blast the land."

By the time he had finished hearing about how Stone

made tiny ploughs, attached them to these creatures and sent them hopping off to cause the deaths of heifers and the failure of his enemies' crops, the plate he returned to had gone stony cold.

"What did he give you?" asked Saunders.

"Same as you got," Greenaway scowled. "A load of old rabbit."

Greenaway went to church the next morning. Not because he had begun to fear for his soul, but because Tombs advised it would be an opportunity to observe everybody in Upper Pendleton in one place. Ironically, on the Sunday that followed the dark deed of Stone's murder they would be celebrating Candlemas, when every family would be given a candle to take home. Once, these would have been placed in every window, bathing the village in flickering light, but under the blackout, they would go on the mantelpiece instead, perhaps illuminating many other witch marks.

They stood at the back, so Ramsey could put faces to names. Meredith Stone, accompanied by Chapman, was among the first to arrive, the vicar folding his hand over hers as they spoke. Happy Batchelor came with his friend Bill and the tiny Mrs Dyer. Calvin Peachey, who had raised the alarm. All Hackstead's workers arrived at St Oswald's before the farmer himself.

Hackstead was a thickset man with untidy curls that had begun their journey from chestnut to silver long before he reached his present age of 40. He stood about five foot tall. His wife was a hard-faced woman in a fox fur, bottle-blonde hair and lipstick a shade too red for this occasion. Both looked like they had woken with a hangover and been squabbling all the way to the church doors.

Hackstead clocked the interloper from Scotland Yard at the back. His storm-grey orbs turned away quickly and he steered his wife to the opposite aisle. Throughout the service, Greenaway watched them all, stealing glances at each other and him, nudging with elbows and knees. The vicar made the best of the occasion.

"As we gather together to celebrate the presentation of Our Lord at the Temple, we come here to be cleansed. The candles we will take home with us today represent the light of Christ. This year, that light has come at a darker time than any I can recall. While the world remains locked in conflict, untimely death has snatched one of our own, and we think of our brother, Josiah Stone." His gaze rested on the bowed head of Meredith. Her shoulders betrayed the silent sobs she made into her handkerchief. Hackstead, on the other hand, fidgeted in his pew, while a row behind him, Batchelor fretted with his cap. "If ever a village needed to be bathed in the light of truth—" the vicar's voice rose in volume "—then that time is now."

On a normal Sunday, Ramsey told Greenaway, the congregation would linger in the churchyard, catching up on the gossip; it was the one time of the week when everyone was guaranteed to be present. But on this, far from average Sabbath, exodus was swift. They only just managed to catch Hackstead, and not in time to hear what he had whispered into Batchelor's ear, his arm clenched around the cattleman's shoulder, before he made his way to where his wife stood, scowling, at the lych gate.

"Plenty to think about, Mr Hackstead?" Tombs called after him.

Hackstead turned. His eyes shifted between the three policemen, an insincere smile forming beneath. "For you, I'm sure," he replied. "Got your work cut out. Did you find any fingerprints, then?"

"I'll have to pay you a visit, Mr Hackstead," said Greenaway. "We can discuss that and a few other matters I think you might be able to shine a light on."

Hackstead's eyes hardened. "I'll look forward to it," he said. "Though I don't know how else I might be able to help, I've already told young Matthew here all I know." He shrugged theatrically. "I'm just a simple countryman."

"Well," said Greenaway, "we'll see about that. Now, don't keep your wife waiting."

She shot daggers in their direction as he scuttled towards her.

"I see they didn't take a candle," noted Tombs.

Greenaway watched the departing flock. "Was there anyone who wasn't here?" he said. "Sid Higgins. I didn't hear anyone mention his name. Meredith told me he was Stone's oldest friend. Thought he might make an appearance."

"Old Sid?" said Ramsey. "Cor, you wouldn't find him in a churchyard."

"Then where would I find him?"

*

Greenaway left his colleagues to the peace of their Sunday lunches. Though he had been invited back for a home-cooked meal by both, he walked instead to Hill View and tried the door again. Once more it appeared empty, no smoke coming through the chimney, the blackout still down at every window, though a well-tended garden attested that someone was looking after the place. A stone mason, Meredith said. If he didn't go to church on Sunday, maybe he kept other heathen habits.

Greenaway went back up Ceon Hill, retracing the route from Conanground to the barn he'd seen the previous evening. As he got closer, he could see flickers of movement inside the structure, hear what sounded like a chisel tapping against stone.

He put his head around the doorframe. A man was up on the scaffold, fitting a brick into the top of the wall, just underneath the eaves. Or at least, that's what it looked like. It was too dark to completely make it out.

"Mr Higgins?" Greenaway enquired.

The head that snapped round had owl-like blue eyes under thick, frowning eyebrows, and a balding pate framed with scant, springy threads of what looked like wire wool. He was certainly old. "You're a hard man to find in such a small place."

"Who are you?" The other man barked. "What do you want?"

"I heard you were Josiah Stone's oldest friend," said Greenaway. "I just wanted to ask you some questions, find out a bit more about him. That's what my job is."

The man started to climb down the scaffold, as wiry and

agile as a cat despite his years. No need for him to walk with a stick.

"Did you know him when he saw the black dog up here?" Greenaway continued. "Did you go back that far?"

"It would be best for you to not ask of such things." He dropped the final couple of feet back down to the ground and stood staring at Greenaway, unblinking. They were almost the same height and up close Greenaway could see that, just like Stone, his trade had kept him strong and fit.

"What, about the dog?" Greenaway said. "Frighten you, does it? You believe he really did see it? Or have you seen it yourself?"

"These are things that lie outside your jurisdiction." His chin jutted, pugnacious as a prize-fighter. Up close, the gleam in his eyes was every bit as bright as that of Greenaway's informant from the Cooper's Arms, but flashing signals ten times more dangerous. He still had his chisel clenched in his right hand. "There are other laws that govern this world than the ones that you know about."

A man who could butcher, or a man who just knew how to cut a clean line?

"You got me wrong," Greenaway said. "I heard you were his friend."

The old man's prodigious eyebrows twitched. In the half-light of the barn, time stretched out like an elastic band as Greenaway awaited his next move. Then the madman threw back his head and laughed.

"He thought so and all," he said.

*

Greenaway came down the hill. He had no certain way of proving it, but he thought he knew how it all came together. What he had to work out now was a way to lure these cunning folk into traps of their own devising. It was time to brush up on his local knowledge, back at the Cooper's Arms.

He went to visit Hackstead the next morning. The farmer greeted Greenaway still dressed in his Sunday best. Only that was a bit more rumpled now, his shirt hanging out and black shadows under his eyes. The kitchen beyond the back door looked like it was missing a feminine touch, and the smell of alcohol hung woozily in the air.

"Where's Mrs Hackstead today?" Greenaway asked.

"Gone to Stratford, to do some shopping." He waved Greenaway through, brushed his untidy forelock out of his bleary eyes and blinked for a moment at the piles of plates and dirty surfaces. "Cup of tea?" he offered warily.

"Just sit down," said Greenaway. "Let me run a theory past you."

Hackstead looked almost relieved. "You've not got a smoke, have you?" he asked.

There was an overflowing ashtray on the table, a pewter tankard and empty bottles of beer and gin lolling about. "Here." Greenaway passed his packet, lit them both up. "Now," he said. "Sid Higgins. He put an idea into your head, didn't he?"

Hackstead inhaled deeply, relief spreading across his ruddy countenance, and with it a measure of his former cockiness.

"About what?"

"About doing some work on the farm, at first," Greenaway offered. "You had a few business meetings about it in the Cooper's. But Sid wanted a bit more than you could afford. ''Cos you're in a bit of schtuck, ain't you, son? We've had a look at your books. Is it the wife, costs so much?"

Hackstead's hand closed over the tankard. It shook as he lifted it to his mouth. He grunted something unintelligible.

"So, anyway, Sid done a deal," Greenaway went on. "You get him something he really wants, he'll do the work for less. Gratis, even. And what does he want? Josiah Stone's pocket watch. Well, it sounds a bit odd, but the next time you see Stone, you ask him for the time. He can't tell you, his watch has stopped. What a stroke of luck, you think. 'Oh, let's take a look,' you say. 'I know a place you can get that fixed—want me to see about it for you?' Against his better judgement, he hands it over. Gives him a sleepless night, so he asks for it back the next day. 'Oh, you can't get it fixed that quickly,' you tell him, 'they have to send away for a part.' Stone don't like this much. 'Give me my watch,' he says. 'Or there'll be consequences.' Yeah, you think, like what? Next thing you know, poor old Happy's knocking on the door. One of your heifers has fallen into a ditch and mangled itself trying to get out—you have to shoot the poor thing. So you run and tell Sid, and all that old pony about magic starts to take on a new meaning: Stone's put a curse on you and your herd. Perhaps I elaborate, but that's what Bill Dyer said Happy told him. Next morning, you get yourself in the mood with a bit of blood-letting down at Barlett's farm. A couple of pints for courage and off you go."

Hackstead's head raised from his tankard. "You got it wrong," he said. "Happy got it wrong. He's so thick, he can't remember one day from the next."

"I did see the back of Stone's head in the morgue, and that blow you landed on him probably would have been enough to kill him," Greenaway went on. "Only you weren't the only person there, were you? And I don't think you reckoned on what that old bastard Sid's capable of—that's why you were still watching out for him when PC Ramsey found you at the scene. You didn't know how far back those two went and how dark it got between them. Maybe you wouldn't have believed it if you did know, but in that watch is a witch's charm that Sid believed gave Stone all these powers, including protection from the devil dogs on this hill. The two of them had a big falling-out sometime over Christmas and Sid thought Stone used this charm to put a curse on him. That's why he had to get it and why he carved him up the way he did. The watch was Stone's grandmother's, did you know that? Someone thought she was a witch and all. Stuck a pitchfork through her head."

Hackstead put the tankard down on the table.

"Where you getting all this from?" he asked.

"Some people down the pub," said Greenaway. "You probably wouldn't have noticed them. They're only little, but they've got very big ears."

"Well," Hackstead said, "Happy got his facts wrong. He's come to his senses about what day it was we found that heifer in the ditch. I've told him to go down the station and clear that up; says he'll swear in a court of law it was

Wednesday. But I thought it was fingerprints you come to talk to me about."

"You knew we wouldn't find any," said Greenaway. "You had plenty of time to clear up after yourself. But there's one thing you forgot. When I find that watch, I'm going to find both your fingerprints on it. Yours and Sid's."

Hackstead laughed. It was a short, harsh sound, not Sid's maniacal cackle. "You reckon the army's gonna find it for you, do you?"

"No." Greenaway stood up. "I reckon I'm going to magic it back."

Greenaway went back to the station, stopping to talk to the troops on Ceon Hill who were continuing their searches. Batchelor had already been in to change his statement and give Hackstead an alibi by the time he got there, along with Dyer to back him up.

Later that afternoon, about an hour before sunset, when the army had returned from Ceon Hill empty-handed and Saunders was on his way back from interrogating Italian grocers, Greenaway got a call. An old friend from London was passing through and wanted to show him something. Telling Tombs he was nipping out for an hour, Greenaway went to where his associate had parked, on the outskirts of the village, by the kissing gate to the Conanground. The cargo was in the back of the van.

"He's a beauty, Alf," he said, smiling in admiration at the huge, black Great Dane. The dog got to his feet, shook himself and looked up hopefully.

"Yes," Greenaway's friend agreed, "he could do with a walk, though."

"I'll take him," Greenaway offered. "Be about an hour."

"Looks like he died of fright." Ramsey knelt beside the stricken figure. Old Sid's face had frozen in an expression of shock, owl eyes staring into infinity. He lay on his back on the floor of the barn, one hand on his chest, the other by his side, chisel still in its grasp. Not being able to find him at home, Greenaway and Ramsey had come up first thing that morning to take a statement on his whereabouts on 14 February. Since they were getting nowhere with Hackstead, Greenaway thought it prudent to get a record from all farm employees. And, as Ramsey spotted on the way up the hill, the barn wasn't all that far from the murder scene.

"Probably a heart attack," Greenaway said. "Wonder what brought that on."

"Still working at his age." Ramsey got to his feet. "That's what did it. Died with his tools in his hand."

"Does seem to happen a lot around here," said Greenaway.

"You don't reckon he saw a ghost, do you?" Ramsey sounded serious. "Got a visit from Stone in the night?"

"Maybe he saw one of them devil dogs," said Greenaway. "Anyway, best leave him to Professor Willis. But as I was saying, I did see him fiddling around with something up here on Sunday. Wonder if it was anything of significance?"

Donning a pair of gloves, he climbed the scaffold to the place where he had first seen the old man. Sure enough, there was one loose brick. Pulling it back, he found a leather pouch hidden there. Greenaway held his breath as he opened it.

Wrapped in a bundle of sage was an old pocket watch.

VIRGINIA RACER

BILL BEVERLY

I was a bastard, there's no debate. My dad met my mama on a bus he was riding downstate to turn himself in for some resale of stolen property. When the state coughed him out six months early, she surprised him at the gate, handed him a just-weaned baby, and climbed into a Buick nobody's seen since. As for my grandfather, he exchanged gunfire with his wife's relations more than once. And my Uncle Burquet got locked in a mine with a girl named Claude McKinna: that's where all the twins came from.

It was said no man and woman in my family ever got together right. I never made no promises on it, but when I was young I figured I could do better. If I just held out, maybe there'd come a girl for me. I didn't know what she'd look like. I imagined she'd sort of drop down, like Wonder Woman without the wrestling tights, and something would send us the same way. I wasn't never good at waiting. But I would wait for that.

I was nineteen and a half, approximately, when I met Mike Mark. That was his name, Mike Mark, like two tires going over a seam. He's dead now, as everyone knows, died last November in Orange. My name is Farquhar. No one can say it.

Mike Mark robbed banks. When I met him, he was robbing a bank, the Wachovia where I was making the afternoon deposit for the one real job I'd ever had. I was first in the line when it happened.

He had a gun, didn't swing it around much. Wore a mask—who doesn't? Any consternation I felt, it was minor; this fellow had a handle on his business. One thing, he got everyone sat down in the easy chairs, even the old guard, with his six-gun he was too shaky to aim. The chairs were low and square and mossy green, and people sat back and crossed their legs and sighed, like they'd just got home after a hell of a day, now they got to see a bank robbed, front row. The only ones standing were him and those two cashiers and me. Simple instructions, no heart-attack hollering *Everyone get the fuck on the floor.* Mike Mark told you what to do like you would want to do that anyway.

I stood in line where I'd been, while the two cashiers cleaned out the drawers.

He noticed me. "Any reason you're standing up, boss?"

"I got twenty minutes only to make this deposit," I said, "or I catch three kinds of hell. So if it's all the same to you, I'll keep my place in line."

Not that it grieved me if Mount Rogers Sandwich Masters lost its lunchtime take. It might do to get robbed in this set of circumstances, of money that none of it was mine.

For a moment he looked at me and the whole bank looked at me. I flared the yellow zipper deposit sack out from my leg innocently, only so he'd see what I was talking about. Bright yellow. I guess I was open to whatever happened.

He saw and came to relieve me of it. All this is true, it's on the CCTV. "How much you got in here?"

Someone asks you a question, most times it don't matter what your answer is. They listen how you answer. They watch you answering. My dad used to say that. I never held with my dad much. But he was a man who answered the hell out of things.

Loudly I declared, like it was money I had made myself, "Five hundred thirteen dollars."

"You certain of that?"

"That's the number the sumbitch counting it said."

He nodded and slipped the zippered sack inside his jacket. A vest in there, black, armored—he could drop whatever he wanted and still have both hands free.

"Thank you, brother. You ain't got to stand in line no more. Head on out if you want."

"Me myself, I'll stay for the police report. I won't do you wrong," I said. "I'm still on the clock."

"I got you," said Mike Mark. I saw his eyes make sure of his crowd in their chairs, cut back to the cashiers finishing their bagging. "Tell them officers I looked a lot like George Strait, will you?"

"Will do," I said, and he took his money and split. I heard a set of tires slicing out of the lot, didn't move to look. The people seemed to know it was finished now, but didn't want to give up their seats. The elderly guard let out a snore and woke himself up.

I got back in the Mount Rogers Sandwich Masters delivery Jeep and it drove itself, finding the little roads as the green mountain got bigger and bigger.

"I clocked you out some time ago," Harvey Kitts reassured me. "I had to, been making sandwiches in your place two hours now." A bit of provolone clung to the weedy moustache he grew. "You're gonna pay every dollar back," he threatened.

"You can't do me like that. He robbered the *bank*. The police took a *police* report."

"I'll see that report," said Harvey Kitts. He was a big man, unpleasantly curious. He was a well-known failure in these parts. But the sandwich shop was working, and it was like he couldn't stop searching for what would stop him this time. "Till I do, you owe the shop five hundred twenty-six dollars. I'll take it out of your next five paychecks."

"Five hundred thirteen dollars. You counted it yourself."

"And thirteen more for the sack."

"Fuck you, Mr. Harvey," I declared. "You ain't taking nothing out of nothing."

This made him mad as hell; nobody but nobody called him his first name. "You said it right." Little spit fireworks dwindled over the cheese slices. "You ain't got nothing to take because you ain't nothing. Get out of here."

"I will," I said, but I didn't go anywhere, chewing my long-earned belligerent minute. I saw my green apron hung up by his office. All I was leaving behind was my dad's old copy of *Guns & Ammo*.

That's when the same two detectives came in, wanting another word. Harvey Kitts changed then, from wanting me out of his store to saying the detectives needed his permission to ask me questions, even if I was off the clock and quit. I took off my *Welcome Sandwich Masters My Name Is* pin and pinned it into the *You Found Virginia's Tallest Sandwiches* banner hanging over the counter, and enjoyed watching the detectives tell my boss it wasn't none of his if they questioned me or not. Two minutes later I was in the back of their Ford, answering the same questions. Something about me they hadn't liked. Something about me seemed cockeyed.

The black detective explained, "Everyone say the man don't look a goddamn thing like George Strait."

"I don't know, something about the jaw," I said.

"Do you, uh, get along with your Mr. Kitts?" the white detective asked. The black one chewed spearmint gum and twitched his nose now and then, like he was picking up a smell that he couldn't place.

"I just quit that sumbitch, so draw your own conclusions."

"Son, I can't say I admire your attitude," the black detective said.

"Brother, you ain't the first," I replied.

I had the feeling it was maybe the most important day of my life: I got bank robbed, I said fuck Harvey Kitts, I decided I'd rather be a cockeyed eyewitness than a sandwich jerk the rest of my days.

I started working pit crew for my cousin Ray Jones. His real name was Ray Farquhar-Jones, but he dropped the Farquhar two years back. He claimed it was because my dad's dad was a rapist and an asshole and did his mother wrong, but more likely it required more painting *Farquhar-Jones* on a race car than just *Jones*. I couldn't deny any what he said about my grandpa Jenkins Farquhar, but if Jenkins Farquhar hadn't made his way with Betsy Brown, I told him, wouldn't be no Ray Jones racing sportsman cars, here or nowhere. "Sometimes them dirty apples is the only apples you got," I said, "so get up out of my face."

Ray Jones pulled his own V-8s cheap from a yard over the mountain, and did fabrication on his backyard slab, so he raced twenty weekends a year on not much. Had an old trailer he won in a bet, and his Dodge Ram Hemi with the X-cab to pull. I worked his pits and tires to make a little cash, two seasons I guess. I didn't know much about race cars, didn't love the noise and the smoke of it, floating like a brown skid mark beneath the lights. Mostly I handled the gas can and fetched Ray the wrench and, since I didn't drink, I could drive home through the night, a half-case of Keystone cans in the back seat with Ray, and he saved the price of the motel and the Shoney's breakfast it took for him to sleep it off. That price saved was the money he paid me, more or less, and his wife Curtsy was happier, comparatively, 'cause I got him home safe.

"You're a godsend, Far," she would say, putting her hand

somewhere up on the back of my hand where it left a little charge, like she'd passed me some kind of chiggers she had.

Wasn't long before Ray's drinking got out ahead of him a little bit, like we'd get to the track, set up and practice, but by the time heats came around, he'd have a mountain of Keystone cans telling on him. The track stewards found out, and Ray got DQed a couple times. Word got around: Ray had to slow down drinking or think of something. What he thought of was him taking over the pits and me driving the car. I was the real driver in the family, he said, the second coming of Ricky Rudd.

I was fine being suddenly a race car driver. I drove well, always could. Ray had one of the better cars out there, but he never won a heat that I knew about, approached prize money mostly when other guys crashed each other or ran their engines out. Me, I went top three in heats pretty steady, ran second in the feature at Shenandoah my second time out.

Didn't bother me the car still said *Ray* on the side and Ray still paid me like his pit man. What else was I going to do? I'd tried to plumb but didn't make journeyman, and the armed forces didn't want none of me on account of one school guidance counselor I never met. I was twenty-one now. If you asked me who I was, I was a goddamn race car driver. If you asked me any question at all, my tongue it was ready. I set about making myself a name, as someone who'd battle you in the corners.

Then one night at a little half-mile right down the road, I had a bad wreck. The right rear wheel came off. It didn't wobble, didn't warn, but all of a sudden it sheared the studs and went zooming off and the goddamn car was a rocking horse with a broken rail and you could balance the weight maybe if you kept going right. Thing is, in racing, go left is all you can do. It was Ray's best car, the yellow number 88 I'd run at Shenandoah. It had just the right slip, you could throw it to a slide with just a tap and a yank as you entered the turn. It was like riding a good horse, a horse that knew what you wanted and wasn't too old to give you some, a horse that wanted a little bit itself.

So the weight tipped and then all the tires slid and I went round once and smacked the wall, hopped and came down sideways, all this goddamn sheet metal scraping down the straightaway like a hundred grinders at once. The engine was still full out because I'd stomped on both pedals, I stomped the whole floor; I didn't let off till the car quit sliding. A pack of three cars went by me just like three kids, that's what I remember, three humming sweaty boys racing for a pitcher of root beer, just racing back to the line. The yellow lights came on around the track, and Ray's car made a sound like it was thinking about rolling over, but it stayed up on its side.

I watched the brake lights, the three cars heading into the turn. The outside wall was above me, the infield grass below, the pavement eighteen inches beneath my cage and the sky damp and shit-brown over my left shoulder. In my head my heart and blood were pounding. But I wasn't scared. Up and down the stands, everyone was watching me. Just before something ends, that's when you see you love it, that it is beautiful. Hanging over the track, the floodlights throwing three, four shadows off of everything, spreading out every which way like you could be all those places at once.

Maybe that's why I never heard the tires screech. They say I put my head back and braced, and that saved me, because the 21 car was coming hard when it hit and blew apart Ray's yellow 88, axles whipsawing free and the metal peeling like a candy wrapper as I tumbled down the front straightaway. I closed my eyes till it was over, though tumbling sideways and thrill-ride flying, you lose your sense of *over*. It might never be over. Or it might be over already.

The track techs were brothers, bumpers of fat lining their brows, like padding on a catcher's mitt. One had a moustache and the other didn't.

"You all right, bud?" said the brother with the moustache.

I had come to rest upside down. "Great," I said. "How come there are two of you? What happened to his moustache?"

The two brothers looked at each other and the one without the moustache began to laugh first. In that moment I could see: he had always been the one without the moustache. This was how their parents told them apart. I could see their life stories.

I twitched my arms and legs, tried to count pieces. I didn't think I'd broken anything but everything buzzed, like lightning had hit me.

The lights around the outside of the track shone red now. There was a picture in the paper of me in the cage and the wreckage trail behind it. I later learned that the photographer wasn't but four years old.

"What's the name of that fellow that hit me?"

"Oh, twenty-one," said the one with the moustache. "Yeah, good on the gas. Not so much on the steering wheel."

Of course we rode the same ambulance. They strapped us on backboards in case of anything. I wouldn't have thought there were two backboards in the whole county. The paramedic seemed happy enough to ride up front.

"Showing your virules are stable," he said.

"Vitals?" said the other driver, but the paramedic had already closed the door.

I knew I'd just about got killed.

"Sorry about that, boss," the other driver said. He had banged his head, had it all trussed up in ice packs, like an organ kept cold for a transplant. "That your car we blew up back there?"

"My cousin's."

"What you doing stopped where you was?"

"Wheel come off. What were you doing still hauling ass?"

"I burnt my brakes out five laps back. Just hoping I could finish. But I ain't gonna drive anymore, starting tonight. That was bad judgment, I can't deny, and I don't have the eyesight you young fellows do. Tell the truth, I was only racing to learn to drive better."

"Learn to drive better," I said, picking this through like someone had asked me to eat a plate of rocks.

"In real life," he clarified.

"In real life? What you do, long haul?"

In half a minute he'd got me off wanting to kill him. Now

I was inquiring after his day job. I was always thinking about getting some day job myself. But most of my life hadn't seen it.

"I know you," he said. But upcountry where I'm from, people say that. Someone says it every day.

"I'd say you do, personally. Seeing as you just drove a car up my ass."

"I met you in a bank one time."

"In a bank?"

"Five hundred thirteen dollars."

I started laughing. I remembered him then, and for the first time since the tangle on the straightaway I felt the bruise in my body, the black bloom of it. I was going to hurt tomorrow.

"Son, you like to drive?" he said. "You any good at it?"

I turned my head under the straps, which it hurt to do, and studied him, masked in ice like he'd been masked in a Lone Ranger mask the first time. He didn't look nothing like George Strait.

I said, "Better than you."

He lived eight miles down from my cousin Ray's where I'd taken the bedroom over Ray's garage, where his mother-in-law used to live. Curtsy's mom's things were still up there, and a few of Curtsy's too. Curtsy used to ask if it bothered me, her old scrapbooks all quilted up like May Day aprons on the shelf over the sink. "It don't bother me, Curtsy," I'd say, and she'd look at me with her flashlight eyes, searching me out for a liar. I wasn't a liar. I didn't mind her scrapbooks jutting out up there.

They were from when she was younger, bits of newspaper or programs from plays and dances at her high school over the mountain, snapshots of pretty girls from ten years back, everything from ten years back, when she was a pretty girl too. A sizable gap between then and now that wasn't explained, but I guess it didn't need any explaining. Nor any of my asking about it either, when she stood behind my chair, hands on my shoulders 'cause we was family now, asking me how I felt.

Truth, I wasn't too good. My concussion stuck around. It used to be hell getting up early, now I could barely stagger around in the afternoon. My skull felt like someone had prized it open and laid a couple shovel blades over my brain, keeping everything out. Just one hit. My dad played football and he fought bareknuckle down in Roanoke back in the day, and he wrapped a few trucks around telephone poles in his life, and I don't think he'd ever had a concussion in his life. Barely even a knot on the head. Or so he would tell you. So he told me. I don't know how much to credit the things he told me. I think these days about the things he didn't tell, what they might have been.

Ray, he was kind, me living out of his kitchen, his wife rubbing my shoulders. He didn't blame me for wrecking his yellow 88 car but once, and that was the beer talking, mostly. He spent his time out on his slab, doing repair and tune-ups, building up a new 88. Maybe he'd start driving again, he said, but that was the beer talking too.

Curtsy Jones's scrap- and yearbooks that showed how pretty she was: they weren't bothering me. She was bothering me. Her mother's Farberware with the flaking coat was bothering me. But nothing bothered me more than those ten years missing, years she'd lived without saving a thing. I was that age now, inside those ten years, and I had nothing but a headache. When it went, Mike Mark came to fetch me, and it wasn't but a gym bag full of clothing I took. I was basically like a child, ready to go.

So I became, for a time, a bank robber's driver. Accomplice. Apprentice. Whatever you'd call it. It ain't like we made me out a badge.

He put me up across the road, another mother-in-law apartment. Everybody in Virginia had them. I learned to cook eggs and cook a chicken in the electric frypan. "You can take two eggs a day and a chicken every week, starting Monday," said the lady, with whom I had not exchanged names. "It's in the rent already. It's the board." I looked out the window then, saw the chickens down there, cracked my knuckles. Same Farberware.

Mike Mark's companion was named Cassie. At first I thought her his wife. Then girlfriend. She was neither. But I'd never seen devotion like that between a male and a female before. Inseparable. One time in school I had to write on *Romeo and Juliet*, which I hadn't read, just watched the movie, most of the parts on YouTube in the library, half asleep the morning the paper was due. Then I looked up 'love' in the Random House dictionary. 'Love' was a long entry. I wrote my paper about thirteen different things love meant, and here and there I tossed in a line from the play. My teacher loved it. Best paper you ever wrote, she said. Gave me a B+.

I went to the library every time after that, trying to catch the same magic. Never did. But watching Mike Mark and Cassie wasn't a dictionary definition of what love was. It was like watching someone invent it in a lab. Even when something bubbled over and blew up, it got cleaned up, they took notes. She walked him back through it. I gave them some distance. Something that rare, I wasn't getting in the way.

This old fellow, Harrison, lived in the basement with his saws. He built custom cabinets in a county where no one needed custom cabinets, the cabinets they had worked just fine. The main floor was Mike Mark and Cassie's, but there was only one kitchen, so Harrison came through all the time. He had his Mason-jar whiskey and his big pick-up. It was his house after all and he was a mountain we had to find ways around. We indulged him his trespassing. He indulged us our beers and hiding all the money in his linen closet, in a fireproof safe that Mike Mark had bolted right down through the joists—it weighed a good five hundred pounds. Harrison always told stories on Mike that ran half like a boast and half like a curse. "I saw this boy steal a mailbag from a mailman once," he said. "December too, all them Christmas envelopes."

"Aw, no I didn't," Mike Mark would say. "You got that story wrong. All them envelopes got delivered, every one."

As bank robbers go, we had our routine. Mike Mark handled the inside. I drove. Cassie rode up front. She would hold the headrest, turned around, talking to him. I wanted to tell her not to ride that way, that if we hit anything she'd wreck her neck. But I didn't dare speak up to Cassie much.

She had bright orange hair and she scared me a little.

We hit a bank about every week that fall. Upstairs at Harrison's, we'd have meetings. Mike Mark told us how it would go, and we'd pace it off on the maps. Then he'd ask if we had any questions, which Cassie never had any questions.

"How many banks you robbed so far, anyway?"

Mike Mark ducked his head to look out through the back window at Harrison standing looking at the mountains, a small white mountain himself. "I don't worry about it." He said crisply, "How many banks *you* robbed?"

"None," I said. "And I'm worried about it already."

"That's the difference," Mike Mark said.

You see bank robbers in a movie: car rolls up, three or four guys leap out, running like they're fighting a fire, in fast, out fast, hit and run. Not Mike Mark. Before he walked into a bank we'd sit sometimes outside for half an hour. Like, meditating. I thought it was wrong, crazy; I thought that's how you got caught. "No," Mike Mark said, "you don't want to rush it. You want a chance to watch people move. Makes you relax." He glanced me over. "You ever rob a place before? Store, church, anything?"

"Me rob a church?" I said. "I'm the kind of people churches rob."

He touched his lips. Mike Mark, he used to be a smoker. It still ran through his body, how he'd bend a few fingers together, pull on something no one else could see.

"You are at that," he said. "You understand, we're a kind of a church, the three of us. We run on faith. And prayer."

"You're the preacher," I said.

"I ain't but the office manager," said Mike Mark. "Cassie, she's the priest."

That made me the bus driver, I guessed. We waited around the corner from the bank. This was once a farm town, now a yard sale town. Big mint-green water tower with the graffiti painted over, the name of the town swabbed out too. A pair of little boys played in the yard, whacking each other with a hollow yellow plastic bat. Neither seemed too unhappy about it. Nor did they hesitate taking their turns.

"See do they have any two-dollar bills," said Cassie. "Christmas is coming."

"Right!" said Mike Mark. He pocketed his pistol in his light fall coat with the vest underneath, and he went. In the long minutes after, Cassie searched the radio for a song she liked. Then she sat still and did a crossword in her lap, in fine-tip ink, never looking for nothing. We were both keyed up and pretending not to be. Myself, I had to keep from staring out at everything. I could see an old, old man, sitting on the stoop beyond the two boys, perfectly still.

A church. A bunch of prayers and rites and sins and devils one had to learn. We listened to the end of 'Tell Me Something Good'. The two boys tired at last and went in the house. Somebody hollered. Mike Mark came back.

I said, unable to rein in my nerves any longer, "You took a while."

"Them goddamn kids," Cassie said.

"That's right," said Mike Mark. "Go."

I moved the car out from the curb, and we all buckled in. It was so calm and slow. Honestly, it didn't figure to me like he'd even entered the bank. "This wasn't the place to park," he said. "Not in front of them two little boys playing. They were gonna remember this. This car. Me. They remember everything. And Cassie. You're too pretty for this town," he added.

"I'm sorry," I said.

"Not your fault," Mike Mark said pleasantly, though it was. I'd picked the space out. He'd hired me on so easy, like there was nothing I had to know.

"Want me stop some other place and we line it up again?"

"No need." Mike Mark reached inside the vest, grabbed a handful of something, tossed it out the window into the wind. When it hit the street it exploded in a pop of velvety red. I almost screamed.

"Dye pack?"

"It was buzzing at me," Mike Mark explained.

Different towns, different banks, different instructions. Stay in place or drive around. He'd jump in outside the bank, or we'd pick him up down the street, once on a ladies' bicycle, once at the Sonic. One time I got lost, other side of the tracks as a Norfolk Southern passed by, but he found me there. We watched each other across the flatbeds until the last car cleared.

The road away, different every time. I knew the Piedmont from driving sandwiches, pizzas. Some rides we took fast. Sometimes we loitered along in plain sight. Once he got out all at once on a curve. "Go on," he commanded.

"What?"

"I hear them," he said, descending the ditch, getting invisible. A mile down, Cassie and me hit the roadblock. They asked us had we seen anything. We said sorry, we had not. Stopped for a cheeseburger, picked up change off the floor. Cassie told me to keep going. Mike Mark got home late with a nice old lady. In between time, he'd robbed a dollar store too.

"I'll go in with you," I volunteered. "Some time."

Mike Mark said, "Mr. Farquhar, that ain't your job."

Only once did they have us for sure—it was a brand-new Ford with dual searchlights and heavy suspension. I had a Subaru that bounced up the mountain nicely in the twilight; sunset was coming earlier and earlier. Behind us the white Ford tracked up the dirt road steady as a bug. "God damn," moaned Cassie, and we headed toward the summit, me crouched down steering, Cassie and Mike Mark braced against the jostling. All of a sudden Mike Mark said, "Run up left off the road and stop once you clear the last post of that fence."

"So what? They can catch us on foot?"

"You ain't got no other choices," said Mike Mark. "I thought you said you knew this road."

"I do," I said, but this fast, sweating myself, nothing looked familiar. "How am I gonna know where the fence stops?"

"Concentrate, boss," said Mike Mark. "Slow down. Use your eyes. Let him get close, don't worry." But the Ford was already close, red and blue lights splitting the air.

I wanted to vomit. I saw the fence cut away just below the ridge and there was something, maybe a two-track, just past the last fencepost. No time to ask questions. I jerked the wheel left and we cleared the fencepost then the car dug in like a groundhog and stopped. Not good at all, but it left the cop Ford nowhere to go but straight ahead. We held still and dark as a rootball as it plowed by. Nowhere to go but through that last line of barbed wire across the peak.

It wasn't a road we'd found. It was a manure pit. A sheep stood across the fence, studying me.

The cop, he hung in air for a moment, then disappeared, down the back side of the mountain where there was no road.

Mike Mark added, surprising me always, "I happen to know there's a nice pond down there."

Cassie said, "Just stocked."

Sometimes I woke knowing it was a dream we were living, that we rode some charm up and down the black roads. What was going to stop us? If you'd asked Mike Mark, he'd have said nothing. He'd say, "We got the exact team you want: me on the people end, Cassie handling the luck and the nerves, and Del Far in the 88 car. A dream team. Better than they got."

If you'd asked me, I would have said the same. Like a movie, where the luck of true believers never runs out.

But underneath those two gravediggers' shovels, I wondered what would catch us. A pack of SWATs running Mike Mark down at the car. Or a curve I'd take too fast, too late. Or a tire strip laid in a shadow across the road, cops chuckling behind a tree. I'd spent my life around Virginia country police. Seen them pleasant, seen them vicious.

They'd all be vicious from here on.

One day I showed up when Cassie and Mike Mark were out, and Harrison asked me—I don't think I'd ever seen him leave the house—"What's gon' happen to you, boy, when you get done robbing banks?"

This old feedbag of a man, demanding answers of me. "I suppose we quit when we got enough."

He guffawed. A guffaw is a laugh that is loud and is boisterous, a dictionary will tell you that. But in Virginia, when a man guffaws right in your face, he is counting you, seeing how you add up. This no-count old bastard with his liver spots and his gut spill.

"How much is that? What's the number," he said. Then when I said nothing, he said, "You quit and then what? Huh?"

"Get a job," I said. "I won't need to rob no banks then. I'll do whatever I want."

"That's what you say," said Harrison. "That is what you'll wonder them long mornings in jail. Like your daddy. What it was, that other thing you supposed to be doing. Because if you were gonna do it, you'd be doing it already."

I didn't ask how he knew my daddy. Everyone knows everyone's daddy.

"Maybe I'll go back and be a race car driver."

"Maybe I'll go back and be quarterback of the Pittsburgh Steelers," remarked Harrison. "That's a job with a salary at least. Driving cars ain't even a hobby. It's a habit."

"Maybe I'll stay here and learn my trade from you," I sneered. Right then Cassie and Mike Mark walked in with a case of beer and a bag of sandwiches, Mount Rogers Sandwich Masters.

"Even you ain't that stupid," Harrison said. "Though I did get a job this week. Set of kitchen cabinets for a brand new mansion up top of the hill."

"Why, congratulations, Harrison," Cassie said. With a stray kindness now and then, she kept him buttered up.

"Giving your boy some guidance counsel," Harrison said to Mike Mark, by way of parting.

"He's found his future," Mike Mark said.

I didn't have the combination. But Mike Mark didn't mind opening it, showing me the piles of money.

"How much money is it?"

And Mike Mark would say, "Almost enough."

Two months since the concussion. Sometimes I was fine. But not that I'd realize at that moment. The sort of fine I'd remember the next day, when I wasn't so fine anymore.

"It's Mike's birthday," said Cassie. She was on the sofa, doing a crossword. I guessed she and Mike Mark had already discussed the job before I came over.

"Why you like them crosswords so much?" I asked Cassie, small talk-like.

"I don't like them at all," she said, with vehemence. "They're what I do."

Took me a while to see that Cassie wasn't a priest. She was a witch. To see that she was the lifer.

The car was a little Pontiac with a strong V-6. It drove fine, but a little kid had placed stickers all around the doors and roof and dash, funny stickers that clung on like a fat wet scab. "It ain't like you got to read them all," Mike Mark said. "Drive it today. We'll never see it again."

Today we were going east. It was a little town called Orange. "You driven that town before, you said," Mike Mark checked me.

"Yep. Used to pick up tires."

"You know the ways."

"I do."

"All right," said Mike Mark. "Well, I might take a shower."

I wasn't one for asking personal questions. My teachers back in school used to note on my reports: *Delbert should feel more confident asking questions when he needs help.* But I asked one now.

"How you get together with Cassie?"

Mike Mark came close and gazed, like he'd spotted something on my face. "What do you mean, *together*? We're roommates," he said. "Ain't that clear to you?"

"I mean—" But I didn't know what I meant. "What's it mean, handling the luck?"

"Cassie is gifted." Then, as if he didn't believe I believed him, he said, "Cassie's not for me. That girl's young enough to be my daughter." He fished a key out of his pocket, checked the writing on the grimy tape. "I am confident we'll be out on the road by nine-thirty," he announced.

I went inside, waited on the sofa while Cassie took her shower. Whenever she was done, I'd be ready. I'd had my lean breakfast and gone jogging around Harrison's yard in my sweatpants, shadowboxing. Though this headache I had, boxing was probably not the best idea.

Harrison knocked twice on the front door once he was already inside. "What are you still doing here? I thought you all were going out somewhere today." He sat down beside me and the floorboards wheezed like they'd been caught in a lie.

"Might soon," I mumbled. "Not yet."

"Sorry about that talk," said Harrison, picking something off his shirt. "Mikey likes you. He's my boy, I got to look after his best interests."

"What do you mean, your boy?"

"What, can't you see no family resemblance?" Harrison cackled again.

"I'll be damned." This weird man who collected rent on these rooms, who thumped around downstairs with his saws and molding and mountain curses.

"It don't mean anything," said Harrison. "It's a fact you ain't ever gonna outrun, like your birthday, but it don't mean nothing to nobody unless you throw a party for it."

"Speaking of which, today's Mike Mark's birthday," I said stupidly, since I had nothing else to say. Like if Harrison was Mike Mark's father, he wouldn't know this.

Harrison seemed pleasantly amused. "Well," he said, "there you go. Y'all doing a job today?"

"I don't know."

He chuckled. "How far away is the job you don't know if you're doing?"

"Over in Orange."

"Good answer," he said. "That's a fair piece. Drive safe."

*

Mike Mark and I stood up on the back porch together. It was a gray day, the sort of not-quite-dark, not-quite-wet day when something is pushing up the mountain ridge, bringing a storm, colors are dark and oily and the tops of the trees move ever so slowly like a large creature just beginning to wake up, when the leaves close up reveal their ancient spines.

"How come nobody told me you were Harrison's boy?" I said.

"Why the fuck would I tell you that?" said Mike Mark. "Who told you that?"

There was something red-faced in Mike Mark today. He had some aftershave on, rich and faraway. Maybe he was allergic to it.

"He did," I said. "Your dad did."

Mike Mark stared down at Cassie in her thin shoes where she was picking her way over to the smudge-painted Pontiac, through the piedmont mud that never really seemed to dry. He seemed, for once, stuck. Like he'd forgotten why he was keeping this secret, could only remember that he was.

For a moment I was ready to call the job off myself.

Then Mike Mark's face tightened and he inhaled. He nodded, as if to say: *You were born ready, right?* Like we were in a band, done tuning. Like the singer has to sing that song, every night. You can't be Bruce unless you remember 'Born to Run'.

He'd already let it pass. "We are what we are," he said.

The bank was a sky-gray stone such as crypts are made out of. We parked seven cars beyond. In front of me, one car length, a right turn around a shattered curb, and I'd be on a road behind warehouses. We could catch a low farm road between two wedges of corn.

It went Popeye quick. Mike Mark entered the bank, then barely a minute later, he emerged onto the sidewalk, between that stone and a shiny line of parked cars. I'd been watching the mirror for him. That was my discipline, watching the mirror.

Mike Mark looked up the street like he was waiting on a bus, then craned his neck and waved. A wild, quivering wave, off one side of his body, like he was flagging down invisible taxis all down the street.

"He want us?" I asked Cassie. "What's that mean?"

She covered her puzzle and turned around. "No. He's telling us to get going."

I began to roll the window down, and she hissed, "Do not. Do not roll the window down. Do not let anyone see you looking. Do not."

"Give me the shotgun. I'm going in."

"No," Cassie said. "He wants us gone."

"Why would he want that?"

"Mike Mark wants what he wants," Cassie said. She added, "You don't even know him."

In the mirror I saw Mike Mark heading back into the bank. We crept out of the gravel.

"How's he gonna find us?"

Cassie looked back at her puzzle. "All this, all this has been discussed."

The rites, the sins. The secrets. I didn't remember anything like this being discussed. But I knew the roads,

the land. I had the wheel, not Cassie. On the old two-lanes, I
cut back, our reversal of course covered by the sunless gray of
the clouds. Came into town the other way.

Out front they had the ambulance, were loading someone
in. A gurney, a sheet. A pair of black boots, streaked with
alluvial mud.

"What is this? What is this?" Cassie said, just now realiz-
ing what I'd done, where I'd brought us. She swiped at me
in her fury.

"Maybe it isn't him," I said.

In the mirror I saw them shut the door on the ambulance.
But they never even turned on the lights.

I took Cassie home.

A neighbor stood outside Harrison's house with a small fire
extinguisher lain in his arms like a prize piglet. All four
corners of the house were on fire.

"What the hell, you tried to burn up our house?" said
Cassie. She went straight past him, went inside.

"He did," said the neighbor, stirring his hand around in a
circle like he was trying to bring the name up out of the mud.
"Harrison."

"You want to try to put it out with that thing?" I asked him.

"Already tried," said the neighbor. "It's empty now. I tried
with your garden hose but it's cut."

Harrison.

"I summoned the County for you."

"Thank you," I managed, though a visit from the County
was the last thing I wanted right now.

"You might want to fetch out your girlfriend, I guess," the neighbor said.

"She ain't my girlfriend," I said. I ran into the burning house.

Everything was as we'd left it, except the smell of gasoline, flames scaling up the corners and poison curling out of the walls. And the safe closet. Cassie had unlocked the door, but there was nothing there anymore. Harrison had sawed the floor out from below, straight through the joists, a big square gap where the safe had been. We looked down into the basement. The safe had fallen, I guess, landed right on the cabinets he was making for the new mansion up on the hill. Smashed them to bits. But it wasn't there now.

The next day it came on the news, a man died of a heart attack right in a bank. He had an account. A gun in his pocket. But it's Virginia. A gun don't mean nothing till you pull it out.

"What are we gonna do," said Cassie. But it didn't sound like a question.

I stood on the other side of the road watching the pumper truck cool down the smoldering timbers of the house where Mike Mark brought us all together. The flares of white water in the dark, the hiss.

The two of us now. I hated her. That winter we went mostway across the country together, made a baby, someone to curse us down the ages. It took months for them to catch us. But to me it felt like years.

That afternoon we searched for Harrison or his truck. We kept to the mountain ridge. Somehow it seemed like the safest place. Somehow we imagined he'd be on it or along it. The sun burnt the clouds off, filled the valleys in green.

Cassie looked out, the sun behind her, momentarily blocking out her face, edging her ruff into gold. We looked down that long road under the nose of the mountain. That straightaway where the trucks coming off the hill let their Jake brakes hammer, and the bikers flashed by like hornets growling in the sun. In a few minutes the sun would duck behind the mountain, begin soaking the road in darkness.

I knew what was waiting for me down there. Cassie rode in the back seat now. Minutes later I stopped the car.

"Give me the shotgun," I said.

Cassie handed it over. I checked the action. She glanced up through the dusty windshield, recognized the banner.

"The usual," she said. Then maybe she realized who she was with. We didn't know each other from anyone. "Turkey and provolone," she added, small kindness.

But you are who you are. I went inside to see Harvey Kitts one more time. And Cassie bent back to her puzzle, weaving answers together with her fine slashing pen.

THE BELL

LAVIE TIDHAR

1

"I told him, of course I know how to use a gun. Everyone knows how to use a gun. He was very cute though." In the booth next to hers two girls of about nineteen had their rifles resting against the changing room's wall as they tried on lingerie, hurriedly.

"Did you sleep with him?"

"We made out. What time is it?"

"The bus is in half an hour."

"I don't know about sleeping with a German," the one girl said, dubiously. Deborah could hear the girls through the thin walls of the changing rooms. She checked her own watch. The girls had Tavor assault rifles, fully automatic. Deborah looked in the mirror but the blouse sat on her like a sack. She checked her own watch. Deborah had a Jericho pistol, 9mm, stolen from an IDF army base a year and a half back. She looked at the blouse again, sighed and began taking it off.

"Do you really want to screw a German? I mean, my mum won't ever go to Germany or use a German car. Because of the Holocaust."

"Well, he's cute." She could hear them changing, the heavy army boots pulled back on their feet. The guns lifting from the wall. "Are you going to get that? Wait, what are you doing?"

"Just act natural," the other girl said. Deborah heard her stuffing something under her uniform. The door opened and the two girls left.

Deborah looked in the mirror again. Should she buy it anyway? She couldn't decide. She checked the watch. It was almost time. She left the changing room and caught sight of the two young soldiers disappearing through the doors of the mall. She thought about crime, small white crime like stealing a pair of thongs or a bra, or selling a matchbox of hash, or killing a man. There was a scale for crime but wasn't it all transgression when it came right down to it? It was all a form of stealing, whether you stole a garment or a breath or a life.

The gun had been nestled patiently at the bottom of her bag. She had let the elderly Russian security guard check her bag on entering the mall, but the examination was cursory, indifferent. He wouldn't remember her. What was there to remember? The important thing was not to draw attention and be quick and stay away from cameras. She went to the busy food court where the men were sitting at a table in the middle together, keys and phones on the table, cigarette packets and disposable lighters, plastic coffee cups and trays with shawarma and humous and chips, pickles, salads. She waited.

Presently the man she had come to see got up and made his way towards her. He passed her and she followed him to the sign that said *Toilets*, through fire-doors into a corridor. A man came out of the men's wiping wet hands on his jeans. She waited for him to pass. Aharoni had his hand on the door when she said, "Excuse me," and he turned, looking at her without really seeing her, a little bemused at this middle-aged woman in the shapeless blouse with the anxious face. "Listen, *buba*, whatever you're asking for I already gave and I got to take a piss." Then his eyes grew just a little bit wider when she took out the gun and she shot him twice, quickly, in the face. *Do you see me now?* she thought. Aharoni fell back against the toilet door which swung inward and his body fell on the toilet floor smearing blood and brain on the door handle and on the door and on the floor someone must have just cleaned, an Arab or an Ethiopian, someone as unremarkable as her. She only took one look to make sure but she was already walking past and out, not hurrying, the gun safely in her handbag.

"I think I'll take this," she told the girl behind the counter back in the shop. The girl rang the top through. There was a commotion behind her. "Thank you."

"Would you like a bag?"

"Thank you, yes."

She took her shopping and left the mall. There were police sirens in the distance as she left, growing closer.

2

It all began with Rafi, always Raphael to her but Rafi to his friends, of which he had many, though none of them were any good. When he was little he was so scared of everything, Deborah used to have to hold him night after night and rock him to sleep. His dad, Soli, died when Raphael was five. Not in the army, for which, at least, there would have been a pension, but in a stupid traffic accident, coming off the Ayalon interchange in someone else's car. She'd met Soli after the army, they were married a year later in Tel Aviv when Rafi was already kicking in the womb.

"But I didn't think you'd be in, Ima," he said. She had walked into the small flat and there was her son, so thin now, his T-shirt ill-fitting and grey, standing in the middle of her living room riffling through her things. "Raphael, I have nothing left to take," she said. Then she saw he was holding the gun and she said, "Not the gun, Raphael, it's not yours to take, it belonged to your father."

"But he's dead," the boy said, with sudden savagery. His eyes were milky, pale, and he was shaking.

"Put it down."

It was an old gun, a Star 9mm, a Spanish knockoff of a Colt, not manufactured since the nineteen sixties. She didn't know who Soli had bought it from but he'd never used it. She had forgotten it was even there. "I could sell it," Rafi said; but she could see the fight was gone from him.

She gave him two hundred shekels, it was all she had, and he left. He crawled back two days later, leaving a tooth and a trail of blood on her kitchen floor. The money had not been enough. It would never be enough. She made chicken soup and fussed over her son, who lay shivering on the couch. "Who did this to you?" she said.

"Leave it, Ima. It's nothing." She touched his bruised ribs with a wet dishcloth and he flinched. "This is nothing?" she said, but the boy did not reply.

She made chicken soup: carrots and potatoes and onion, celery and parsley roots from the market, chopped into chunky cubes, a chicken carcass from the butcher's across the road. The smell filled the tiny flat as it used to, every Friday night, when Rafi was a boy.

"Is it over?" she said. The answer, unspoken, was in his eyes.

"How much do you owe?"

"Does it matter?"

"This can't go on, Raphael."

"What do you want me to do?" he said. He sounded indifferent to her. "I need it." He looked around for his cigarettes. Deborah said, "I threw them away."

"Ima!"

"How much do you owe?"

There was something new in her voice. Something colder and harder than he was used to. "Twenty thousand," he said, softly.

Twenty thousand shekels. How could you owe so much money—how could you have so much money to lose? She imagined stacks of fifty-shekel notes, with the writer S.Y. Agnon staring up from each one, the only Israeli writer to ever be given a Nobel Prize by those Swedes far away, in their cold land, stacks of them fitting into a briefcase, how much did twenty thousand shekels weigh? "What are you going to do?" she said. Her son looked up at her. "I want a cigarette," he said, sullen.

That night she sat on her bed and listened to his breathing in the living room next door. *You could make all the chicken soup in the world*, she thought, *but you couldn't fix a soup bowl if it broke. Where am I going to get twenty thousand shekels?* she thought. How am I going to save him, my little boy who is dying, moment by moment, from that poison.

She knew in the morning he would be gone, and whatever valuables she still had. And a week or a month or a year later they'd find him dead and apologetic against a drain or a municipal rubbish bin or in the dunes. Somewhere, anywhere, but dead all the same.

"Who do you owe this money to?"

"Leave it, Ima."

He looked embarrassed that she'd ask.

"Who is it, Raphael?"

At last she extracted a name from him. Chamudi, an Arab dealer in Jaffa. A mobile phone number. "Hello?"

"Is this Mr Chamudi?"

The voice on the line sounded amused. "Who is this?"

"I am Raphael Ben-Zion's mother. I want to talk—" her voice shook, then straightened. "I believe he owes you money."

"Rafi?" a laugh on the line. "Rafi's mother? Mrs Ben-Zion, I don't know what you hope to achieve with this, if I were you I'd let your son speak for his own actions." He spoke Hebrew without an accent, he sounded as Israeli as she did.

"He is my son," she said, simply. There was a short silence as he considered. "What do you have in mind?" he said, at last.

"Can we meet?"

"Do you have the money?"

Silence on her end; speaking her answer loudly enough.

"Then I don't think—"

"Please."

That simple word; or maybe he was just curious.

After she hung up she gathered her things and left the apartment. Raphael was still sleeping. She took the bus to Jaffa. Along Jerusalem Avenue the new Scientology headquarters and cafes where men sat smoking shisha pipes. Greengrocers' produce lolling on tables spilling on to the pavement. She went behind a rundown block of flats and no one paid her any attention. Into a dark hallway and up a flight of steps to the first floor and the first flat and she knocked.

"Come in."

He was alone in the flat. She thought it must be his mother's flat. It had carpets on the floor, framed photographs on the walls. Chamudi sat in an armchair away from the window, facing the entrance to the living room. He didn't get up. He was young, a few years older than her son maybe. He wore a red T shirt and had bony, hairy arms. His hair was cut short all over with a standard number two machine cut. He didn't smile.

"Tfadal, Um Rafi," he said, in Arabic. *Come in, mother of Rafi.*

"I think you speak very good Hebrew," she said, and he shrugged. "This is my home," he said. "This is what I will speak."

"I didn't mean anything by it," she said.

"What can you offer me?" Chamudi said, in his good Hebrew. He looked at her curiously. "Are you sure you want to replace your son's debt for yours."

It wasn't exactly a question. She said, "He is my son."

"He's a junkie," Chamudi said. He said it very matter of fact.

"But he's still my son."

"Do you have my twenty thousand shekels."

Again it wasn't entirely a question. She shook her head, slightly.

"Then what do you want, Um Rafi?"

"Here," she said. She took the money out and pushed it at him. It was two thousand and six hundred shekels. It was all she had. "I could pay you the rest when—"

Chamudi didn't rise. He *tsked* his teeth. "It's no use," he said. "Your boy will just owe more, then. And more."

"Then don't sell him no more."

He sighed. "I have to eat," he said.

The money was still in her hand. She held it like it could offer salvation. There was no one else in the flat. "Please," she said.

"I'm sorry. I really am."

She took off her wedding ring. "Will you take this?" she said. He looked curious again. He reached for the ring and took it and examined it in the light. Then he laughed.

"This is worth shit," he said.

It was the only thing she had left that Soli had ever given her. He'd bought it honestly. He'd bought it from a jeweller not far from where they were now. Chamudi threw it in her face. It hit her and stung and fell to the thick carpet without a sound. "Tell your boy to get me my money," Chamudi said dispassionately. "Or next time it won't end in just a beating."

She bent down and picked up her wedding ring and slipped it back on her finger. Maybe it was the wedding ring or maybe it was the threat to her son. The sunlight rippled in the room and it was very quiet but for the sound of children in the distance outside playing hide and seek. She took out the gun. At that Chamudi moved very quickly and he was reaching under the armchair when she shot him. She shot him in the chest, once, then stood back and watched him. He opened and closed his mouth several times. There was a hole in his chest and blood poured out over his red T-shirt. He looked surprised.

"This isn't—" he said and her finger tightened on the trigger again and she put one, two bullets in him, one in the chest again and one in the head. She didn't know what he had been going to say. She realised she didn't care.

She held Soli's old gun and turned it over in her hands. She'd not used a gun since her army service and that was more than twenty years ago. She looked at Chamudi but Chamudi was dead. She noted the fact but didn't feel anything about it. She put the gun away in her bag and left the room and left the flat and closed the door behind her. An old homeless man by the municipal rubbish bins was squatting awkwardly on the ground, his dirty white underpants around his ankles. He was holding a roll of toilet paper in his right hand. He didn't pay her any attention.

She caught the bus back. When she got home Rafi, and the last of her jewellery, were gone.

3

A week later she was crossing the road back home with her shopping when a man stopped her. He was about her age or a few years older, with grey short-cropped hair. He was a large man with a paunch. "Let me help you with those bags," he said.

"Thank you, but I'm fine," she said. By then she was across the road and at the door to the block of flats. The man said, "I insist." She looked behind him and saw a black four-wheel drive coming to a halt at the curb. She couldn't see through the windows. The man said, "You could invite me up for a chat, or we can go in the car, Mrs Ben-Zion. It's your choice."

She didn't say anything, she just waited him out. He smiled. Despite everything he had a nice smile. "What will it be?"

She let him take the shopping bags and opened the door. He followed her inside and up the stairs, uncomplaining. She unlocked the door to her flat and they went in.

The man put the shopping bags on the table in the kitchen and stood and surveyed her little flat. "It's very nice," he said, conversationally. "Keep your hands where I can see them, please."

"Who are you?" She'd had the drawer with her kitchen knives casually open. She closed it.

"Do you follow the news, much, Mrs Ben-Zion?"

Deborah shrugged. "It's not like you can avoid them," she said. Every day there was something, a terrorist attack or tension on the border or problems with the African immigrants or with the Bedouins or with the Settlements—anyway something.

"Read the papers?"

"Sometimes. Not often."

"Last week there was a news item—a small news item, admittedly—about a man found dead in Jaffa."

"I don't think I saw it." She was very tense. His face looked familiar, though she had never met him before. Now that she was in her own place she noticed more things about him. He wore expensive but understated cologne and an expensive and ostentatious gold watch on his left wrist. There was thick black hair on his arms. She wondered how he'd found her. Later, she figured it must have been the homeless man by the bins.

"His name was Chamudi. He wasn't anyone's favourite person. But he was working for someone."

"Who was he working for?"

"Me."

Sunlight slanted in through the window. Deborah took a deep breath. "So?" she said.

"So I was wondering why anyone would wish Chamudi dead. What did he ever do to anyone? Beyond being a piece of shit nobody loved, not even his mother."

"I'm sure she did," Deborah said, softly. He looked at her keenly. "You have a son, don't you, Mrs Ben-Zion?"

"Yes."

The silence bore its own implications. "Who are you?" Deborah said, again.

"My name is Binyamin Pardes. Benny."

The name jolted her memory. The man's face, surrounded by men, coming out of the doors of the courthouse on Weizmann Street, a beaming smile. The television cameras had followed him avidly, hungrily. A lawyer, young and bland: "My client has always maintained his innocence against these spurious allegations—"

"Oh." She began to move around the kitchen, to put away the shopping. He stood there watching her. He had the ability to stand very still. "You're an interesting woman, Mrs Ben-Zion."

"Deborah," she said, putting a bag of sugar on the top shelf above the sink.

"Here," Benny said. "Let me help you." He took the bag from her hand. For a moment his fingers touched hers. She could smell his cologne.

"Thank you."

He moved away. "Your son owed twenty thousand," he said. Deborah unpacked celery and potatoes. "Owed?"

"I'm willing to cancel the debt," he said. "But of course, you still owe me for a life." She looked at him directly, then. He had brown eyes as cold as Jerusalem in December. "I have to ask you a question," he said. "What did you feel when you put three bullets in Chamudi?"

She had to think about it, for a moment. Then she said, "Nothing. Isn't that strange? I didn't feel anything at all."

4

She didn't know why she didn't go home after the Aharoni shooting. She took the bus and the murder was already on the news, reporters had descended on the mall in north Tel Aviv and were broadcasting excitedly of another gangland assassination in the escalating fight between the families. There were so many crime families it was hard to keep track of them, co-existing in a complex network of rivalries and co-operation that shifted and changed with old grievances and new alliances.

She got off by Charles Clore Park, the southern beach where once the Arab village of Menashiya stood. She walked along the promenade and smelled the sea. A young Orthodox couple sat chastely on the rocks. Kids on skateboards rolled past, sharing a joint. Black-clad Muslim women walked past pushing prams, chatting. Deborah followed the pathway. Salt spray flew in the air from the waves pushing against the rock wall. She thought of Aharoni's face, his surprised eyes, that condescending tone when he called her *buba*, doll. All that time back when Benny found her, she told him she felt nothing when she pressed the trigger. But that was a lie. There was a heightened sense of perspective, somehow, even an exhilaration, and she knew that he knew, that he felt it too. It was a bond between them.

But still, she couldn't help thinking about it now. There was something so vulnerable in men's eyes the moment before you shot them. A dumb surprise that it was a woman. And disbelief, till the very moment, that it was happening at all. No one ever thought they were going to die. She followed the trail to Jaffa and walked away from the sea, along Salameh, where tiny factories and junk and scrap metal yards flourished like industrial flowers. Motti's was just around the corner, it was one of Benny's places and they had a working furnace where she sometimes disposed of the guns, but she didn't do it now.

Something changed and she didn't know what.

She took out her phone and called her son. "Raphael? It's me."

"Ima!" He sounded happy to hear her. His voice pinched her heart. "Are you coming for Friday dinner?"

"I don't think so, sweetheart," she said. She took a deep breath. "In fact, I was thinking—why don't you and Galit go on holiday?"

"Holiday? What, in the middle of—I mean we don't even have the m— What?"

"I have some money put aside. Wouldn't it be nice if you and Galit went away, for a while? Italy, maybe. It's so pretty this time of year."

She had gone two years before, to Rome and then Naples, with Benny.

"That's crazy," Rafi said. "I can't just leave work and—"

"Please, just think about it. I'll come by."

She hung up abruptly. She decided to do it now, before she could regret it. But it still took some time. She took another bus to the bank and took out the money, all the money that she'd saved away in a safe deposit box all those years. Then, feeling suddenly flush, she took a cab. On the radio they talked about the shooting and she asked the driver to switch it to another channel, the army's one, that played music and didn't have commercial breaks.

"You look happy," the cab driver said, apropos of nothing.

"Do I?" Deborah said. She looked at her reflection in the window. Was she happy? She saw the crow's feet at the corners of her eyes. The loose skin of her neck. She realised she had been humming without knowing it, an old song, Arik Einstein's 'Avshalom', with the refrain, "Why not, Why not now?"

She'd never thought of it before. She said, "I suppose. I suppose so."

"That's nice," the driver said.

"Yes," Deborah said. "That's nice."

She sat back against the seat and looked at her reflection in the window again, and she was smiling.

5

It must have been a month or two after Binyamin Pardes first came to see her that the job came up. She'd not seen him since the first time he came. For some time she did not hear from her son and she was sick with worry. Then Rafi called her, and he was in a rehab clinic—he had been checked in by people. He was vague on the details, but he assured her everything was fine.

So when Benny finally came again to see her she wasn't surprised. Again, he was alone. This time, he was waiting in her flat as she came in. He was sitting in the armchair by the window where Soli had liked to sit, and he was smoking a Noblesse cigarette, the cheapest, local brand. He looked up when she came in with her shopping and his eyes crinkled with amusement.

"Mr Pardes," she said, awkwardly.

"Benny, remember?" he said. He got up and helped her put away the shopping, courteously, and then he stood by the window and finished his cigarette. "Rafi is ok?" he said.

"Yes," she said.

"Good, good," he said. "He's a good kid."

"Yes."

"Listen, Mrs Ben-Zion—"

"Deborah," she said, and he laughed. "Deborah," he said. "How would you like to do me a favour?"

"What sort of favour?" she said.

"Have dinner with me."

"What?"

He laughed again. He had an easy laugh.

"Nothing fancy," he said. "I know a good fish place. What do you say?"

She said yes. Later, they went downstairs. His car was parked a block away, on a side street. The car wasn't fancy, it was one of those Japanese cars. He opened the door for her.

They drove along the sea to Bat Yam and to a little fish restaurant overlooking the sea. The food was good. Deborah found herself laughing when he told jokes, when he told her stories about famous people he knew from his nightclubs, or funny incidents from his military service. He was easy to talk to. He wasn't at all what she'd expected.

The restaurant was near-empty. It was early. As they were drinking coffee he reached for her hand under the table. His hand was dry and warm. He took her fingers in his and put them against the underside of the table and she felt something cold and hard attached to it. She didn't flinch. Benny nodded.

"A man is going to come in here in about five minutes," he said. "A short, fat man wearing a brown-coloured toupee. He has a mole on his left cheek. He runs all the drugs this side of town and I need him out of the way."

She didn't say anything. He said, "Are you listening?"

"Yes."

"Good. I'll wait in the car, around the corner. Don't run. Do it quietly. He'll have his boys with him but they don't know you." His fingers left hers and he got up, quickly. She saw him look at the proprietor and nod and the proprietor nodded back, nervously, and looked away. Then Benny was gone. She sat there over the remains of her coffee and her hand under the table, touching the gun metal, tracing the Velcro straps that held it to the underside. Five minutes later, with a final piece of baklawah swimming in honey and rose-water before her, a man came into the restaurant with two younger men behind him, who looked at her momentarily with cold hard eyes and lost interest. They swept into the room and sat by the windows, far from the door. She waited, watching them. The older man had a mole on his cheek. Salads and dips and warm pita bread arrived as soon as they sat down. She sat there for a while not thinking of anything much in particular before reaching under the table and pulling the gun free. It felt so heavy. She checked it blindly, under the table, and put it into her handbag. She got up at last and pushed the chair in and went to the toilets and waited. Presently he came, as she knew he would, puffing a little as though he found even the simple exercise tiring. He stopped when he saw her in the shadows, then smiled without warmth and said, "Are you lost, lady?"

"I think so," she said. She took out the gun and pressed it against his chest and shot him, at close range, and he didn't even react until he fell back from the impact. She shot him again at close range in the head—what in the army they used to call a confirmation kill. She didn't know how loud it was. She didn't run but she walked away and outside and she saw the two younger men still sitting by the windows—they didn't even glance her way.

6

It made her smile even now. Men were always most vulnerable on the way to the toilet. They paid no attention, they were in a hurry, being shot came as almost a relief. They'd never need to pee again. In a way, she was doing them a favour.

"Here is fine," she told the driver. He stopped the cab and she paid the fare. She walked the rest of the way to Raphael's house. He was living with Galit now, she was a nice girl. It wasn't the best neighbourhood but it wasn't the worst, either, and she could smell the sea in the distance, you were never far from the sea in Tel Aviv.

She rang the bell and Rafi answered almost immediately. She gave him a hug and pulled back and looked at him, holding his head between her hands. He was taller than her. He had Soli's eyes.

"What's going on, Ima?" he said, puzzled. She followed him in. Galit was there, in the kitchen making coffee, and she gave her a hug and a kiss, too. "I won't stay long," she promised.

"Ima, what's going on?" Rafi said again.

Deborah said, "I just thought it might be nice if you…" she hesitated. She didn't know how to put it, exactly. She could still change her mind, she knew. But she also knew she wouldn't. "I think it might be best if you went on holiday," she said. "Just for a little while."

"Why, are we in trouble?" Rafi laughed. The idea was absurd. His bad times were behind him. At least, she hoped so.

"No, I just… I have some money put aside, and you two haven't had a holiday and, well, I thought you might like to see Italy."

"Well, I suppose," Rafi said. "But—"

He and Galit exchanged a look, the way couples did. It made Deborah feel at a loss. She and Soli never spoke much between them. A look was all he needed from her to know what to do.

"Coffee, Deborah?" Galit said.

"Yes, thank you."

They drank it in the kitchen, all standing up. No one said much. It was obvious they were concerned about her. Finally she took out the envelope she'd prepared earlier, when she'd left the bank. "Here," she said. "It's all there. I want you to call me when you get to Naples."

"Naples? Ima, are you crazy? Who is going to Naples? Where *is* Naples?"

"I've never been out of the country," Galit said, dreamily.

"We can't just— What's in the envelope—" He tore it open and looked inside and then, in horror, "Where did you get this, Ima?"

"I told you, I saved it up."

"It's too much!"

"I would give you everything, Raphael. You know that."

She turned, quickly, so they wouldn't see her cry. She walked to the door. They followed her, bewildered. "Are we in some kind of trouble?" Rafi said again. She hugged him, holding him tight. "Nothing I can't handle," she whispered. She hoped she was right. She couldn't tell him they weren't in trouble, yet. But that they will be.

Outside it was hot and humid but she walked, she didn't mind walking today. It gave her time to think. All she knew was that she was tired doing men's work. She also knew there was only one way out, and that way was death.

It would have to be done right.

7

Deborah Ben-Zion and Binyamin Pardes became lovers the night she killed the man in the fish restaurant. Later, on the news, she found out his name was Modechai Saakashvili; that he was born to Jewish-Georgian parents in Bat Yam; that he was married and a father of two; and that the Tel Aviv YAMAR, or central detective unit, suspected him not only of involvement with drugs and prostitution but also to have had a direct hand in several executions carried out in the past several years, but to which no witness has ever come forward.

That evening, however, she simply walked out of the restaurant and found Benny in his car and got into the passenger seat and they drove to Jaffa, to a scrapyard. She waited in the car as Benny went in there with the gun wrapped in cloth and then he came back without the gun.

"Did you destroy it?" she said.

He didn't answer. She thought that he may have kept it, to always hold it over her. It was what they did in the movies, didn't they? But she couldn't get worked up about it if he did. It seemed to her not to matter much, anyway.

They drove away. The radio was on, playing Arab music. A weight of unspoken words lay between them in the stillness of the car. A fat moon rose above the dark sea.

"Stop the car," she said, minutes or hours later. He pulled over to a lay-by. Black waves crashed against the shore. She fumbled with the seatbelt. Why did she need a seatbelt? What did a seatbelt protect you from? It didn't stop bullets. She found that she was laughing. It was all so funny. Benny reached over and calmly helped her with the belt. She reached and took hold of his hands. She looked into his face, his eyes. She wanted to hit him. She knelt into him and kissed him on the lips. His lips were warm. He was warm all over. His big hands ran over her body. She pressed into him, urgently; he smelled of aftershave and sweat, his skin tasted of salt. They were tangled up, as hopeless as teenagers. Somehow they pushed the seats back. She fumbled with his belt. His fingers, impatient now, all but tore the buttons off her shirt. His mouth devoured her skin, her hands ran through his short, cropped hair.

Later, much later, she nestled against him, her fingers playing idly with his chest hair. Benny lit a cigarette and rolled down the window. Warm air came in carrying the smell of salt and tar. She took the cigarette from him and took a deep drag and then coughed, and he laughed, and then she was laughing too, laughing and coughing, and the lonely lights of cars travelling on the road passed them by, briefly illuminating them each time.

8

It'd been a strange day and when she got back from Raphael's place she ran the shower and washed her hair for a long time, thinking she could still take it back, still change course; that nothing was set.

And yet she had been set on this course, she realised, almost all her life. Certainly since picking up Soli's old gun, but much earlier on, a question of morality. She had been brought up to kill, trained to kill in the army, but only in service, only for an ideal, but an ideal, she realised, she never truly believed in. Perhaps most people didn't, they just did what was expected of them, what the state told them had to be done.

But she didn't want it any more. None of it.

Since that first time with Benny they had established a routine. He had given her a phone, a disposable, and she topped it up with credit once a month, using cash. Benny was the only one to have the number. He never came to her flat again. They'd meet every month or two, each time at a different place. Sometimes they went to a restaurant, then a hotel. Other times they just drove.

The second job he'd given her was a woman. She never learned what the woman had done to bring it on herself. The death never made the news, beyond a footnote in one of the newspapers about a corpse found, about six months later, buried in the dunes beyond Ashdod. Deborah remembered the woman's pale, frightened face, her blue eyes. She had been very pretty.

She stepped out of the shower and dried her hair and put on a robe. She felt calm. She picked up the phone and called him.

"I need to see you," she said.

9

Later, when it had all gone wrong and she was running for her life, holed up in that B&B in the kibbutz in the north, she still couldn't regret anything she'd done. But she was glad she'd sent Raphael away.

10

Her plan depended on the same principle that had seen her work successfully in the intervening years since Chamudi, her first. That men fatally underestimate women. Even Benny.

And she wasn't that wrong, she thought later.

They met in a bar near the Carmel market, at dusk. The bar was quiet, it catered to an older clientele. There were candles on the tables, bottles lined up in rows behind the bar. It was dark. The radio was playing, the army station again, Galgalatz.

Benny was there when she arrived. He had that habit of always getting to a meeting early, of never being caught by surprise. Once she asked him why he always travelled alone, without bodyguards like the other men of the families. And he laughed and told her he didn't need to, he always took care of himself.

Paranoia was a way of life for those men. Benny's rivals employed bombers, young serious men trained by the army, and heavy Russian bodyguards who were ex-Spetsnaz and ex-Afghanistan and who emigrated to Israel after the glasnost. The bosses changed cars and routes, kept safehouses, arrived to meetings as though they were on patrol on the Lebanese border. They always went armed: to the toilet, to synagogue, it made no difference. But most of them were afraid of a car bomb or a sniper, an ex-army job. Not of some old woman with a gun.

Benny smiled and kissed her on the cheek, like an old friend. He sat facing the door. She sat sideways, half looking at him half at the exit. "Why did you call?"

His voice was cool but she could see he was unhappy.

"I wanted to see you."

"We should not meet so soon after a job."

"I was scared. I thought I was being followed."

He shifted in the seat. Put all his attention on her. "By whom?"

"I thought it was that detective from the YAMAR again."

"Ehud Sela?" Benny said.

"Yes."

It had happened a couple of years into her work. When

she came home a man was waiting for her. She thought he might be one of Benny's men, then he flashed her a badge and asked to come upstairs.

She let him in. What could she do? She made coffee and he introduced himself as Detective Ehud Sela, of the Tel Aviv central unit, the YAMAR. He took out photos and placed them one by one on her coffee table. "Do you recognise this man?"

The photos showed Benny and Deborah together, at some beachside restaurant. Deborah shook her head. "I don't know who that is."

Detective Sela looked suddenly amused. "You have dinner with random strangers?"

"If so, what's it to you?"

"Listen to me, Mrs Ben-Zion," Sela said. "You don't look like a stupid woman, and I don't want to waste your time, or mine."

She supposed she should feel flattered. What she felt was scared.

"What does Benny Pardes have on you?" the detective said. "What does he want? I see your son—"

"You leave my son out of it!"

"Has a history," Sela said. "But nothing recent. Is he in trouble again? Is this what this is about?"

Deborah shook her head. "I can't," she said. "I won't."

She felt an overwhelming desire to talk to him; to tell him everything; but he was just a man.

"You look very comfortable with Mr Pardes, if you don't mind me saying so," the detective said. He looked at her quizzically. "Are you linked romantically?" Then he laughed and lumbered to his feet, the idea apparently ludicrous. "He's a dangerous man, Mrs Ben-Zion. I hope you know what you're doing."

He reached into a pocket. Gave her a card. "Do the right thing," he said. "Call me. Day or night. We're going to get him, sooner or later, you know."

"And there'll just be someone else in his place," she said, with sudden bitterness, and Detective Sela's face hardened. "Help us catch him. We can protect you."

She almost laughed. She escorted him to the door. He left the pictures on her coffee table. She looked at them for a long time, but she felt nothing. She threw them in the trash along with the detective's card.

Benny shook his head. "It wasn't Sela," he said. "My people watch him even more than his people watch me." He laughed. "You did fine," he said. "You did good."

She breathed out tension. "I want to go," she said. "Let's go. Now."

"All right."

He put money on the table. He'd been drinking scotch. There were people outside but not many. The market was closed and the nightlife hadn't yet started. She leaned into him as he opened the door of the car. Tasted his lips. His aftershave stung her nostrils. Her hand was in the handbag and she brought out the gun. He said, "What are you—"

The gunshot went through his side and into the back window of the car, which exploded. Benny pushed her with more force than she'd expected and she fell back and her next shot took out the front window but missed Benny. He reached for his own gun, screaming with pain and rage, and brought it up and she was on the floor, winded, and she fired low and hit his shinbone or his knee.

He screamed and fell, his back to the car, the gun still somehow in his hands, aimed at her: aimed at her head.

He pulled the trigger.

She rolled and felt the bullet pass so close, or maybe she'd imagined she could feel it. Distantly she heard people scream. His car was parked in shadow but beyond where they were a street lamp had come alive, casting down a pool of yellow light.

She desperately wanted to be in safety of the light.

For a moment they stared at each other across the distance between them.

Then they both fired.

11

She had a bag full of cash in the back of the car, two guns with ammunition, a road map on the passenger seat and the radio playing 1990s rock music—Ha'atzula, or The Nobility, some band she'd never heard of. She'd not driven in years but at least the car was an automatic.

She'd half walked, half ran from the shootout. Benny was lying at the edge of the pool of yellow light. His blood was a darker puddle around him. She thought she'd got him but she couldn't be sure.

It hadn't gone the way she'd planned.

She threw the phone he'd given her into a bin on her way

home. She didn't have long, one way or the other. When she got back to the flat she turned on the television news. "A man identified as suspected crime family head Binyamin 'Benny' Pardes has been taken to hospital in critical condition..."

She packed up a bag and took one last look at the flat. Her life depended on a coin toss, now. She rang Raphael and he answered.

"Why are you still here?" Deborah said. She could hear Galit in the background. "We're just on our way to the airport now," he said. "We're waiting for the taxi." He sounded happy, happier than she'd heard him in a long time, and she sighed with relief.

"You have your passports? The money?"

"Stop fussing, Ima," Rafi said, laughing. "We're fine."

"Are you sure you called a taxi? You have to leave plenty of time for security checks at the airport."

"We're *fine!*" He laughed again. "Is that Deborah?" she heard Galit in the background. "Thank you so much for the tickets!"

"You're welcome."

She wished them a safe trip. She hung up the phone. She stared at her flat as though she had never seen it before.

Her life depended on a coin toss, now. On how good the doctors were at the hospital.

"Police are anxious to talk to a woman, who may be a witness, who was seen speaking to Pardes shortly before the shooting."

She made sure the gas was off. The windows were closed. Wiped dust off the coffee table.

"The attempted assassination comes shortly after the successful murder of suspected gangland boss Ephraim 'Ephi' Aharoni in a Tel Aviv mall earlier this week, in what police are calling 'a possible escalation of tension in the criminal underworld'."

She switched off the television. Unplugged everything. Stared around her with a vague sense of loss, and left the flat, locking the door behind her.

Now she drove with the window down, the hired car like a beetle on the strip of dark asphalt. Tel Aviv's lights receded behind her. What *was* that music? She switched stations. Something melodic, in English, she didn't know what. It didn't matter.

The lights of the Hadera power plant ahead. After the Rabin assassination they changed its name in his honour but everyone still used the old name. It was an eyesore in the day but at night the lights carried forever. She had not been back north in years, she forgot how dark it gets out in the country. She was so used to Tel Aviv, that press of people.

Caesarea, then fish pools gleaming dark under a hesitant moon. She turned away from the seashore inland, past an Arab village with eternally uncompleted houses, then through trees and fields and solitary cars passing in the night, and all that silence: who knew the world could be so silent.

Finally she came to the dark turn to the kibbutz and took it.

*

12

Seven days and seven nights Deborah resided in that humble bed and breakfast on the kibbutz. Seven days and seven nights in which she was not once disturbed.

The kibbutz sat on top of a low hill, an island surrounded by a sea of greenery. In the day birds passed on their annual migration overhead, ancient pilgrims of a long-forgotten crusade. She'd read somewhere that over 530 species of bird transited through Israel. She was ashamed to realise she knew none of them.

On the second day she bought a common guide to bird spotting, and spent several hours identifying redbreasts, coots, egrets, buntings, nightingales and a goldfinch. Then she got bored and turned on the television.

The nights on the kibbutz were very dark and very quiet. The B&B sat on the edge of the kibbutz and from her chalet she could look out over the lights of the Arab city of Umm al-Fahm in the distance and the Hadera power plant marking the border of the sea. In daytime she saw fields of marigolds and lupines, cyclamen and irises. Their colours startled her, the air felt thick with honey.

Sometimes she saw the members of the kibbutz go past, children laughing with a football, a dog barking, a middle-aged couple taking a stroll. She saw an old man drive past in an electric buggy. She saw young mothers pushing prams.

It was very restful.

"Doctors are saying Mr Pardes has regained consciousness today, though his condition remains serious."

The television screen flickered. It was only eight in evening but outside it felt like the middle of the night. A horsey blonde woman and two grown children by the bedside. The wife wore chunky jewellery. The daughter, straight from the army, still in uniform, her hair pulled back in a ponytail. The son had his father's face. Police in the background, she thought she recognised the detective, Sela. But it was hard to tell the gangsters and policemen apart.

"Well, that's that," she said, to no one. She put on the kettle and made a cup of coffee and sat outside on the veranda, though it was getting chilly. She looked out over the lights. The coffee was sweet and strong. All around her the crickets chirped, she wondered how many of them there were. They only chirped at night.

She wondered who it would be.

13

Seven days and seven nights Deborah resided in that humble bed and breakfast on the kibbutz. Seven days and seven nights and she was not once disturbed.

On the eighth day a man came walking unhurriedly up the path to the chalet. He was not young but he was not yet old. He was like her; something in between. He was perhaps sixty years old, ten years older than her. His shoes were black and polished and his trousers rustled slightly as he walked. They were crisply ironed. His hair was white but luxurious. It was combed back. He wore a light shirt and a sober jacket and no tie. In his hands he held the day's newspaper rolled up. He came and knocked on the door.

"Who is it?" Deborah said from inside.

"Maintenance," the man said, apologetically. "I've come to check the cable, Ruth—" she was the B&B manager "—told me it was out."

"I hadn't noticed anything wrong with it," Deborah said. "Just a moment."

She came to the door and opened it a crack.

He was brutally fast. The newspaper fell to the floor and in his hands he had a Beretta M9 with a suppressor. She slammed the door on his hands, hard, as he fired. He fired two shots. The door slammed on his wrists and the gun dropped from his hands to the floor. He was already moving when the door opened fully and Deborah stepped out, her Jericho in one hand, the Beretta in the other, both raised, searching for him.

There was no one around and the kibbutz seemed asleep in the honeydew air.

She fired after him just as he disappeared around a corner and the bullets didn't catch him.

"What's your name?" she said.

From behind the corner, his voice. "It's Max."

"Max," she said. "So it's you. He mentioned you, sometimes."

"He must have trusted you."

"Yes," she said, wonderingly. "I suppose he did."

And why wouldn't he, she thought. She was his, from the moment she took up a gun she was his. Where could she go? She could never leave him. But men always overestimated their own importance.

"Max," she said. Remembering Benny in bed one night, his head against the pillow, the moonlight catching his tanned face. A cigarette in his hand. The smoke smudging the air.

"He's French," he told her. "Came over to serve in the army when he was eighteen. Afterwards he was a contact point with the Marseilles gangs, and did some cleaning up jobs for—" he mentioned the name of an old boss, now serving twenty to life. "He came to work for me, finally." He smiled and ashed the cigarette. "He's old school, Max."

Unspoken on her lips: Then what do you need me for.

She was pressed against the wall, the guns raised, picturing Max on the other side. Or was he moving? Was he even now doubling back, hoping to catch her by surprise?

"How did you know I was coming?" he said.

"Your shoes, Max. No one here wears city shoes."

He laughed. "So you were his ace in the hole?" he said. She gripped the guns. Was he moving away? Was he waiting? She edged towards the corner.

There were ten chalets clumped together in the B&B, single-storey wooden buildings, like something assembled out of an Ikea catalogue. Pine trees dotted the pathways between the buildings. It was low season, a weekday. Only onc of the other chalets was occupied, by a couple of bird watchers from Tel Aviv, and they'd gone down the hill earlier that morning.

"I suppose I was," she said.

"So why?" Max said.

"Why what?"

"Why did you do it?"

"I quit," she said, and she pushed herself off the wall and stepped quickly around the corner and levelled the guns.

"Nice try," Max said. His voice came from the veranda.

At that moment she heard the annoying jingle of a bicycle bell. She turned and there was a boy riding past, ringing the bell. He looked over curiously, stopped, and got off the bike.

"What are you doing?" he said.

Deborah froze. The world was still. She could hear Max moving, unseen.

"Are those guns?" the boy said.

"We're just playing," Deborah said.

"Who are you playing with?"

"My friend."

"Well, where is he?"

"He's hiding."

"Are you playing hide and seek?" the boy said.

"Yes. Yes, we are."

"Is that a real gun?"

"Get lost, kid!"

The voice came from somewhere behind and overhead. The boy blinked resentfully.

"Why should I?" he said.

Deborah gripped the gun, her hand white where the blood was blocked. "Why don't you go off," she said, gently. The boy looked into her face, then stuck out his tongue and got back on his bike. He rang his bell insistently as he rode off towards the kibbutz houses.

"He's gone," Deborah said. She sighed with relief.

"Good," Max said.

His voice came from directly overhead.

She pushed from the wall and raised her head and her guns at the same time.

Max was standing above her on the chalet's roof. He had a gun in his hand. They fired almost at the same time.

The bullet caught her in the arm and spun her. It felt like being punched by a giant.

She stumbled back, the gun wavering. It seemed to happen simultaneously, she was aware of a dark shape like a sooty falcon (which was one of the 530 species of bird in her book) swooping down, and she cried out, in fear and pain.

Max hit the ground. His shirt no longer looked perfectly tailored, the crease in his trousers was gone. Deborah could still hear the boy's bell dinging faintly as he rode off. She sat back heavily, dropping to the ground, one arm useless, the other still holding a gun. Max lay still on the ground. Then he shifted, his hand edging with the gun still held in his fingers, the barrel pointing at her.

She said, "Don't."

14

She tied a tourniquet on her arm above the wound, stemming the blood. She dragged Max's body across the grass, one-handed, holding him by his lapels. He was surprisingly light; she thought he must have hollow bones, like a bird's. He left a trail of blood on the grass. Her whole body hurt and she was losing blood too. Pulling him up the few stairs to the door was the hardest thing she'd ever done. Once inside, she shut the door and sat down on a chair, breathing hard.

Max moaned. It was a terrible sound, like a tortured cat. He blinked. Ran his tongue around his dry lips. "Water," he said.

"You'll have to wait."

"Benny said you were good."

"Good at what?" she said. "Good at what!"

"Good at not dying." Whimpered with the pain. He looked a mess. It was a miracle he was still alive. She sat on the chair breathing hard.

"What now?" Max said, from far away.

"I don't know."

"Help me," he said.

She came back from wherever she went.

Got up, though it took everything. Went over to him and knelt down and ran her good hand over his body. She made a small pile of guns on the kitchen table. Her Jericho, his Beretta, and the gun he'd shot her with made three. He had another gun strapped to his ankle, a Browning .22, and a Bowie knife, like Rambo. He screamed when she touched his ankle. He'd taken a shot in the chest and broke his leg in the fall: his leg lay at an unnatural angle.

She tried to remember her army training. Went to the kitchen and got plastic shopping bags and some tape. Her bullet must have gone through his lung. She taped the plastic on his chest and back, momentarily sealing the wound. "Stop screaming," she said. "Someone will hear."

He bit his lips until they bled. "I need a doctor," he said.

"I know."

He blinked. "What are you going to do?"

"Take a shower."

She left him there. He would manage, or not. In the bathroom she ran cold water and put her hand under it. She needed a doctor too, she knew. She put her head under the cold water and gasped when it hit her.

When she came out she saw Max had dragged himself upright enough to lean his back against the door. His hands were by his side. He looked at her. He looked ridiculous with the shopping bags taped to his bony chest.

"So," Max said.

"So."

"Got anything to drink?"

"I don't really drink."

"You Sabras," he said, but without bitterness. His face was locked in a painful grimace. She knew he was trying hard not to scream. He was covered in sweat. His chest rose and fell rapidly.

She sat back in the chair and cradled the Beretta in her good hand. Her hair was wet.

"Your jacket is ruined," she said.

"Could I have some water?"

"Bullet could have torn your gut," she said, dispassionately. "I'm afraid it's nil by mouth."

"My phone's in my jacket pocket," Max said.

"So?"

"You could call him."

"Why would I do that, Max?"

"It was easy enough to find you, Deborah." He sighed. "How hard do you think it will be to find Raphael and that girlfriend of his?"

She froze. Max's lips moved like they were trying to

drink from a glass that wasn't there. They looked rubbery, like whale flesh.

"Galit," she said. "Her name is Galit."

"Call Benny," he said. "It's too late for you. But it's not too late for Rafi."

"Raphael's away," she said. "He's safe."

"In Italy?" His eyes were sad. She looked away. Looked into nothing. "Rafi?" she whispered. It was the first time she'd called him that. When she closed her eyes there was nothing but darkness.

"I need a doctor," Max said. "Call Benny. Make things right."

She opened her eyes and saw him. Her hand gripping the silenced Beretta. Though guns were never silent.

"Someone would have heard the shots," Max said. "We haven't got long."

"I've got long enough," she said. She looked at him down the barrel of the gun.

Max's chest rose and fell, rose and fell. The plastic bags made a weird rustling sound.

"My hair," Max said. "My hair."

"It looks fine," Deborah said, absently. "It looks good, Max."

A bird landed on the windowsill and peered inside curiously. She thought it might be a sparrow or a wagtail. She didn't really know anything about birds. Outside the window she now saw the damn kid was cycling back on his bike. The gun felt warm in her hand.

The kid was still ringing that goddamned bell for all it was worth when she pulled the trigger.

BORROWED TIME

R. J. ELLORY

I paused, right there in the doorway of the bookshop. To my left and right the street was empty. During the night it had rained, and the pavements gave off a dull gunmetal sheen. Sounds were muted, as if coming from a distance. I heard voices—distant words—but could make no sense of them.

I knew that something was wrong. I could not identify what it was. I seemed to be looking through the prism of the past at something that was trying so very hard to be forgotten.

And she was there among my thoughts. Elise. So many things we had shared returned to me. This was where she and I had met. Remembering her face was like remembering a dream.

I opened the door of the bookshop and stepped inside.

I breathed in that atmosphere. That unmistakeable haunt of paper and ink, of every tale ever told, of every thought committed by hand or typewriter or printing press. So many stories, so many worlds to discover.

So many books, so little time.

The memory of everything was here, as if the walls and the floor had absorbed fragments of my own history and preserved them As if I could not be trusted with my own memories, and so they had been stored here—safe, in perpetuity, never again to become faded or jaundiced with the passage of time.

Everything I once was, everything I had become was right here in this little bookshop in the suburbs of Paris.

I looked out through the window. The street was still empty, though curved and twisted through the aged glass.

I had returned from Morocco. It had been a brief photographic assignment, the repatriation of displaced Algerians to their homeland. I was commissioned by the *Sunday Times* magazine, and though the photos were moving and profound, though the faces I had captured would join the ranks of all the others that haunted me, I knew that the world was already desensitised and inured to the plight of such people. The lost, the homeless, those stricken with famine and plague, the Cambodians who fled the Khmer Rouge, the Ugandans oppressed under the tyranny of Idi Amin, the masses whose human rights were abused as if no such rights existed—I had witnessed all of it through the viewfinder of my camera. The spilling of so much innocent blood.

At the beginning, it had been a crusade. That word was

in my thoughts as I followed endless conflicts across unforgivable terrains. Seeking refuge in makeshift shelters and burned-out buildings, I had witnessed the slaughter of fathers and sons, mothers and daughters. For me the worth of a human life was shown to be of no real worth at all. Crusade. It meant that you were marked with a cross. Branded.

But I became blind to the horror. I lost myself. A man witnesses sufficient crimes against humanity, and somehow he loses a part of his own. I was no longer surprised by any inhuman act. I sought danger. I chased the ghosts of the dead. I woke up each morning believing that this would be my last, and then the day would close, the light would fade over some other battlefield, and I would understand I had made it through. I would feel not only a sense of relief, but also a strange sense of disappointment. Borrowed time. I lived on borrowed time, and yet I did not know from whom it had been borrowed, nor how to repay it back, nor what charge would be made for the loan.

People told me I lived wildly, dangerously, as if testing the very patience of God.

I would smile and say, "Tell me now, is there any other way to live?"

They would smile as if they understood, but they did not.

There were moments of profound importance, moments when I really believed I had accomplished something of value. These were scattered randomly through my life. Much of my time was spent waiting for something I could neither predict nor determine. It created an emotional vacuum, a hollowness, an abyss. I thought of Nietzsche: "And if you gaze long into an abyss, the abyss will also gaze into you." The hall of mirrors folds in upon itself; you see what you believe is there, and reality becomes something else that others experience.

Some of us walk a dark road expecting to find light at the end. I was still walking, still looking. The only lights I saw were muzzle flashes.

And then I came here. Paris. This little bookstore in a suburb I did not know. It was an escape, a day or two in the city of lights before I returned to London. I wanted to breathe air that was tainted neither by the stench of blood nor the acid of cordite. I wanted to drink red wine in small cafés, eat oysters and entrecôte, smoke bitter French cigarettes and convince myself that I would once again recover my sanity, my imagination, my sense of humour.

Perhaps I was fooling myself; perhaps my mind had finally slipped its moorings and I had drifted into the open sea of delusion. It did not matter, and I did not care. I was feeling different things, and that was all that was important.

I just walked the streets, camera in hand, snapping photos of people, places, moments that would never be repeated. I was Cartier-Bresson, Capa, Doisneau. I was in a daze, my thoughts numbed and broken. I wondered if some people went crazy simply because that was the only place left to go.

And then I stumbled upon this doorway, and through it found the very bookshop in which I now stood. It was as if nothing less than Fate had guided my feet. I stepped inside, seduced, as always, by the promise of the written word. Even as a child, I was never without a book. "The best pictures are on the radio," my grandmother would say, and I believed her. The mind's eye. The power of imagination. The way in which we can take a word, a sentence, a paragraph, and from it spin images and emotions, sensations and feelings, and a million other human realities that are as real as anything we could touch or taste.

In a book the people look just how we wish them to look. They smile the way we want them to smile. Their voices are the voices we want to hear. When they succeed we feel their happiness, and when they grieve we grieve with them. We mourn their loss, we celebrate their passions, we live some small part of their lives within our own. Rare is it to read a book that does not change the way we think about something, however insignificant it might be.

Had I known then that this moment would be the moment my entire life would change, I would never have believed it.

But it happened.

I remember what I was wearing. A dark reefer coat like a longshoreman. Suede boots, scuffed and dirty. My hair was unkempt. I was unshaven. I had taken a room at the Hotel Scribe, simply because of its history. It was there— on the night of August twenty-fifth 1944—that members of the Press Corps had gathered to record the liberation of the city. Bob Capa, Ernest Hemingway, William Shirer, Lee Miller, Noel F. Busch and so many more. I wanted to stay somewhere meaningful, somewhere once frequented by those as crazy as myself. But I had not slept well, perhaps haunted by the ghosts of those who had slept there before me, my mind tumbling back and forth through things seen, things imagined, the violent collisions of humanity that represented so much of my life.

I lived in places where there were no laws, only agreements, and yet those agreements were broken with the same significance as superstitious men break spent matches. Thoughtless; a matter of routine. People spent their entire lives trying to make sense of life, and then died ignorant and exhausted.

I had taken a book from the shelf, unthinking, unaware.

"You enjoy this kind of book?"

I glanced sideways, uncertain whether it was I who was being addressed.

She smiled. She was French, no doubt. Her accent, her manner, her dress.

"Sorry?"

She smiled again. "You are English."

"I am, yes."

"You read French?"

I looked down at the book. *Dix heures et demie du soir en été* by Marguerite Duras.

"No," I said.

"Perhaps it is a gift for your French mistress," she said.

I laughed. "I do not have a French mistress."

"You know what this book is about?"

I shook my head.

"It is about an alcoholic woman who is trying to get her husband to have an affair with someone. They are trapped in a hotel in Spain. There is a murderer on the loose. There are flamenco dancers and a suicide and then the woman disappears altogether and no one can find her."

"You should write blurbs," I said.

"Blurbs?"

"The back of the book. It tells you what the book is about."

She laughed.

"What is your name?" I asked.

"Elise. What is your name?"

"My name is Robert, but everyone calls me Dante."

"Why?"

"It's a long story. It has to do with always finding myself in Hell."

"So why are you selecting a book in a language you do not speak?"

"I wasn't thinking about it. My mind was elsewhere."

"Where was your mind, Dante?"

I frowned. I could not understand why she was asking me such questions.

"I am interested," Elise said, as if she had perceived my thought.

"Sorry?"

She laughed. It was a beautiful, infectious sound. "Only the English do this."

"What?"

"Apologise all the time. You must have done some terrible things to feel that it is always necessary to apologise."

I didn't know what to say.

"I am interested," she said again. "Your expression. I could see you were asking yourself what this crazy French girl was doing, asking you these personal questions, invading your careful English manners and making you uncomfortable."

"I am not uncomfortable," I said.

"But you are curious."

"Well, yes, to be honest. I am curious."

Elise stepped a little closer. "You look like you are carrying the world on your shoulders," she said.

"Not the whole world," I said. "Just the heavier part of it."

"Do you live here in Paris?"

"No, I live in London."

"And why are you here?"

I turned and looked at her, perhaps for the first time. She was not beautiful—certainly not in the classic sense—but she possessed a manner that was both self-assured and charismatic. That was where her beauty resided, in her presence, her persona, her very being. And yet in her eyes I could still see the child that she'd once been. Even though there were merely a few years between us, seducing her would have felt like a crime.

She looked at me unerringly, as if seeing right through me. For some unknown reason, I knew that such a woman could never be lied to.

"I am on the way home from North Africa. I am a photographer." I showed her the camera that I had slung over my shoulder, as if needing to prove my credentials.

"What were you photographing?"

"Human misery," I said.

"And this is what you do? You travel the world and take photographs of the misery of others?"

"Yes. War, civil conflict, famine, natural disasters, epidemics. The worst the world can offer."

"And you carry the ghosts with you even when you leave?"

I looked away towards the window. People were now walking in the street. As they passed the aged glass of the store's façade they too changed shape, became twisted in the middle, their heads elongated. They became caricatures of themselves, and all the more interesting because of it.

Time stopped. Everything stopped. There had never been any other moment than this, and there never would be.

"Yes," I said. "I carry all the ghosts."

"This is a difficult life."

"Perhaps."

"Why do you do it?"

I shrugged. "Why does anyone do what they do? Because they believe in it, because they think it's a good idea, because they want to feel that they matter. Maybe we all share the same fear, to walk the earth unseen, unknown, unremembered."

"No," she said. "We do not. Some of us wish to remain unknown, unseen and unremembered."

"So what do you do?" I asked.

"I am a nurse," she replied.

"Then you must also see some terrible things."

"Yes," she said. "But I do not follow it. Such things come to me."

"And they stay with you?"

"Sometimes."

"And how do you deal with it? How do you exorcise the ghosts?"

"I talk to people. I live each day as if there will be no tomorrow. I try to be unafraid of everything. I try always to do things I have never done before. I remind myself that the dark corners of humanity are small and difficult to find, and once you find them you do not need to stay there."

I smiled. "I think I could learn something from you."

"Then put the book back and we will go and have a glass of wine together. Perhaps I will teach you how to exorcise your ghosts."

She smiled. I knew I would not hesitate.

She left the bookshop. I followed her without question.

I loved her in a way that I did not understand.

I loved her for all that she was, and all I imagined she could be.

I loved her despite myself.

For a year and a month I stayed in Paris. I did not think of war and death and famine. I thought of life and light and Sunday morning streets, of fresh bread and good wine, of bistros and brasseries and late night walks along the banks of the Seine. I learned to love the quiet winter light of this city. I learned how to smile. I remembered how to laugh. I rediscovered the meaning of being alive. In truth, I believed that I had never been so alive as when I was with her.

I worked for magazines and newspapers. I even went to the hospital where Elise worked and cultivated the finer arts of surgical photography. I earned good money, and we rented an apartment together in Montparnasse. We thrived among the ghosts of Duchamp, Apollinaire, Varvoglis and Giacometti.

And then the dreams came back. They came back with fingers like tendrils of mist and they dragged at my soul. They worked their way into the veins and arteries of my body and they found my heart. They pulled at me like the song of sirens, and they whispered words that challenged all that I was, all that I had become, all that I had ever hoped to be.

And I could not escape.

"But why?" Elise asked.

I shook my head. I did not know. The seed had been planted in my mind. It had grown in the fertile soil of my imagination and was now bearing fruit. Perhaps the fruit was sour and blemished, but the nourishment it offered possessed its own strange capacity to seduce and cajole me into that all-too-familiar addiction.

"It won't be for long," I said. "A month is nothing."

"Africa."

"Yes."

"Civil war."

"Yes."

"I thought you had given up on this life," she said.

"I did. However, it seems that this life has not given up on me."

"I fucking hate you and I can't understand why you are doing this to me."

"I love you, Elise."

"Love? You love me? You don't understand this word, even less the action. To be loved is to give everything. You have to let yourself be reached. Every part of you."

"There are things about me that you do not need to know. Things I never want you to know."

"Then you will always be lonely. You see that, don't you?"

"I have booked a return flight."

"I cannot talk to you anymore."

"I understand."

Elise sneered. "No, you don't."

"I am trying to understand."

"Go back to your hell, Dante. I think that's where you belong."

We fought for a week. She screamed at me, and then she cried, and then we fucked like we were trying to climb inside one another and never escape. I drank cheap cognac and I smoked cigarettes and I got sick. She told me I deserved it. She told me that sometimes she wished me dead. Then she would hold me and kiss me and cry and tell me she was sorry for thinking such terrible things, but it was my own fault because I was an English whore's son and that she could never forgive me.

And then she told me she forgave me and made me promise than I would come back.

I promised.

"Whatever happens, I will come back," I said, "and I will stay with you forever."

I left in May. The light of Paris was that of painters, sculptors, photographers.

I chased the ghosts of the living and the dead across a bleak and bloody terrain. For the first time I felt that I was looking for something that could never be found. Or perhaps, if I found it, it would be something empty and of no value. I could not permit myself to think such a thing, so I tried not to think at all.

I sent pictures back to the Sunday Times in England, to magazines in France, Italy, America, Spain. I received a telegram. I had been nominated for the Robert Capa Gold Medal. I wrote letters to Elise. Many of them. I told her that I loved her, that I had needed to do this—not only to prove something to myself, but also to remind myself of why I did not need to do this anymore. I told her I was coming home, and this time I was staying, and I would never leave again. I believed my own words. I believed myself. Beyond everything, this is what Elise had returned to me: a certainty in my own thoughts that I thought I had lost forever.

The bookshop, I said. *Remember? The one where we met. That's where I want us to meet again. It will be like starting our love affair all over again.*

I mailed that letter. I could see myself standing in that doorway of the little shop in the suburb of Paris, and my heart swelled with love and every imaginable promise for the future.

Every shelf carried a wealth of books, and every book carried a wealth of voices, and every voice was a life all its own, and we belonged to that, and it belonged to us, and we would begin our second life together from the very same place.

And so here I am.

I stand in the doorway. That unmistakeable, unforgettable atmosphere. The dust, the pages, the stories that wait so patiently to be discovered. They are all here, and will be here forever.

I find a quiet corner, and I wait for Elise. I am early. Despite all that I have lost, my English manners remain steadfast and true.

A man arrives with a box. He sets it down and has a discussion with one of the booksellers. Together they arrange a table, set out some chairs. From the box they take books and arrange them across the table. They cover the books with a deep burgundy cloth. People start to arrive. They seem reserved, reticent. I do not understand what is happening.

No one seems to pay the slightest attention to me. No one asks me why I am there or if I need any assistance.

A man with a camera arrives, then two more. They talk with the proprietor. Someone sets up a light that illuminates the table at the far end of the room.

More people arrive. There must be thirty or forty.

I am puzzled.

And then they close the door.

The proprietor stands ahead of the table of books that have been laid out, and then he draws back the burgundy cloth.

I see my face on the cover of the book.

"Ladies, gentlemen," he says. "We are here for the release of this collection of photographs by the celebrated war correspondent, known only as Dante. The driving force of this project, as you all know, was Elise Lévêque, Dante's confidante, lover and muse. It is as a result of her appearance in his life that the later period of Parisian street photography was inspired, and it was here that they met, in this very bookshop. Hence we are so very proud to be presenting this book to you, a very select audience, and to acknowledge and celebrate the lives of two extraordinary people."

I step forward to speak. I want to know what is happening. I do not understand. I have not published any photographs. I do not know what this man means when he says that Elise has been the driving force of this project. What project?

I open my mouth to speak.

Dante.

I turn at the sound of my name.

Elise looks back at me. She smiles, that smile so unforgettable.

What is happening? I ask her.

She presses her finger to her lips. *Quiet,* she says.

She looks back towards the proprietor.

"And so," the proprietor says, "we commemorate the life of Dante, killed so tragically in Africa just five months ago, just one day before he was due to return to Paris to be reunited with Elise. And Elise, so devoted, so heartbroken, who threw herself with everything she possessed into making this book a reality. No sooner had the first copies of this exceptional volume rolled off the presses than she took her own life, hoping perhaps that she would follow Dante to wherever Death had taken him. We salute them as lovers, as soulmates, as artists, as human beings, and we recognise in them the true spirit of passion and adventure that epitomised their lives."

I turn and look at Elise.

Everything I had become was right here in this little bookshop in the suburbs of Paris.

You promised me you would come back, she says. *And you did.*

I breathe slowly. My mind is clear and calm.

And this time it's forever.

I feel her hand in mine. I close my eyes.

I am no longer living on borrowed time.

The debt has been paid.

IN THE BELLY OF THE BEAST

JOHANA GUSTAWSSON

Translated from the French by Maxim Jakubowski

Anna gazed in fascination at the hand flattened against the door. It was stretched wide open like a sun, a wedding ring strangling the ring finger, a pink scar running from the thumb to the forefinger.

Anna turned her head and swallowed, as she looked into the windowless room. A man, sitting behind a table, offered her a dry, tired, reluctant smile. Collapsed into the chair, he looked as if he was about to fall asleep.

The assistant moved her weight from one foot to another and sighed heavily. Anna brushed against her sweat-drenched uniform, its buttons straining against her prominent chest. *"Look, darling, are you going to step on it? I'm not holding this door open forever for you, you know!"* That's what she wanted to say to her, the woman with the scar and the malevolent expression.

"Mrs Hellenström?"

The man's voice was as weary as his smile. Lingering, like a slimy kiss on the cheek, or the lips.

Anna acknowledged him, pulling at her jacket.

He pointed to a chair facing his. Inviting her to come forward, to sit in front of him. To begin the conversation. Or, rather, his confession. It was a matter of just a few metres before deliverance. To cross the metaphorical threshold. Then it would become easy.

As it closed on itself, the door blew a gust of air in the direction of Anna's back.

A gust of air... fresh... breathing... breath... last breath...

That's the way she functioned: by word association. A mental game that allowed her to map out a person's mind in just a few seconds. What would the fat scarred woman have said if they had begun to discuss her damaged hand? The scar? The sense of touch? Scratching? Soothing?

Anna wetted her dry, raspy, cracked lips.

"Should I ask them to bring you a glass of water?"

"No. No. Thank you, Inspector."

The man ran the tip of his fingers across his clean-shaven chin without looking away from her.

Anna tried not to grimace. The contact of the nails against the hard bristle: a deafening, indecent sound.

"Could we go over what you have told my colleague again, please?"

"From the beginning?" she enquired, crossing her legs under the chair.

"From the beginning, yes."

Anna thought of the first thing that had crossed her mind: how were they going to transport her? Her wet hair plastered against her skull, like a swimmer emerging from the water, her skin streaked with red, her arms hanging loose, the ambulance staff's shoe soles splashing through the pool of water surrounding the bathtub. Would they lay her out on the stretcher before covering her with a sheet? No, the material would absorb all the blood and stick to the body. Would they zip her into a body bag? One of those wide black bags you saw in crime movies, which looked just the right size to carry ski equipment. They would zip it closed over her bloodless face, catching a few stray hairs between the zip, a blond and greasy clump like an unwelcome spike of corn against a lacquered head.

Lacquered... organised... clean... polished... waxy...

The inspector drew back into his seat, prompting Anna to sigh heavily and begin.

"I... She had been unstable of late. Although she hadn't shown any previous signs of it, before."

She loudly gritted her teeth together.

"Before what, Anna?"

He'd asked her to start again from the beginning. But the beginning had actually been set in motion a long time prior to the initial signs of uneasiness.

"Maybe I should go back further in time, before she became ill. Otherwise I won't be able to explain things properly. All I would be doing is stating the facts. And everyone will believe she is guilty, responsible for her actions, when of course she clearly wasn't. Do you understand, Inspector?"

He nodded in acquiescence, edging his glasses up across the bridge of his nose with a single digit. His forefinger brushed across the lens, leaving a greasy print.

"She was an accountant and worked from home. She seldom saw her clients in person. She wasn't very sociable. Something of a loner. Like Tomas, her partner. Both were true homebodies."

Anna's lips sketched a smile.

"How did she meet him?"

"In high school. I would like some water, actually."

The inspector raised his arm, like a customer hailing a waiter. Anna started and brought her hands to her face. The wide one-way glass wall reflected a terrible image: her hollowed cheeks like craters, her fringe swept to the side unveiling her lined forehead, her eyes puffy from lack of sleep. Guilt was eating her from the inside. Sorrow too.

Anna adjusted the collar of her Liberty blouse and took a first sip to wet her lips. The taste of blood flooded through her mouth.

"You were telling me about her partner."

"Yes, sorry, Inspector."

She shook her head to banish the memories of the bathtub. The water red and thick as gravy.

"I... They'd been living together for eight years. He's an estate agent."

Anna pulled off the elastic band holding her hair back. With the tip of her fingers, she ordered the strands layered across her scalp and formed them into a ponytail.

"He... He didn't see anything. He didn't understand that her weariness connected with something deeper."

Anna swept her hand across the top of the table.

"But it's not his fault, he's not a bad guy. Men just don't have the emotional talent necessary to read a woman's signs of distress. Or anyone else's, for that matter."

"Did it begin with him?"

"No. Why... Oh, sorry, Inspector."

She smiled sadly at the table.

"They say that trauma and fears have their origin in childhood, don't they? This must certainly be the case, in his case as well as hers, I mean."

Childhood... roots... parents... transmission... unrooted...

"Are you thinking of anything in particular?"

Anna swallowed. A stabbing pain radiated from her throat all the way to her ears. She looked up at her interlocutor; he appeared to be more alert. He must have reached the limits of his weariness and was now functioning on his energy reserves. But it worked for him, he now appeared attentive and keen. On the other hand, though, under the fearful yellow light bathing the room, the stain on his lens shadowed his right eye.

Her eyes moved to the one-way mirror. Dear God, she looked a mess, as if she had just stepped out of bed. She longed to be herself again! She suddenly noticed a sort of lump deforming her front: a fold under her jacket. She'd buttoned Monday against Wednesday, as her mother would have put it.

As Mummy would have put it.

"I was thinking of my mother, Inspector. What happened to his mother?"

He remained silent, his head slightly to one side, his forearms supported by the elbow rests of his chair, as if body and face belonged to two separate entities altogether.

"His mother grew up with a handicapped sister. Mentally retarded. Truly feeble-minded. The sort of person that if you asked her to call the lift, would shout out 'Lift!', if you see what I mean."

Anna interrupted herself. The man had now adjusted his sitting stance and was rubbing his fingers into his forehead.

"I'm not taking the piss, Inspector, not at all. What I told you did actually happen: she genuinely cried out 'lift' when she was… Anyway, his mother had to endure this painful situation and did so with much difficulty. Her parents would not allow her to do anything her sister couldn't, which didn't leave her with much to act on; no afternoons with girlfriends, no going out or innocent relationships with boys. She lived as a recluse until her sister drowned at the age of seventeen. You don't get over such a trauma overnight, Inspector, and it took her years before she could feel comfortable in society. It's a bit like her sister had retained a hold over her life, even following her death. Tragic, don't you think?"

"It certainly is, Anna."

He, in turn, took a sip of water.

"You can imagine the consequences. Being socially handicapped, but unable to leave the home where she had been held back, she married the first man to come along. And quickly became pregnant."

Anna suddenly closed her eyes. A migraine had dug its claws into her temples and the brutal pain held her cranium in a vice.

"You never tried to see if she was alive? To take her pulse? Touch her? Hold her hand?"

Anna straightened in her chair. He was judging her. He'd come forward, leaning across the table, his hands held flat down on its surface, gazing at her, his eyes aligned with her forehead. Weighing her inertia.

"No, I didn't try to. No. I stayed by the side of the bathtub, waiting. For help. Even though I knew she was dead."

"What made you think she was?"

This time, he was looking straight into her eyes. He wasn't judging her, he appeared to be accusing her. She jumped out of her chair, the noise of its scratching against the floor drowning his words.

"Anna, please sit down again."

"I don't appreciate your tone of voice, Inspector! I could have remained at home, but here I am! I'm trying to salvage her reputation! Her conscience! And here you are accusing me! You're saying I should have... Tried... Attempted what, in truth? I called for help, the emergency services, didn't I? I was at her place even though I shouldn't have been! The authorities took a long time to get there, it's not my fault if..."

"Anna, I'm not accusing you of anything. Absolutely not. And I'm grateful you came here tonight. Please, would you sit down again."

Anna stood behind the chair, gripping its back, her eyes fixed on her own hands.

"I just stood there, Inspector. Watching her body in the water. Listening to the silence. That silence was truly terrifying. As if I were the one inside the bathtub. Right then, all I could think of was of that mother who had spoken so eloquently on the radio about the death of her son. She'd stated that the silence was the worst part of it. No more small footsteps rushing down the stairs, no more crystal laughter, or sounds mimicking fire engine horns or the triumphant victory roar of pirates, no more loud TV or tears, toys colliding or plates shattering down on the floor, or bath water splashing. No more sounds of life."

She stepped around the chair and sat down again.

"They laid her out on the stretcher. Here and there, her skin was covered by a brown film, not unlike the deposit at the bottom of a bottle of wine. When they folded her arms across her body, one of her hands fell onto her thigh, as if attempting to conceal her nakedness. Could I have some water?"

He raised his hand.

"What did you do next?"

"What I did? What do you mean?"

"You went to the police? You went home?"

"I went back home."

This time around, it was a young man who brought in the water. No longer two plastic glasses, but two small bottles. Anna unscrewed one of them and began sipping from the top of the bottle.

"Maybe I should continue with his mother's story, no?" she suggested, setting the bottle down.

"If you wish to do so, Anna."

"You're not interested in the story?"

"Of course, it helps me understand what happened. But I also realise you must be tired and might prefer continuing later."

She opened her mouth and promptly closed it again.

"Yes, Anna?"

She peered at him with a look of discomfort.

"Maybe you're the one who is tired?"

He smiled back at her. Wrinkles stood out in the corners of his eyes. He took his spectacles off, picked a handkerchief from his pocket and negligently cleaned his lenses.

"It's true, I am tired. Night work doesn't agree with me. I've never been able to get used to it, I must confess. But I'm here until seven tomorrow morning and I'm happy to listen to the story of Marta's mother. Her name was Linn, wasn't it?"

Anna nodded, agreeing.

"Do you want something to nibble on before you begin? I'm sorry, but I haven't had anything to eat and I'm starving."

"No, thank you, Inspector."

"Do you mind awfully if I do eat something?"

"Not at all, please do."

He never even had to raise his arm. The young man almost immediately walked into the room, with a couple of slices of polar bread with cheese and a cup of coffee on a tray.

"You're sure you don't want anything, Anna?"

"No, thank you."

"Not even a coffee?"

"No, I'm fine, thanks."

He quickly ate the first slice of bread and tentatively sipped his coffee.

"Can I begin, Inspector?"

"Yes, please go ahead, Anna. You were telling me that Linn married the first man to come around and quickly became pregnant."

Anna's lips broadened into a grateful smile.

"Indeed."

"What happened afterwards?" he asked, biting into the second slice of bread and cheese.

"The pregnancy was dreadful. Like a descent into hell. Linn was certain she was about to give birth to a handicapped child, just like her sister. She was convinced that the nightmare she had endured all the way through to adulthood was about to repeat itself. That yet again, she would become alienated. That someone was about to destroy her life, as her sister had. She even... She even thought of interrupting her pregnancy. Aborting."

"But she didn't?"

"No. She couldn't summon the inner strength... To rid herself of it."

"Was it a boy or a girl?"

"I was just referring to the baby. 'It' for *the* baby."

"Was the baby born handicapped?"

"Not at all, no. It was in perfect health."

"And this child was Marta?"

"Yes, Inspector, it was Marta."

He sat back in the chair, which leaned backwards, and he balanced the coffee cup over his knee.

"Anna, who told you about Linn's life? Was it Linn herself? Marta? Or maybe Tomas?"

"Linn."

"You were close?"

Anna's gaze moved from his hands to the one-way mirror.

"Were we close? I'd say so, yes, for her to be able to tell me something of such an intimate and disturbing nature. We must certainly have been. To be capable of confessing to someone you were planning to get rid of an unborn baby, it requires a measure of trust, I reckon."

"How did Marta's childhood unfold?"

Anna shook her head.

"It's difficult to say. I'm not sure I'm in a position to properly answer your question. All I know is that Linn lived in constant terror that anything could happen to her child. She was a very protective mother, suffocating even. What's ironic about it is that she was repeating with her children the exact same process her own parents made her go through: the feeling of being locked up, the depersonalisation, that sensation of giving up on life. Somewhere inside her, she was conjuring all those factors, for different reasons altogether, but recreating them nonetheless."

"What sort of impact did this have on Marta?"

"She inherited all those seeds sown by her grandmother. She kept on deliberately destabilising herself."

"But you were telling me earlier that her instability was a more recent factor and that she had previously displayed no signs of it?"

"That's correct. What was subconsciously happening inside her was not visible to her or anyone in her close circle of acquaintances. Tomas didn't see it coming. Nor Linn."

"What about you, Anna?"

She swept the flat of her hand across the tabletop, as if wiping off dust.

"Neither did I. I too didn't catch the signs that might have set off an alarm. You know, it's a bit like when you have debilitating migraines and the doctor tells you that your headaches are due to stress; he advises you to take up sport, or meditation, and six months later they discover you have a brain tumour the size of a peach. Initially, I thought her tired, then later tense and worried. It's when she began to show signs of depression that I realised something was radically wrong. Something was off. But it was already too late."

"Why?"

Anna moved her head from side to side to blow aside the strands obscuring her eyes.

"Because she was already pregnant. Four months in."

She pulled on the flap of her jacket, which was bunching up around her waist.

"She hadn't realised she was. Her periods had always been irregular and no specific symptoms had manifested themselves."

"You said it was too late? I don't understand why you say that."

Anna appeared surprised.

"Because it's too late to have an abortion when you're four months down the line."

"So it was her state of pregnancy that was causing her general distress?"

"Yes, her pregnancy reopened all the family scars inhabiting her. She had no wish to be colonised by something that was going to consume her from the inside. She came to that understanding when she learned she was pregnant; she had never thought that carrying a child would generate such feelings, or she would have avoided falling pregnant."

"How did she convey this to you?"

"I'm the one who brought it up. I had…"

Anna bit her upper lip.

"It was the way she was assuming her pregnancy. She felt she was harbouring a parasite eating her out from the inside, like a tumour."

"Did she use those specific words? *Parasite, tumour*?"

Anna nodded in agreement, her eyes fixed on her hands that lay across her thighs.

"She felt a foreign body had taken control of hers. She felt deformed. She even confessed to me that she had looked up how to generate an abortion on the Internet."

"What was your answer to her?"

"I wanted to warn Linn and Tomas, but she begged me to keep silent, that it would alarm them unnecessarily. She assured me that her dark thoughts were merely due to hormonal imbalance, and that given time matters would revert to normal."

"What did you do?"

"What I shouldn't have done: believe her. One week later, she cut her stomach open in her bathroom."

The memory of Marta spread out in the slimy bath water returned, clear as daylight: every single detail in terrible focus. Until now, her brain had occluded the more painful details, polished the uglier ones away, those that gnawed at her soul.

Anna's eyes were full of horror.

"Anna, are you OK? What's the matter?"

She opened her mouth wide, searching for words appropriate to describe what she had seen, but it all died in her throat.

"Anna?"

She closed her eyes, tightening her eyelids, then opened them again. She seized the water bottle and drank it dry. She only stopped when the plastic neck crinkled between her lips under the pressure of her suction.

"Anna?"

"I'm fine... I'm fine..." she reassured him breathlessly, setting the bottle down. "I'm sorry, Inspector."

"What happened?"

"I think I... I'd hidden away some of the memories of the day I discovered Marta. There were three razor blades on the floor by the bathtub. In a pool of blood..."

She swept the tears from her cheek.

"I thought I... I could picture the scene again and I was almost certain the bath water was almost opaque and that I couldn't see Marta's body inside it. But... That wasn't the case, Inspector."

A sob took shape in her throat. She swallowed hard to chase it away.

"It's not the case! The bath water was not cloudy at all: I could see Marta's body, Inspector! Her mutilated stomach! She'd slashed away, all the way to her sex! Her round stomach... Her round stomach..."

She leaned her elbows on the table and vigorously massaged her temples.

"How could I have forgotten that, Inspector?"

She looked up at him, imploringly.

"It's a frequent mechanism of self-protection, Anna: your brain blanked it out, as you were unable to cope with the emotional violence of the situation. It was protecting you, filing those terrible images out of sight, until you'd reached the stage when you could finally live with their brutality and face the trauma. It's not your fault, Anna."

"It's not my fault…"

"No, it's not your fault. Anyone would have reacted the same as you did."

"Anyone, I know. But the two of us were so close."

In turn he settled his elbows on the table.

"Anna, could you tell me a little about your relationship with Marta?"

Anna immediately frowned.

"My relationship with Marta?"

"Yes, your relationship. You said you were very close."

"We were."

"How long had you known each other?"

Anna had a tired smile.

"Forever. That's the way it felt to us, at any rate."

"You didn't have a specific reason to visit Marta that morning, did you? She wasn't expecting you, but nonetheless you woke up with an urgent compulsion to go and see her."

"Indeed."

"How can you explain that?"

"The bond between us was very powerful."

"So it seems. You told me earlier that you woke up

with such a strong inner feeling circling your thoughts. An uncontrollable impulse, a sense of urgency, so acute that—I quote you—you felt you had 'written it down in capital letters in a notebook'. You desperately had to see her. How can you explain that feeling to me, Anna? That imperious need to go visit Marta?"

Anna shook her head from side to side, her lips puckering.

"I don't know."

"Anna, earlier you were telling me about Linn and the problems she had experienced about her pregnancy and her impending motherhood."

"Yes."

"Maybe I'm wrong, but I get the feeling you were resentful of her, as if you thought that she wasn't supporting her daughter as a mother properly should."

Linn's features stood invisibly between them, her wrinkled cheeks, the permanent state of anxiety that lent a form of sadness to her eyes, the way she had of clenching her lips to express her disagreement, putting forward her own version of events, always bathed in pessimism; her hand holding on to Marta's shoulder in an attempt to comfort her but only serving to reinforce her disapproval, tormenting her even further.

"You're not wrong, Inspector."

Anna looked him straight in the eyes.

His head shifted to the side, as if in readiness to acknowledge what she was about to say, or maybe avoid it.

"She's the one who dug her grandson's grave."

His right arm stretched towards the tabletop, palm set

upwards, like an invitation. *Like a supplicant's hand*, Anna thought. She imagined it full of water, like a cup, her lips resting across the callous flesh, slowly sucking up the liquid. The freshness of the water reviving her face all the way from her throat to her ears and causing her to smile.

She set her own hand down in the hollow of his. He closed his fingers, catching her in his grip. This was no sexual moistness, no lubricious caress. Just a reassuring form of contact, as if this hand embodied the essence of succour of a parent.

"Anna, earlier you referred to Linn's children; you said 'her children'."

"Yes."

"Her children. Plural."

A tremor ran across Anna's face.

"I know, yes, I know. It's just that it's so difficult to talk of the others."

"*The others.*"

"The others, yes. I was one of them, I know."

"Yes, Anna. Linn is your mother, you too."

"Yes."

Linn had cast a seed of doubt above Marta's shoulders, as she had done to herself; she had maintained that heavy brass blanket above their heads until both had been crushed by it. Anna had attempted to set aside her mother's toxicity. That acid bath which gnawed away at all feelings and joy. She pretended to be a mother, but she clearly wasn't. Giving birth doesn't necessarily make you a mother. And neither does motherhood come into life with the child: it grows alongside it. It's a learning curve; the art of abnegation, or rather the capacity to be able to conquer your fears, your anxieties and your doubts so they are not passed on to the child; the talent to protect them without suffocating them, to love with no holding back.

"And Marta?"

"Marta is my sister. My twin sister."

"Yes, she is, Anna. Marta is your sister."

"Marta is my other half."

They had just celebrated Linn's birthday. That particular year, Anna and her sister had prepared things in a rush; between the end of year exams and organising the celebrations for the *Studenten*, they just about had time enough to devote to their mother. Throughout the meal, Linn's face had been drawn, tentatively blowing on the candles with pursed lips, barely eating any of the cake. She'd begun to open her first present when she interrupted herself. She'd crossed her arms with slow deliberation, gazing firmly at each of her daughters in turn, and then had told them the story of her own hellish pregnancy. How distressed she had been to become a mother. Her wish to have an abortion, to rid herself of the twins. And then she continued to unwrap her presents. Mother Linn. Linn.

"Marta is my sister, yes."

"That's why the pain she endured became yours."

Anna lowered her head towards the desk, pressing her cheek against the lukewarm surface.

"What about the baby, Anna? Could we talk about the baby?"

"Marta's baby. He was inside her tummy when she lacerated herself with the razor blades. Three blades."

"Did the child have a name?"

Anna freed her hand and straightened up.

"Could one even call it a 'child' at that stage?"

"Some babies are born at only seven months, Anna."

"No, he had no name."

No name. No room. This 'child' who only existed so far when it moved inside its mother's womb. Marta was submerged in her anxieties. Tomas was insistent they prepare for the baby's coming. As for Anna, she was trying to lighten her sister's mood, bringing her home decoration magazines and humorous books on the subject of pregnancy, but Marta kept on saying they still had enough time, that it was tempting fate to organise everything in advance. If anything did go wrong, the ensuing fall would just prove more painful. So Tomas and her had retreated back. After all, she was the one who was carrying this 'child'.

"So, what was inscribed on the gravestone then, Anna?"

Her mouth went dry.

"I don't know. It's Tomas who dealt with it."

Tomas had selected the tiny coffin, the gravestone, the lines from the Bible the pastor had read out. She'd never thought to ask what he had had carved into the stone. She had not found herself capable of taking her eyes away from the coffin, thinking how the baby had just been moved from one form of container to another, from the womb to this box. From one dark coffin to another.

"What would you have called it, Anna?"

"Marta and I had prepared a list of names. Or rather I'd made a list for her."

"What was your favourite? And hers?"

"Oscar. We both liked Oscar."

"Do you think that's what Tomas had carved on the gravestone? Oscar Hellenström?"

"Oscar Ljung."

"Ljung?"

"That was Tomas's family name."

Her head slumped over her shoulders.

"Anna?"

"I was thinking of the burial. The baby's burial, Inspector."

He leaned towards her, his hand reaching the tabletop.

"Do you want to talk to me about it, Anna?" he asked her, looking straight into her eyes, trying to connect.

She could recall the smell of the damp earth that lingered in the air, similar to the smell emanating from fallen tree branches and bark debris after a storm; the heavy barrier of clouds suspended above their heads; the smoothness of silk on skin; the hands intermittently gripping her naked shoulders; the pain chewing through her stomach; the unpleasant tone of the pastor's voice; her mother's smothered sobbing.

"All four of us were there."

"All four?"

"Yes, that's what I just said, Inspector, all four. Tomas, Linn, Marta and me."

"Marta too?"

"Yes, Ma—"

Anna jumped up, throwing the chair back. With a trembling

hand, she pulled her skirt up all the way to her navel. Scars streaked across her stomach down to her pubis. Pink and blistered, they covered the whole surface of her abdomen. Even her navel seemed stretched into an abominable smile.

She emitted an animal shriek. It died inside her throat and tears took over. Shaking her like an earthquake, turning her into a bush caught in a violent storm. She swung from front to back, her dishevelled skirt still gripped by her hand.

"It will be OK, Anna. It will be OK."

He stood right by her. She hadn't noticed he had moved alongside her. She buried her face in his chest and kept on crying. One of his hands settled on her shoulder blade while the other stroked the top of her head. He waited for the flow of tears to come to an end and her breath to settle down before assisting her back onto the chair.

She sat, wiped away the tears and snot running across her face, and looked over to him, lost.

"I don't understand. I don't understand. Is it me, Inspector?"

He moved his chair to face her again and sat himself down.

"Your name is Anna Hellenström. You're thirty-two. You're an accountant. You live with Tomas Ljung. You've known him for a long time, since..."

"Since high school," she continued, her voice like a rasp.

He looked at her sympathetically.

"Exactly, Anna. Do you remember your address?"

"Bokvägen 37, in Kållered."

"Perfect."

"My mother's name is Linn Hellenström. My sister is Marta Hellenström. She is my twin sister. They also live in Kållered."

"That's it," he answered, smiling. "That's very good, Anna."

Anna's eyes moved swiftly from left to right as if she was following a tennis match.

"Shall we have a rest?"

"No, no, I want to continue. I'm fine. I can see it all now. I wish to continue."

She sighed heavily and then spoke again.

"That morning, I woke up after Tomas had left for work. I had my only coffee for the day while listening to the news on the radio. I remember hearing a mother speaking about the death of her two-year-old son. The terrible emptiness it left behind. I envied her that sense of emptiness. The baby wasn't born but was already taking over so much space in my life. Too much space. When I rose to clean up the kitchen table, the baby moved. He was wedged against one of my ribs and my breath was briefly obstructed. It felt like having a snake in my stomach. A snake who was kicking against me in an attempt to burst out. And, as if he could read my thoughts, he began moving even faster. Trying to make me understand my own body no longer belonged fully to me: he inhabited it and was in charge. I was no longer the captain of my own ship. He would decide what I was allowed to eat, how long I would sleep, how much strength I was allowed and how heavy my breasts would feel. He stretched the skin of my stomach like a drum and turned all attempts to make love into a laborious and insipid parody. He was preventing me from being a woman and turning me into a mother."

Pregnancy... baby... fish... toxic...

Anna's lips twisted in a show of disdain.

"I decided I should take a warm bath to sooth the pain and calm down. I had no alternative but to accept the child's reality; I had become aware of it too late to arrange a termination. I had to live with it. With him. Or her. I walked over to the bathroom next to the spare room as our bedroom only had a shower stall. I was wearing my nightshirt with the thin straps; it was white with pink dots, and four buttons down my chest and a silk bow. One of those awful garments I'd had to purchase to accommodate my growing stomach and my misshapen breasts."

She looked up to the ceiling as if profoundly exasperated by this forced dereliction of her fashion sense.

"I ran the bath. Or, more precisely, I ran *our* bath. When I lay down in the bathtub, I reflected on how much the baby was already interfering with my lifestyle, my tastes, my desires. I hate taking baths. Which is why there was no bathtub in our own bathroom. It's a waste of time. It's only Tomas who uses the bathtub when he has to shave his chest or pubes, because it annoys me intensely to find hair in the shower stall. So, anyway, I settled inside the damn bathtub. With my enormous breasts and stomach emerging provocatively from the water. It began to move inside me, forcing an elbow or a knee from inside against the skin just above my navel, creating yet another deformity. It had to stop. That's what I told myself as I gazed at my absurdly shaped belly. I no longer wanted a parasite to harbour inside me. I could no longer stand this tumour eating me out from the inside. After all, it was my body. *My* body."

With one hand she straightened the folds of her skirt.

"I took hold of the glass where Tomas kept his razor and blades. There were three blades left. I placed them on the edge of the bathtub. I unwrapped them, then began to cut into the taut flesh of my stomach, as it signified to it that it still belonged to me alone. I continued until I fainted, I suppose, because when I woke up I was already at the hospital and Marta was by my bedside. She explained how she had found me. She wanted to know if I had been assaulted, but I could see in her eyes she had no belief in that having happened. She knew I had slashed my own stomach. That I was the one who had killed my baby. Because I knew it was dead. Everything was returning to normal inside me. I could feel it. The parasite had finally been chased away."

"How do you feel now?" the man asked, following a moment's silence.

She looked back at him with serenity.

"Much better, Inspector. My mind is clear. I'm relaxed."

"Good, very good, Anna."

"I don't know why I repressed it all. Why it all became jumbled up. Why I thought Marta was dead. My wonderful Marta. I am so sorry."

There was tenderness in her thin smile.

"Did you know that after we were born, we were quite unable to sleep separately? The only thing that could soothe us was being physically close to each other: my head cushioned against her neck or my arms threaded through hers."

"You talk of Marta: do you miss her?"

"A lot."

Anna frowned. Her forehead wrinkled.

"Yes, Anna?"

Her head moved to one side, she rose and slowly stepped towards the mirror. She watched her own reflection and then, suddenly, her heart filled with joy. She could recognise those hollow cheeks, the fringe of hair swept to the side to reveal the ever-wrinkled forehead, the eyes puffy and tired. She recognised the tender, anxious, full-of-loving smile. The maternal smile. She flattened her hands against the glass, on either side of her face.

"Marta," she whispered.

"Yes, Anna, it's Marta, on the other side of that pane of glass."

Tears began running down her tired cheeks.

"I thought it was me. I thought I could see my reflection in the mirror."

"Do you want to see her, Anna? Do you want to see your sister?"

Anna impatiently nodded, her eyes full of innocent and joyful expectancy.

He made a sign to Marta, who pointed with one finger at the room where Anna stood. Anna ran to the door, opened it and fell into her sister's arms. She buried her nose in Marta's neck, pleasurably closing her eyes as fingers combed through her hair.

"*Hej min älskling*. My little darling. My Annita," Marta whispered, punctuating each word in turn with a kiss.

She placed her hands across Anna's cheeks, their noses almost touching.

"I missed you, little darling. God, how I missed you."

"I'm sorry, Marta, so sorry. I just don't know why I thought you were dead. I don't know. Sorry," Anna muttered, her voice unsteady.

"By endangering your life, you buried, altogether forgot a part of you, and that part was me. You just needed the time to find your way back to yourself, *min älskling*. And, look, now you've managed it."

"You're not angry at me because of Oscar?"

With the back of her hand, Marta swept her tears away.

"No, of course not."

"I'm so sorry, Marta. I couldn't… carry him inside me…"

"Don't worry. How do you feel?"

"It's strange. I'm not sure. I just don't understand how I could forget, mix things up, be so wrong. What about Tomas?"

Marta's eyes peered deep into her sister's.

"He's left, hasn't he?"

Her delicate fingers drew a line from Anna's forehead to her cheek.

"Yes, he's left, *älskling*."

Anna briefly closed her eyes. When she opened them again, they were shining with childish exuberance.

"Do you want us to go and have something to eat?"

"I'd love to, but it's too late, darling. I'll return and come see you tomorrow, before I go to work, OK? You should get some sleep too, no?"

"OK. I can't wait for tomorrow. Will you walk me to the door?"

The man approached the two women.

"I have to speak to your sister, Anna. I'll have someone walk you back, is that OK?"

"Yes, thank you, Inspector."

The young man who had earlier brought in the bottles of water was standing by the door.

"Would you accompany Anna home, please, Peter?"

"Of course, would you like to come with me, Anna?"

Anna nodded, cuddled her sister and disappeared down the corridor.

Marta collapsed onto the chair.

"Is it OK? She's not about to start screaming and assaulting the nurse when she realises she's being taken to her room and not her 'home'?"

"Her room is her home for now and Peter will explain things to her. It will be fine, Marta, don't worry."

"The scar she left on that poor other nurse's hand doesn't help reassure me."

"Anna is now well past the violent phase. There have been no incidents of that kind for over two months now."

"Anyway, she appears to have taken great steps forward from what I've witnessed this evening, don't you think, doctor? Or am I celebrating too early?"

"Yes, it's a good sign, truly. Much will depend on how tomorrow's session unfolds. It's quite possible she will act out again the police station scenario as she did tonight, or call herself Marta, like in the early weeks of her confinement. But tonight, she has made a journey back from her fantasies towards reality. It's great progress, even if she still lacks any form of empathy for her son."

Her son...

Anna, if only you could see the delightful mischief in his eyes when he readies to spit out his evening food; his tiny shoulders shaking like a grown-up's when he bursts out with laughter; how his thumb slips past his lips when he sleeps and bunches his fist. If only you could experience his wet kisses on your hollow cheeks, Anna, the silkiness of his blond strands of hair, his innocent smell, of spring, of eternity. If only you could, my Anna, that child would mend you forever...

Our little Oscar, already sixteen months old, she pondered as she closed the door of the psychiatric hospital behind her.

Your son. Our son.

MY son.

IN ADVANCE OF DEATH

A. K. BENEDICT

Thwunk. The sound of a book landing on her welcome mat. Ten or more came through Lucy's door every day. Uncorrected proofs, they're called, or ARCs. Advance Reader Copies, sent by editors hoping for a juicy cover quote. Ellis, her assistant, usually dealt with them, but she was on holiday in a rainy corner of Cornwall. Lucy wished she were with her: hiking to shore-huddled pubs; peeling chips from salt-licked paper; watching waves rise and die. Instead, she was at home, finishing her latest novel. Supposed to be finishing it, anyway. Only ninety-two words had been eked out that morning. She had, however, eaten fifteen Hobnobs, spent two hours researching methods of hanging and another trying to find the exact word for the smell of death. Words never came for her. She had to lasso them, drag them to the page.

Enough. She stood and stretched, arms locked above her

head, mirroring the hands of the clock. Lucy leant back until her spine ticked. Words could wait till after lunch.

There was nothing unusual about the package. Her name and address were printed dead centre on the brown envelope. Proofs were sometimes accompanied by bribes—bars of chocolate or tiny bottles of gin—but this one came alone. Not even a begging letter from an editor. Just a plain white proof in a Jiffy bag shroud.

Lucy carried the book through to the library and was about to add it to the hundreds of other ARCs when she remembered—Ellis had a system. All ARCs were recorded in a blue notebook: date received, title, author, publisher, editor, date of forthcoming publication. Ellis would love it if Lucy actually followed her method. Before Ellis (B.E., as Lucy called it), she had piled books in teetering columns that swayed like the trees from which their pages were made. The rest of the house had been no better. Her clothes had been kept in one mourning-black mound on her bedroom floor and she could barely step into her study for all the paperwork. Ellis had changed all that. Ellis had changed everything. She sorted books, cooked, placed paperwork in one of the filing cabinets and laid out clothes on Lucy's bed every morning and night. Maybe Ellis would be so pleased that Lucy had followed her system, that she'd let Lucy call her by her first name. Love stories began like this. It had the weight of fate behind it.

Sat in her favourite armchair, Lucy opened up the notebook and followed the curve of Ellis' cursive with her ring finger.

Underneath, letters straying into the line above, she wrote down the details of the new ARC: *13th April; 'In Advance of Death'; Anna E. Masters; Corpus; editor not mentioned; 13th April.*

Who sent out proofs the same day as publication? Magazines and journals needed six months, minimum. The artwork would be sorted by now so there was no chance of a cover quote. A PR intern at Corpus, whoever *they* were, probably forgot to send out copies. *In Advance of Death* would sink like a mobster wearing concrete Dr. Martens.

Lucy laughed, even though there was no one there to hear her. She'd use that line in her book. Who said she'd gone off the boil with the second DCI Imogen Shaw, the follow-up to her debut? She was doing better than Anna E. Masters, that was for sure. Where did she know that name from? She met hundreds of writers at awards ceremonies, signings, panels, while sprawled on the lawn at Harrogate… It was hard to remember specifics after being plied with Prosecco by publishers on the poach. She may even have promised Masters that she'd take a look at her book. After all, a best-selling writer had raved about Lucy's debut. It was how Lucy had made it as an author, give or take a technicality or two.

Lucy turned to the first page and settled back to read. Her armchair gave a leather-breathed sigh.

Lucy Horsley sits back in her chair, red leather creaking beneath her. She cradles the book in her lap as if it's a paper cat. All that knowledge in the library around her yet Lucy doesn't know one important fact: in seven hours, she'll be dead.

Lucy gripped the book tighter. Her name. Right there. First line. Coincidence, that's all. Couldn't be anything else. If Ellis were here, she'd laugh and say that was typical— putting herself at the centre of everyone's story, taking space on someone else's page. She read on.

Lucy had always wanted a library, ever since she was a girl. Her childhood home in Pocklington had possessed two tomes: The Karma Sutra *and a Delia Smith cookery book. Both came from charity shops and both were lost on her parents: they favoured fighting over fucking; divorce over duck à l'orange.*

Lucy froze. She was from Pocklington. Not that you could tell from her accent. Her flat vowels had risen like a Yorkshire pudding when she moved to London. She'd left parents, friends and a lover behind, getting away with what fitted in her backpack.

When her first novel, The End of Julia McCleod, *was made into a film, she'd sold her flat and bought an elderly house in the arse end of Medway. Half of her next advance went on filling the dark-beamed dining room with shelves and books, the rest of it on elocution lessons. She sits in her library now, reading these words. Knowing that she is a liar. A murderer. A plagiarist.*

"What the fuck?" Lucy jolted up to standing. The book fell to the floorboards. She fumbled in her pocket for her phone and pressed on the last used number.

"I'm afraid I can't answer the phone at the moment," Ellis' recorded voice said. It had a lightness to it that Lucy hadn't heard before. The holiday was obviously agreeing with her. A thread of jealousy sewed Lucy's heart shut.

She phoned Simone, her editor. Same thing. Straight to answerphone. A message came through shortly after: *In a meeting. Will call ASAP! S. x* She was probably in acquisitions, wrapping Sales and Marketing round her tweeting finger.

Lucy then did what writers knew best, other than procrastination wanking and judging the perfect number of coffees in a day: she Googled. Lucy's fingers spat the words into the search bar: *Anna E. Masters.* A guide leader in Orpington; a chef in Auckland; and one writer, with one of those greyed-out Twitter silhouettes with the profile name, Writer_in_ Law. No mention of her books. No tweets. As for Corpus, her publisher, not even a smell or whisper of them existed.

The phone rang. Let it be Ellis.

"Lucy! Can't be long, I've slipped out for a vape," Simone shouted. Her voice and, no doubt, her signature vanilla vape fumes competed with the Embankment traffic. Cars had no chance against her.

"Something weird's happened," Lucy said.

"Good weird or bad weird?" Simone asked.

Lucy curled back into the chair. "Have you heard of a book called, *In Advance of Death*?"

"Don't think so. Not a bad title, though. Why, thinking of it for your next one?"

"Someone got there first. I got an ARC of it today. By someone called Anna E. Masters."

"If *I've* never heard of it, or the author, no one else will have," Simone said. "You could use the same title, no problem."

"That's not the problem."

"What is, then?"

Lucy tried out the words in her head. It was no good. How could she tell her editor that a book was stalking her? Or that it was accusing her of plagiarism? Or that its claims were true? "Nothing," she said at last. "I'm being silly."

"You don't sound like you're being silly," Simone said. "You sound…" She paused for a moment. "Scared."

Lucy tried to smooth the shakes in her voice. "Don't mind me. Ellis is away and I'm spending too much time in my own head."

"You know my advice in these situations?"

"Gin?"

"Gin. And if that doesn't work, go for a walk. To a bar that sells gin."

"Thanks, Simone."

"Any time. Now bugger off and write me some words."

Lucy pulled a throw over her goose-bumped body. She couldn't stop shivering. She tried Ellis again. No answer. Who else could she call? No one.

Dark pressed its face to the windows. So many windows. So many eyes that could lie behind. Someone had been watching her. Maybe they'd been watching her a long time, maybe they were watching her now. Lucy pulled all the curtains, checked all the locks, switched on the chandelier that hung in the centre of the library. Its crystals threw light onto books like confetti at a wedding.

What would DCI Shaw do now? There was only one piece of information to hand. Only one thing Shaw could go on. The proof. She picked up the book and paced as she read.

Lucy stuffs the pages into her bag along with the teddy bear that Marta gave her for Christmas. 'I'll keep it close,' she says. 'It's like taking you with me.'

'I'll come with you,' Marta says, reaching for Lucy's shoulders.

Lucy steps away. 'I'll call for you, when I'm safe and set up somewhere. I promise.'

'Wait, your shoelace is undone.' Marta bends down. Ties up Lucy's shoelaces for the last time.

Lucy then kisses Marta with winter lips that feel like paper and walks down the stairs.

Lucy comes out of the front door and hurries towards her car. She then drives away with the only copy of Marta's manuscript.

Lucy choked on the words that lay her as bare as the victims in her books. Her mind chased itself, going through permutations. The only people who knew all this were deceased. And the dead spilled nothing but decomposition chemicals. Marta herself had died fifteen years ago, the year that Lucy's debut came out. She was found, hanging from a noose, in her dining room, a copy of Lucy's book on the floor. Lucy had spoken about it in interviews; how she was glad she'd been there for a fan in need.

Anna E. Masters. The name kept whispering to her. DCI Shaw was always able to join the dots. That was her USP—a preternatural ability to turn seemingly impossible things around in her mind until they could be explained. Lucy did not have this facility. The dots floated before her eyes, unjoined.

Poor little Lucy. She still doesn't know what's going on. Still unable to tie things up by herself.

"Leave me alone!" Lucy shouted. The library said nothing, only held the echo in its pages.

She should stop reading. The book couldn't affect her, couldn't *hurt* her, if she stayed well away. One of the tips she gave wannabe-writers was to never read their reviews.

But Lucy never follows advice, even if it's her own. She picks up the book, In Advance of Death, *and flicks through. Her stomach twists like a thriller at every line. Every reminder of what she's done. And still she hasn't worked it out. It would be as easy as a slip knot to undo if she only had the brain. All she knows is that this centres on the manuscript. Marta's manuscript.*

Of course. Lucy ran into her study. Post-Ellis, it was already returning to its default setting: crumbs and mugs multiplying; Post-its vying for wall space. Feeling under her desk, she found the mound of Blu-Tack and peeled it off. She crawled back out and sat cross-legged on her rug.

Buried deep in the Blu-Tack was something she hadn't looked at for fifteen years. She picked the stiffened blue stickiness away, revealing a small silver key. The key to her other filing cabinet, the locked one. Not even Ellis had been allowed access.

The drawer shunted open. There it was. The handwritten manuscript of *The End of Anna Masters*. And, on top of it, a note in Ellis' handwriting. *She was all I had. I've left what you should wear on your bed.*

*

It took two hours for Lucy to gather the courage, another one to gather the rope that Ellis had left on the bed into a noose. She then walked slowly downstairs and into the library.

Lucy dragged her armchair under the chandelier. Her heart beat quickly, as if trying to use up its allocation before it was too late. She climbed onto the chair's back. It wobbled, as she knew it would. Everything does. And she's no different. She got away with nothing, after all.

She placed the book on the arm of the chair then threw the rope over the beam. She knew how to tie the knot. Of course, she did. She knew the beam would hold, that she didn't weigh enough to trouble it. The only variable, the only possible plot twist, was whether her indecision would have her feet reaching for the chair. She gave herself over to the story and stepped into the air.

The weight of fate pulled at her feet. Her throat was closed by the rope's choke. Her arms flailed a hundred times in the chandelier's crystals. Her leg kicked the proof onto the floor. It fell open.

She knows what comes next, even as her brain sparks its last. She has done her research. Her tongue will swell. Her eyes will dot with red petechiae: unjoined. And now, at last, she can smell it. It is waiting for her, has been waiting all this time. The word. The smell of death. A yellow smell. Tallow lit and extinguished. The word welcomes her as no one else will again, it sweeps over her like love. Her tongue swells with it. It is all that is left. The smell of death.

YESTERDAYS

A Charlie Resnick Story

JOHN HARVEY

"They're all dying, Charlie."

Ed Silver's words echoed across the years, across the near-empty room in which Resnick stood, remembering. He had been about to go off duty when he'd been called to a disturbance at Emmanuel House: a man threatening to take a butcher's cleaver to his own bare feet—first the left and then the right and heaven help anyone who tried to stop him.

At first Resnick hadn't recognised him, and then he did. Silver. Ed Silver. Up on the bandstand at the Old Vic on Fletcher Gate, shoulders hunched, alto sax angled off to one side, fingers a blur of movement as he blitzed through an up-tempo blues with sufficient speed and ferocity to make the eyes water. Now the same hands, purple and swollen, were scarcely able to hold the cleaver steady, never mind a saxophone; Resnick had reached out slowly but firmly and taken the cleaver safely into his own hands. Taken Silver home and fed him, made coffee strong and black, talked long into the night.

"They're all dying, Charlie. Every bugger!"

Just as Silver himself was to do not so many years later. February 16th, 1993. On the anniversary of which date, Resnick would habitually take down from the shelves an album Silver had made with a local rhythm section: Richard Hallam, piano; Geoff Pearson, bass; Mike Say, drums. Half a dozen numbers associated with Charlie Parker, a couple by Thelonious Monk, one Silver original, and a Jerome Kern ballad, 'Yesterdays'. But now those albums he hadn't sold back to Music Inn were boxed up by the front door and ready to go, the stereo alongside.

He'd put it off long enough; longer, probably, than he should. Rattling around in that place, Charlie, must be. All them rooms. Time to do the sensible thing, downsize. Downsize. The word made him shudder. But that's what he was doing, nonetheless. Contracts signed and exchanged. An upper-floor flat in a newish building just off High Pavement: ten minutes' walk to the city centre, twenty tops to the Central Police Station on Maid Marian Way. The land at the back sloped away towards the canal and the railway tracks, and he could clearly see the floodlights at the County ground at Meadow Lane and those at the Forest ground beyond. Another forty-eight hours and it would be home.

He poured a small shot of 10-year Springbank into a whisky glass, sniffed, tasted, and poured a little more. Carpet removed, the stairs creaked beneath his weight; dust had gathered in soft curls in the corners of the upper rooms. He stood at the window, staring out, still not really able to believe he was on the point of leaving. A wife, four cats, a lover: that's what this house had been. A life. While there had been just the one cat left, arthritic, blind in one eye, he had found reason to cling on. But then, just shy of Christmas, the inevitable had happened. Resnick had dug a burial place deep in the garden, deep enough to keep out the foxes, and, that done, contacted an estate agent, put the place up for sale.

"Bit of a do, then, Charlie," some wag had said, catching Resnick as he was leaving the station canteen. "Want to mark movin' in with a pint or two I'd reckon. Celebrate, like."

"Celebrate, buggery!"

"Thought as you'd be well chuffed. One of them smart new apartments in city, in't it? Single bloke like you. Out clubbin' afore you know it."

Resnick cut him off with a stare and continued on his way.

These last few years, ever since his official retirement, he had been clocking in as a part-time civilian investigator, in which role he was kept busy interviewing witnesses, taking statements and processing the necessary paperwork, aware that the majority of the cases requiring his assistance were relatively minor and anything regarded as serious was no longer likely to come his way. It smarted, but what could he do? He kept his head down and shuffled paper, offered an opinion when asked but not before.

He was in the process of shutting down his computer, tidying away at the end of his shift, when a young PC put his head round the door. "Somebody to see you down front. Been there a while."

"Why the heck didn't someone let me know?"

The constable shrugged and went on his way.

She was waiting in the reception area. Dark hair cut raggedly short, piercings, rings; denim jacket over a pale blue T-shirt; jeans with the obligatory tear below both knees; faded pink trainers, bright yellow socks.

"Mister Resnick?"

He held out a hand. "Sorry to keep you waiting. Nobody told me."

She shrugged slim shoulders. "S'okay."

"What was it you wanted to see me about?"

A smile slipped across her face. "You don't know me, do you?"

"No, I'm afraid not..."

It was the smile that did it. Fleeting. The eyes, like her mother's eyes, bluey-green like the sea.

"Rebecca, isn't it?"

"Becky, yes."

When he'd seen her last it had been a photograph. A beach somewhere. Mablethorpe? Filey? Seven, eight years old. Now she'd be nineteen, twenty. Older?

"How is your mum?"

"Not so good."

"I'm sorry."

"Do you think," she said, a flick of her head towards the door, "we could talk somewhere else?"

They walked alongside the theatre towards Wellington Circus and found a table outside the Playhouse bar. Anish Kapoor's steel sculpture crested over them, reflecting clouds passing slowly across the sky.

"You were saying, your mum's in a poor way."

"She's in hospital. Cancer."

"I'm sorry." Resnick fidgeted forward on his chair. "How serious is it? I mean…"

"Look, do we have to talk about it?"

"No, no, of course not, if you'd rather…"

"She's dying, okay."

Resnick drew a slow breath and held it in. Becky stared at the ground. A pigeon fluttered down from the curve of bare trees behind them, pecked aimlessly, then flapped away.

"Can I get you something?" Resnick nodded in the direction of the bar.

"No. I mean, yes. Yes, okay. Gin and orange, then."

"Gin and orange, it is."

"No ice," she called after him. "No ice."

When he got back with her drink and a half of Castle Rock for himself, she was chipping at the polish on the fingers of one hand with the thumb of the other.

"This bloke," she said, not looking at him, still fiddling with her hands, "this bloke Mark, Mark Brisley. I was going with him best part of a year. More'n that, I suppose. Together, you know? This place I was living, I was sharing, right, so it was easier to stay at his. Stayed over more and more till I was more or less living there." She picked up her glass, swirled the contents round then set it down. "It were fine at first. And then, after a bit, I don't know, he'd get all quiet. As if he were angry with me for some reason, something I'd said or done. I'd ask him an' he'd say, shut up, just shut the fuck up, and I did, but then, this one time when he still wasn't speaking, wouldn't as much as look at me, I asked again and that was when he hit me. The first time. I mean, hard. Sudden, out of the blue. Knocked me halfway across the room."

She glanced across at Resnick, held his gaze then looked away.

"He said he were sorry. Didn't know what'd got into him. Promised it'd not happen again."

"But it did."

"Not right off. He were lovely then, Mark, more than before. Fun, you know? And then, this one time, we'd been down the pub with his mates, laughing an' that. Soon as we got back he started accusing me of trying to get off with one of his pals. I tried telling him it was nothing but he wouldn't listen. Ended up called me a dirty whore and worse, and all the time hitting me, kicking and punching." She ran a hand up through her hair. "Course he was all over me after, sorry, sorry, I'm sorry, it won't happen again. I promise, I promise."

"You believed him."

"I wanted to." She lowered her head, her fingers trembling a little as she reached for her glass. "The next time it happened I had to go to Queens. A & E. One of the nurses there, told me I should report it to the police, which, in the end, after I'd talked to me mum an' that, is what I did. Saw this copper. Woman. Thought she might've been a sight more sympathetic than she was. Did I have any proof of what I was saying? Accusing him of. As if I was making it up. So I showed her these photos, selfies like, I'd taken when I come out of hospital. This copper, she brightened up then, as if she might be taking me seriously."

"The officer, you remember her name?"

"Thomas. Dawn Thomas."

Resnick pictured a youngish woman, early-mid thirties. Hair tied back, glasses. An accent of some kind? Geordie, maybe.

"Mark," Becky said, "when the police went to question him, he denied everything, said I was making it up. Called me—what was it?—a fantasist, that's it. Bloody fantasist. Reckoned I'd done all that to myself to get back at him for dumping me, chucking me out on street. Copper, I'll say this for her, she wasn't having any of it. Didn't believe him and told him so. Next thing he was arrested and charged. Assault, actual bodily harm."

"He's out on bail?"

"Pleaded not guilty, didn't he? Magistrates' court. Trial's less'n a month off."

"You're due to appear."

"Yes."

"And that's what's worrying you?"

Becky nodded. "He keeps sending texts, leaving messages. Telling me what will happen if I go to court. Warning me, like."

"Threatening you?"

"I dunno what else you'd call it."

"You kept them, these texts?"

Becky shook her head. "I know I should. I know it was stupid, but I just wanted rid of them. There and then."

"And did they continue?"

"I changed my number, got a new phone."

"That put a stop to it?"

"Yes. Only since then he's tried calling me at work, going round to where I'm living. I wake up in the night sometimes and there he is, parked across the street."

"Harassment. Intimidation. You can apply for a restraining order."

"Thomas, she told me about that, only I wasn't... I wasn't certain. I thought it would only make him more angry. I didn't want to make things worse."

Resnick leaned away. "I can talk to her, see if there isn't anything else can be done. But without a restraining order it's going to be difficult, I'm afraid."

"You can't, you know, have a word with him yourself?"

"Warn him off, you mean?"

"I suppose so, yes."

"Not really."

"No, no, course not. I shouldn't have asked."

"I'm sorry."

"S'all right. I just wanted someone to talk to, that's all. Mum being sick an' that, it in't right to worry her. And she always spoke of you as if you were a friend."

"So I am."

"Yeah?" Pushing back her chair, she scrambled to her feet.

"Becky, please…"

He watched her walk quickly away.

Night came nudging in. As Resnick crossed the ring road towards the hospital, rain began to fall steadily. The oncology ward was on the fourth floor.

"Are you a relative?" the duty nurse asked.

"No, a friend." Remembering Becky's earlier scorn, the word burned on his tongue.

Elaine was in one of four beds partly screened off at the far end of the ward.

"She's sleeping just now," the nurse said.

"I'll not wake her."

In the years since he'd last seen her, she seemed to have aged threefold. Skin like parchment. Hair like straw. Her face hollow and lined. When he leaned over her, an eyelid fluttered then was still.

Tubes ran in and out of her body.

With sudden clarity, he remembered the first time he had met her, shy of twenty years before. A basement wine bar, evening. Music meandering between innumerable conversations. Her hair auburn tumbling loose over her shoulders. Her mouth generous and wide. Those eyes. She had not long been married to Terry Cooke, Becky's father: Cooke a career criminal, a medium-weight chancer in and out of trouble since he was first excluded from school.

Resnick had glanced at the near-empty glass near Elaine's hand, guessed Bacardi and Coke, and carried a fresh one across, along with a Scotch and water for himself.

"Copper, aren't you?" Elaine had said, but, accepting the drink, had shifted sideways to make room.

Getting familiar with the criminal fraternity, drinking in the same pubs, the same bars; a word here, a misplaced remark there; friendships, betrayals. It was part of the job, went with the territory. Not so long after that meeting, Terry Cooke, under growing pressure, would take his own life rather than go back to prison, leaving a wife and young daughter. For several years while growing up, Becky would be in and out of care.

With a slight moan, Elaine's head shifted sideways and a dribble of saliva snailed across her cheek. One hand twitched.

After Terry Cooke there had been others, chosen, to Resnick's estimation, with a similar lack of care. She had moved away from the city, moved back. Once, in too deep and in fear for her life, not knowing where else to turn, she had gone to Resnick for help and he had taken her in. Shelter from the storm. Somewhere around two on the first night, she had slid out from the bed he'd made up for her and slipped in with him. Her legs lithe and surprisingly long, her hands knowing and cold. Just before dawn, Resnick awake, she had pressed her face close up against him and whispered a name that wasn't his.

"Charlie?" Her eyes blinked open now for an instant, closed and opened again. "Is that really you?"

"Really me."

"Thought I must've been dreaming."

Sitting cautiously on the edge of the bed, he rested a hand gently on hers. Bones and skin.

"How long've you been here?" she said.

"Not long."

She coughed, a raw scraping of sound, and Resnick lifted a water glass and straw from alongside and brought it to her mouth.

"You've seen Becky?" she asked once she had settled.

Resnick nodded.

"I told her to go and see you. She didn't want to but I said you might be able to help."

"I'm not sure if I can."

"Oh, Charlie…" A small shake of the head. "The apple don't fall far from the tree."

"I'll do what I can."

"I know."

Settling back against the pillows, she closed her eyes and seemed to fall immediately back to sleep.

"You shouldn't stay too long," the nurse said quietly over his shoulder. "She tires easily."

After several more minutes, Resnick lifted his hand gently away and set off down the ward. Outside the rain had slackened and the wind risen in its place.

Dawn Thomas was at her desk early, glasses nudged forward as she peered at the computer screen. Hair pulled tightly back and held in place by a tortoiseshell comb. Resnick had picked up a brace of flat whites from The Specialty Coffee Shop on his way in.

"Bribery, Charlie?"

"Kindness of my heart."

"Bollocks!"

She removed her glasses, touched the mouse and the screen went blank. "What can I do for you?"

"Becky Cooke."

"What about her?"

"She came to see me."

"Whining, was she?"

"Why d'you say that?"

"Sort she is." Distaste clear on Thomas's face.

"She's frightened."

"Of him? Brisley? No one to blame but herself."

"How so?"

"Taking up with him in the first place. In and out of trouble since he was sixteen, seventeen. Violence, often against women, intimidation. Not the first time he's been pulled in for abusive behaviour."

Thomas tasted her coffee, nodded approvingly, took a mouthful more. "Look, I sat with her, Charlie, talked her through everything, the process, coming to trial, what it'd mean. Warned her he might do what he could to get her to change her mind. No, she says, no. It'll be all right. Then, next thing, she's back in here, he's been texting her, sending threatening messages. Show me, I said, then maybe we can do something." Thomas shook her head. "Deleted them, hadn't she? Silly cow."

"He's been following her, she says, turning up where she lives."

"No surprise."

"Restraining order, not an option?"

"Went through that with her as well, didn't I? Didn't want to know. Not that I'm convinced we'd have got one, anyway."

"So, there's nothing?"

"Look, Charlie, you know what these girls are like."

"Do I?"

"Bloke's older, good looking in that kind of way. Bit of a reputation. Seen around with him, people notice. Enough to make her feel good, something special. Slaps her once in a while, well, part of the territory."

"Bit unfair on her, maybe?"

"I don't think so."

"She came here. Came to you. Dropped him in it. Wanted to press charges."

"After he put her in hospital, yes."

"And that's wrong?"

"What about all the times before? Tells her mates she walked into a door then takes him back."

"Once, maybe."

"Once? What she told you, was it?" Thomas shook her head. "Girls like Becky, sometimes I think... Oh, I don't know."

"You think what? They get what they deserve?"

"I didn't say that."

"I should've thought she'd have got a bit more sympathy."

"Because I'm a woman, you mean?"

"Yes."

"It's maybe because I'm a woman, I find it hard to have much sympathy. Weak, isn't she? Where she should be strong."

"Easy for you to say, maybe."

"Is it?" Thomas's voice was fiercer, a sudden light in her eyes. "You'd need to know a sight more about me—about my life—before you could say that. And then you might be surprised."

Swivelling away, she set her glasses back in place, reached for the mouse and brought the data she'd been reviewing back on to the screen.

A motorcyclist had swerved to avoid someone who'd stepped off the kerb against the lights and had been broadsided by a lorry. So far, Resnick had interviewed the driver of the lorry, the pedestrian and two bystanders; an appeal had been made for any other witnesses to come forward. The motorcyclist was in intensive care: touch and go.

Dawn Thomas knocked and entered.

"I didn't want to leave it like that."

"Okay."

Thomas pulled round a spare chair. "She did come forward, Becky, I'll give you that, and that's more than most. Less than a quarter of women in her situation get that far."

"And those that do…"

"Those that do are putting themselves at risk of further violence, yes, yes, I know."

"So we should do what we can to protect them."

"If they'll let us." Thomas sighed and looked away. "Not easy though, Charlie. Coercive control, that's the fancy name for it. Men like Brisley, one way or another, they exert it right up to the courthouse steps. Survey not so long back, you probably saw. Northumbria, maybe? Just over half the cases where defendants stood accused of abuse, the complainant didn't turn up at court and the case was dismissed. That's why so many of them choose to take the course they do. Play the system. Plead not guilty so it has to come to trial. Knowing full well there's a good chance the case'll get thrown out."

"And you, that's what you think'll happen? Comes down to it, Becky'll not show and Brisley'll walk free."

"If I was laying bets, yes, fifty-fifty at best."

"I'll try and talk to her again. Bolster her confidence if I can."

"Okay. And I'll have a word, see if I can't get one of the local patrols to do a drive-by or two. If Brisley is hanging around, that might scare him off."

"Right, Dawn. Thanks."

"Owe you a coffee, Charlie."

"Two shots, no sugar."

"Got it."

They went back to work.

Becky was living in a shared house in Sneinton, two up and two down, front door opening straight onto the street. Working two jobs, part-time, plus occasional bar work, enabled her—just—to pay her share of the rent and expenses. The first time Resnick called round, she'd asked one of her housemates to say she wasn't home; the second time he arrived just as she was fitting her key in the door and she agreed to go for a quick drink with him, one drink that grew into two and then three; Becky happy to talk about anything and everything but Brisley and the forthcoming trial. Before Resnick left her back at the house, she agreed to go with him that coming Sunday to visit her mother in hospital.

The day proved cold, Becky shivering in a short skirt and a denim jacket that didn't fasten at the front. No hat, no scarf, no gloves. Resnick, in contrast, wore a heavy overcoat and a crumpled felt fedora, a black and white Notts County scarf, somewhat incongruously, round his neck.

Despite her best efforts to claim otherwise, Elaine seemed to have slipped backwards. Her breathing was laboured and heavy, her voice rarely rising above a whisper; for minutes at a time, she seemed to lose all awareness they were there, responding to their presence in slightly startled surprise.

As they were getting ready to leave, Elaine scrabbled one bent hand across the sheet and beckoned him close. "Look after her, Charlie."

Resnick gently kissed her cheek, her skin damp against his lips.

Tears in her eyes, Becky stood waiting at the end of the ward and they rode the lift down in silence. A blast of cold air struck them as they stepped outside.

"I don't know," Becky said, as she fumbled for her cigarettes. "I don't know how many more times I can stand to see her like that."

The flame from her lighter quivered then caught. She drew deeply then released smoke upwards, fanning it away from her face.

It was a week and a day until the case against Mark Brisley was due to be heard in court.

"Why don't I pick you up?" Resnick said. "Give you a lift in?"

"It's okay. I'll be fine. No need to bother."

"You're sure?"

"Sure."

"Meet me then."

"I am gonna be there, you know."

"I know. But just to humour me, if you like, let's meet beforehand. Coffee, maybe. Go over what you're going to say. Can't hurt."

Becky half-smiled. "All right, then. If it's just to shut you up."

"Best make it eight o'clock then."

"Quarter past."

He nodded. "Quarter after eight, the Old Market Square."

"Where exactly?"

"By the Left Lion, of course."

"Like a date, you mean?"

Resnick laughed. "Yes, just like a date."

It was where, traditionally, couples met, by one of the two stone lions guarding the Council House steps on one side of the square: one to the left, one to the right. When, early on in their relationship, Resnick had arranged to meet the woman who was to become his wife, she had been standing by the wrong lion, right and not left. "It depends," she had said in her defence, "if you're coming or going." Going turned out to be the case, though she'd taken her time about it.

Resnick liaised with Dawn Thomas during the week: staff shortages notwithstanding, she'd successfully arranged for a patrol car to do a number of drive-bys past the house in Sneinton. Resnick phoned several times and Becky reassured him that everything was fine. Not only had Brisley not been seen, he had made no attempt to be otherwise in contact. No texts, no messages via social media, no calls.

"Eight o'clock tomorrow, then," Resnick said on the last occasion.

"Eight o'clock."

The morning was bright but cold. Buses shunted busily from Friar Lane around the corner into Angel Row. Trams came from opposite directions into South Parade, disgorging their passengers into an already busy Market Square.

Resnick stamped his feet, clapped gloved hands.

No Becky.

Five past eight.

Ten.

He checked his watch, the Council House clock.

At a quarter past he called her mobile. *The person you are calling is unable to answer your call.* When he tried the house phone, no one picked up.

The nearest taxi rank was on Wheeler Gate, just off the Square. Morning traffic was heavily congested, the one-way system a nightmare. After ringing the bell a number of times and hammering on the front door, he finally roused one of Becky's housemates sufficiently to come down and open up. A face stared out at him from under tousled hair.

"Becky, where is she?"

"In bed, I s'pose."

He pushed past her and hurried towards the stairs.

"Hey! Where d'you think you're going?" A tall woman, sweatshirt hastily pulled on over pyjamas, met him halfway.

"Becky's room. Which is it?"

"Why? What's happened?"

"Just tell me." He showed ID and she stepped aside.

"Up there on the left."

The bed was empty, unmade. Drawers half open, a scattering of clothing on the floor.

"She's gone." A third woman appeared in the doorway. Asian, small features, dark hair.

"Gone where?"

"I don't know. I asked her but she didn't say."

"When was this?"

"Last night, late. Must have been close to one."

"And what? She just up and left? She must have said something."

A shake of the head. "Someone called her a little earlier. Twelve? Somewhere around there. We were in the kitchen and she went out into the hall to answer. Closed the door. I could hear her voice but not what she was saying. A couple of times she got louder. And then I think she might've been crying. She ran upstairs and slammed the door and when I went up and asked her if she was all right, she said, 'No, no, what did I fucking think?' There was a lot of banging around and then, next thing I knew, she was pushing past me with this holdall and she must have called a taxi because when she went outside there was one waiting."

"You sure it was a taxi?"

"Yes. I'm sure."

"Know where she might have been going?"

"That time of night, no."

"Friends?"

"There's this girl she works with. Wilko's. She's stayed over with her a couple of times. Too out of it to get back home. I can't think of anyone else."

"This girl, you know where she lives?"

"Top Valley somewhere."

"Name?"

"Nat? Nat-something. Natalie. Nadia. I'm sorry, I just don't know."

"Fuck!" Resnick said. "Fuck, fuck, fuck!" Then, steadying himself, "Thanks. Thanks for your help. Here's my number. If you do hear from her, if she rings or anything, please get in touch. As soon as you can."

Knowing that no matter how soon it was, it would be too late.

"It's over, Charlie. Done and dusted. Should have placed that bet after all."

"You don't have to look so damned smug about it."

"Smug?" Thomas laughed derisively. "You should have

seen the expression on Mark Brisley's face if you wanted smug. Grinning from ear to fucking ear."

They got the address from the taxi firm, the workmate's name, Nadia Jagoda, from their place of employment. Becky had called late, asking if she could come round, sleep over. When she got there she'd been in a real state, Nadia said— agitated, frightened, something to do with an old boyfriend, she thought, but Becky hadn't wanted to talk about it, wouldn't say. Early next morning, really early, she'd left for the station. Train station, bus station, she wasn't sure. And no, she hadn't said where she was going.

Thomas was right: it was over.

In common with most other areas of the country, the number of officers leaving the Nottinghamshire force without being adequately replaced had increased, meaning the workload of those remaining rose in proportion, Resnick's included. Despite which, come summer, he found his days reduced from four to three. He sought to fill the extra time by taking self-improving walks alongside the Trent and around the Arboretum; going to the occasional afternoon movie; reacquainting himself with the intricacies of County Championship cricket from a seat in the Upper Stand at Trent Bridge, where the conversation around him took in everything from the beauties of left-arm spin to hip replacements and problems of the prostate.

The move into his flat complete since the spring, he no longer woke in the mornings wondering where he was. Most of his possessions were out of boxes, shelved, hung up, tidied away. Herman Leonard's photograph of Lester Young, taken in Paris in 1959, hung, framed, above the stereo. Everything compact, close at hand. He missed the accumulation of clutter that only came with time; missed having to walk up or down several flights of stairs to retrieve something misplaced or mislaid. He missed the cats.

In early autumn and desperate for something to do, a new project, he decided to catalogue what remained of his collection of vinyl albums and CDs, now that it was down to a manageable size. Catalogue properly: track titles and composers; instrumentation and personnel; place and date of recording; label and date of original release. He got as far as G for Dexter Gordon before giving up. *Our Man in Paris*, 1963. Gordon, tenor; Bud Powell, piano; Pierre Michelot, bass; Kenny Clarke, drums.

Paris again.

He'd never been.

Wouldn't that be a better use of his time than this? He promised himself he'd set it right. A long weekend at least. This year, next year? Maybe next year would be best. Next year in the spring.

Once, passing through what remained of the Broadmarsh Centre, he thought he glimpsed Becky Cooke heading in the opposite direction, but when he called her name there was no reaction other than to carry on walking. He thought he might have been mistaken.

He went several times to see Elaine in hospital, her mind increasingly vague and logged back in time. "You're a cheeky bastard, you!" she called out once, clutching at his arm, and he knew she meant her ex-husband, Terry, and not him at all. The last time he went she was sleeping and he stayed the best part of an hour waiting for her to wake, then left.

She died a week later.

There were leaves loose in the air as the coffin was lifted into the chapel. Becky sat in the front pew, alone. The voices of Resnick and a dozen others faltered to silence before the end of the hymn. When the service was over, Becky stood on the path outside, turning a cold cheek to strangers' kisses and whispered words of commiseration. She held Resnick's hand for a moment then let it go, never looking into his eyes.

At home afterwards, dusk masking the windows, Resnick poured the last of the Springbank he'd been saving into a glass, set an Ed Silver album on the turntable and sat back to listen.

'Yesterdays'.

Becky's friends weren't going to let her mope around miserably for ever. "C'mon, Becks. Shift off your moody arse and come out wi' us. It's Tricia's birthday, for fuck's sake."

They met in the Square and headed up to the Suede Bar; five of them, all reckoning a slice of pizza would stop their stomachs rumbling, provide the necessary balance for what was to come. If you were going to throw up at the end of the evening, best to have something other than just white wine or vodka and cranberry juice inside you.

From the Suede Bar they went on to Revolution and Das Kino. Pitcher and Piano was too crowded, too noisy. There were only three of them by now, Becky, Tricia and Nadia.

"Let's go to Propaganda," Tricia said.

"Feeling gay, are we?" Nadia said.

Tricia grabbed hold of her and kissed her on the lips and they stumbled back, spluttering with laughter.

Becky linked arms with the pair of them and they sashayed, still laughing, along Broadway towards the entrance to the club.

Once inside they were swept up in the crowd, dancing, singing, pausing only for another vodka cocktail. After an hour or so, head throbbing, Becky went outside for some fresh air, chatted with the bouncers on the door, bummed a cigarette. By the time she went back inside, neither Nadia nor Tricia were anywhere to be seen. Half an hour more and she decided to call it a night.

She was heading down Barker Gate, looking to pick up a taxi outside the Arena, when she heard footsteps behind her and quickened her pace.

"Hey! Wait up! Becky. What's your rush?"

Mark Brisley.

"Slow down, why don't you?"

If she stopped long enough to pull off her heels she could run.

"Becky, come on. Don't be so daft."

One shoe off, she wobbled unsteadily, close to losing her balance. A hand reached out to steady her and she shrugged it away.

"No call to go rushing off like that. All that stuff from before, forgotten. Put it behind us, eh? New start."

He circled his hand round her arm and this time she let it stay.

The incident in the opening paragraph refers back to my first published short story, 'Now's the Time', commissioned, like 'Yesterdays', by Maxim Jakubowski, and published in London Noir *[Serpent's Tail, 1994].*

CONNECTING THE DOTS

JEFFERY DEAVER

"I've asked for some help on this one."

"Oh. Okay."

The two detectives were in the war room—really, just the Wayne County Sheriff Department's smaller conference room—and staring at the corkboard on which were pinned the crime scene photos of the Joshua Musgrave murder.

The images were graphic to say the least.

Gloria Athens continued, "There's something wrong here. This one's different."

That may have been but, in truth, Henry Trimble was surprised that his boss was calling in hired guns. Her skill in investigating violent felonies was renowned throughout the state. If this homicide was 'different' it was way different.

He also knew that Athens—the Senior Criminal Investigations Division Detective of the WCSD—had an ego; for her to share the spotlight on a gruesome murder like this one meant the stakes were high. The nature of the murder suggested that the killer might strike again.

"Who'd you ask?" Trimble's thumbs were hooked through his belt, a 32-incher, with the metal tongue in the last hole. Been skinny all his life. With the mop of brown hair, which had a mind of its own, he could be a youthful farmer, if you swapped out the Macy's suit for faded blue denim Oshkosh. And a dark suit and white shirt it was today, every day; Athens had told him, "Appearances intimidate. Look like an FBI agent with a warrant. And never, ever smile on the job."

He had an idea Athens could sense his confusion, or concern, even if he himself wasn't sure what his reaction to the outside help would be.

"They're good people, Trimble. You met 'em last month. Chatham County CID." Athens's voice was rough, as if she'd chain-smoked. But she never had, at least in the year Trimble had been assigned to her.

"That workshop?"

Athens confirmed with a nod.

Chatham was two counties over and similar in geography, demographics, and size to Wayne, though more rural, but that was splitting hairs.

"Barney Stand and his junior partner. Can't remember his name."

Trimble did. "Dan Gebbert."

"Right. They had something similar a couple months ago," Athens said, eyes still on the corkboard.

"Knifing?" Trimble asked.

"I think it was a beating, but a homeless man. Or woman.

Random, it looked. No theft or other reason they could see." She glanced at her watch, a big, old Timex. "They'll be here soon."

Henry Trimble was getting a sense of how policing was also about power and image and career, as much as solving crimes. A lot of outsiders wouldn't have wanted to make the trip to another jurisdiction—they'd be seen like hired help—but an invite from the famed violent-crime-expert Gloria Athens? That'd be a feather in Stand's cap.

Uniformed and suited deputies were leaving for the evening; several waved through the large glass windows that were the conference room's walls, in sore need of Windex. Trimble wished he could leave too, to get back to his modest ranch house in the hinterland of Wayne County for dinner with his wife and young son, Todd. But it would be yet another late night.

That was the downside of working with Gloria Athens.

The upside was you were working with Gloria Athens.

The forty-five-year-old, or so, detective now slipped her hands into the pockets of her bulky dress slacks. Her white blouse was large too. She would occasionally bring to work plastic containers of tuna, without mayo, and carrots and baby tomatoes. The diet then morphed back to pizza and burgers, more from convenience than indulgence. She was a large woman, freckled and redheaded, and she had better things to do than trouble herself about the transit of calories into her body.

She now paced back and forth in a gentle sweep, her eyes on the board that described, in cold, bloody detail, how

Joshua Musgrave had come to die in the abandoned Harper Manufacturing plant.

His death had been among the more unpleasant ways to depart the earth.

Trimble was sweating. The March day was cold, which meant the unstable heating system in the Wayne County Public Safety Building was working overtime. Both officers had doffed their suit jackets, but that was doing no good. One window overlooked the gray, damp evening, but it had been painted shut years ago.

As always, Gloria Athens wasn't paying attention to the heat, like she didn't pay attention to the cold.

All that mattered to her at the moment was the corkboard.

Joshua's last hours.

She was staring, staring, trying to force herself into the mind of the person who had slashed Joshua to death.

She'd explained to Trimble how she did this, a harrowing and edgy practice. But it was necessary. She had to *become* the person who'd committed this terrible crime, and that, in turn, might point her toward where he was living, where he worked, where he was going to strike next. Who he was sleeping with. What he did for hobbies.

Now, Trimble could see that Athens returned again to the pictures of the bloodstains.

The blood.

That was the thing.

The blood.

*

Detective Barney Stand was a solid man, fifties, broad shoulders and a round belly that enhanced his stature; his lean face would have given him a gaunt look if he'd weighed less. He was six foot two inches and had dark eyes beneath white brows, which matched his mane of hair. Stand had presented one of the lectures at the seminar last month—on forensics.

His junior partner, Dan Gebbert, was smaller, but built like an athlete. A baseball player, Trimble assessed. They'd had lunch together, this foursome, at the conference. Stand was somber but smart. Gebbert, younger, had a sense of humor.

Stand wore black slacks and a dark, dusty, and wrinkled sports coat—it was plaid when you got up close—and Gebbert was decked out in a snug-fitting suit, which would have been stylish if it weren't some odd shade of beige. It nearly matched his sandy hair.

"Detective Athens," Stand began.

"Aw, we've got a history. Practically married. Let's do Gloria and Barney."

Hands were shaken all around. Trimble was amused that both of the visitors glanced toward Athens with a modicum of awe.

"Appreciate you coming to our small burg."

Stand said some pleasantry, but his eyes had moved from Athens to the case board, and he was regarding it with still eyes.

"Coffee. You'll have some coffee?"

There was a pot in the room, in the corner. Athens lived on it. She admitted it was an addiction. She liked it black and bitter and strong. The smell suggested the brew had been sitting for a spell, which it had. The newcomers declined. Athens poured a cup and sipped.

Stand, eyes still on the board, said, "Brief us."

"Henry?"

"Sure. Two days ago a homeless man was wheeling a bag of cans and bottles—for the deposit? He had a cart like movers use?"

Trimble reminded himself to can the questioning tone; he fell into this sometimes—mostly when he was nervous. Detective Athens had told him to watch it. "Makes you sound weak."

"We think he stole it from the Home Depot. He was wheeling it along Fourth Street. Tough part of town. Used to be the mills and warehouses, but when the work got sent over to Japan or China, the place went downhill."

"When he got to the Harper Manufacturing plant he left the bags out front and went inside."

"To pee?" Stand suggested.

Athens said, "Joshua—we've known about him for some time—wouldn't need someplace private. He was disposed to pee wherever he wanted."

"Middle of Thompson Street once," Trimble said. "Rush hour." To the extent they had rush hour in Wayne County—even here, in Garvey, the county seat.

Trimble continued, "Probably looking for a place to move into. There's a camp under the train trestle but there's been some complaints, so the homeless're moving."

Athens took up the narrative. "The killer got him just

372

inside." She pointed to a diagram and a series of photos of the interior of the plant.

"He was stabbed to death beside a wall that separated the plant floor from the warehouse."

"Who found him?"

"Our one lead," Athens said. "Except it isn't."

"Anonymous call from a pay phone," Trimble explained. "Somebody saw a white male, light hair under a stocking cap walking out of the factory fast. He was holding a rag that looked bloody."

Units had responded and found Joshua inside, dead.

"We got the rag but no other DNA, other than Joshua's, or prints. Some fibers consistent with cloth work gloves, but no way to trace them."

"CCTV of the unsub?" Gebbert asked.

"That part of town," Athens said, "is lucky to have electricity. High tech does not figure in the picture."

Trimble added that he'd canvassed a tent community near the trestle and a shelter where Joshua had spent some time. "Like a lot of homeless, he avoided the shelters. They get bullied, robbed."

"Ice or fent heads hit him for change?"

Meth and fentanyl were the bane of small, rural towns, where unemployment could reach 25 percent. Garvey was lucky, though, in that most of the young people—the sort who'd be tempted to smoke and shoot up—headed elsewhere for college or work. Wayne County was known as a fine place for growing up. But when you hit eighteen it was best to put the town in your rearview mirror.

Athens said, "We've got a few cookers and users, but we talked to the usual suspects and none of that panned out. Anyway, he wasn't robbed. He still had twelve dollars on him."

Trimble added, "Nobody knew of any disputes he'd been in with anybody. He was a feisty guy, not particularly pleasant, but there was no reason we could find to murder him."

He was not, in Athens's term, 'kill-worthy'. But Trimble wasn't as hardened as she was and tried to avoid flippancy. His day would come, he supposed. He took another look at the bloody crime scene and took a deep breath, controlling it.

"So," Athens said, "random, I'm thinking. Thrill kill."

"Vigilantes?" Stand asked.

Athens said, "People around here don't like homeless. They rough 'em up a little bit, toss a soda on them. Usually it's drunk college kids from Fayette. Never heard of murder."

"Luck tracking down the caller?" Gebbert asked.

"We dusted the pay phone, but it was near a call center— immigrants and migrant workers phoning home. There were seventy-two partials. The ones we could read were negative at IAFIS. No footprints. No car tread marks. Canvasses were zero. But here's where we hope you can help." Her eyes turned to the crime scene photos. "Look at the blood spatter."

Athens was the preeminent violent crimes investigator in this part of the state, but her skills were mostly psychology and general detection. She wasn't a forensics expert—she found the subject work boring.

Barney Stand, on the other hand, was known for his skill in crime scene analysis. And his main specialty: blood pattern analysis.

From his days at the academy, Trimble knew something of the technique. Using physics and the science of fluid dynamics, experts can often learn volumes about a crime by examining how blood hits a surface when the victim was stabbed or shot (or blown up, though that happened with zero frequency in Wayne County).

BPA—bloodstain pattern analysis—traces its modern origins to a Polish professor and criminalist, who wrote a paper on the topic in the late 1800s: 'On the Formation, Form, Direction, and Spreading of Blood Stains After Blunt Trauma to the Head', which while not the snappiest of titles succinctly and accurately described content. It attracted the attention of law enforcers around the world.

The two visiting detectives turned their attention to the photographs on the corkboard.

Athens said, "The spatter seemed unusual to me. But couldn't exactly say how." Stand walked closer. "There was a case I ran a few years ago. The perp used a knife he'd made himself. It had a hook at the end. He slashed and then pulled."

Gebbert said, "The pattern's similar, sure."

"Helpful. Maybe a homemade weapon."

Gloria Athens wore her hair piled up on her head in a carefully arranged nest, which she kept in place with pencils—the old-fashioned yellow kind. She extracted one now and pointed out several portions of the blood spatter photo. "Now, this is the big mystery. Here you can see the droplets and streams were all traveling in the same direction. Away from the Joshua's body. But look at these."

She touched round dots of blood at the top and bottom of the photo.

"They don't indicate any movement at all," Gebbert said, frowning.

Most blood spatter in a violent crime appears like a comet, or sperm: a head and tail.

The dots Athens was pointing out were round.

"They hit the wall straight on."

Stand moved closer yet. "Maybe Joshua managed to get to his feet and some of the drops hit the wall at ninety degrees."

"No," Trimble said. "Once he was down, he stayed down."

Stand said, "Do you have close-ups?"

Athens nodded toward Trimble, who went online and called up the digital crime scene photos. Stand was apparently familiar with the photo software and sat down at the keyboard to enlarge the images he was interested in.

Gebbert beside him said, "The hell is that?"

Stand gave a soft chuckle. "They're not drops. Look."

Athens leaned closer. Trimble too. The roundish, red marks were uneven, a rough circle with a random pattern inside.

Athens said, "I don't understand."

Stand eased back. "They were put there intentionally. Like from an ink stamp. Probably he used a stick, because it's uneven. He dipped it in the victim's blood and pressed it into the wall. You can see some dots're faint, like he ran out of, quote, 'paint' and had to replenish the brush."

There were dozens of the marks on the wall.

"Why on earth would he do that?" Athens asked, focused

on the hard-copy photos. Joshua Musgrave's killer was apparently one perpetrator whose mind she wasn't able to slip into.

It was Henry Trimble, staring at the photo of the wall, who suddenly understood. He said, "He's writing a message."

Athens turned a cool glance his way. He knew she didn't like unsubstantiated theories, especially those that were just plain weird.

Trimble said, "If we draw lines between them, I think they'll make letters, or numbers, or maybe it's a drawing."

Athens seemed less skeptical now. She asked Stand, "That homeless killing you had a few months ago? This case parallel anything about that one?"

"Other than being homeless, not really." Stand explained that the body of a fifty-year-old woman had been discovered in the woods beside the Chatham River. They didn't have an ID for the woman, officially known as UF, or Unknown Female, though Gebbert and Stand gave her a name: Chatham Mary. She had not been stabbed, but had been beaten to death with what was probably a hammer—never recovered. There was virtually no evidence in that case either, and no witnesses.

"She'd lost plenty of blood but the body'd gone undiscovered for at least a month. If there were messages, they'd've been washed away by storms."

Athens looked at the photo of poor Joshua. "So, Barney," she said, with a cynical tone in her voice, a sound Trimble recognized, "you still getting pressure to back-burner the case?"

He chuckled. "I am, yep. From the chief to the County board to the mayor. The attitude was: she was homeless, who cares? Let's go after the druggies."

Trimble vaguely remembered that he'd mentioned something about that at the lunch during the conference last month.

Athens sighed. "I'm getting the same thing from the top."

Trimble hadn't known that the powers that be in Wayne County weren't happy with the case. But, at twenty-eight, he wasn't privy to the politics of policing.

She added, "But I see your posts for requests on the wire. Basically, you're telling 'em to hell with it; you're following through."

"Homeless or not, she was a human being. I'm going to close it."

Athens nodded. "And we're going to canvass till we drop, to find that guy with the bloody rag. Aren't we, Trimble?"

"We are, Detective."

She turned to the photo of the bloodstain. "Message, hmm? What're you saying? *If* you're saying anything?"

Stand said, "Let's figure it out."

Athens said, "Give me a pen. And some paper."

Trimble jumped to. He always did when she asked for something in this tone. Athens was in what he called her volatilely obsessive mood.

She plucked the largest picture of the bloody wall from the board and set it down on the table. She placed a white sheet of printer paper over it.

"Shit. I need to see through it. Tracing paper. I want some tracing paper!"

"Well." Trimble too looked around, though it would be a futile search. The Wayne County Sheriff's Department was not like Todd's third-grade class, with art supplies at every turn. "I'm not sure—"

She said, "The glass," pointing to the window of the conference room, overlooking officers' cubicles.

An impromptu light table, Trimble realized. He taped the blood pattern photo onto the glass and the blank sheet over it. He placed a desk lamp on a chair just outside the room, shining at the image and paper. Athens took her hair pencil and began drawing small dots on the white sheet. In a distracted voice, as she labored, she explained that it wasn't odd for homicidal sociopaths to leave messages at the scenes. Postmortem arranging of the corpse was the most common, but many killers left written notes, either explicit or word games that needed to be unpacked to make sense.

She finished and pulled the paper off the glass then replaced it on the corkboard. There were two-dozen dots, in two horizontal bands, suggesting words or sentences.

But no obvious letters, numbers, or images appeared.

Trimble pulled a large glossy whiteboard from the corner and reproduced the dots in the exact position on it. He realized that, without thinking, he'd marked them in dark red, similar to the shade of blood they were based on. He then took up a black marker and, as they came up with ideas, he'd draw lines between them to try to make words.

The first letter was likely a *V*, though it might have been part of a *W*; the letter to the right was unidentifiable.

Trimble believed the last letter on the top band of dots was probably an *S* or a *5*.

They got an *O* or a *Q*.

Trimble said, "*Wheel of Fortune.*"

Gebbert smiled, but Athens stared at him blankly.

"A TV show."

Gloria Athens was known for working, working, and more working. Trimble had no idea what she did for relaxation and entertainment, but suspected television was not on the agenda.

"*D,*" Stand said. "I see a *D.*"

"And that's a *G,*" Athens said. "No. I think a *C.*"

In ten minutes, Stand snapped his fingers.

"Got it!"

He took the marker from Trimble and wrote out:

VAYA CON DIOS

The Spanish farewell: *Go with God.*

Gebbert said, "The perp's religious? Killing in the name of religion?"

But Trimble could see Gloria Athens looking off, with a frown. Her mind was racing. She looked to Trimble and said, "Little San Juan?"

Ah. Interesting.

"Could be."

She explained to the out-of-towners that a poor Latino neighborhood was not far from Fourth Street, where the killing had occurred.

Trimble said, "There's been some growing gang action there."

Athens said, "Initiation?"

Stand was nodding. "That could be it."

To get jumped into a gang, a prospective member sometimes had to commit a crime, even occasionally a murder, to prove he had the steel to be part of the crew.

She was nodding slowly. "We have some contacts there. I know some of the players. Trimble, let's go talk to some people." A glance toward Stand. "You two stay here and see if you can figure out the rest of the message." Then she paused. "Trimble, you *do* speak Spanish, don't you?"

"Uhm, actually, I took French."

"French? What the hell good is that?"

Stand's younger assistant, though, Gebbert, said he had a working knowledge of Spanish.

Athens asked Stand, "Okay if he comes with me?"

"Sure." The detective was distracted, staring at the blood pattern pictures.

"Better if Mr. Wheel-of-Fortune stays here anyway," she muttered, with a nod toward Trimble.

She and Gebbert took their coats and headed out the door.

For the next half hour, Stand and Trimble tried to decipher the rest of the clues. He kept in mind that even though the top message was all letters, the lower one still might involve numbers or images.

They weren't having much luck. The bottom line was considerably harder. They came up with a few possible letters, but no words jumped out. Trimble was half-thinking he should call his wife (they both loved the TV game show, watching it every night—when he was home; she was a much better player than he was). But he decided not to call her. He wanted to keep her as far away from the seamy side of his job as possible.

His mobile hummed. It was Gloria Athens.

"Detective," he said.

She asked bluntly, "What've you found? Any more messages?"

"A few letters, but they don't make any words. We're still at it."

"Dan Gebbert and I're back at the scene. The Harper plant. We're looking for the stick he used as his paintbrush. After that we'll get over to Little Puerto Rico. Call me if you find anything."

He said, "I will," but she'd already disconnected.

Stand and Trimble stared at the whiteboard and, through trial and error, wrung a few more letters out of the pattern of the dots. They got a *J* and an *E*.

The minutes rolled past slowly.

A letter *A* emerged. An *N*. A number: *4*.

And finally, with a jolt in his gut, Trimble saw the answer.

"It *is* a gang initiation."

"What?"

The young detective strode to the board and took the marker, then added the final sentence.

VAYA CON DIOS

YOU AND MARY — the MT-14s.

The MT-14s were a vicious crew, with affiliates in a dozen states. Drugs, guns, prostitutions.

Trimble said, "Mary would be your victim."

Stand nodded. "So, the cases *are* related. The motive..." His voice faded.

Trimble realized that Stand had stopped moving. In fact, it seemed he'd very nearly stopped breathing.

"No," Stand whispered.

"What, Detective?"

Stand, his face awash with confusion, said, "When I said Dan and I called the victim 'Chatham Mary' I meant that literally. *Only* we did. We came up with that ourselves. Unknown Female was too cold, not respectful."

Trimble's thoughts were arriving at the same place that Stand's had. But it seemed impossible.

Trimble asked, "Somebody else must've heard."

"Who?" Stand asked sharply. "Maybe the name's in case notes, but it's not public. Nothing in the press. Jesus."

"How long have you known him?"

"Not long. But it doesn't matter. Dan's the most straight-laced cop you'll ever find."

"And Ted Bundy was the most normal, cheerful law school student you'd ever find."

Trimble thought to himself: And he speaks Spanish. If you wanted to blame a Latino gang for a killing you committed, that skill would come in handy.

Stand swept up the phone. He said to Trimble as he waited for an answer, "Dan's not married. He lives with some roommates in an apartment near the sheriff's headquarters. I'll find where he was on the night of Joshua's murder."

When he got through to somebody, he had a conversation. Trimble could easily see his face was troubled by what the person on the other end of the line was telling him. He disconnected.

He nodded to the board. "Your victim was killed on Tuesday."

"Right."

"Every Tuesday, Dan works out. He starts at the gym and then goes for a fifteen-mile run. He was out last Tuesday from six through ten."

The exact time Joshua was killed.

Trimble muttered, "And the man spotted by our witness, the man with the rag. Blond. How many blond Latino gangbangers do you know?"

"Shit. I should've thought of that."

Trimble was pulling out his phone. "Maybe there's another explanation, but I'm calling Detective Athens."

She picked up on the third ring. "Trimble. You figured out the rest of the message?"

"Listen to me carefully, Detective. Is Dan Gebbert near you?"

She paused. "That's correct." Her instincts had kicked in immediately and she'd forced her voice to sound normal.

"It's possible he's the killer. Maybe not likely. But possible."

"I see."

"I can explain it all later. But you have to get out, without letting him know you suspect anything."

In a light, carefree voice she said, "Oh, I'm sure that can be worked out. Thanks—" Her voice stopped. Then she barked, "Wait. No!" There was a thud. She screamed, a wrenching sound.

The phone went dead.

*

A new blood pattern, fresh and bright crimson, was spread across the floor of the Harper Manufacturing Company.

The splashes and splatters were quite evident; the Sheriff's Department crime scene unit had set up fierce halogen spotlights inside.

In this display of blood there was a communication too, though it was not delivered via a mysterious code to be deciphered. The message was simple and straightforward: that the person that had lost this much blood could not possibly still be of this earth.

Stand and Trimble stood silent over the green bag enwrapping the corpse.

Other officers and deputies were arriving. Medical people.

The press too, of course. How they loved their serial killers. Nightly news just can't get enough.

The figure appeared in the doorway and walked toward them, limping.

Trimble looked toward Gloria Athens. He'd debated embracing her. That concept was alien in the extreme and he settled for a sincere nod.

She turned to Barney Stand. "I'm sorry."

He said nothing. His face was grim.

The County Sheriff arrived. Tom Bodwin was a massive man, whose gruff, scowling visage deceived; he was soft spoken and a kind, fair, thoughtful boss.

Athens said, "I was looking for the stick he used to leave the messages." A glance to Bodwin. "I'll explain that later.

I'd found one that might've been used and was bending down to pick it up. That's when Detective Trimble called and told me they suspected Gebbert might be the killer. I tried to play it cool but there must've been something in my body language... Gebbert came up behind me and hit me across the shoulder with that two by four."

She pointed to the beam, tagged with an evidence note.

Stand asked, "He say anything?"

"Just, 'Son of a bitch.' Maybe something else. I was on the ground, stunned, you know. He turned away for a moment and I managed to roll away and get to my feet. Over there." She pointed. Crime scene numbers littered the floor. "He was holding that."

An evidence bag held a wicked-looking weapon. It was like a razor-sharp filleting knife with a hook on the end.

"Ah," Stand muttered. He seemed shell shocked.

"I went for my weapon and he thought he could beat me. I fired three times, four. I really don't remember."

One of the slugs had torn through Gebbert's neck, hence the cascade of red.

"I tried to stop the bleeding. But..."

Bodwin said, "So, he's responsible for the homicide in Chatham and ours here. Left the message to blame the MT-14s for it. Why? What was his motive?"

Athens reminded, "Thrill kill."

Bodwin cocked his head. "You know, I seem to recall there were three other homicides in the western part of the state. We should cross-reference Gebbert's whereabouts when they happened."

Stand said, "Better if I don't handle it, though. I'll probably be on administrative leave till they get this worked out."

Trimble was thinking: Yeah, having your partner of several years be a serial killer *is* going to create a big stew pot of problems.

The detective from Chatham County just stared at the body bag. Trimble supposed he'd be running through the times that Dan Gebbert had acted odd, been particularly reclusive, had spent just a little too much time in the autopsy room or morgue, maybe let his gun linger on the body of a suspect, debating whether or not to pull the trigger. Wondering when the young man had snapped and decided to start recreating crimes of the sort he'd been investigating. Trimble had learned this was a phenomenon, police feeling they were justified in stepping over the line.

Maybe Gebbert had asked for the assignment to be Stand's protégé because of the blood.

Gloria Athens winced as she rubbed her shoulder. Henry Trimble had the absurd idea to wrap his hands around her muscles and massage. But he, of course, did no such thing.

The sheriff said, "Take a couple days off, Detective."

She looked at him as if he'd said, "I heard the moon is a Hollywood prop," and Trimble knew she'd be back in the office at 8:00am tomorrow.

Trimble said, "You want me to get you some coffee, Detective?"

"I'm good, Trimble. Go on home to your wife."

*

The only thing Gloria Athens didn't like about the precious soak she took nearly every evening was walking past the full-length mirror in the hallway between bed- and bathroom.

That extra fifteen pounds, which absolutely refused to go away, sat like a sluggish reminder of the passing years. Still, it didn't bother her enough to remove the damn mirror, which she could do pretty easily. Being handy with tools. And strong.

Time was a precious commodity.

Tonight, her hair tucked up under a shower cap decorated with daisies, Athens now sank into the expansive tub, a whirlpool model, though today the jets were silent. She was concerned the shooting water would be too powerful on her shoulders, sore and raw from the incident earlier tonight at Harper Manufacturing.

In the bathroom of the thirty-year-old Colonial, there was a two-sink vanity and a wicker laundry hamper, on which Jack, her Maine Coon cat, presently sat preening and studiously ignoring his mistress. She could hear the purring from here. Jack was content.

And so was Gloria Athens.

She believed that she'd pulled it off.

What people often didn't realize was that studying something intensely can lead to an obsession. And that obsession, like any addiction, often means that simply studying is no longer enough. She thought of the famous concert musicians: years and years of training, devoting themselves to mastering the literature of the great composers. Yet simply practicing in the dull, dim rehearsal space, or your living room, hour after hour, while you ignore the fragrant smells of dinner being prepared by the neglected wife? That would be hell.

At some point musicians know it's time to launch themselves into the real world.

A phenomenon, Athens had learned, that applies to murder too.

She knew exactly when this moment occurred within her.

Six years ago.

Athens had studied psychology, pathology, medicine, police procedure, interrogation and interview techniques. She practiced transforming herself, mentally, into the most heinous of killers. She learned nearly every theory of why violent criminals were violent. How they killed or maimed to achieve the more intense high. What a killer might do to sublimate his or her urges and lead a straight life (very, very little). She had used these skills to become the most successful violent crimes investigator in the state.

That night six years ago, a chill October, she was walking home and reflecting on a case she'd just closed: a domestic abuse homicide, a husband who'd tortured his wife to death.

She was, for sure, pleased she'd collared the perp. The chief had praised her for the arrest, as had the press. She'd earned the tearful gratitude of the victim's family.

But Gloria Athens had been nagged by something else, and couldn't figure out what.

Until it occurred to her: Envy.

She *envied* the husband who'd put his sadistic and lethal urges into practice, while all she could do was study, observe, analyze.

She felt empty. And angry that the satisfaction of completion was denied her.

It was like watching cooking shows on TV and never stepping up to a stove.

She needed more.

But she dismissed the thought immediately. She didn't dare commit a violent act herself.

No, no. Of course not.

Walking through the cold, dark night on her way to home and kitten Jack, she thought: What a foolish idea.

On the other hand.

If anyone was suited to getting away, literally, with murder, it was Gloria Athens.

For one thing, she knew homicide investigation techniques cold. She wouldn't make any of the classic mistakes that most murderers did: in the areas of forensics and surveillance, for instance. And—the kicker—there'd be no motive for committing the murders. With no apparent reason to kill the victim, she wouldn't fall into the bag of initial suspects.

Her motive would be killing for the thrill of it, the rush. Blood would be her fentanyl, her cocaine.

Something to ease the churning need within her to graduate from student to practitioner.

Did she dare?

She revised her answer to a tentative, Yes.

And so, a few days later, she used a hammer to beat to death a young man who was in a small-time crew about fifty miles away.

Oh, it was a high like nothing else she'd ever experienced:

no longer tepid professional satisfaction at observing carnage. Now, she reveled in it.

About twice a year she'd travel discreetly around the western part of the state, targeting those whose deaths wouldn't draw much attention, always in locales where there was no CCTV, no witnesses.

She tried telling herself that she was doing them a favor—the homeless, the druggies—killing them, putting them out of their misery. But that was a lie. She didn't give a shit about them. She wanted them to die and die bloody, at her hand, hands armed with tools and baseball bats and knives.

But then came the homeless woman, dozing beside the Chatham River after a binge. The woman who became Unknown Female, or Chatham Mary.

Hers had been a very satisfying, and very bloody, death.

All good.

Until Detective Barney Stand got on the case.

She always made a note to read the interagency police reports in the jurisdictions where she'd killed someone, and she learned that Stand was looking at the case as a holy grail.

How to stop him?

She signed up immediately for the law enforcement continuing education seminar last month, which would give her an excuse to meet Stand and to find out about the case. She'd learned about his little puppy dog assistant—Dan Gebbert—and decided the odd kid would make a good fall guy.

If Gebbert was revealed as the killer, Stand would be

disgraced for missing the man's guilt. And the police brass, uninterested in solving the Chatham case, would drop it. Stand might even be fired outright.

One could always hope.

While the seminar was underway, she'd slipped into Stand's office and rifled through the files; his notes suggested that only Stand and Gebbert referred to her as 'Chatham Mary'.

A perfect clue to plant to draw suspicion to the young detective.

But Athens knew it would look better if somebody else came to suspect Gebbert. That's why Joshua had to die: to get the Chatham detectives here and have Stand and darling Henry Trimble connect the dots—literally—to implicate Stand's unfortunate protégé.

With her dawdling at the crime scene in the factory, looking for the 'paintbrush' branch (which was long gone), Stand and Trimble, back at headquarters, finally deduced that Gebbert might be the killer.

Trimble had called to break the news to her. And she had given a grunt and a desperate scream, then disconnected the phone (she could only imagine what Trimble's expression would have been).

Dan Gebbert, who'd been outside the factory, came running, with his gun drawn, eyes wide.

Athens had laughed. "Only a rat, sorry."

He'd smiled and put his gun away.

Which was when Athens drew hers and shot him in the face and neck.

He dropped so fast, he didn't even have a chance to look astonished.

When he was down, Athens—in latex gloves, of course—took from her purse a plastic bag containing the weapon she'd used to kill Joshua, an ornate knife with a hooked blade (she'd stolen it at a flea market). She pressed the handle and blade against the dead cop's fingers and left it there, then she'd fallen backward against the two-by-four beam, as if he'd hit her with it. This too she placed against his hands, to transfer prints and DNA.

One final touch: she'd taken the hammer she'd used in the Chatham Mary killing from her trunk and transferred his DNA and prints to the tool. Tomorrow she'd pitch it into the backyard of the house where he lived in Chatham.

All nice and tidy.

She now asked, "What do you think, Jack? Did I pull it off?"

If his purring were any indication, she had.

Any other issues?

Well, only one.

Her own assistant. Henry Trimble.

He was a smart kid and he tended to stick to projects he'd been assigned and see them through to completion, which was, in a way, her fault. She insisted on discipline.

If anyone would notice inconsistencies about the Joshua Musgrave murder, it would be clever Henry.

But she'd keep an eye on him.

She wasn't going to give up her addiction. Somebody else in a different county would die in a month or two. And Trimble might become curious.

So she had a plan for him too, though Gloria Athens hoped it wouldn't come to that.

One thing she'd learned in the business of policing: good assistants were hard to come by.

ABOUT THE AUTHORS

A. K. Benedict read English at Cambridge and Creative Writing at the University of Sussex. Her debut novel, *The Beauty of Murder*, was shortlisted for an eDunnit Award and is in development for an eight-part television series. Her second novel, *Jonathan Dark or the Evidence of Ghosts*, and a tie-in novel for *Doctor Who* spin-off *Class*, have since followed. Her short stories have been published in anthologies including *Best British Short Stories* and *Best British Horror*. Before becoming a writer in 2012, A. K. Benedict was an indie-rock singer/songwriter and composer for film and television, with music played on BBC 1, Channel Four, Sky, XFM, BBC Radio 1 and Radio 3 and in award-winning films. She now sings with The Slice Girls, a group of female thriller writers singing songs of sex, death and crime. She is currently writing scripts, short stories, a stand-alone psychological thriller and the sequel to *The Beauty of Murder*. She lives in Rochester on Sea with writer Guy Adams and their dog, Dame Margaret Rutherford. Visit www.akbenedict.com for more.

Bill Beverly lives in Maryland and teaches at Trinity University in Washington, DC. He is the author of *On The Lam* (2003), a study of the criminal fugitive figure in 1930s and 1940s American fiction and film, and also of *Dodgers: A Novel* (2016), winner of the Crime Writers' Association (CWA) Gold Dagger, a *Los Angeles Times* Book Prize, a British Book Award, and the Mark Twain American Voice in Literature Award. A new novel, a cousin to *Dodgers*, is due in late 2019.

Ken Bruen is the author of thirty-eight books, twelve of which have been made into films, with a television series on Swedish Noir aired on Sky Atlantic. He served a prison term in South America and received a Doctorate in Metaphysics. His new series is ready to launch. He says: "The best profile of me own self was where top journalists described me a benign thug." He has one daughter who has Down syndrome, and works in a school as a reading tutor.

Lee Child has more than a dozen number-one bestsellers under his belt. *Forbes* calls the Jack Reacher series, "The Strongest Brand in Publishing"; not bad for a guy out of work and on the dole when he first conceived of being a writer. The fictional Reacher is a kind-hearted soul who allows Lee Child lots of spare time for reading, listening to music, Aston Villa and the Yankees. Lee was born in England but now lives in New York City. Visit Lee online at LeeChild.com for more information about the novels, short stories, music, and movies *Jack Reacher* and *Jack Reacher: Never Go Back*. Lee can also be found on Facebook: LeeChildOfficial, Twitter: LeeChildReacher and YouTube: leechildjackreacher.

Jeffery Deaver is an international number-one bestselling author. His novels have appeared on bestseller lists around the world. His books are sold in 150 countries and translated into twenty-five languages. His is currently the president of the Mystery Writers of America. The author of forty novels, three collections of short stories and a non-fiction law book, and a lyricist of a country-western album, he's received or been shortlisted for dozens of awards. His *The Bodies Left Behind* was named Novel of the Year by the International Thriller Writers association, and his Lincoln Rhyme thriller, *The Broken Window,* and a stand-alone, *Edge*, were also nominated for that prize. *The Garden of Beasts* won the CWA Steel Dagger and he's been nominated for eight Edgar Awards. Deaver has been honoured with the Lifetime Achievement Award by the Bouchercon World Mystery Convention, the *Strand Magazine*'s Lifetime Achievement Award and the Raymond Chandler Lifetime Achievement Award in Italy. His book *A Maiden's Grave* was made into an HBO movie starring James Garner and Marlee Matlin, and his novel *The Bone Collector* was a feature release from Universal Pictures, starring Denzel Washington and Angelina Jolie. Lifetime aired an adaptation of his *The Devil's Teardrop*.

Stella Duffy has written sixteen novels, seventy short stories, including many for BBC Radio 4, and fourteen plays. She has twice won the CWA Short Story Dagger. Stella has also worked in theatre for over thirty-five years as an actor, director and writer, and is the co-founder and co-director of the Fun Palaces campaign for cultural democracy. She was awarded the OBE for Services to the Arts in the Queen's Birthday honours 2016.

R. J. Ellory has authored fifteen novels for Orion UK and is translated into twenty-six languages. He has won the Livre De Poche Award, the *Strand Magazine* Novel of the Year, the Mystery Booksellers of America Award, the Inaugural Nouvel Observateur Prize, the Quebec Laureat, the Prix Du Roman Noir, the Plume d'Or 2016, the Theakston's Crime Novel of the Year, the St. Maur and Villeneuve Readers' Prizes, the Balai d'Or 2016, and the Grand Prix des Lecteurs. He has received a further eleven award nominations, including five from the CWA, two Barrys, the 813 Trophy, and the Européen Du Point. He is the guitarist and vocalist of The Whiskey Poets, and they have recently completed their third album, *Native Strangers*. His musical compositions for Universal Records have been featured in films and television programmes in more than forty countries. He has two television series and a film adaptation in pre-production.

Christopher Fowler is the multi-award-winning London-born author of fifty books, including twelve volumes of short stories, and the Bryant & May mysteries. His novels include *Roofworld*, *Spanky*, *Psychoville*, *Calabash* and two volumes of memoirs, *Paperboy* and *Film Freak*. He won the Green Carnation Award for *Paperboy* and the CWA Dagger in the

Library for his Bryant & May mysteries. His collection *Red Gloves*, twenty-five stories of unease, marked his first twenty-five years of writing. He has written comedy and drama for BBC radio and the national press, graphic novels, the play *Celebrity* and the *War Of The Worlds* video game for Paramount. His short story 'The Master Builder' became the movie *Through the Eyes of a Killer*, starring Tippi Hedren. Among his other awards are the Edge Hill prize 2008 for *Old Devil Moon*, the Last Laugh prize 2009 for *The Victoria Vanishes* and again in 2015 for *The Burning Man*. His most recent non-fiction work is *The Book of Forgotten Authors* and his latest novel, *Hall of Mirrors*, is his fiftieth book. He lives in London and Barcelona.

James Grady's first novel *Six Days of the Condor* became the Robert Redford movie *Three Days of the Condor*. Grady has received Italy's Raymond Chandler Medal, France's Grand Prix Du Roman Noir and Japan's Baka-Misu literature award, two *Regardie's* magazine short story awards, and been a Mystery Writers of America Edgar finalist. He's published more than a dozen novels and three times that many short stories, been a muckraker journalist and a scriptwriter for film and television. In 2008, London's *Daily Telegraph* named Grady as one of "50 crime writers to read before you die". In 2015, *The Washington Post* compared his prose to that of George Orwell and Bob Dylan.

Born in Marseille, France, and with a degree in Political Science, **Johana Gustawsson** has worked as a journalist for the French and Spanish press and television. Her critically acclaimed Roy & Castells series, including *Block 46, Keeper* and, soon to be published, *Blood Song,* has won the Plume d'Argent, Balai de la découverte, Balai d'Or and Prix Marseillais du Polar awards, and is now published in nineteen countries. A television adaptation is currently underway in a French, Swedish and UK co-production. Johana lives in London with her Swedish husband and their three sons.

John Harvey was born in London, where he now lives, while considering Nottingham his spiritual home. Poet, dramatist and sometime publisher, he is best known as a writer of crime fiction, the first of his twelve-volume Charlie Resnick series, *Lonely Hearts,* having been selected by *The Times* as one of the 100 Best Crime Novels of the Century. The first of his Frank Elder novels, *Flesh & Blood*, won the CWA Silver Dagger in 2004, and his story 'Fedora' won the CWA Short Story Dagger in 2014. In 2007, he was awarded the CWA Cartier Diamond Dagger for sustained excellence in the crime genre. He has been awarded honorary doctorates by the Universities of Nottingham and Hertfordshire.

Lauren Henderson was born in London and worked as a journalist for newspapers and music magazines before moving to Tuscany to write books and party; after a ten-year stint in Manhattan, she returned to London. Lauren has been described as both the Dorothy Parker and the Betty Boop of the British crime novel. She writes for many UK-based publications, including *Grazia* and *Cosmopolitan*, and several national newspapers. Together with Stella Duffy, she edited the anthology *Tart Noir*, a groundbreaking collection of twenty short crime stories by leading female crime writers. Lauren has written seven novels in her Sam Jones mystery series, which has been optioned for American television, three romantic comedies, the non-fiction *Jane Austen's Guide to Dating* and two YA mystery series. As Rebecca Chance, she writes *Sunday Times* bestselling sexy thrillers.

Her interests include watching Bravo shows with fellow crime writer reality TV fans while drinking cocktails. Her books have been translated into over twenty languages.

Mary Hoffman has written 120 books, mainly for children and teenagers, including the much praised Stravaganza series but also two adult novels under pseudonyms and several short stories. Her books have been translated into more than thirty languages. She is a passionate Italophile and many of her books are set in that country. Sadly, Mary has no home there but lives in a converted barn in Oxfordshire, which is also pretty nice. She runs the History Girls blog and is on the management committee of the Society of Authors.

Maxim Jakubowski worked for many years in book publishing alongside his career in writing, editing and translating. He is the author of twenty novels, the last being *The Louisiana Republic* (2018), and five collections of short stories. He also opened the UK's first mystery bookstore, Murder One, which ran for over twenty years. He has edited a number of major cult imprints and well over 100 anthologies and is a regular broadcaster and contributor to national newspapers and magazines. A past winner of the Karel and Anthony awards, he was also co-director of London's International Film and Literary Mystery Festival, Crime Scene, at the National Film Theatre for ten years. A vice-chair of the Crime Writers' Association, he lives in London.

Denise Mina is a Scottish crime writer and playwright. She has written the Garnethill trilogy and another three novels featuring the character Patricia "Paddy" Meehan, a Glasgow journalist, in addition to six other mystery novels with a strong social background, and true crime narrative *The Long Drop*. Described as an author of Tartan Noir, she has also dabbled in comic book writing, having written thirteen issues of *Hellblazer*. She is two-time winner of a CWA Dagger and her work has been adapted for television.

Jason Starr is the international bestselling author of many crime novels, psychological thrillers and comics. His novels include *Twisted City, Tough Luck, Hard Feelings, The Follower, Panic Attack,* and *Fugitive Red* (published in the UK as *Too Far*). Additionally, he's the author of the acclaimed *Pack* series of urban fantasy novels. His work in comics for Marvel and DC includes *Batman, The Punisher,* and the entire *Wolverine Max* series. He has also co-written several novels with Ken Bruen for Hard Case Crime, and is the writer of the official *Gotham* novels, based on the hit FOX series. Several of Starr's novels are in development for film, television and theatre. He has won the Anthony Award twice, as well as the Barry Award. He lives in New York City.

Lavie Tidhar is the author of the Jerwood Fiction Uncovered Prize winning and Premio Roma nominee *A Man Lies Dreaming*, the World Fantasy Award winning *Osama* and of the Campbell Award winning and Locus and Clarke Award nominated *Central Station*. His latest novels are *Unholy Land* and first children's novel *Candy*. He is the author of many other novels, novellas and short stories.

Cathi Unsworth is the author of six highly acclaimed pop-cultural crime novels, *That Old Black Magic*, *Without The Moon*, *Weirdo*, *Bad Penny Blues*, *The Singer* and *The Not Knowing*, all published by Serpent's Tail. She began her writing career at the age of nineteen on *Sounds* and has since worked as an editor on *Bizarre* and *Purr*. She has written on music, film, pop culture and general weirdness for *Fortean Times*, *Financial Times*, *The Guardian*, *Mojo*, *Sight & Sound* and *Uncut*, among others. Her latest book is the co-authored autobiography of the first woman of punk, *Defying Gravity: Jordan's Story* (Omnibus Press). Find more at www.cathiunsworth.co.uk

EXIT WOUNDS

EDITED BY PAUL B. KANE AND MARIE O'REGAN

CRIMINALLY GOOD

A brand-new anthology of crime stories written by masters
of the genre. Featuring both original in-universe stories and
rarely-seen reprints, this collection of masterful short stories
brings together some of the genre's greatest living authors.
Tense, twisted and disturbing, *Exit Wounds* is a visceral and
thrilling collection showcasing the very best modern crime
fiction has to offer.

Featuring stories from

**A.K. BENEDICT · MARK BILLINGHAM · STEPH BROADRIBB
LEE CHILD · JOHN CONNOLLY · FIONA CUMMINS
JEFFERY DEAVER · PAUL FINCH · CHRISTOPHER FOWLER
ALEX GRAY · SARAH HILARY · LOUISE JENSEN
DEAN KOONTZ · JOE R. LANSDALE · DENNIS LEHANE
VAL MCDERMID · JAMES OSWALD · MARTYN WAITES**

PHANTOMS

EDITED BY MARIE O'REGAN

STORIES TO DIE FOR

Explore the world of spirits, phantasms and ghostly apparitions
in this new anthology of ghost stories. These eighteen unsettling
tales from the some of the best modern horror writers will send
a chill down your spine like someone has walked over your
grave… or perhaps just woken up in their own.

Featuring stories from

**KELLEY ARMSTRONG · A.K. BENEDICT · M.R. CAREY
JOHN CONNOLLY · GEMMA FILES · HELEN GRANT
MURIEL GRAY · JOE HILL · MARK A. LATHAM
TIM LEBBON · ALISON LITTLEWOOD · JOSH MALERMAN
GEORGE MANN · LAURA PURCELL · ROBERT SHEARMAN
ANGELA SLATTER · PAUL TREMBLAY · CATRIONA WARD**

TITANBOOKS.COM

For more fantastic fiction, author events, exclusive
excerpts, competitions, limited editions and more

VISIT OUR WEBSITE
titanbooks.com

LIKE US ON FACEBOOK
facebook.com/titanbooks

FOLLOW US ON TWITTER
@TitanBooks

EMAIL US
readerfeedback@titanemail.com